Acclaim for SALAH EL MONCEF's

THE OFFERING

"El Moncef's prose startles with quiet brilliance.... The nature of truth and deception (willing and otherwise) is ever at the forefront, and the way el Moncef weaves his story, subtly accruing suspense through the accumulation of Tariq's memories, creates a reading experience that is simultaneously weighty and invigorating. El Moncef seeks to explore what it is that we may construct with our pain and what it is we may have buried beneath it. The result is a literary enigma of the highly satisfying variety. An immersive, finely wrought mystery of tragedy, loss, and recovery."

—*Kirkus Reviews*

"Although *The Offering* is at times painful and even heartbreaking, it is consistently beautiful.... In this stunning novel el Moncef's prose often rivals that of today's most poetic and accomplished word-smiths. A myriad of passages in *The Offering* rival those in the work of a writer like John Banville, where one is simply dazzled by the sheer virtuosity of the language, the structure, and the rhythm. This soon evolves into a feeling so intense and delicious that one simply must pause to take it all in."

—*The Los Angeles Review of Books*

"*The Offering* takes on the scintillating form of a psychological thriller, the dissociation of the protagonist recalling the best of J. G. Ballard's fiction. The Left Bank of Paris with its distorted perspectives, hidden courtyards and tropical gardens becomes the phantasmagorical setting for a miraculous, masochistic and all-consuming love affair.... El Moncef's novel is an exquisitely drawn chara
and intelligent, this is a beguiling story of
and sacrifice."

"El Moncef's book is rather tragic in its sensitivity to loss, albeit with something like the affirmation of love's value.... It is this affirmation that *The Offering* puts forth for its readers, not so much on the level of content as on the level of expression, where el Moncef's stunning craftsmanship and his virtues as a writer of timely and relevant fiction for a neoliberalized global order are so much in evidence."

—*Angelaki*

"Like Job, Tariq Abbassi has lost everything; and yet for all his desolation, he tries to find an escape within himself—in the words that bring meaning and structure to his life. The quest for beauty becomes Tariq's only guide in his distress and we find ourselves drawn into his mind, fascinated, mesmerized. When describing the style of Salah el Moncef, one adjective comes to mind: dazzling. His poetic prose makes us experience the world in all its sensual beauty."

—*The Amazon Review*

"Beautiful and spellbinding in its capacity to shock and seduce at once. *The Offering* is a triumph of the art of storytelling in an age shaped by digital technology and global cultural exchange.... El Moncef's psychological thriller is a fine instance of the literature of dissociation, recalling the best of J. G. Ballard's fiction."

—Jason Barker

"Here we have a young novelist amazing the world with a mystery novel he should not have reasonably achieved. But genius does not heed reason. *The Offering* drops us into the lower depths of destitution and a Camus-like loss of self before the world. At the same time, there is the possibility of salvation dangled before us like a redeeming but elusive oasis of escape. That promised haven is beauty—esthetic elegance of the highest order. Read this ravishing book and learn how to survive in the face of trying pain and loss. The breadth and depth and poetic power of *The Offering* will enchant you."

—Willis Barnstone

"Readers who welcome challenges, I believe, will be captured by *The Offering*—by its narrator's intelligence, his fight to surmount his sufferings, and his linguistic magic. You can open this remarkable novel anywhere and find passages, long and short, that are so precise, so evocative, and so polished that the prose sometimes becomes indistinguishable from a particularly controlled, sharp-edged form of poetry."

—John Glendenning

"An exciting conception of the novel. Rare, these days, to pull off such a trick."

—Rebecca Gowers

"A highly compelling novel. *The Offering* is remarkable in the sustained intensity of its poetic sensibility. One is haunted by its capacity to plumb the abyss of loneliness, anguish and horror; enchanted by its power to evoke the magic of love and 'the mysterious alchemy of people and places.' A must-read."

—Gerard Greenway

"True to Gustave Flaubert's pronouncement on the importance of being 'violent and original in art,' this book is a mesmerizing tale of tales, inscribed from one pen to another, growing with the intentions of its voices into a singular piercing work of art. A tough, uncompromisingly ambiguous novel. And the sheer beauty of it—loads and loads of breathtaking beauty. This is a magnificent opus by an author whose glorious time has come."

—Khaled Mattawa

"This book is quite simply excellent! It ends with admirable purpose and finality. All questions resolved in one fell swoop. And yet the ambiguity lingers till the last word and beyond. A brilliantly layered and nuanced story that develops the way any great novel should."

—Stefan Mattesich

"Besides the intensity of its esthetic vision, this haunting book presents us with an urgent and novel statement on the fluctuating world in which we live, a world defined by global migration and the digital age. Through *The Offering*, el Moncef gives us not only a diasporic drama of profound beauty; he also creates a completely new literature of mobility for our digitized epoch, a literary electrokinetics born from the startling encounter between the diaspora experience and the electrifying rhythms of technology."

—Thomas Nail

"This is a book about the power of beauty as a healing source that allows us to go on in the aftermath of unspeakable pain. The streets and parks of Paris, the Moorish houses and sun-drenched beaches of Tunisia, the fine drizzle and furtive fog of Brittany, the ever-shifting shades, shapes, and tonalities of the ocean. *The Offering* is filled with mesmerizing visual passages—passages where the reader can lose herself in rapt contemplation of the sheer elegance of expression. El Moncef is endowed with the gift of making the finest, most elusive sensory experiences leap off the page with so much vividness that the reader has the uncanny sense of stepping right into the world of *The Offering*."

—Mari Ruti

"What a great novel! *The Offering* is alternatively painful and exalting, inferno-like and redemptive, traumatic and sublime; but it is consistently beautiful. In this stunning and, finally, shocking novel, el Moncef's prose rivals that of today's most poetic wordsmiths. For me, *The Offering* reaches that horizon of stylistic excellence we find in a writer like John Banville. One is dazzled by the sheer virtuosity of the language, the structure, and the poetic rhythm as the reading experience evolves into a feeling so intense and delectable that one simply must pause to take it all in."

—Stephen Watt

Salah el Moncef

THE OFFERING

Salah el Moncef was born in Kuwait City, Kuwait. Raised in Tunisia and educated in the United States, he is a Fulbright Fellow and a recipient of the Presidential Award for Excellence in the Humanities. One of the few North African fiction authors to write in English, his works, largely focused on the Arab diaspora experience, have been published in numerous British and American magazines and anthologies. More recent publications include his novelette, *Sleepwalking*, and his highly acclaimed debut novel, *The Offering*. El Moncef teaches English and Creative Writing at the University of Nantes, France, and is editor at *Angelaki*.

The Offering

—

Salah el Moncef

PENELOPE BOOKS

LONDON . NEW YORK . PARIS . SYDNEY

Penelope Books
36A Norham Road
Oxford OX2 6SQ, United Kingdom

Penelope Books
2, bis Rue Dupont de l'Eure
75020 Paris, France

Portions of this novel appeared in *Jadeed* and *Post-Gibran: Anthology of New Arab-American Writing*.

Grateful acknowledgment is made to the following for permission to reprint previously published material: Alfred A. Knopf Inc.: excerpt from *Journal of Katherine Mansfield* by Katherine Mansfield. University Press of New England: excerpt from *The Best of Rilke* by Rainer Maria Rilke. HarperCollins Publishers: excerpts from *Tao Te Ching* by Lao-tzu.

ISBN: 1500859443
ISBN 13: 9781500859442
Library of Congress Control Number: 2014915507
CreateSpace Independent Publishing Platform
North Charleston, South Carolina

For my mother

And he took bread, and gave thanks, and brake it, and gave unto them, saying, This is my body which is given for you: this do in remembrance of me.
—*Luke*, 22:19

Introduction

I was reading the second half of *The Offering* on the plane from Los Angeles to Boston and, for the first time in my life, I wished there would be a delay in landing so that I could find out "who done it." The novel that had started as a painful story about love gone wrong—and about a father trying to find a way of relating to his two estranged sons—had suddenly turned into a gripping detective story of murder, mayhem, and mental illness. When we approached Boston, my wish was granted: the captain announced that bad weather in the city was placing us in a holding pattern for an hour. *Great!* I thought, as I settled back into my reading, aware that the circling of the plane above the storm clouds mirrored the spiraling rhythm of the novel's ever-darkening plot: layer by layer, the story brought me closer to the (terrifying) landing zone. It's just that when I finally landed, I discovered that I was not where I expected to be but had, instead, landed in Carthage, Tunisia, where the story both begins and ends. The novel, in short, culminates in a plot twist that changes everything, leaving the reader breathless and disoriented even as it offers the satisfaction of revelation (and therefore closure).

I am up against a challenge here: how am I to discuss this novel without giving away the plot elements that make it such a rewarding reading experience? The obvious answer is that I cannot talk about the narrative—about what "happens"—but must stick to the story's emotional and existential resonances. There is much to choose from in this regard: love and its loss; the bitterness of finding oneself betrayed by those one has trusted; the tenuous, ever-threatened bond between parents and children; the insane (but sometimes wonderful) things that happen between siblings; the fierce loyalties of friendship; the sensual details of cooking; the harsh realities of immigration, displacement, and racism. This last topic alone could fill the pages of a scholarly tome, for the novel's protagonist, Tariq Abbassi, has left Tunisia to study philosophy at the Sorbonne but ends up, after completing his doctorate (and by the time the reader catches up with him), running a high-class Middle Eastern restaurant in Bordeaux while aspiring to be a poet. Tariq's highly cerebral nature, along with his literary ambitions, war against the stereotype of the Arab immigrant to France, and for the most part he seems to experience French society as enabling rather than oppressive—a respite from the traumas of his family history and the political struggles of Tunisia. This, however, does not prevent French society from wounding him. Some of the most startling moments of the novel arise when Tariq—who sees himself primarily as a mild-mannered poet-intellectual—comes in contact with a racist culture that by definition bars an Arab man (the angry, raving fanatic) from this self-definition.

Most fundamentally, however, *The Offering* is a contemplation on the relationship between loss and creativity, trauma and rebirth. The novel's enigmatic title functions on multiple levels, the most philosophical of which is arguably the question of what one has to "offer"—to sacrifice, as it were—in order to conjure something truly worthwhile into existence. *Everything*, Salah el Moncef seems to suggest. In the course of the novel, Tariq loses more and more, to the point that there really is nothing left to lose, yet each loss seems to replenish his creative powers so that, at the end, in a state of unimaginable suffering, he finally attains what he has been after all his life: a perfect poem of pristine formal beauty. The poem is called *Night Owl* and I reproduce it here:

> Oh, you know: that hour.
> The smeared rim of heaven
> has turned to cold crystal;
> it is the last champagne blush
> in the opalescent sky:

The light-dregs of day
at the bottom of a lonely glass.

But the owl has descended,
preening on his perch;
a few last touches before the night hour—
his time of glory,
when all the rest of creation
will be floundering, floundering
in formless mud and murk.

Oh, you know, you know:
When his gaze begins to brim up
with a thousand sparks of amber,
crackling with the memory of a million noons—
the encapsulated sparkle of eons
at his command,
lighting up his voyage into the night.

This poem, which arrives with incongruous gentility in the novel's final pages, when the reader is galloping toward the finale, is worth waiting for. And the novel's narrative makes it clear that it is born of pure loss. This is not to say that *The Offering* fetishizes loss as the ultimate kernel of creativity. It manages to convey the stark brutality of loss so effectively, so relentlessly, that it forces the reader to wonder whether, in the final analysis, there is anything that could ever compensate for the pain undergone. That is, it is not at all clear that the creative impulse that arises from the wreckage of Tariq's life can even begin to make up for what he has had to give up—to "offer." Yet there is also a strong sense that something unfathomably precious does emerge from the debris. Interestingly, the fledgling Phoenix rising from the ashes is ultimately not (or at least not *only*) the poem I have cited but—and here I cannot help but give away a bit of plot—rather an unexpected connection to a mother whom Tariq has long experienced as a forbidding fortress of silent suffering but who is mercifully revealed as a kindred-spirit in possession of an immense imaginative capacity and an equally immense reservoir of emotional generosity that has been carefully tucked away from the prying eyes of those capable of causing devastation. If trauma—the agony of loss, betrayal, solitude, and suffering—has been passed intergenerationally from mother to son, the reader discovers that something more affirmative has also made the passage, something that was in danger of getting lost in translation (between generations, between genders, between cultures, between languages), and that is the gift of being able to touch the other, reach the other, comfort the other, and even caress the other, through the written word (a poem, a letter, a novel).

The Offering illustrates what French thinkers—Jean-Paul Sartre, Jacques Lacan, and Julia Kristeva, among others—have been particularly good at expressing, namely that at the core of human "being" resides nothingness, and that in order to continue to "be," one must find a way to translate this nothingness into *something*: a word, an image, an affect, an attachment. The melancholy message of French thought has repeatedly been that there is no meaning without non-meaning, no sense without nonsense, no creativity without despair, and no love without loss. Simply put: if human beings were completely devoid of lack, they would also be completely devoid of desire, with the result that the world would have nothing to offer them; their arrogant self-sufficiency would generate a debilitating, soul-stifling boredom. From this perspective, the nothingness at the heart of being, while certainly a source of a great deal of misery, is an existential opportunity: what forces us to venture into the world in search of things—objects, lovers, friends, passions, ambitions, and so on—that might (however temporarily, however tentatively) make up for our gnawing sense that something is missing from our lives. Sadness, in this sense, is the somber lining of everything that is meaningful about human life. As Kristeva explains in *Black Sun*, the ability to "remake nothingness"—say, to pluck a poem out of a confused, feverish stream of consciousness, as Tariq manages to do—is "the royal way through which humanity transcends the grief of being apart."

On the one hand, Tariq's trials exceed the limits of "ordinary" human suffering: his losses are irredeemable, his anguish incurable, and his grief irrepressible ("uncompromisingly rigid and willful," as he himself puts it). On the other, poetry—and the written word, more generally speaking—functions in his life as a means to manage misfortune, to create a barrier against utter abjection. This barrier is terribly flimsy; it is always on the verge of collapsing under the weight of the pain pressing on it. But against all odds—miraculously—it holds, for the novel repeatedly foregrounds the manner in which writing, for Tariq, serves as a lifeline to meaning in a world that seems hell-bent on depriving him of it.

Besides writing poetry, Tariq keeps a journal where he jots down not merely the events of his life but also the minutest movements of his interiority. The journal in fact functions as a site of an almost obsessive cathexis, the place where Tariq records everything from his anger, resentment, and disillusionment to the trusting sweetness of his sons and the electrifying jolt of fresh romance. Regardless of how the day ends—in hopeless desolation, drunken revelry, passionate love-making, or banal weariness—the journal is where Tariq stops before sleeping (or, as is often the case, instead of sleeping). The reader quickly realizes that the journal serves as a collection of scraps of thought, emotion, and impression that Tariq hopes will one day become a novel. In this sense, the journal is a metaphor for the (actual) novel that the reader is in the process of devouring. Indeed, through the rambling journal entries of his protagonist, el Moncef offers the reader a torrent of observations about the demanding craft of writing, such as the following: "You have to keep your eyes on that something you want to net—hard as it is to do that. Setting up the right conditions to create that fragile something out of nothing—the first embryonic seed that will keep you going. The initial doubts of writing are what's most exhilarating *about* writing in the first place: it's a gamble most of the time. You start something even while you're in the dark about what it's doing and where it's going."

Noteworthy here is the theme of creating something out of nothing that I have sought to tease out. But equally noteworthy is the fact that one of the many pleasures of reading *The Offering* is the sense that el Moncef has indeed managed to "net" something that is exceedingly difficult to net: the very scraps of thought, emotion, and impression that Tariq is so desperate to trap between the covers of his journal. Beyond this, what el Moncef captures with unusual dexterity and deftness are—and I again quote his own metacommentary on the process of writing—"even the most commonplace scenes and sounds—especially the most commonplace scenes and sounds." Perhaps the most exquisite parts of the novel are the intricate evocations of place—of the streets and parks of Paris, the houses and beaches of Tunisia, the fine drizzle and furtive fog of Brittany—that form the backdrop of the story's unfolding. The author manages to bring the Left Bank of Paris, particularly the narrow lanes, cafés, and restaurants of the rue Mouffetard neighborhood, alive in such vivid detail that the reader has the uncanny sense of stepping right into the scenes that the characters inhabit. Likewise, the depictions of the ever-shifting hues, shapes, and tonalities of the ocean—both in Tunisia and Brittany—are painted with such a delicate but controlled touch that the reader experiences them in all their sensuous richness. The textures of Tunisia—its sights, sounds, scents, and other sensory qualities—leap off the page with agile but robust intensity. Brittany, in turn, is shrouded in muffled mystery, as in the passage below:

> On a blazing summer day, coming out of the water:
> The gentle curves and the shadowy hollows of the Breton country east of the gray-ribbon coastal road—pulsating ever so quietly in the shimmer of the afternoon heat, sprawled like the soft forms of a sleeping woman;
> the salt-and-fern fragrance of a land baked and burnished in all the hues of gold, copper, and bronze;
> and those wind-dwarfed, weather-braving lone pines—still now, in the scorched stillness.

El Moncef's prose, in short, achieves the quality of poetry, which is fitting for a novel about an aspiring poet. Consider, for instance, the following depiction, this time from Tunisia: "To our right, the craggy mountainous country was a pinkish pale green in the afterglow—the smoky green of sparse Mediterranean brush; and to the left, there was the massive sheer cliff that formed the eastern face of the Korbous Cape with the darkening ink-blue of the bay at its bottom, gathered into a ruffled strip of snow-white froth shimmering on the puckered hem of the shoreline." *The Offering* is filled with such mesmerizing sentences—sentences where the reader can lose herself in rapt contemplation of the sheer elegance of expression. In this context, I cannot keep myself from fixating on a seemingly insignificant aspect of the narrative: the fact that, in his most traumatized state, Tariq discovers that English is the language that allows him to best communicate his emotional turmoil. English in fact becomes, for Tariq, a sanctuary of sorts, a way to gain some much-needed distance from the traumatic events he is navigating.

As an immigrant who many moons ago deliberately adopted English as an armor against trauma (albeit not trauma of the same acuteness as what Tariq experiences), I find this narrative detail fascinating, particularly as it counters the expected story: the story of a foreign language as a desolate place of alienation and dislocation. Tariq exchanges Arabic and French for English because there is something about English that brings him solace. The fact that the language is English may be unimportant—or it may be immensely important. There is no way to know from the story. But the larger point is worth lingering upon: speaking a foreign tongue is not always the forlorn, tragic experience of inner erosion that it is frequently assumed to be, particularly for immigrants. Though it is certainly true that, for those who have been violently displaced, the alien land with its alien language may feel inhospitable, for others—particularly those who have moved voluntarily—it can be a way of finally forging a life that feels livable. In a narrative about loss yielding to creativity, trauma yielding to rebirth, Tariq's embrace of English as a means to go on in the aftermath of unspeakable pain may not be an insignificant detail after all. And it must surely hold a special meaning for el Moncef, who chose to write *The Offering* in English even though he had other languages—languages, moreover, that are illustrious for their literary achievements—at his fingertips.

On one level, *The Offering* is a story about the struggles and hard-earned joys of everyday life: lazy, meandering days at the park, on the beach, and in the maze of city streets; family reunions, family recipes, and family squabbles; the anxieties and rewards of fatherhood; and the promises and betrayals of love. On another level, it is a story about—to once again borrow Tariq's words— "the pyrotechnics of fate," about sudden events that change absolutely everything so that there is no going back, no return to how things once were. In el Moncef's novel, that sense of fatefulness is poignantly expressed in the equivocal joys and sacrifices of the creative mind torn between the "place of convergence where the miracle of beautiful creation is born" and the sinking realization that "every miracle comes with a price tag." It is hard to come out of this story feeling hopeful. But it is also hard to come out of it feeling completely hopeless. This, I would say, is one reason this novel is so riveting. At the end, one is left with a profound sense of perplexed ambiguity—just as is often the case in "real" life.

Mari Ruti

Foreword

I am an impatient writer, which means I am no writer at all. Every time I try to express my thoughts in writing, I feel cramped and clumsy and out of place, tripped by the words and angry at them. The written text is an element I've never learned to tame or to trust. And so at the risk of being unclear and uninformative, I will be brief—not because there is wisdom in brevity, as the proverb has it, but simply because writing is beyond me.

The first thing I would like to say here: if you're holding this book in your hands, if you're thinking of reading it, you need to know up front that it is the work of a dead poet. Before he committed suicide, the man who authored *The Offering*, Tariq Abbassi,[1] made me sole legatee but failed to leave instructions about what to do with his legacy. When I discovered the stunning typescript of Abbassi's novel on his computer (along with the appended self-addressed e-mail that he calls "the letter"), I assumed that since it formed a full narrative, titled and almost completed, its author probably intended to share it with his fellow humans and be remembered by it. This book was conceived on the faith of that assumption.

The second thing I would like to include in this introductory note is a brief reference to the agonizing circumstances in which Abbassi's opus came into existence as a printed text. Soon after discovering *The Offering*, I tried to make it available to the general public through the conventional channels of publication, but the publishers I contacted didn't want anything to do with the dead man's story. The fruit of his labor was like a luckless foundling: rejected by all. And

---

[1]Abbassi drowned himself in the ocean and his body was never recovered. He had left a suicide note.

so I decided to be its ultimate guardian, this unwanted brainchild. I sent Abbassi's work to an American copy editor, a fiction writer herself and a French-to-English translator—she edited it and sectioned it and patched it up as best she could. Then I e-mailed the copy-edited text with its translated foreword to a typesetter in Manchester. Finally, when the text was press-ready, I took it to a printer here in town.

And now the story of the dead poet is a full, material book: three-dimensional, delivered from the vast electronic prison house designed by its author—a labyrinthine multimedia mosaic of collaged diary excerpts and pictures and audios and videos sprawling endlessly in the recesses of a near-defunct laptop.

Unfortunately, not being a writer myself, I will never find the words to express why and how the reproduction of that mosaic—the sad and somber tale narrated in these pages—has become the center of my existence. Suffice it to say here that Abbassi's story means so much to me that it has quite literally driven me to distraction. (I will, of course, spare you the circumstances of *that* narrative—it being another story, as they say, and none that you would care to hear: the sad vicissitudes of distraught and distracted men do not make for good storytelling.)

This is the book of a man who, in spite of immense handicaps, was not only able to quest after the truth and live for the truth; he was also willing to *die* by it. Abbassi was most certainly aware that the truth, like a too-potent medication, was going to kill him, but he never stopped questing, despite the many flaws, inaccuracies, and outright fabrications of his narrative. Flagrant and misleading as they are, those obvious failures should not be viewed as moral shortcomings, nor should they be used to bear judgment on the man who committed them. They were motivated by three factors no human being can control: guilt, illness, and fear of prosecution.

I don't think Abbassi was much of a storyteller, but that doesn't mean he didn't have a story to tell.

This book is the story of that story—that's what it became the moment the printer gave me a boxful of it and I stopped and sat down in her lobby and pulled one volume out of the box to hold it in my hands and feel the full mass and heft of it.

Now, if you are the kind of reader who thinks, "Since the truth is such a sinister drug why on earth bother with it," this book was never intended for you, and this is probably the point at which you're going to close it and dismiss the case—pull the plug on the story of "The Man from Tunisia."

But if you happen to be the other kind of reader—a steadfast lover of the truth—this book is about to become your life companion.

Sami Mamlouk
Rodez, France
March 2017

"**M**y brothers were even worse," I said. "They treated me like a freak. The fear and the revulsion were almost physically palpable, like a mean smell that kept filling the air between us."

Zoé and I were lounging on our favorite bench in Square du Vert-Gallant, an escarped garden at the northern tip of Ile de la Cité. That solitary bench, we both liked to think, was a unique spot on the island—perched at the end of a promontory high enough to give you the only open view of Pont des Arts and the river traffic below.

Sitting there was like being on the prow of an ocean liner: if you kept your eyes on the bridge and on the water, it was easy to sustain the ship illusion and ignore the riverside bustle on either side of the island—rush-hour traffic pouring out of the Right Bank *Quais.*

"Terrible," Zoé said. "Would they rather you showed up alone? They're your kids, after all—their nephews; and the three of you need a solid old-fashioned sense of family belonging at this point."

I remember the moment and its meaning very clearly: the shadows around us were long and the lawn a deep green in the late afternoon. The breeze was almost autumnal, and our mood was darkening like the colors of the garden, the crisp Paris sky.

I felt Zoé stiffen at the thought of how alone I was: she clasped her hands and leaned forward with her elbows on her knees, staring into the grass between her feet.

Then she turned around and sat back, looking into my eyes—her face tired but tender.

She put her hand on my shoulder: "You can always count on *me.* You know that, Tariq, don't you?"

"I know I can."

Shams came over from the sandbox.

He was thirsty and I gave him the bottle to refill, looking over my shoulder to see if he still remembered the tap by the gate.

He looked even lankier in his oversized overalls, with the seat flapping slightly below his lean buttocks—a boy claiming his share of the world, walking with an attitude, each forward-leaning stride a statement.

Zoé wanted to know the latest news in my divorce lawsuit.

I said, "I called Le Bel before we went down to Tunisia: she told me we'd never get the judge to set a date before the fall, gave me the usual crap about the slow wheels of justice, and we left it at that. That's all the news there is, I'm afraid. Think of the irony, though: now that the basic facts have been established in the finding, it's the judge who is stalling the lawyer!"

"You mean there's nothing she can do to speed things up? What about Shams's schooling this fall? Why didn't she use *that* as an argument?"

"Completely irrelevant at this point. You know the story: there's no abduction charge against Regina, and since kidnapping your own kids isn't a crime in this country, the judge decided the boys are in a stable enough environment, living with their mother and her parents. I think they're dragging their feet on the final hearing *because* of Shams's schooling. They'll wait and open the file long after summer recess; then they'll say, 'Wait a minute, this boy is already enrolled in a German school—*there's* another factor of stability.'"

The barges and the scenic boats glided along with a faint rustle, their sounds muffled in the strange hush of the riverbed—the aquarium stillness of its depth. On the Left Bank, Paris went on about its business, but it all felt remote and vacuum-sealed, like the sounds of the Seine down below.

I kept going back to Tunisia: "It's astonishing how little we know our loved ones—the secret personality traits that a sudden twist of fate can bring out in them. I never thought my mother and my sisters would be so deft at hiding their pain. Although I knew damn well how much they suffered inside, it was such a relief to see them put up a good front. It took a lot of strength, I'm sure—some sort of stoic, understated power I never suspected in them."

She threw me a teasing wink and a smile.

"That's women for you. It's called the power of resilience. They showed greater tolerance for the out of the ordinary than the men. Your brothers and your brothers-in-law saw only weirdness in your situation—and it must have spooked them. I guess they were scared—*and* confused."

She took a deep breath.

"To them, you had suddenly turned into something unrecognizable. The way they saw it, your life had taken a bizarre turn—you were metamorphosed into something unthinkable to them as men: some sort of *male* mother—something they couldn't name or conceptualize. They must have found that very unsettling to their male identity."

Zoé stood up and walked over to the trash bin.

She tossed the empty bottle and said that she wanted to play— her way of telling me she had had enough.

I picked up the rucksack and followed her down the path.

The Ceylon tea scent of her skin wafting on the breeze, the white spaghetti-strap sundress, the shadow of her legs shimmering behind the see-through fabric: I felt a pang of guilty desire walking behind her.

Womanlessness hurts: you see a beautiful woman and it is that sinking-in-the-heart again—counting the days and the months of loneliness, feeling sorry for yourself.

She kicked off her sandals and hopped into the sandbox while I stood back and watched them in the corner: Zoé hovering around the boys at first; then getting into the game little by little—holding the bucket for Haroon, dumping the sand where Shams was squatting, making sand patties with the plastic molds.

———

I had parked my car near Place d'Italie on my way here, and so we took a taxi.

I struggled with Zoé to put the double stroller into the trunk—the driver would not help.

We lifted it up and slid it in over the rim of the trunk, and Shams kept reminding Zoé how aged it was: "Daddy calls it the rickety rickshaw," he said.

We all laughed.

I sat in the back with Haroon in my lap and Shams right by my side.

The drive down Boulevard Saint Germain was very slow—it was sundown when we reached Place du Panthéon, with Saint Etienne du Mont a deep copper in the afterglow, its slate bell tower veering toward black.

The memory of that moment—the temporal threshold of that something heavy with happening that is just about to hit us; the still-unknown bend in time that the moment is; the twist that will take us into the territory of the utterly new:

It is the first evening of our vacation in Paris—the beginning of something that will leave our existence forever shattered.

A few days from now, on August 30, my sons will be murdered.

None of us knows it yet, but that taxi ride in the summer of 2007 is the first step in a set of events that will seal the boys' fate just a few days later, destroying them and destroying everything that the four of us mean for each other.

In time, the unthinkable will come to pass, and within the time span of one night so many things will occur (so swiftly, so uncontrollably) that do not even have a place or a name or a concept or an image within me yet—not in my darkest fears.

How does one tumble from one state of being into another, from one page of utter clarity into a numberless leaf of illegible cipher?

And the unstoppable succession of things and faces and places—the mathematical rigor of their concatenation, like a row of dominos minutely lined up by a Master Hand, choreographed to fall flat in perfect succession:

The monstrous death of my children.

My traumatic brain injury and the psychiatric complications.

My transfer from the Paris trauma center to the holistic institution in Brittany.

My work with holistic psychiatrist Dr. Cohen and the hypnotherapy team.

The providential role of Sami Mamlouk, my associate.

The ambiguous role of Police Commissaire Pierre Collin.

The redeeming role of my mother's letter—for all its unspoken terrors, its deliberately naïve swiftness and platitudinous illusions of closure.

And Zoé Selma Brahmi—the terrible things that will happen to and through her.

All these things will soon come to pass; in one night, they will become our only reality—the reality that will possess us completely.

But in this moment, riding together through the sun-gilded streets, we are happy without knowing it—filled with the invisible joy of our free-floating freedom and our togetherness.

At this point in time, I still don't know that an erroneous letter will become the center of my life—entire passages from it echoing in my head, as if it is something I have written myself.

I still don't know that an injury will alter my existence in language and my prose beyond recognition.

The dark things are not here yet; they are still crouching in the Womb of Time, still only about to happen—the things that will keep us pent up in terror, that will make us broken and bleak-minded with despair.

We are still dancing on the rim of the abyss, and we do not know it—still riding the happy wave of here-and-now.

———

Even in my Sorbonne days I used to find the narrow lanes behind the Panthéon sad and strange at the end of a summer day: there was always a resigned and melancholy feeling about those moments, when the buildings east of the Place took on the last flush of sunset—a short-lived miracle of enchantment on the facades of pale stone, too fickle and passing to be true.

On both sides of Rue Clovis, the alleys were choking with the early diners, tourists mostly—strolling from restaurant to restaurant and studying the menus, holding hands, kissing, laughing.

It was Summertime Paris, Romance Paris—the Paris of the willingly self-deceived tourist: they knew it, and they were alive and adrift on the giddiness of the deception.

We got out of the taxi at the top of Rue Descartes.

On the terrace of the Verlaine, the tables were all taken: the beautifully dressed women and the chatter of merry conversation—couples about town with time on their hands and money to spend, their libidinal heat almost a palpable exhalation in the air.

And the accordion player sitting in his customary spot—this side of the menu board and the wooden geranium planters, a top hat between his feet and the red carpet, the sheet music stacked up next to his canvas stool.

We passed the crowd outside Di Angelo's and Zoé said that we should all go for ice cream.

"Good idea," I said. "Let me get some dinner for the boys first."

On Place de la Contrescarpe, Zoé walked over to the churchyard with the boys in the stroller, and I went and bought dinner from Sarkis'.

The shadows were thick on Rue Mouffetard—it felt almost as if night had fallen, but the iron bench and the gray cobblestones were still full of the heat of the day.

We fed them rice and kofta and listened to the street band playing for the crowd on the bistro terraces around the square, probably taking their cue from the stand-up poster and the big sign by the American Bar—"Billie's Way," it read.

I have always placed you far above me,
I just can't imagine that you love me.

Once or twice I tried to imagine Billie's voice rising above the music, but I was distracted by Haroon—he was tired and grumpy and kept getting off the bench, making for the fountain behind us.

———

I gave Zoé two pajama sets for the boys and she took them to the bathroom.

I went to the kitchen, put our ice cream in the freezer, dished out the mezze in small plates and set them out on the table.

She called me into the room when she got them dressed and ready.

Zoé was trying to talk to them, but they were too excited— Haroon saying something about the Rhine and jumping on the couch, Shams toying with my laptop and talking to him: "It's *not* the *Rhine*, it's the *Seine.*"

"Stop it you two," I said. "Let's have a nice bedtime story, shall we? Come, boys, give Zoé a good-night hug."

I pulled out the couch bed while they cuddled up with her, put out the pillows and the bedspread (I noticed Haroon rubbing one eye with his fist, leaning into her).

Shams patted his brother on the shoulder, told him not to be sad, but Haroon shook him off and hid his face in Zoé's bosom as she knelt on the rug with her arm around him in a loose embrace.

I knelt down by my son's side, leaned over, and murmured in his ear: "What's the matter, my son?"

He shook his head with a muffled sound.

"He mixed the Seine up with the Rhine," Shams explained. "I was just telling him *Grossmama*'s apartment was on the *Rhine* not here."

More head shaking and muffled sounds from Haroon.

"He thinks he's come back to the *Rhine*," Shams went on.

"This isn't Cologne," I told him, putting as much softness into my voice as I could. "We're in Paris, Haroon. It's still vacation time and we're going to have a lot of fun here. You're right, though, the Rhine does run through Cologne; and the river that runs through Paris is called *La Seine.*"

He turned around and looked at me—with condemnation in his eyes, I thought, and something like a terrible discovery: rivers do go their separate ways after all—the revelation came with a truth too crushing for him to bear.

He started to cry, silently at first—his lower lip curling out and trembling, his cheeks sagging with sadness; then he was moaning and saying he wanted to go to *Grossmama.*

I picked him up and put my arm around his shoulders. "Let's go to bed, young man. I'm going to read you the wonderful story of the straw ox."

I put him on the bed and lay down beside him. I ran my fingers through his soft brown curls—that was all I could think of to console him.

Zoé sat down behind me and reached out over my shoulders to hold his hand.

The brown eyes, glistening with tears, their hopelessly disconsolate expression—my own mirrored image: Haroon.

"Tomorrow you'll see how beautiful the Seine is," I whispered, almost singing. "We'll go for a walk along the quays; we'll take a boat and see Notre Dame. Would you like to take a boat with me and Shams tomorrow?"

He nodded and rolled up his eyes a little.

Shams sat up. "Really?" he wanted to know.

I told him to lie down and hush up. "We'll talk about it tomorrow. Now it's story time."

Zoé turned on the reading lamp and switched off the ceiling light. She tiptoed out of the room, leaving the door ajar. I sat in the armchair by the lamp and commenced to read "The Straw Ox."

Haroon fell asleep almost immediately. A few times, his head rolled slightly across the pillow and into the light—his eyes, surprised, lighting up for a split second then withdrawing behind the golden-brown eyelashes.

Shams lay curled up on his side, facing the wall, listening intensely—I knew he was.

When I finished "The Straw Ox," I sang him an Egyptian lullaby and a German lullaby, very softly.

Then I kissed him on his forehead and stood up.

"Sweet dreams," I said.

"Sweet dreams," he drawled, as he always did on the edge of sleep.

I walked out of the room and left the door cracked, the way they always wanted it.

———

(*Betrayed*: it was the word I used in my first diary entry for that night.

Rather maudlin—the tone and manner of that entry:

The condemnation was written in his eyes, I wrote. *"You failed me. How could you do it—make the rivers part?"*

I still recall the moment I discussed that passage with Dr. Cohen. It was the first time we broached the muddled question of my guilt feelings—a sense of "residual debt," she said, which I am not yet ready to "assume."

"It's interfering with the unfolding of the grief process," she said.

Guilt, complicated grief, loss—the ravages of a life in ruins, and the tools deployed to put it together again: analysis, self-image and speech therapy, cognitive skills reconstruction, motor skills therapy.

And that other possibility—looming in my stormy consciousness like a haven of redemption, one that only Dr. Cohen's team could offer in a clinical setting: hypnotherapy—my only hope of recovering the night of August 29 from the pits of amnesia.)

———

I found Zoé in the living room, stretched out on the couch with a glass of rosé in her hand. She had just taken a shower and seemed pensive, or maybe simply tired.

I poured myself a glass of wine and sat down in the armchair.

She asked me if everything was okay.

"Haroon went right off to sleep," I said. "He's had such a hectic day, poor kid."

There was only a little light, from the kitchen and the lamp in the corner. The half-dark put more depth into our voices somehow.

For a second, she appeared changed, unreal lying there on her side—her skin looking dark and grainy as scoured bronze, her teased locks a deeper shade of blond.

She eased herself against the armrest and slid down a bit, staring past her feet.

Her toenails were painted with dark polish—they had the depth and hard sheen of onyx, but there was no telling what color they were.

———

Zoé said, "Forget the future—for the time being. It seems to me the more urgent question is, what's the problem *now*? I think it's important for you to be able to put your finger on what's ailing you at *this* point in your life."

We were done with dinner, I realized, but when I offered to put away the dishes she said she would do that later. I sensed a hint of impatience in her tone; and I thought it was probably very important for her that the moment not be interrupted: she had mulled over the situation for some time, wrote out our conversation in her meticulous mind, and now she wanted me to sit down and listen to the full script.

"First, you need to spend many, many months listening to your pain—the *loss* of your relationship with Regina. That's how you start putting it behind you, I guess. Getting on with your life—rebuilding it actually, from scratch. You'll have plenty of time to think about the future—*after* you've sorted out the past."

Then she was quiet for a while, staring at her glass and turning the stem between her thumb and forefinger.

I was not quite sure how to interpret her silence now: was she collecting her thoughts? Was she still irked? Or was she waiting for me to say something?

I decided to speak: "I guess what I still have to work on is my bitterness at Regina's duplicity."

Her eyes came alive, lighting up with an inward smile—she did expect me to say more, after all.

I told her, "Theoretically, I can accept that she was not feeling at home in France. Also, her worries about not being able to fulfill herself. But to come home in the middle of the night and find the apartment half-empty. To spend three days not knowing where they were…emotionally, I still can't manage it somehow. It keeps coming back into my mind, over and over. It's creating so much emotional blockage, I can't even *think* of writing poetry. That kind of secretive premeditation, that double life she was leading—it's incomprehensible to me. It has left me with so much unprocessed anger."

I offered Zoé some water. She shook her head.

I poured myself a glass then I said, "The other problem is my apprehension about the boys: I don't think I can live with any long-distance visitation arrangement, even a generous one. I want them to live close to me. I don't want to be a vacation father. I *hate* the idea. I guess my fear is waking up one day and finding myself a total stranger to them. I think I'd rather stop all contact than see that happen. Then again, in my better moments I think maybe this feeling is just what it is—an irrational fear."

"Well, hold on to your better moments, Tariq. It would be tragic if you didn't—and you know it. After I broke up with Yann, I was angry, too—*and* I could not write any poetry, for months. When you hate you can't create. Creating is exactly like having babies. It's love that does it."

She drank up the last drop of wine and put down her glass, a bit theatrically. There was a twinkle of self-satisfaction in her eyes as she stood up.

———

I was leaning against the worktop and watching her put the dishes in the dishwasher:

"I really don't know how to explain the temptation," I said, "if that's what it is in the first place. The thing is, after those flashes of anger, when I'm totally worn out with rage, I'll find myself worrying about how long I have to live with this. It's terrifying—the idea that I might actually spend the rest of my life nursing this sort of righteous pain on and off, like an allergy or a migraine. That's why I can understand how some fathers are very tempted to give up—walk away altogether. I'm not saying I find that acceptable. In fact, I believe it's neither acceptable nor respectable. But I can understand it just the same."

She took the ice cream out of the freezer and scooped it out into the bowls.

"That's exactly where I disagree with you," she said. "What you're describing to me is deep hurt and the resentment and anger that go with it. What I'm talking about is the courage and strength it takes to come to terms with both—to avoid the denial that comes from being a victim. In order to do that, you'll have to take a deep, hard look within and discover what it is *in you* that contributed to the collapse of your marriage. Obviously, walking away from the pain won't do it. But I agree with you: it *is* very tempting to walk away."

Suddenly, the thought crossed my mind that this moment was all too familiar—Zoé bustling about and I standing close by, gabbing on: it was like an acted-out scene from my childhood—whenever I wanted to wheedle something out of my mother, I would always do it in the kitchen, while she was busy cooking.

What was I trying to whine out of Zoé, I wondered—guiltlessness?

For some reason, I felt irritated at the turn that the conversation was taking.

I was glad when we switched to small talk.

———

I told her, "The restaurant is keeping me very busy, as usual, but since I hired this assistant I can get more writing done in the morning. He handles the shopping and bookkeeping fairly well. I can rely on him. You know how it is, though, the lifestyle. Sometimes I wonder how long I'll be able to keep the secret life going—the life of the mind, as they say. Most nights I get home very late. Then it's the diary and lights out. That leaves Sundays for everything else—mostly reading and writing, or a film sometimes. But who's complaining? When I think about how bad we both felt about our job prospects after the dissertation..."

"It was dreadful," she said, shaking her head. "'The academic job market is tough on Deleuzean freaks,' remember?" She chuckled.

"Good old Geffen. That man is so special, you know? The only truly supportive professor I've ever known."

"Oh, yes. Geffen is a stand-up guy, all right. Too bad he couldn't help us much with the job search. He fought my dissertation committee even *before* the defense. They told him the subtitle was too self-indulgent for a doctoral student. What, 'A Poetic Machine'? 'They make it sound like I'm spoiling you,' he told me. The hell with them, though. I liked it then and I still like it now—my poetic machine."

"You wrote a great thesis—and he was very proud of you. I wonder if there was some sort of father figure—"

"Now we're getting psychoanalytical, eh? You did wonder before and I already told you. He *has* a daughter-philosopher—in case you don't know."

"Of course I know," I said, still teasing her, "but she's not a *genius*."

"Oh, please. The genius who ended up in her mom's lingerie shop. But as you said, who's complaining? Those rich woman's undies are paying my bills and putting bread on the table, bless them. Plus, I get enough time to think and feel and write."

———

She got up off the couch, stretched, and said she was going to bed.

I asked her what time her train was leaving and she told me she would be heading out around eleven.

"I'll take the subway—Gare d'Orléans. Remind me to give you the American Bar voucher tomorrow. And don't forget to take your stuff to Monique."

"What did you show her?"

"Three photopaintings and the video you gave me for my birthday."

"Oh, no."

"Oh, *yes*! It's great material, Tariq, you know that. Please go see her. She's extremely interested—and not just in the photopaintings.

She loved the video, too—that grainy underwater quality. Her gallery is right opposite the park. You can take the boys to the carousel."

"Parc Monceau."

"Yes."

I stood up and went to get my sheets and my pillow from the closet in the corridor.

Zoé had said all she needed to say: she had been very concerned through all our discussions, but never emotional or intrusive. I was glad of that. No excessive outrage, no second-guessing or blaming, no specific advice—just listening and pointing out where my priorities should be.

She stopped in the middle of the corridor on her way to the bathroom—stood there for a while, looking down at me.

I stopped rummaging and sat down on the floor, my hand still on the bottom shelf.

She gave me a long smile and I smiled back, even though I could not quite decipher the meaning of that smile—not necessarily a scrutinizing smile, I thought. Maybe an understanding smile, at once penetrating and compassionate. A tipsy smile? I was a bit confused by her expression. I expected her to stagger off.

Instead, she said she found it interesting—what I had told her on the square: Billie Holiday singing in my head.

"Well, I think you'd do well to remember the other song for now. Lock your heart and throw away the key for a while, Tariq. I know it's going to be tough, but I think you need that emotional vacuum—helps you stay focused on yourself. Who are *you*? How are *you* feeling about yourself? Where do *you* go from here? You can think of that special somebody later, when you've settled your—quarrel with yourself. Sleep tight."

———

(Traces of things gone, echoes of voices that have ceased to carry any direct living meaning for me—their only life an artificial reconstruction from the diary, the files on my laptop, the labyrinthine directories of the external hard drive.

A massive archive of words, sounds, and images: the sum of my sad, sad life—in scribbles and bytes.)

———

I made up the couch and wrote in my diary, thinking how empty I felt in the face of Zoé's impending departure.

We were two close friends—lying in bed after hours of intimate sharing and reassurance; and yet here I was, shaken with sudden unexplainable anguish at the thought of her leaving.

All at once, I realized that I had an overwhelming need to get up and share my emptiness with Zoé—so forlorn I felt at the nameless loss already forming within me.

But even if I walked up to her room and opened up, there was no telling what she would say: that it was all a lot of pathetic mush? That I could e-mail or pick up the phone and talk to her any time?

Again, I remembered my guilty sexual craving in the garden, my secret childhood recollection in the kitchen, and again, there was the saving urge to withdraw into my stillness.

Some things are best locked up inside.

———

I am in an arcade somewhere in Venice.

On my arm is a slender, pale-skinned woman—a prostitute.

We are walking down a long gallery—endless shops on our right, their tall oak-framed display windows cluttered with antiques and gilded furniture.

"I'll even kiss you and be very tender with you—for a small extra fee," she's saying, leaning into me with teasing tenderness. "All these cheap hustling girls you see around you—they're just after your money. I'm going to take good care of you, because I work with feeling—and there's nothing I hate more than a half-ass job."

Now I can see streetlights in the distance just outside the gallery gate—dim, foggy, shaky, like faraway lanterns seen from a tunnel.

We press onward until we are outside and heading down a dark back lane so narrow it feels like an underground passageway—the stifling presence of moldy old stone walls on either side, leaning so close, as if they were about to collapse onto each other any minute.

The street reminds me of those Tunisian roofed alleys in the Medina that you can span with your arms stretched out.

We come to an intersection of four alleys, and I say, "Tra le vie."

The woman does not seem to have heard me.

"Here we are," she says, brisk and businesslike. "But before I take you to my place, I'm going to ask you to do one more thing—a pure formality, really. Everybody in the business here does it. You need to give me your mask. It means you're with me."

So, I hand her mine—a rough reddish Phoenician face made of grainy plaster or clay.

There is a white plastic armchair on one of the street corners: she crosses over to it, upends it, and puts the mask on the underside of the seat.

"Now take my hand and let's run to my place," she says with girlish glee.

But the moment I grasp her hand and we start running, I realize how bony and stiff it is—and hard, stone hard.

I stop and turn to look at her, and what I see is a face that has turned the color of grayish-brown parchment: the woman is a mummy—that is what I am thinking in this frozen second of horror.

Her cheekbones sticking out of the brittle skin, her mouth set in a dead grin.

It was the morning of August 26, 2007.

Total darkness in the room, except for a crack of yellow street-light between the curtains—the leaves of a balcony plant like long blades silhouetted against the fabric.

The blood beating in my ears, the rustle of my body between the sheets.

I fumbled for the switch and picked up my diary.

I began to record the nightmare.

———

The boys dragged me into a playful scuffle just after Zoé had left.

We had a rowdy pillow fight in the living room and I let them wrestle me down to the floor.

They were all over me—screaming and pulling, and I played along with a lot of dramatic effect: I would grunt and strain and pull funny faces, make believe I was struggling hard to get them off me, then I would let myself slump back under their push.

I went through the same routine several times, and the whole act got them so excited that I did not know how to get them to stop.

"Uncle, uncle, *uncle!*" I screamed after a while. "I have to clear the dishes and fix your lunch, boys. We're eating in the garden."

I gave them color pencils and paper and went about the apartment opening the windows and tidying up. When I got to the breakfast table, I found a handwritten note under my plate:

> *If you want to become whole,*
> *let yourself be partial.*
> *If you want to become straight,*
> *let yourself be crooked.*
> *If you want to become full,*
> *let yourself be empty.*
> *If you want to be reborn,*
> *let yourself die.*
> *If you want to be given everything,*
> *give everything up.*
>
> *Take it easy on yourself, Tariq. And never forget: I'm with you.*
>
> *Love,*
>
> *Zoé*

I sat down with the piece of paper in my hand:

Haroon was drawing on the rug, Shams hunched over the piano, playing random notes—very gentle, balanced, and surprisingly self-restrained for a child with no musical training.

Those steady fingers moving softly on the keyboard. The fine-chiseled features earnest and intent—so much at odds with the intense twist of his pitch-black eyebrows warping like two wild streaks of charcoal drawn above his dark eyes.

Zoé was obviously talking to me in that slip of paper, through it, but I could not help staring at Shams's fragile frame instead, thinking of him:

Can I learn to give *him* up—if only for a time, the better to find him again? And the price? A sacrifice too heavy to bear? A risky wager on an uncertain future—the wait between holidays, the emptiness of a home without their presence, the gaping wound of time lost forever, irredeemable?

I kept sitting there, taking them in—my flesh and blood.

The urge to hug them swelling in my chest like a tumor: to make a gesture, say something that would seal a bond between us lasting through our lives.

Instead, I just sat there, my hands clammy with the hemmed-in emotion—watching them play, two boys basking in the languorous mood of a carefree summer morning.

There was something deeply rueful beneath the peaceful surface of this moment—the vast distance between their serenity and my somber ruminations as I contemplated the forces raging around us: we lived in two different universes and I was a powerless prisoner of mine—hoping desperately to reach out to them yet holding back, fearing that the second I tried, something of my sorrow would mar the beautiful equanitmity of their world beyond repair.

Shams must have sensed my torment: "Dad, aren't we going to the boats?"

"That's later," I said. "We'll go to Jardin Carré and have lunch first."

———

(I have never hated Zoé for what she did—never even blamed her.

Commissaire Collin is convinced that her father, Faisal Brahmi, was involved in the plot that led to the murder of my sons. The commissaire's theory: "He is a facilitator."

Zoé chose to protect him and lie to my family—not of her own free will, most likely; she was quite possibly acting under threat of death when she visited my mother in Tunisia—ostensibly to brief her on the circumstances of my sons' passing.

I never shared my thoughts with Collin, but I am positive that the murderers of my sons were behind her trip to Tunisia: the Zoé who went to see my mother was a dogged and harried woman—not just a protective daughter appalled at the prospect of seeing her family sullied with the tarnish of a heinous crime.

She lied to my mother, and as far as I know, none of my siblings had ever tried to verify the facts of her story:

They came under the same the threat, I am sure. I can see their terror—Zoé, my family—encoded in my mother's words, feel it every day, like barely visible cryptograms inscribed between the lines of her letter: mother's references to the network of evil men from my past—sinister ominous patriarchal figures driven by dark satanic designs, striving together toward the achievement of horrific goals.

What the ciphered words are saying—the words within the words: she is in dread of them, the men; for only terror can explain the rushed glibness with which she closes the case of her own son, the brutal vanishing of her own descendants.

It is all too simple, too dubiously simple: the pacing and progression of the letter; the pseudo-facts; the solidary, emotional get-together in my mother's home; my family's attitude of pained, tragic acceptance; the cut-and-dried elucidations and the illusions of closure.

Ultimately, however, there is something far more significant than the fear and the glibness encoded in her letter: an intimate, secret yet incessantly reiterated invitation embedded within the trite discourse—to see the real threat lurking behind the facile hopes of closure that she proffers, the warning intimations of a woman who is telling me that she was under pressure when she sat down to write those words.

In spite of all the murky manipulations that took place in Tunisia, I have never doubted Zoé's sincerity in our friendship, her love of my children. I am certain that she was as trusting and as unknowing as we were when we set foot in her home that summer, that she did not have an inkling of what was in store for the three of us.

I never told Collin about my mother's letter, because as soon as I was able to digest and come to terms with the contents of that letter I was fully convinced that neither the visit to Tunisia nor the story were Zoé's idea: the lie she told my mother was too complex, too strategically self-serving in its complexity to have come from her.

She was terrorized into both the visit and the lie—I remain convinced of the reality of that lie to this day.

And my mother's urgent secret desperate hints at it: I am convinced that someday I will know under what terrible circumstances she had to accept Zoé's story.

Someday, when the time is right, I will know—there is nothing more certain in my mind.)

———

The mysterious alchemy of people and places.

On any given Sunday in winter, you will find Jardin Carré no different from any neighborhood garden in Paris: just another sleepy green patch in the sleepy city, its snug dull commonness curling about you like a well-worn blanket—the drifting eddies of tattered leaves; the water spots on the dry fountain; the quiet shuffle of bourgeois families walking through, going home from church—to lunch and afternoon coffee and cake.

Sitting there on one of those wrought-iron green benches under the sycamores, you could be in any hinterland village.

Then in the summertime the tourists would take over: lovers from all over the world streaming in and out every day from nine till eight, and the garden would metamorphose into a parade ground of libidinally charged bodies.

It was never excessive, embarrassing, or flashy; yet you had to struggle to keep your gaze from getting trapped in the rites of intimacy that went on all about you: feeling at once drawn in and repulsed by the raw poetry of the moment, the sheer animal energy around you—those lovers caught in the charge of their erotic vibrations, the gravitational attraction of their constellated bodies.

You (the testimonial eye against your will) always find yourself capturing their presence there in furtive mental snapshots—immaterial flashes of the mind, your gaze secretly framing those scattered nodes of lustful heat pulsating through the garden: the passion and power it took to bring them all together in this place where you stand like an unwilling witness, too proud and too visible to linger on any one face.

And yet sometimes it would just happen—the hard implacable fact of looking, of lingering with your eyes:

The amber-skinned woman (African American, Jamaican?) straddling the rim of the fountain—the carefree charm of that long skirt pulled up almost waist-high, that foot splashing the water. Her girlfriend sitting behind her, stroking the small of her back and leaning over her shoulder to put the joint between the proffered lips—head tilted sideways tenderly, copper-colored hair dangling in long thick oily curls. Taking a deep drag, she closed her eyes and let go, settling back into her lover's bosom.

Or the teenage lovers—standing there unavoidable, in the middle of the shady side path (sun beating down hard on the main path along the central lawn as we came trundling around the trees into the shade): it was perhaps not the most beautiful kiss I had ever seen, but it was certainly the fiercest—driven by a passion that was like desperate thirst: these two had found the spring of love and they were drinking ravenously—their vibrations intense, almost aggressive; but beautiful beyond words—and filled with a primal eloquence that was alien to you, a floundering long-distance father, a failed husband, a man with the bile of shattered relationships still caked in his throat like dry clay.

When they were behind us, Shams wanted to know what they were doing, of course.

I told him that they loved each other very, very much and were saying it with a big slurpy kiss.

The two of them laughed.

———

I unpacked our lunch on the bench under the sycamores: we had a nice view of the lawns and the flower beds and I wanted the boys to run around barefoot when the sun started going behind the trees.

Haroon was grinning with mischief: "Give me my slurpy," he said. "I can eat all by myself."

"Slurpy! Did you hear that, Dad? He called the sandwich slurpy! Isn't that funny?"

I said, "A slurpy sandwich? Yummy!"

"But it's a tuna sandwich, yes Dad? It's a tuna sandwich?"

"Yes," I said. "Haroon was just kidding, you see."

"*Noooo*," Haroon said, "it's a SLUR-*PY!*"

We all had a good laugh about that, and I told him I had to hold his sandwich for him because the tuna mixture inside it was gooey.

It was a hot day and the boys were constantly asking for water.

After a while, with the sun edging behind the treetops, I told the boys that if they felt like it we could all take off our sandals and loaf around on the lawn.

Haroon said it was a good idea.

We strolled around and named plants and flowers at first, then I spread out a towel in the shade and we played Mikado.

Shams was relentless with Haroon and I had to remind him that it was all right if his brother moved the sticks a little bit.

"Let him warm up," I said.

Haroon was positive that he could play better if he took off his cap. I told him to leave it on; then Shams moved a bunch of sticks and said he was warming up, too.

Behind the chestnut trees by the east gate, the rattle of something nasal and screechy, like a distant flight of geese. Somebody rolling up a creaky window shade.

My mind was not quite focused on the game—the secret tug of all those bodies, the nameless nagging of the recurrent questions: is there some One for me here—or anywhere? Who is She? Where is She? Can I even imagine Her?

Maybe the hush hovering over everyone in the garden (as if the conversations here were prayer) had something to do with my sudden feeling of aloneness: the motions of complicity between the lovers were like secret rites in consecrated territory, and I was sitting this side of their hallowed grounds—a stranger to their faith, alien and uninitiated, helpless to penetrate the code of their worship.

Maybe it was that, ultimately: feeling like an intruder in a place of communion where I sat awkward and misplaced, as if I had never known what being together meant.

I thought, "One is always lonely for the first time."

———

We left the garden through the gate on Rue Descartes and headed for the taxi stand by the Contrescarpe market square opposite Zoé's building—the din and glare of life outside the garden jarring even on a Sunday afternoon, the sidewalk cafés filling up already.

Haroon made me cross over to a creperie on the sunny side of the street: he had seen a woman eating outside the shop and started whining for a crepe.

I got him one with Nutella and we went and sat down on the same bench where Zoé and I had fed them yesterday: the crepe was not such a good idea—sticky, messy, and simply bad.

Before us, the marketplace was scattered with wrappers, empty plastic bottles, bits of food and fruit leftovers: a chaotic jumble of multicolored trash scattered over cobbled space the size of two basketball courts—in plain sight of the café crowds, at the height of the tourist season.

At some point I saw a taxi pull over to the stand and went to speak with the driver: he was hypocritically crass about not taking us—not enough room in the trunk for a big stroller, he argued. A patent lie.

After a while, a station wagon taxi came along and took us. He drove us to Pont Neuf.

———

I had seen him many times before—the bearded man standing silent and motionless under the bridge, his eyes, shadowed by the dark overhang of his bushy eyebrows, were always fixed on the river traffic; his face devoid of any recognizable expression or emotion, as rough and shadowy as weathered metal.

Today he was talking to himself.

I sat down on the bench next to him, took the water bottle out of my rucksack, and handed it to the boys.

His words at first were no more than hoarse incomprehensible mutterings, rushed and mechanical—uttered to himself a bit frantically but with a certain tone of humility, like penitential prayer.

Then he started sort of chanting—loud enough for me to hear:

"You always think you're going somewhere. But you're not *getting* anywhere, I can tell you. You think you can deny me. You think you can disappear me and turn me into a nothing. But I have already willed *you* into nothingness—long ago. The curse I cast on you—it's the curse of annihilation by invisible decay. And it's already eating away at the foundation of your existence like a cancer. You may not know it yet, but it is *eating away*. Open up your manholes and you'll see it: in the arteries of your waterpipes, in the cables that feed your eyes with sight and your ears with sound. You'll see it in your tunnels, in your subways, in the worn-out *joints* connecting the rails of your subways. The stitches that hold you together. You think they're strong? You seem so damn sure. You just wait and see. You'll see the full power of my will when it bursts right in your faces."

It was painful to imagine the state of his body inside that confusing jumble of rags into which he was bundled up—the smell of rotting shellfish and smoked herring almost unbearable.

He wore at least two pairs of torn ragged pants, two jackets, and several shirts—all torn and twisted beyond recognition, so grimy and hardened with filth that they looked like a muddy cast loosely wrapped around him. His espadrilles were almost unidentifiable: dark with patches of ingrained oil and dust, their rope soles all wispy with the hemp sticking out in feathery tufts from underneath, like clumps of dry grass.

The man's attitude was meek as a saint's, his voice mild; but there was something very disturbing about him—the disconnect between the soft tone and the rage of his intentions was eerie and unsettling.

He was such a symbol, it seemed to me: the dark consciousness of the city—a shattered testament to the many it had left behind.

And yet it was so easy to pass him by—the way you would overlook a familiar monument.

———

It is painful to watch the videos and the photos from the boat tour, to read the diary words on those moments. But they were beautiful moments and we were happy being together, happy at the sight of the wonders unfolding before our eyes.

My mawkish diary recollections, written the night of August 26:

The reddish ochre glow of the buildings along the quays reflected like abstract watercolors in the oily mirror of the Seine: Notre Dame rising before us in the ripening sunlight—straight, raw, and pure as a burnished mass of sheer cliff towering over the water; the skaters and the promenaders on the Rossi Garden esplanade; the aluminum twinkle of the Centre Pompidou (the boys and I joked about its structure—turned it into a water factory complete with pipes and vats).

In his need for attention, Shams was persistent and exhausting, but sweetly charming: he had a story for everything that captured his eyes (he knew that his voice was tiny in the baffling din around us, so he kept pulling at my sleeve every time he wanted to say something—I would obligingly tip my head over toward his side and listen).

Haroon was silent most of the time, taking it all in with his big wide-open eyes. Just every now and then, whenever he spotted a potted palm along the quays, he would shout: "A banana tree," as if that was his one duty for the rest of the day—to wait patiently and point them out one by one.

All of these things enveloped in the chugging noise of the boat, the excited yammering of the sightseers, the mechanical drone of the PA system (literally nobody was listening to the commentary). This and having to constantly pay attention and respond to Shams made me weary.

On our way back to the wharf, I felt them both press against me in silence. They, too, were tired so I put my arms around their shoulders and let them snuggle up and rest their heads in the hollow of my shoulders.

For a second, I felt Shams look up at me and I looked back: for just one second, I saw a flutter in his dark eyes—that flutter said more about his love for me than anything he could have ever expressed in words.

———

After the relaxed dinner and cartoons, the excitement of bedtime and the endless exhilarated chatter about the boat ride:

A sudden hush had fallen over the apartment, the shift to silence almost unbearable—the same silence that I had begun to fear since the night of our separation.

I opened the living room window and stood on the balcony for a while: the muffled chatter from the bars down below; the clinking of glasses and the clatter of silverware from the restaurants; the abstract laughter of people having an amusing conversation somewhere around the square.

A moment of nameless longings: Mouffetard sounded invitingly alive and merry, full of stories and promises.

I felt guilty almost immediately, thinking of what Shams had said in bed just before he nodded off to sleep:

"When are you going to marry Zoé?" he asked me, staring into the ceiling. His voice, hoarse with fatigue, had a disturbing quality of profundity about it—an urgency beyond his years.

"Zoé is my best *friend*," I said, laughing uncomfortably.

In the wedge of dim light slanting through the bedroom door, it was impossible to read any expression on his features. The contours of his face were statuesque and remote, shining with a thin dusty glitter. His nose was like an arrowhead carved in dark stone.

"Don't you have anybody to marry?"

"No."

"Then you'll have to marry *me*."

Southwest '06

There is something oddly stark and unqualified about the memory of pain visited upon others: a feeling of guilt and unworthiness that is so pervasive it becomes an integral part of everything you are; so total that it strips you of every sense of nuance and proportion, every shade of self-justification that might alleviate your feeling of culpability.

Also, when in remembrance you come to grasp the reality of the pain that you have caused and take full cognizance of your unworthiness, you begin to sense something altogether new coming over you: the realization that it is your natural lot to be the sole bearer of all that suffering, like a sacrificial beast on its way to slaughter.

In some way, you also find inexplicable peace in assuming your position as object of sacrifice: a reconciled acceptance of your fate that slowly grows into a form of cold faith and certainty within you, as if your whole life has been a rehearsal for that walk to the sacrificial altar.

Strange, how every trace of selfish personal pain or loss or outrage fades in the face of suffering visited upon others: your most intimate, most real dolor—indeed your very existence as a sorrowful entity—has a stupefying way of vanishing into blank irrelevance.

This has been my condition since I began to understand the loss that I had inflicted on Regina in the summer of 2007: as I started to come to terms with the deeds that I committed on August 29 of that year, I found myself speechless on the events of our separation, powerless to deal with the months of pain and fury that followed from it.

And yet there was a time before that summer when I used to spend many moments scrutinizing my diary with the frenzy of obsession, trying to make sense of our breakup.

How agitated I felt in and around those private pages—both recording my own torment and going over the record of it—at times spending hours of agonized contemplation over a few lines jotted in anguish, despair, or sheer anger.

(Now the very physical presence of those traces is a hollow shell emptied of all emotional meaning, not even an abstract residue of self-pity left—the spectral memories of a fictional man.

But there is that one exception: my last entry before the calamity. In themselves, the words are downright elated—thoughts of an enamored man slowly drifting off to sleep, a man looking forward to the sun rising over a new morning, in the new life.

August 29, 2007.

Then nothingness—an ocean of silence.

That stretch of blank paper beneath the words: the open wound of amnesia begins there—in that ocean of blankness lapping at the final stretch of recorded memory, my first beachhead of genuine happiness with the other woman.)

Still, unworthiness or no, the breakup has to be revisited somehow, without the rage and the anger and the agony now—swiftly and dispassionately, the way a deft mortician embalms a badly mangled body for its last resting place.

It began with an envelope taped to the door of a half-empty apartment, Regina's surreally titled "Farewell Note" inside the envelope—an indictment in disguise:

My wife said that by leaving me, she was trying to rid herself of years of emotional battery and begin a new life. In my selfishness, I stifled her potential and never acknowledged the sacrifices that she had to make for the sake of my career. Over the years, my "persistent attitude" of "pathological withdrawal" and my "systematic tactics of emotional battery" had become increasingly damaging, "reaching such a degree of gravity" that my very presence in the home was a "serious factor of emotional and psychological instability for our sons."

That was the beginning: Regina's letter and I running through the streets of Bordeaux at two o'clock in the morning, all the way to the Riverside precinct—the officer at the front desk asking me to wait with the others in the lobby.

My glasses were fogged up and I could not make out her face at first.

I tried to tell her that it was very urgent—a child abduction case, but her machine-gun voice crackled right through my words: "You need to keep calm. Have a seat in the waiting area. We'll start processing your complaint as soon as we can."

Across the lobby from where I sat: a dim corridor with a row of neon-lit offices that had transparent glass doors and blindingly white paneling inside.

In the first office, I saw a policeman behind his desk, busy with a plaintiff.

Slumped in my seat, watching the soundless interaction between the two men in that glaring box of neon light, it was all I could do not to fold my arms across my knees and lay my head down and go to sleep.

My mind was reeling—the fatigue of a long hard workday, the shock of the letter. I suddenly wanted this whole situation to go away—caught myself dreaming that it was just a desperate plea from Regina, an angry warning.

I wanted to be in bed, waiting for the phone to ring.

But there was no getting away from the reality of this place, with its sinister business of sad late-night stories.

The neon light fell so harshly on everything inside the office that the police officer's pale face seemed to shine with a phosphorescent halo.

The policeman who took my statement, a Maghrebi, wouldn't hear of child abduction: "Sir, I have no way of ascertaining that," he said. "I am not empowered to put the term 'abduction' in the wording of your statement. That's for the competent authorities to decide."

I could not take my mind off the heat even as he spoke: I was sweating, I realized, wondering how he could stand it in here—in his thick blue sweater, trapped within the stark plastic-paneled walls of this room.

The officer's voice was gravelly from smoking and sleeplessness but his tone was even, in a self-preserving way—the voice of a man who had seen too much madness and had learned to rise above the turmoil of tormented stories like mine.

Facing away from the screen, though, he looked much older than his years, the lines of his face dark and deep.

"And who are the competent authorities?" I said, feeling rather silly for asking.

"The justice system, I suppose."

Then, as if he were trying to ease my agitation, he told me that he had specified it was "spousal conflict."

I tried to explain that I was not even there, but he nodded and went on typing the report.

He handed me the slip and said that I had to go to the Prefect's office first thing in the morning: "They will enter the names of your spouse and your children in the missing persons database."

———

Standing outside the building, I began to realize what had happened tonight—and with the realization came the nameless understanding that nothing would ever be the same again, the thought creeping into my mind with a peculiar feeling of misery—persistent as the pace of my restless heart, sticky as the sweat on my body.

Regina and I had been living in Bordeaux for more than six years and our children were born here, yet I was certain that from this moment onward the town would grow strange and unreal for me.

The strangeness was all around me already: in the icy aspect of the long white lights reflected in the river; the sinister shadowy silence of the garden in the island further downstream; the lonely drone of the Riverside traffic on the opposite bank; the spindly skeleton of the bridge arching over the river and the esplanade with its latticed girders—a cold mint green in the floodlights.

They were all there, these places, as familiar as they had always been—tangible space referents during our Sunday walks along the river; and yet, as I stood on that embankment, I knew something in me had shifted, throwing a pall of sad opacity over those marks of meaning: a malignant mood of estrangement was beginning to settle deep inside, and with it this silent inward shattering—as if my innermost being was quietly coming apart at the joints, like a structure disintegrating in a weightless environment.

Something deeply disruptive was gradually dismantling my sense of mental space, my mind flying in all directions, and once again I yearned for disappearance: somewhere away from all this—back in Paris, or Tunis; anywhere but these endless minutes of severance and this indefinite nowhere in which I stood completely aimless, suspended in time, a witness to my own unraveling—an unmoored atom drifting in vacuity.

(This cluster of alienated emotions was nothing that I grasped mentally at the moment—a sensorial state more than anything else: feeling as if I was literally walking on new ground—shifting, treacherous, foreign.

The realization was as sudden as it was unfathomable.)

———

I crossed the Esplanade, walked over the bridge toward the left bank, and took the steps down to the cobbled strip by the trolley line.

The river exuded a malicious chill and this was beginning to put an even deeper fear in me: I found myself wondering about what the police officer had meant when he mentioned the justice system, coming to grips for the first time with the concrete consequences—the real-life effects of Regina's act.

He knew the full extent of my predicament, of course. To him, I was yet another instance—another man who had passed the point of no return, entering a new space and having to deal with a new form of existence: my family and I were a legal case now—numbered, filed, and crunched into a monstrous information machine: the Justice System.

Every decision in our lives, every solution, every daily arrangement would have to be handed down by It—the Justice System.

———

The moment I stepped into our apartment, my longing for the illusory peace of sleep had evaporated: I was now a creature of raw disquiet.

There was no other action I could take at this point to keep my mind occupied, and it was still a long time till morning—in a city where I had no friend, not even a good acquaintance.

Alone, caged in with my wound, I discovered that I had to wrestle with a new kind of pain: my sense of loss and confusion was now a palpable bodily presence—a physical sensation that squeezed the familiar air out of my lungs.

I kept pacing around my stripped home in circles—feeling like a pent-up animal, scouring the emptiness for any sign of sense, trying to decipher the blank spots where the furniture used to be, over and over. It was as if I was struggling to fend off my own mental vanishing by sheer force of physical motion, as if revisiting those patches of deserted space was the key to my existence.

At some point I decided to force myself to sit at the kitchen table and have a stiff drink.

I poured myself a Scotch and struggled hard to mentally step away from the mad whirling circles of my mind—tried to think of Regina instead, tried to figure out her motives, her fears, what she wanted to tell me through this.

But it was all as futile as my escape longings at the bridge: there was no getting away from the sinking panic of the here and now—and in these terrible hours the here and now was like a wave endlessly crashing.

———

That was when I made my second decision:

Zoé picked up the phone just after the first ring—her first word muffled by a deep-throated gasp, as if she had been awakened with a splash of cold water.

"I'm terribly sorry to call this late, Zoé—I'm in a fix. I need to talk."

She responded with a sort of deep hum—halfway between a question and a faint snore. For a moment, I thought she had gone back to sleep.

"I'm so sorry. I feel terrible about this."

"That's all right," she replied. "What happened?"

I could hear her sitting up in bed.

I said, "Regina walked out on me a few hours ago—I mean sometime today; I don't know exactly when."

"That's terrible," she said. Her words were inarticulate—she was still trailing in half-sleep. "How did this happen?"

I said, "I got home a few hours ago and found a note on the door. She took her things—almost everything. She wants out, I suppose."

More silence. I felt obligated to fill in the emptiness and give her time to weigh up the terrible situation: "I just can't stand being alone with this. It's killing me. You don't have to say much. I understand it's awfully late and there isn't much to say anyway, but I just don't want to be alone with this right now."

"Of course—you don't have to."

I heard rattling sounds on the other end and asked her if she would like to take some time to get dressed.

"No," she answered. "I'm making a cup of coffee."

There was kitchen clatter in the background.

She said, "I can't believe it. How did this happen? I mean, how did it come to this?"

———

Zoé said, "Nobody walks out on a marriage like that—on the spur of the moment. I know it's too soon to start discussing this, but at some point you'll have to do a lot of soul-searching, ask yourself a few tough questions. Of course, I'm not trying to justify what she's done—or minimize the gravity of it. I think it's totally wrong. What I'm saying is, if she didn't have the courage or the strength to confront you with some crucial questions about what wasn't working in your relationship, maybe you should be doing that for yourself now—for your own sake, I mean. But I have to admit, I am terribly shaken by this. I find her behavior deeply shocking."

We talked about what could have made her act the way she did: I told Zoé things about our marriage that she had never suspected—the disillusions of the last two years, Regina's obsessive feelings of uncertainty about her future, the tensions in our relationship and the terrible chasm of selfish indifference that can grow between two people plunging deeper into their inner worlds of self-doubt and lonely apprehensions.

Discoursing with such level-headed self-criticism, I must have sounded like an understanding husband who genuinely empathized with the fears and self-doubt of his wife—her dread at the thought of a life devoid of self-fulfillment; an understanding husband, but a wronged and baffled and angry one nonetheless—wronged and baffled and angered by a desperate, extreme, and ultimately irresponsible act.

In fact, my apparent self-questioning could not have been more selfish nor more self-serving—and in the pettiest, most manipulative way.

Through a secret intellectual subterfuge, I managed to steer the whole conversation away from me, kept it revolving around one single theme (Regina and her apprehension about the future), as if I was talking about a single woman.

(Eventually, though, I came to see how despicable my attitude was.

I was a man who had managed to keep his wife in a state of emotional deprivation for years, but by displaying some form of hypothetical empathy with her fear, I was secretly exonerating myself from all personal responsibility for the failure of our marriage.

For months I kept rambling about Regina's "problem." But what about mine? Was not my total self-involvement the worst of all problems?

This utter failure to see beyond the horizon of my impotent struggles: my incapacity to find a balance between work and writing; my incapacity to get any poetry published; my incapacity to listen to Regina's hopes and dreams; my incapacity to allow her to take some time away from our children.

I was the perfect example of the struggling, incapable husband; and the sad terrible irony was that over the months following our separation, through a cunning strategy of self-deceit, I managed to turn my own inadequacies into someone else's "problem.")

———

Zoé and I spent several hours talking, but there were also moments when I just sat in silence, holding the phone to my ear and marking the passage of time in the sky over the rooftops—the first diffuse grayness, the flush of dawn, the distinct streaks of early morning between the wispy clouds.

It looked like another unusual December day—crisp-blue sky and cold dry wind.

The longest day of my life.

Sometime toward eight, I told Zoé that I had to get ready for my Prefecture appointment.

As soon as I hung up, I called Fatma and asked her to substitute for me at the restaurant.

Then I wrote in my diary, shaved, took a shower, and left home around midmorning.

———

("Bordeaux": a file that I found on my laptop in a directory titled "T Bio." The notes were written shortly after my transfer to Le Croisic:

Salah el Moncef

The move to Bordeaux

Tariq meets Regina—Sorbonne 1997. R: Socrates exchange student. T: writing doctoral thesis—philosophy.

By end academic year '98: R & T very much in love—R decides to leave philosophy dept at Univ. Cologne. Moves in with T—Paris, late '90s.

Spring '99: R completes B.A. T defends thesis. Wedding.

Academic year 2000: T applying for positions in France, Europe, US. Job market very bad.

Early summer 2000: T decision to focus on poetry, philosophical writings, pursuing longtime dream: restaurateur career.

R and T decision: move to Bordeaux—cost of living more affordable. R to pursue doctoral degree—Univ. Bordeaux. Epistemology.

R parents, T mother financial help: move into apartment in Bordeaux. T opens Middle Eastern restaurant: The Cypresses.

February 2001: Shams conceived—unplanned. Spring semester 2001: R quits univ. Decision: resume her studies when S starts going to kindergarten.

Poetry going poorly: frequent submissions to magazines—repeated rejections. Enthusiastic feedback in poetry workshops—Bordeaux, Poitiers, Nantes, Paris. But rejection hurts. T frustrated, bitter but persevering.

T cultivates convenient suspicion. Convinces himself editors find it disturbing not to be able to discern specific national, ethnic identity behind poetry: thinks his work is seen as too incompatible with his name/ethnicity—disturbingly "un-Arabic, unexotic poetry"; too daringly experimental with language; too self-assured; too involved in playful linguistic abstractions; not "third-world-naïve" enough; not "third-world-committed" enough—no mention of his prodemocracy activism, no sense of region, identity, cultural memory.

Many variations on this explanation run through entire diary—deep-seated obsession: mistrust = coping strategy? Ruse of battered ego? T full of resentment + righteousness + powerlessness, but intensely prolific.

Full of secret sense of persecution—running on rage.

Does not share inner crisis with R. Convinced solution within him: purer poetry, more disciplined writing. Definition good verse: "Crystals of poetry so scintillating in rhythm and construction that they stand on their own, without any need for meaning, like a beautifully lighted city that beckons you from a distance by sheer force of fascination."

T tries to palliate humiliation of rejections: hard work, monastic vision of poet. Result: increasing isolation from R and S, brutal self-abusive workload.

Convinced self-inflicted pain form of symbolic sacrifice: "surcharge" that artist must pay "if he is to leave something to be remembered by."

Diary shows increasing alienation from R: T gloomy in infectious way. R passively abused, T admits in diary: "This terrible silence between us—continents of it. So many degrees and latitudes of distance: they're sapping her energy, I know it all too well—weakening her will. What a Black Hole I have become!")

The missing persons notice on December 18 and the hours that followed:

It was brainless, blind, blissfully stupefying work—the expression of pure nerve, muscle, and bone.

Right after my Prefecture errand, I went to the central police station: told them I had never searched for anyone before, asked them to help me find my sons.

I was immediately escorted upstairs, to the office of a lieutenant whose name I could not make out on the tag.

The lieutenant had straight brown hair and shockingly dark bags under her eyes.

Her manner was gentle and graceful, but she had this odd way of looking at an indefinite point between the edge of the desk and her lap while she spoke—as if she was reading out loud from notes that she had placed there.

Whenever I made a comment or asked a question, she would look up, a shade startled, as if she was not expecting any interruption.

Lieutenant: "There is no abduction case here, I'm afraid, even if that's how they've posted it at the Prefecture. I think they were mistaken to specify that."

She shrugged her shoulders, sympathetically I thought—a fluid rise and fall, barely noticeable as a meaningful gesture.

Lieutenant: "I understand your disarray. This must be a terrible shock for you. To tell you the truth, we're not at all empowered to search for your wife. I know this must strike you as unjust and absurd, but we're restricted in how we can investigate such cases. It is not illegal for a mother to leave the conjugal home with her children."

Tariq: "What if she leaves the country?"

Lieutenant [defensive, but not at all in a peevish way]: "I know, I know, and I fully sympathize with your frustration. This has happened again and again with German spouses leaving their homes and the country. But we're powerless to do anything about it. The way the laws are written, we're obliged to work from the assumption that the wife has left the home only. And a situation in which a spouse leaves the home is not a case of child abduction, but a case of marital conflict."

Her deep dissatisfaction with the laws was sincere, but with her subdued voice and her strangely lowered face, she looked as if she was reading a part from a third-rate film script.

She suggested that I contact the battered women's shelters—meager advice, but I did take it, almost with enthusiasm: I was glad that I had another task, something that gave me some sense of purpose.

On my way to the south side of town, I dropped in at The Cypresses. I spoke briefly with Jacques, gave him money for tomorrow's grocery shopping, and looked in on Fatma in the kitchen.

Then I was gone.

———

It was a fool's errand, of course.

I was convinced that Regina was heading out of France by now, but deep down I must have found a measure of solace in the physical drudgery: witnessing time itself unfold in slow motion with the plodding progression of my feet, from street to street and shelter to shelter—the clock ticking toward that ineluctable moment when I would have to admit to myself that the search was over, that there was nothing more to do now except face up to the inevitable.

The inevitable was going home and searching the Internet for a divorce lawyer.

Géraldine Le Bel:

She was a thin-lipped chain smoker who spoke with an intense tremor in her voice—short-haired, sharp-featured face, dressed in a white linen blouse and a black ankle-length skirt.

The outfit, the longish chiseled face, the stiff gait—there was an air of timeless monasticism about Le Bel that was very much at odds with the businesslike briskness of her manner.

Her office had an open view of the old harbor and the sunlight streamed in through a window behind her—the glare like an aura of luminescent gray dust hovering behind her face and shoulders.

With the blood still pounding in my head and my eyes burning from sleeplessness, it was hard not to squint—the effort made my eyes water up.

She quickly noticed that and suggested we sit in an alcove where there was a coffee table with two leather armchairs around it.

Sitting closer opposite her, I was able to see the color of her eyes behind the silver-rimmed glasses: they were a sharp steel blue—very cold and very intelligent.

She spoke with a nervous voice, but that was probably due to my appearance: my sleep-deprived eyes, the quiet look of animal bewilderment on my ashen face.

Le Bel had her secretary bring us coffee, for which I thanked her emphatically.

Still, I found it hard to warm up to the woman: I sensed a disturbing air of struggling artificiality in the way she was dealing with me—as if something violently negative in her was straining to burst through the carefully erected façade of aloof professionalism.

When I was done narrating what had happened to me, she expressed nothing and handed me a checklist.

Then we went over the paperwork, and she said that it was in my best interest to preempt Regina and file for a divorce as soon as possible.

"There isn't much we can do in terms of abduction," she added. "At this point, our best bet is malicious abandonment—the fact that she deserted the conjugal home and the injury that will result from her negligence toward the children and yourself. The thing I would worry about at this point, though, is which way Mrs. Abbassi will go."

When I frowned in incomprehension, she did not respond right away. Le Bel looked down theatrically with the palms of her hands open slantwise, as if she was miming an open book.

"What I mean is, will she file for a divorce in France or in Germany? If Mrs. Abbassi chooses the second option, the case might get very complicated, because at that point it *does* become a child abduction situation, which, theoretically, should strengthen your position. The problem is that the Germans refuse to cooperate with our courts. Actually, I don't know of a single case when they chose to work with us. As soon as the French judge issues an injunction, they systematically demand that the case be prosecuted in a *German* court. They also turn down orders to show cause. At any rate, for the time being we'll have to assume your wife will file in France. We'll develop a two-pronged approach: abandonment and negligence."

That was her way of summarizing, I thought, and I assumed it was time for me to leave; but I could not help making one last statement, an irrelevant afterthought that I mumbled with my head down—something about how absurd it all was.

It was obvious that she was unwilling to engage in small talk, but she chose to respond, nonetheless: "I know, it's senseless," she said, in a flat perfunctory tone—a get-over-it, I've-got-things-to-do tone.

And then she stood up. After all, why should she waste any words of indignation or outrage on the senseless? It was actually her job to work with absurd laws and brush the rest aside—the ethical indignation, the moral outrage.

She was that kind of person, this timeless nun: a terrifyingly selective mind.

———

Outside my lawyer's office, there was city life again on Place Sainte Croix—teeming, confusing, unrelenting.

It was past three o'clock and I decided that I needed a nap.

I took the streetcar to Cours Victor Hugo and when I got to The Cypresses, I went straight up to my office.

I sat behind the desk, put my head down, and fell asleep with my coat draped over me like a blanket.

A few hours later, my cell phone rang and I awoke in complete darkness.

It was Zoé and I told her there was nothing new except that I was filing for divorce (the blood was still hammering in my head).

She said that my voice sounded awful: "You should make yourself a cup of herbal tea and go to bed immediately. Read something nice and get a good night's rest."

"Fatma doesn't substitute for me evenings. Plus, I'm better off keeping busy."

"Be strong," she said. "Call me whenever you feel like talking."

She hung up and I sat in the dark for a while—still disoriented, cold, and in great misery of soul. It was tempting to linger here in the dark room, wrapped up in my coat, but I had work to do.

I stood up, switched on the light, and made some coffee.

———

Cooking has a lot to do with structure: the ritual gestures of cleansing and dressing prior to the act; the synchronized progression from the fragments of the ingredients to the cohesive totality of the prepared dish; the finished work on the serving plate.

Cooking has a lot to do with giving, too: the moment of the offer—when you, the host, set out the plates before the guests and see in their eyes that spark of gratitude mixed with hungry anticipation, grasping in that unique instant the relevance of your work.

This evening I felt that I needed the structure more than the giving, and I knew that for a long time to come the meaning of cooking was going to be just that for me: putting order into the muddled mess that my life was turning into.

On my way to the kitchen, I saw Jacques doing paperwork by the cash register and stopped by briefly to say hello.

———

Sami Mamlouk, the second cook, was chopping up parsley for the tabbouleh.

He shook hands with me and went straight back to work.

I washed my hands, put on my uniform, and went to work.

I put on water to boil in the steamer, for the fine bulgur. (Most French people use boiled couscous for tabbouleh—it is outrageously inappropriate.)

I opened the fridge, took out the Tupperware container with the HUMMUS tag on it, and discovered that there was not much left over from lunchtime.

I took out chickpeas from the overhead cabinet—the only thing that came in a jar at The Cypresses (I was never able to get split chickpeas in the local markets, and soaking and boiling whole dried chickpeas was labor intensive).

Most of the hummus that you eat in France is made with unpeeled chickpeas—another outrage. The purpose of making the puree with split chickpeas is precisely to enhance the smoothness that the tahini adds to the mix. Those coarse bits of peel, which no mixer or masher can reduce to anything smaller than irritating fibrous flecks, ruin the creamy texture of your hummus.

And so if you cannot find split chickpeas on the market, there is no alternative: you have to peel your boiled chickpeas by hand.

I put a large plastic bowl in the corner sink and another one on the counter. I ran warm water into the first bowl.

It felt good and comforting to lose myself in the measured delicateness of the movements:

Rolling each handful of those chickpeas between my cupped palms; exerting just enough pressure to work the peel off the pea; dropping them back into the water; picking up another handful and rolling it again until the surface of the bowl was covered with husks floating like bits of dead membrane; skimming the husks and dropping them into the other bowl.

———

Jacques came down with my first order—a royal mezze (the one that included the exquisite and dreadfully time-intensive pickled eggplant—stuffed with crushed walnut, parsley, and garlic).

It was the deputy mayor and three guests, he said.

Royal gets two sorts of bread—Berber bread with black anise seed and unleavened raghif bread.

I took two loaves of each out of the freezer and put them in the toaster oven.

Sami was busy fork-mashing carrots for the torshi, so I laid out m'tabbal pickles, octopus, and olives on the partitioned crockery plate. With wooden spoons I lifted two pickled eggplants out of the jar and carefully placed them on a flat white plate. I drizzled the eggplants with olive oil and garnished the plate. I cut up the bread, put it in a basket, and sent Jacques out with the tray of appetizers.

I took the hand-pressed garlic out of the fridge. I pressed one lemon and mixed the lemon and the garlic into the hummus. I seasoned the mashed carrots for the torshi—garlic, cumin, coriander, salt, lemon, olive oil, and pimento paste. I asked Sami to put four portions of kebbe sinyieh and spinach-feta borek in the oven and to start frying the kebbe mo'lyieh and the falafel. Then I went to work on the kebbe nayieh—pounding the fat-free lamb meat and bulgur in the wooden mortar till they turned a livid pink, spreading the steak wafer-thin on a flat plate, topping it with a dash of lemon juice and a drizzle of peanut oil.

I cooked and Sami dished and decorated, and the whole process unfolded in a structured, smooth, redeeming way—punctuated by islands of the keenest heartbreak, the kind that grips you every now and again like a raw nerve of pain in a cracked molar.

———

(Back in the days when I had a life, I used to run one of the best Middle Eastern restaurants in France.

Bread and pastry were the only things that I did not make with my own hands—it was Fatma and her Lebanese sister-in-law who took care of that for me.

I paid them very well, because their work was impeccable and time-consuming—excellent artisans who did everything the traditional way.

There used to be a sign hanging above the swinging door of my kitchen: *EXCELLENCE SPEAKS FOR ITSELF.*)

———

Jacques called it "chummy time": that particular lull in the bustle of kitchen work when I took the time to go out and mingle with the patrons—greeting the regulars, swapping pleasantries, sharing brief comments on the food.

As I said, being a restaurateur is about giving: you lend your ear to the patrons and you give your time, and they eat and pay and leave with that unmistakable sense of warmth and contentment.

The more time you give to the food and the patrons, the more grateful they are.

Give your time unconditionally and you get unconditional loyalty, trust, and gratitude in return: that is an absolute rule in the world of distinguished restaurants.

So, after having given my time to the food, I took off my toque and began to dole out time to the diners.

I welcomed the deputy mayor and his guests, asked them how they liked their meal, exchanged the usual bland but necessary pleasantries, and hopped over to the next table.

A businesswoman from out of town was interested in the fattat dajaj but did not know what particular ingredients went into it:

I explained what it was and how Fatma would prepare the unleavened, wafer-thin bread the traditional way—on a terra-cotta pan over a coal brazier. I told her about the pine nuts and green onion shoots that went into the turmeric-and-saffron sauce. And I described how and when the sumac, which is served in a separate bowl, is to be sprinkled over the fatta.

———

After a while I went back to the kitchen: the air was saturated with the dense smell of fat particles.

I called Annette, Regina's mother: she told me Regina and her two brothers had flown in with the boys this afternoon, but Regina had told her that she did not want to talk. She would call me.

She sounded curt and cold saying this, like someone forced to deliver bad news.

I said thank you and went back to cooking.

———

Then, after the cooking and the sharing and the talking and the last words of reckoning and organizing, it was closing time—and the terrible reality of having to go back home, to the ghosts.

And so home it was, again—and the torture of walking around the bedrooms, again, contemplating the empty spaces where the beds used to be.

I kept dragging my body around in a daze, sitting on our bedroom floor and staring—the drip pattern of the wallpaper like white raindrops; the lone pillow left in gray underbed dust, on my side; the cracks between the floorboards—straight black lines stretching to infinity.

Moments of utter unreality in which I tried to recapture some sense of my disappeared family by sheer fantasy—a desperate effort to conjure up a mental presence of the people who used to inhabit this nullified home. My own family.

I did not want to know how late it was, the sleeplessness burning in my eyelids.

I could have put the air mattress in the living room and made my bed and called it a day, but I chose not to.

Hours later, I was still sitting on the floor in the children's room, staring at what was left of Shams's corner: the spot that he had filled with his dreams, his nightmares, his illnesses, his excited morning cries.

There were his random pencil and crayon marks on the wall; there was Bea, the beady-eyed brown teddy marionette that I had made for him, with her yellow string half-buried in a heap of dust bunnies; there were his self-drawn cutouts, pasted on the wall above the yellowish line of the spot made by the head of the bed—an airplane in flight with its nose pointing upward, a house with a gable and a turquoise window, his name written in uneven letters and cut out with astonishing care (Shams's private kingdom, done in paper and neatly attached to the wall with clear tape).

I kept staring at these remnants in a dumb alcoholic stupor— as if there was hidden meaning of great depth and consequence in the crooked pencil lines, in the ink dots bunched together like far-flung constellations, in the trailing streaks of drawings hardly begun.

———

Sometime before dawn I went up to the attic and took out the air mattress.

I slept in the living room—deep dreamless sleep. The sleep of the dead.

———

Regina's call came on Wednesday, December 22.

Sami was not in and I was sitting by the table where we put our green groceries—the fruits and vegetables Jacques would bring in every morning from the market.

It was early morning, and the table was still heaped with produce, smelling fresh and sappy—scent of dew and crushed grass.

She said she was terribly sorry, but she had to do it for the sake of the boys—and for her own sake.

Those were her very words. I wrote them down in my notebook—later in the diary: *I'm terribly sorry, Tariq, but I had to do this for the sake of our children—and for my own sake.*

Regina spoke with sincere sadness, but there was a strange dissonance between the tremor in her voice and the starchiness of her tone: she sounded like a vaguely sympathetic boss who was about to fire a likeable but expendable employee—a painful but necessary decision.

She talked about Shams at length.

She said, "I tried and I tried and I tried. I wore myself out trying to tell you: he is starved for some sense of bonding—anything. He admires you so much—his entire *world* is built around you, but you never pay attention to him. Remember when I asked you to do your reading in the living room? I wanted him to get some meaningful—*sense* of your physical presence at least. You did it for a couple of days—quite literally. Then you went back to locking yourself up in your study. God, I could feel how he hated that—he basically told me. It made him feel so—*rejected.*"

She had told me about his need so often, she said, and in the strongest terms: the poor child was feeling cheated out of me, emotionally betrayed. But I was impervious to arguments—the subtle arguments, the blunt arguments, the shrill arguments. It was *hopeless.*

I was withdrawn, living by myself and for myself, she said. I *was* already divorced—from them, in my isolation, living in this maddening impenetrable vacuum.

She said she had grown frightened of me—that loneliness, that terrible sense of a dark emptiness spreading *out* of me, growing darker and sadder by the day, "like a black hole threatening to suck us all in."

There came a point when she could not take it any longer—she decided to save herself.

I was deeply hurt by the fact that she would speak of us in the past, and with such diagnostic aloofness, but I chose to remain silent on that matter—out of pride, I suppose.

I kept staring at the edge of the pine table, letting my eyes wander between the swirling patterns of the wood grain—crushing a mint leaf between my thumb and forefinger until the smell was gone and the leaf turned dark and rusty-looking; the produce on the table far away and out of focus—a green blur with a vaguely cool fresh exhalation.

"So you've been planning this for a while?" I said.

"Tariq, please let's not fight. You call it planning. I've been *suffering* this for a while—and I've been trying to tell you to help me save *us*. But you were so lost inside yourself. Even our Sunday walks—anyone could tell, you were just *walking* with us—you weren't *being* with us. Planning this. As if I never told you these things before—over and over, till we started *fighting* about them. All those fights: I was fighting for *us*, can't you see?"

She broke down and there were more tears, I think, quiet tears.

"But you never mentioned divorce," I said. "At no point did you ever bring up the word. That's what I find so disgusting about this. It stinks of betrayal. There's no other name for it—no matter how hard you try to justify it in words. I mean, no matter how unhappy you felt, you didn't have to *do* it this way. We could have *talked* it over—I mean the split-up."

Regina said that she did not think I would ever understand—and she did not blame me; but now she sounded unsure of herself—in a nervous and defensive way, as if I was going to cut her short any second.

She told me that she had gone over the options with her lawyer so many times: the mere memory of those conversations made her sick to her stomach. She was going to pieces inside, but she had no choice. If she had decided against opening up and telling me about her plans it was because she was unable to even contemplate the possibility of joint custody.

She said, "For me joint custody meant having to stay in France, and that was the bleakest of all options. I don't want to have anything to do with France anymore. I *have* no future in France. I want to start over here—with my children. I have a right to it after all these years—trying to be supportive, trying to adjust to your lifestyle, trying to patch up our marriage. I'm sick and tired of trying—I want something different now. I have a right to it."

"So, your lawyer—you're actually trying to tell me that you spent months hatching this scheme with your lawyer, *while* we were sharing the same bed."

I stammered a great deal through the conversation—as I always do when I am angry and fumbling for words.

"You're trying to make all this sound so—beyond your control, but face it: what you've done is filth—there's no other name for it. It's filth. You, Regina Schmitz, have turned yourself into *filth*, and from here to the end of your days you'll be stuck with the consequences of your filth."

"Let's not *fight*—please? I haven't called to fight. I'm sure a day will come when you won't be so harsh—when you've managed to put all the hurt behind you. You'll be able to understand how shattered—how painful it was for me to make the decision."

(Regina had judged the situation accurately of course: those words of anger were an expression of thoughtless hurt more than anything else, but it was terrible of me to have uttered them just the same; because she was right, of course—about the warning signs, about her own pain, about all the failings that had led to our separation.

She did try to save our marriage, brave soul. She did it all by herself, while I stood by and watched.)

I told her that I had seen a lawyer myself, that she had suggested I file for a divorce first.

Regina asked me for my lawyer's name and telephone number—said she would forward them to her lawyer.

"Don't you want to talk to the boys?"

"Of course I do. You make it sound like I've forgotten all about them already."

"Tariq, please."

"Well, what else can I say? With the kind of letter you posted on the door of all places: it sounds like you're trying to convince yourself of my non-fatherhood already, create a solid narrative in your mind, you know—a nicely consolidated scenario for future use."

There was a sigh and a clunk.

I kept the phone against my ear and held on—waited with that distinct soft swishing sound in my ear like the suppressed wail of wind in an elevator shaft: the unmistakable, always awesome interstellar whisper of a vacant line waiting to be filled with words.

———

When I got home from work that night, it was the same misery all over again—the same downward spiraling of the mind; only now my ruminations were darkened with rage.

I was a prisoner of my warped view of what had happened—furious at Regina's supposed duplicity and the extent of her falseness:

What kind of woman was she—to be able to share my bed and kiss me good-night even as she was deliberately planning to destroy my world?

How could she treat me with such cold-blooded duplicity?

Did I deserve to lose my children, no matter how self-obsessed I was?

All the years I gave her: what was their weight—and their worth?

And the boys: my failure today to get across to them in simple, accessible words was putting me in a state of panic: there was no *recognition* in their voices, as if my presence in their lives had been one single chapter of blankness, as if their new existence out there at the other end of the line was just one more empty page in the blank desert that I represented—an abstract space filled with baffled silences and white noise and static.

Was that what I was as a father? Was that what I *had* been all along?

The White Noise Man?

Dead-end questions, dark ruminations in tight concentric circles—it went on and on, for hours.

———

I wanted out.

Once again, my breathing had grown short and unsteady and my mind was a live node of jarred overloaded nerves.

I took a big drink of Scotch and called Zoé, late again—told her what had happened.

"She really wants to do it," Zoé said after a silence, as if she had been in doubt these past days and was just now facing up to the reality of the deed—there was something close to startled awe in her words.

"Of course she wants to quit," I said, shrill and impatient, feeling immediately ashamed at my tone: here I was calling my only friend in the middle of the night, and I had nothing better to say than screech at her.

"Forgive me," I added, "I didn't mean to raise my voice."

"Well, at least now you can't say you're in the dark," she said, ignoring my apology. "As for the boys, I've been thinking about them. All this *will* blow over, Tariq, and when it does, I'm sure *they* will know how to reconnect with you—emotionally."

"How do you mean?" I asked.

"You need to focus on the bright side. With you separated, you'll get to cherish their presence so much more than before—give them more of your time: cook for them; entertain them; think about their emotional needs; reprioritize your life to put them first. The bond will follow naturally, you know."

They would be more real in my life, she said, and I would be more real in theirs.

She told me that I needed to envision my renewed priorities without obsessing too much about what Regina thought of me as a father: "Forget about *that*. No matter how solid your moral position is, it would be quite simply unhealthy to look back on the past in terms of right or wrong. It's vital for you to think beyond the usual poison that comes with these situations—the finger-pointing, the mind games, the blame games. Just refocusing, and basically asking yourself what went wrong between you and your boys, in the most honest terms—trying to do something tangible about it, something they can recognize and appreciate in their own way."

There was a brief silence, then a darker note in her voice: "Obviously, what went wrong between you and Regina is another story, isn't it?"

I said, "It's this sudden *hole* in my house, in my life, and this entire dark side of her exploding in my face: it's like dropping into emptiness. There's no bottom anymore. There's this burning knot in my stomach—I've been dragging it around for hours now."

Zoé said, "I think you need to let off some steam, Tariq: scream, cry, kick things around. Get the poison out of your system. You *have* to scream—acknowledge the pain and the anger."

At first, I thought it was some vague suggestion, but when I switched back to my relationship with Regina, she told me to forget about her now; forget about everything and everyone at this moment: I needed to let my howling voice be an expression of my whole wounded being.

Zoé paused for a few seconds then she started reading—a passage from the book of the Tao:

> *Express yourself completely,*
> *then keep quiet.*
> *Be like the forces of nature:*
> *when it blows, there is only wind;*
> *when it rains, there is only rain;*
> *when the clouds pass, the sun shines through.*

Then, with the ease and authority of a self-help guru, she went on talking about the virtues of self-expression through screaming—a shaman urging me to submit to the necessities of my deeper nature, to exorcise the evils trapped within me.

———

Oddly enough, I did find myself willing to submit and follow her logic: hanging on every word she uttered, I began to yearn for the possibility of "letting off some steam" as if it was the key to my salvation.

That was how I ended up walking along Quai Louis XVIII and down the pedestrian underpass at the bridge past the island garden: walking in big strides until the asphalt dipped into cobblestones—the strip of old embankment that preceded the wooded path stretching for kilometers, broken only by the footbridges that spanned the tributaries flowing into the Gironde.

Soon the trees closed in overhead:

I was on the Gironde Trail and already beginning to feel the change within me (a hint of vaguely euphoric madness), but I did not know how the sensation had come about—was it the hashish mixing with the whisky, the rages of my body in motion, or the echoes of Zoé's words in my mind?

I called Zoé when I reached the first bench: "Here I am," I said.

From where I sat, the river was only a few steps away, but the surface of the Gironde appeared like an expanse of blank nondescript space behind the thick blackness of the trees—its dull gray shimmer in the gaps between the foliage, like a stretch of faded asphalt road in the middle of nowhere.

All at once, it felt ridiculous to have come this far and I told her so.

"Remember what we said," she shot back. "You have to work yourself into it—*that*'s when it'll start making sense, bit by bit. Just think of all the shit you've been through, and think how unfair and impossible it has been for you."

She said, "You've got to think: I can't take this. This is not for *me* to take."

Her words must have sounded like a shaman's invocation indeed—although I did not consciously grasp them as such then and there.

Sitting alone on a lonely remote bench with the magic of her machine-mediated words to sustain me in this strange endeavor: I began to feel a sudden sense of purpose in this place of emptiness, where it was so easy to nullify and banish the world of sorrowful things and people that I had left behind in Bordeaux, existing solely through the soft rustle of her voice on the line—Zoé's words of guidance and healing.

And so she went on saying her soothing words and I went on listening—until the breaking moment came and I allowed myself to let it all out at last.

I still cannot remember exactly how it started, but at one point I found myself agreeing with her long after she had stopped—uttering a few words that I went on repeating many times until they were nothing but meaningless sound: "You're right, you're right," I kept whispering to myself.

Yes, Zoé was right: I did *not* deserve to carry this poison within me, I was now convinced, to have to bear it like an irredeemable debt.

Something in me (rich, plentiful, giving, merciful) must have gushed out and spilled over at that precise moment; for the next thing I knew I was curled up on the bench, crying hot tears with my face wedged between the seat and the back.

Then I was bawling and choking at the same time, loud and deep, like a bull stuck in the throat—sounds I never thought I would be able to utter.

I cried generously and my tears flowed for all the sad failures of my life—as if the bench, lost in this nameless tunnel of trees, had now become a receptacle for my darkest emanations: the harm inflicted on others and relegated to banality; the harm done to me and forced into the silent recesses of thankless labor; the gifts ill-reciprocated and the losses, like Shams handing me the oak leaf and telling me to put it in my dictionary—and me not finding it when he asked me to show it to him, not knowing what to tell him, not hugging him and consoling him and telling him I'll make it up to you, I'll make it all up—the emotional ineptitude and the icy retreats and the silent frowns and the cold-shouldered indifference. I'll make it all up.

There I was, unbelievably childish I: curled up and crying and not even knowing why—swept away by this sad voice that had begun to speak within me in the strangest of tongues, recalling my flaws and failures to me, my unravelings past and present; and I had no sense of shame or guilt to witness that darkness again, relive it again in recollection.

It felt not so much good as appropriate to be emptying out with such primitive abandon, and I don't recall trying to make myself quit, but I believe there came a moment when my voice went into a low hum.

Then I stopped altogether. Those tears were the closest I came to screaming that night.

On my way back home, Zoé told me that it was close enough, sounding like a contented instructor.

"You're coming over here for Christmas," she said, after a pause. "I can't let you go crazy out there—spending Christmas all by yourself."

———

So there was Christmas after all, and I did celebrate it with the Brahmis (Faisal, Sophie, and Zoé) in the big sumptuous Rue Descartes apartment, only a short walk from Zoé's place on Place de la Contrescarpe.

My account of our December 24 walk through Jardin des Plantes, before the festive aperitif and the holiday meal—one of the many written reflections on the visit:

My first Christmas with the Brahmis:

Despite our frequent visits up here, our cozy familiarity with Faisal and Sophie, there was something rather awkward about arriving at number 12 today—getting into their apartment as a single man. Felt strange.

S was kind enough not to put me up in the usual room. "I prepared the boys' room for you," she said, right after we greeted each other—eager to get that out of the way.

S not a practicing Christian: for her, Christmas is an occasion to be together, share in ritual of togetherness, giving, cherishing one another. "Communing," I suppose, is the word—vague and grand as it sounds.

I like that spirit a lot—spiritual spirit, as opposed to "religious," I guess.

A new spatial perception of their apartment: after the eerie sparseness of my place, S and F's apartment feels strangely "overloaded," "overfurnished"—only an impression, though. I have always loved their place.

Tea and Xmas cookies, beautiful fire in the fireplace, gorgeously thick but understatedly decorated tree: much like R's idea of a Christmas day atmosphere.

At some point, F started talking about "the walk," saying not to be put off by their silence. "It's sort of a family tradition," he said.

"Each one of us deep in their personal assessment," S added, a bit unnecessarily, I thought.

F [looking abstractly into fire, about to say something symbolic—you could tell from the quality of Z and S's silence]: "This moment, before the dinner and the sharing and the gifts, is the most significant ritual for me—when I look around me without really looking, you know, and see these two ravishing women life has given me and I think: yes, this is the way it is meant to be."

Z [teasing F, giving him a deliberate—very funny—you-can-do-better look]: "You know, Papa, I've always hoped there would be a little more thinking along those lines. Or is it actually feeling? Was that the word you were looking for, Papa?"

F [winking at me]: "Yes, yes, Miss comfortable-expressing-her-feelings. Feeling is the word. I have to learn to use it—make it part of my daily vocabulary, right? I look around me and I feel—there I said it. Happy? Ah, my two women—always lecturing me on how to show my feeling side."

Jardin des Plantes—"The Walk":

Z and I talking—a comfortable respectful distance behind S and F. Discussed private rituals: Z said that is what this walk meant to her—it was one of those affect-loaded rituals she had always cherished, since childhood.

Another strange unusual thing: Jardin des Plantes looks spring-like. It is hard to grasp the feel of the garden today—there is no sense of winter cold at all: an unseasonably dry, sunny day for this time of year.

Reptile Pavilion: the limestone piers and arches of the pavilion so stark and powdery in the slanting sunlight—starch-white, almost, against the brick walls.

We walk safely behind S & F and so the "rule" of silent meditation/ assessment does not apply—talk a great deal actually: the new situation, the boys, my options.

Eventually, I bring the conversation around to the book of poems she has put together.

Z simply says there is a publisher who is interested—no further elaboration.

There is an uncomfortable silence for a moment. I have the impression (wrongly?) that she is trying to spare my feelings by being silent about her book. I do not like that.

T: [speaking perversely?]: The only book I have put together so far is the diary—my endless poem.

Z: Not true. There's your novel.

T: It's not a novel yet. I'm still gathering material—taking notes, ruminating in circles. I'm certainly learning a lot about whacky esoteric cults and circles—human sacrifice, orgiastic sex and supernatural energy, occult cosmic power, morgues and criminal investigations, detention cells and interrogations. Museum of Horrors—there's a working title for you. Honestly, most of the time I don't even know what the hell I'm doing with the material—my own notes from underground.

We walked all the way across the garden—from the Ménagerie side along Rue Cuvier down to the labyrinth and the Muséum d'Histoire Naturelle.

By the time we came out through the Muséum gate and headed back up to Contrescarpe through Rue Buffon, the bottom of the sky toward the Panthéon was one clean saffron streak.

Strange, it felt like a brittle spring evening in the South (my South): a desert-dry kind of chill setting in; crystal-cold stars in the sky—and the ravishing enamel of that cobalt blue horizon, like the shimmering rim of an immaculate bowl flipped upside down.

Last (rather somber?) thought:

"This is the way it should be," F said—"it" being the ideal of/for every man, I suppose.

I do not think there was either petty irony or smugness in his words (hope not at any rate). The man was just counting his blessings.

Still, in the back of my mind: I could not help comparing—and feeling the sting of the comparison.

Talking to Zoé in Jardin des Plantes—Rilke rumbling inside my head:

Wer jetzt kein Haus hat, baut sich keines mehr.
Wer jetzt allein ist, wird es lange bleiben, wird wachen, lesen, lange Briefe schreiben
und wird in den Alleen hin und her
unruhig wandern, wenn die Blätter treiben.

New Year's Eve:

Zoé suggested we go to Caveau des Nostalgiques in the Quartier Latin: "Another chance for us to escape, forget, heal," she told me.

It was not hard to guess who was in need of forgetting and healing. I thought it was very kind of Zoé to include herself.

She had an exciting plan and I found it easy to let myself be carried away by her ebullience: the party at the Caveau was billed as Charleston Night, she told me—a nostalgia-theme costume party.

It was the last Thursday of the dying year, and we were sitting in her living room after breakfast.

Sprawled on the couch, waving her arms about with a flush of excitement on her face, she looked like a director pitching a film with a big concept.

Since the idea was to forget and let go, she explained, why not gratify our escape desires in the most indulgent way possible: she wanted us to rent the costumes from La Maison du Festin—a flapper outfit for her and a Roaring Twenties suit for me, with a tight-waisted jacket and stovepipe pants.

Random reflections on New Year's Eve with Zoé [return train from Paris]

La Maison du Festin—shopping for Jazz Age clothes on the Champs Elysées!
Her plan was at once thrilling and outlandish, I thought. Facing her there in the living room, I felt it would be beautiful to be able to project myself beyond my obsession with what had happened in Bordeaux; to mentally step into the event she had willed in/through her mind—the dream she had brought into existence through the infectious power of her words, as if Zoé's vision was now invested with the indisputable authority of commonsense itself.

We started late in the afternoon: Zoé kept running between her room and mine—slicking my hair back with gel and brush, helping me with the cufflinks and the bow tie, insisting my outfit looked so much better with the fob watch, which meant I had to wear the vest even if it was going to be too warm at the Caveau.
Then there came a moment when she went into her room and I did not hear one single word from her any longer: silence—so sudden, so dense and prolonged that it made me feel uneasy.
"Zoé?" I said, in a purely tentative move. There was nothing in particular that I wanted to tell her.
There came an abstracted Yes from her—no more. But that was all I needed to hear, I suppose, because in that rushed Yes I recognized the familiar too-busy-to-talk tone of a woman lost in the mystic rites of self-transformation—the alchemy of makeup.
Abstracted or not, though, I liked the feeling of familiarity in that single word—and with it the comforting realization: knowing with absolute certainty, in a split second, why Zoé had put so much generosity, creative will, and imagination into this evening.
Belonging: it was all about belonging—Zoé wanted to put so much "ritual" into the whole thing so that this year's celebration would be a mark of her loyalty, of her refusal to do what most people would have done under the circumstances: treat me like a disease-stricken man and propose a "low-key" celebration at best.
Instead, she went for the craziest, most festive scenario imaginable. I was grateful for that—her obstinate affirmation of my "normality"—and I

suddenly felt this sappy urge well up in me—felt like I had to do something: a gesture, a word—some kind of "move" to signify my gratitude, anything to express my thankfulness.

(I did none of that, of course, fearing that it would all melt into mush and cheap sentimentality.)

As if she had access to my broodings, Zoé interrupted my thoughts with her playful but firm warning: "Don't you dare come anywhere near this room, Tariq. Sit down and relax. Grab a book."

After a while, she came out and stood between the kitchenette and the living room, at a deliberate distance from me—looking so metamorphosed that I felt my own self grow unreal, everything around me fading out of focus.

She was the center of everything all of a sudden!

More than ever, there was that hauntingly compelling gap between Zoé's garçonne face (the bold lines of her mouth, the Flapper bob hairstyle) and the sensuous Venusian bearing of her body—its forms gorgeous behind the surreal outfit: the sensual, odalisque-like roundness of her shape wrapped up in old-fashioned silk and lace; the misty textures of her powdered face and neck; the dashing bright red of her lips—so full and alive and sensual with a touch of African toughness.

There she stood, the new Zoé—enfolded in the loveliest envelope as in petals of poppy: the dress that we had painstakingly chosen together at Maison du Festin the day before—a sleeveless, low-neck evening gown of scarlet silk with ruffled shoulder straps and silver bullion lace draping down cape-like over her shoulders and upper arms.

For jewelry she wore a five-strand necklace of faux hematite beads with teardrop earrings to match.

Even the air around us was changed—Zoé's presence renewing it in a breath of primal forest: her perfume distinct yet vaporous and subtle in the way it filled the living room—a whiff of orchids you catch in passing.

My new electrified mood and rapture went right into her, like a blaze blasting through a broken door; and she still stood there, with that stealthy gleam in her feline eyes—basking in her own aura, relishing my entrancement in dainty sips.

Underneath it all, though (the theatrics of her flirtatiousness and the levity of her charms), there was the unmistakable essence of Zoé set deeper within her than the streaks of time in stone—the Celtic angle of her mother's jaw, the dramatic protuberance of her cheekbones, the slightly Asian slant of her eyes: a warrior girl—she was that ultimately—a warrior girl with an artichoke character: rough and cutting on the outside, but silk-soft and furry within.

She went back into her room and brought out the hat, holding it up with a prestidigitator's flourish.

It was a tall-crowned cloth-and-malines slate blue hat with irregular trim. The flowers (smooth, fluttery, touch-inviting) were made of silk and feathers.

"Ready" was all she said.

There was a damp drizzle outside—the lights of Rue Mouffetard shining in soft grainy smudges on the cobblestones.

We decided to stay away from the crowded boulevards, but even the backstreets were teeming with partygoers on their way to dinner.

Zoé was quite a sight, drawing admiring glances all the way to Rue Saint Séverin. By the time we walked into the Caveau, I was feeling self-conscious— all those relentless eyes (male mostly) fixed on us.

For some reason, I thought we should make straight for the basement, where the party was going to be, but Zoé insisted we drink our aperitif in the Shakespeare & Co. corner by the bar.

She threw me an impish sideways smile as we walked over to the only empty table, yet I felt the lightness of her expression was just veneer; underneath it I sensed a darker, more ambiguous urge stirring, both imploring and relentless: don't let me down now, it said. Be as grand as I mean this to be. [Was I imagining all this then? Am I still now? Don't know—write it now, figure it out later in Bordeaux!]

We sat down where you could watch the beautifully polished miniature guillotine by the alcove window.

There was something fascinating about the dull brilliance of the oak, the glint and fine edge of the steel, the hanging heft of the blade tugging at your attention.

Something of that edge must have gone into her now. Or was it only an undercurrent of diffidence—hers as much as mine?

But the tenseness was not meant to last.

I remember a distinct, resolute thought after the second glass of champagne: Zoé had made all this possible for me, and it was now my turn to bring my own magic touch to her performance—the evening that she had dreamed up and organized against all odds.

I decided that I was going to take us back to the days when we could not afford the astronomically expensive soirees in the basement, the days when we would spend hours in this corner under the gaze of Sylvia Beach and the others—talking about philosophy, poetry, art, beauty.

So it was my turn to perform now, to act against the stream of time, as it were, and speak as if nothing had happened between our student days and the present moment.

Talking about the old Sorbonne days:

T: I started by reminiscing about our rebellious determination to write for ourselves first and foremost, and the risks of remaining faithful to the demands of what we had once called the Free Poetic Impulse. I talked about the importance of surmounting the ego-bruises of repeated rejection, the importance of remaining fresh for the work, as if each new poem was the first.

Z: The childlike excitement of going to bed with the idea (the hopeful desire) of "netting" something tomorrow morning. Then the rush of panic when the alarm clock goes off: is it all worth it? Why get up and hit the typewriter (again) before I throw myself into the madness of the world out there? Everything about writing seems so unreal and tenuous in those first moments of waking—with you pent up in that kind of infertile panicky self-doubt.

T: Even so, you have to keep your eyes on that something you want to net—hard as it is to do that. Setting up the right conditions to create that fragile something out of nothing—the first embryonic seed that will keep you going. The initial doubts of writing are what's most exhilarating about writing in the first place: it's a gamble most of the time. You start something even while you're in the dark about what it's doing and where it's going. Faith?

Z: Agrees it's a leap of faith—trusting in one's creative instincts, in the creative process taking care of itself. One also needs a lot of faith in oneself— one's capacity to feel: the Feeling Self registering the beauty all around us, open to the poetry of scents and images, even the most commonplace scenes and sounds—especially the most commonplace scenes and sounds. [The passive receptiveness so crucial to creating.]

The barroom was full by now, wonderfully noisy and cozy. Full-costumed latecomers heading straight for the basement.

The whole space had an air of the stage set about it—just before the curtain rises and the play begins: nervous bustle of the manager and the waiters, echoes of the band tuning up downstairs, patrons studying their costumes and chatting frantically.

Only the bartender was his usual cool-and-aloof self, except that tonight he was impeccably costumed and made up to look like a replica of Al Capone— scars, bulbous nose, and all.

Zoé reached out and gave a slight touch to her clutch purse, her mind veering within—toward the basement, the thrill of the festooned setting, the throb of the band, the excitement of the gathered dreamers.

The setting in the big stone-walled basement was as I imagined it: round tables laid out in a crescent around the dance floor opposite the bandstand; decoration hanging down from lamps and ceiling; ferns and wildflowers arranged around the candlelight at the center of the immaculately white tablecloths.

It was all very beautiful—and the champagne working its magic: the people and their sounds were now safely wrapped up in many layers of softness; depthless those bodies—flat and foreshortened almost, their glamorous presence like occasional clouds of glittery color stirring in a kaleidoscope.

And then, all of a sudden, the first splash of music—a beautiful burst through the layers of fuzz in my mind.

A few minutes before midnight, we got off the dance floor and went back to our tables and the band started playing "Saint James Infirmary," while the waiters paraded around the dance floor, shouldering a makeshift black coffin with 2006 painted on it in white.

Then it was the countdown, and the champagne springing out of the coffin as if by magic, and all sound vanishing in a collective shout and a foamy slow-motion shower of confetti and ticker tape flying in all directions.

We were all on our feet toasting each other. A few minutes later, we were dancing to "Ain't She Sweet"—holding Zoé in my arms, clumsy as ever, swaying with her in our cocoon of tangled paper. I might have been the worst dancer in the world, but tonight I was the happiest.

Looking at her radiant face: glowing with something new—a glow that was more than bliss.

Triumph, I suppose—that's probably what it was; and it was written all over her—in the mellow mien of her tipsy body, in the candid flash of her pearly teeth, in the smooth swinging of her gorgeous hips. And her eyes: you see, they said, we've done it, after all. We've fulfilled the promise of ecstasy despite everyone and everything, carved out a beachhead of happiness for ourselves, in the middle of the turmoil.

We danced boldly and fearlessly—kindred souls, conspiratorial siblings, united in a common bond.

We got back home in the early hours of the first day—drunk and happily tired.

I thanked Zoé for everything, gave her a good-night kiss before she went to bed, and told her not to even think of getting up when I left.

I said I would call her when I got home.

In my room, I dressed into my clothes, folded up my costume, packed, and called for a taxi.

It was still raining when I stood waiting out on the sidewalk.

The taxi driver went along Boulevard Saint Germain (streets totally deserted), and it was within a few minutes that we reached the Cour Carrée: looking at the deep glow of the red light; the bright-orange crowd-control barriers along the curb (dripping with red rain); the sad flattened out gobs of many-times-trampled paper cups scattered all over the rain-darkened square.

Why must everything come to an end? Why must people part ways? Why this cruel orphanage, every time?

Feeling suddenly raw and vulnerable in that taxi—disconsolate.

(Surely there must be a way of saving the beautiful moments within—a hedge against the loss and the emptiness; preserving the moments, treasuring them, revisiting them like clusters of diminutive flowers fossilized in amber— rich and inexhaustible in their many facets, in the way they offer themselves

to our gaze and inhabit it, their light filtered through the ripened lens of time, the wise memory of the ages.)

Starting to nod off again—done for now.
 Train hurtling forward, humming.
 Peace to the world.

———

I found Le Bel's e-mail the day after I got back from Paris: Regina's lawyer, Franck Hardy, had called her and there were a few seriously damaging sworn statements.

She needed to talk to me.

She did not say more, but the pieces were beginning to fall into place.

I began to realize the extent of my naïveté in interpreting Regina's call. In my emotional blindness, I had failed to see it for the guilty warning that it was: *Get ready for tough tactics.*

When she had said that she did not want to follow the normal procedure, I was unable to intuit the obvious fact that in court she would need at least one legitimate reason for not doing so.

That legitimate reason was me, now I knew.

———

(Weeks later, waiting in the courthouse atrium, I saw Regina walk in through the main door and sit by herself on a bench close by the entrance—a thick slab of polished dark-gray granite.

I walked over to where she sat, stood before her, and held out my hand.

She stood up, shook it, said that she was sorry, and immediately melted into tears. As I recall that moment now, I realize that they were doubtless tears of sorrow, an unadulterated expression of the keenest pain.

But I was blinded by rage and confusion then—at what I saw as mere weakness of character and moral decay in her reaction.

Today I am firmly convinced that Regina had no alternative.

She did not trump up the charges out of evil intent; she was just human, that was all, a vulnerable woman acting under the pressure of terrible and extraordinary circumstances: hers was a very shaky position—she knew it, and she knew that she was in need of legitimizing the actions that she had undertaken with her brothers' help.

From her point of view, the arguments that she had set up against me were not even attacks on my person: they were merely formal moves within a fuzzy legal game in which her strategy was not so much to hurt me as to hedge her bets, optimize her chances of success.)

———

As soon as she was seated behind her desk, Le Bel got straight to the heart of the matter, starting with the standard good-news-bad-news opening.

With poorly rehearsed enthusiasm, she told me that Mrs. Abbassi was filing in France.

The bad news was much worse than I had expected:

"Mr. Hardy," she said, "told me her action didn't constitute grounds for divorce. What she did was justified by your attitude, he said."

"And what *is* my attitude?" I asked—too quick, too nervous.

Le Bel was silent for a few seconds.

"Apparently *you* were planning to flee to Tunisia—taking Shams and Haroon with you."

She said this with a poorly suppressed squirm, and seeing the sideways flutter in her eyes, I knew that she was beginning to have her doubts about my character.

"Of course, this is what *they*'re saying," she added correctively. "These—maneuvers are to be expected, but I just wanted to make sure that we both agree on the facts, that there's no information gap between the two of us, if you know what I mean."

I let her know my position immediately: "This country is the only country where I want to reside, Mrs. Le Bel. I'm glad we both have decided to take this fact for granted and brush all the cheap talk and manipulative tactics aside. I have no intention whatsoever to change my country of residence."

For all the firmness in my tone, though, I was dumbfounded and hurt to the quick: the shock was so sudden that I did not know what to make of the revelation. I was trapped between my lawyer's misgivings and my wife's betrayal.

I could still feel her eyes gauging me—no longer with that unnerving fidgetiness now, but with the deliberate self-distancing of someone who is about to hit you with very bad news.

"The problem is," she said, "we've got more than *talk* to deal with here. I suppose you know Mrs. Henriette Braun."

"Yes, I do. She's a friend of ours."

There was another nervous switch in the angle of her gaze, another quizzical look on her face.

"Here's what she wrote," she half-whispered. "It's your copy."

She handed me the statement with a photocopy of a page from Henriette's passport stapled to it.

"Deeply disturbing aggressiveness verging on physical violence." That was how she described my "behavior" during her summer visit. Every time I went into a rage, Shams and Haroon would run terrified to their room, she wrote.

And yes, she did witness them—the words I uttered during one of my terrifying tantrums: "He screamed at Regina with tremendous anger and told her that there was no future for them together as a couple, that Tunisia was the only future for him and his sons. Then he went into his study, slamming the door behind him."

Henriette went on to say that she had seen it coming—watching and feeling my "anger," my "peevishness," and my "discontent" grow increasingly "menacing" and "uncontrollable" over the years.

Hearing me talk of leaving, she felt very unsettled but not at all surprised: "I have always had the impression that Tariq was very unhappy with his life in Europe."

She stayed up that night and had a conversation with Regina, talking into the early hours: "She told me everything about the abysmal misery she had endured over the last four years. Later when I went into my room and thought about Regina's confession, I could not help but conclude that my closest friend was leading a secret existence that I had never suspected: the life of a terrified woman."

———

(Shouting, threatening, planning to return to Tunisia: it was, of course, pure fiction—and of the cheapest kind.

But it was credible fiction nonetheless; for even though Henriette's words were anything but truthful, there was a quality of crucifying eloquence about them that gave her testimony so much authority—a mixture of pity and clinical detachment in this swift and deft profile, the sketch of a man who had deviated from the path of normalcy.

And the repugnant strategic cunning underneath it all—the way she used the boys to drive home the idea of an established pattern of domestic violence.)

———

I looked up from the statement and was surprised to see a helpless expression on Le Bel's face—a what-now look.

That was when I discovered the thing about her face: she suffered from a melasma-like disorder that made her rash up with faint dun patches around her cheeks every time she grew pale.

Those patches were, I thought, her way of expressing negative emotion.

She handed me the second statement, written by Mathilde, our downstairs neighbor.

She had multiple sclerosis, was soft-spoken and effaced—a successful journalist and single mother of two since her second husband had left her for a man.

I never thought anything so destructive could come out of her—infinitely heinous in intent and yet understated and unemotional in its banality, its report-like matter-of-factness.

She had managed to turn all our verbal quarrels into scenes provoked by *me*—scenes of mounting rage, typically culminating in what appeared to her as physical violence.

Mathilde's only emotional indulgence came at the end of her testimony, and it was brilliantly orchestrated: "Often, Regina would call me after a violent event, apologizing for Tariq. She would say that for a perfectionist like him, the demands of his restaurant were becoming almost unbearable. Deeply pained and preoccupied by my friend's predicament, I once pressed her, asking if Tariq was *physically* abusive. I only got tears in reply. Without asking for her permission, I stepped out of my apartment and went up and knocked on her door several times. Eventually, she opened up the door, standing there distraught before me—and there was not a shadow of a doubt in my mind: Regina was an emotionally *and* physically abused woman—and she was in urgent need of professional help."

———

"Do you think this is one of those divorce situations that wind up spiraling out of control?" I said in a parched, brittle voice, still staring at the statement—not a question, but merely a low indiscernible mutter. In fact, even as the words tumbled out of my mouth, I did not know what they meant or why I had uttered them.

Suddenly, it dawned on me that my lips had felt dry and hot all along—rigid, too, like a lifeless thing plastered on my face.

The mysterious alchemy of anguish.

"What we need right now," she said, "is to regain control of the situation and counteract their strategy. We need the testimony of people who are willing to vouch for your kindness and decency—to go on the record and say that you're *not* the man depicted in these statements, that the man portrayed here is a fictional being who has nothing to do with the real Tariq Abbassi."

She sounded withdrawn as she spoke—listless also, not putting as much energy into her words as she should.

Her mood was hard to decipher, but it seemed to me as if she was not quite prepared to deal with my physical reaction, that it was making her weary (or discouraged) to find me this vulnerable after all.

We talked strategy and procedure for a while and when I started going in circles (out of anxiety, I think), she sat back in her swivel chair and started fiddling with a letter-opener. It was time to leave.

I stood up and was rather surprised to see her still sitting behind her desk.

Le Bel sat there for a few long seconds—staring at me but not quite at me (it was more like the pensive gaze of somebody looking through your body and beyond).

"This is not going to be easy," she blurted out at last—her voice flat, a touch gravelly.

She sounded as if she was blaming herself.

There were more statements in the folder that she had given me (other neighbors, Regina's therapist, a doctor and his wife—parents of Shams's classmate).

They all depicted Regina in a favorable light, which I did not mind, of course. In fact, I agreed with most of what had been written about her character.

The real sting came from all the filth that they had managed to write about me—people who knew nothing about my inner life.

I felt betrayed by them—even if there was no bond of friendship between us, with the possible exception of Mathilde. (Emotions ran high between us during our fights, but the physical violence was crass fabrication.)

I was discovering that there was violence and violence, and in my case it was the violence of these lies that I could not cope with: I found it nauseating that our acquaintances would be capable of harboring so much resentment, so much negativity, beneath the facade of civility.

And the unreality of the situation—as if matters of fact and procedure did not count in the reckoning of the "attestants," as if it was all a game of role playing, with one chosen person assuming a predefined role for them: all-purpose scapegoat.

Things have taken another dramatic turn, a simpler and starker twist in perspective: it was not just me against Regina now, but me against this shadowy world of hostile others that she had ushered into my inner space—this cast of duplicitous figures stepping out of their darkness, to inhabit my consciousness.

(And how do I feel about this today?

I still hate those people—more than I care to say here, and I still find the whole thing namelessly sickening. With time, however, I have come to exonerate Regina at least, to understand that her initial design was not to cast me as a horrible individual who lived outside the realm of human decency.

There is no doubt in my mind that her lies were not fabricated with malicious intent: they were just part of a desperate defense strategy.

It is the deeds of the others that I still find profoundly disturbing: the memory of what they wrote lingers like an aftertaste of rot—the work of those banal beings creeping out of the shadows: what interest did they have in stepping beyond the bounds of their ordinary lives, in acting so destructive? That they would try to bolster Regina's case was perfectly understandable, but why target me with so much useless filth?

My judgment on their motives may be inaccurate or simplistic, but it is as comfortingly clear as an equation: sick pleasure. There was a margin of perverse enjoyment in it for them, otherwise they would have never written what they did—the meticulous zeal to do a thorough job, but also the orgiastic euphoria with which they did it.

So much for Regina's attestants.

Some things are best relegated to silence.)

And now I had to prove myself with positive judgment—to gather testimony on my capacity for peacefulness and civil behavior, if nothing else.

I had to look for people willing to help me put a human face on the man who was being crafted by Hardy.

In Bordeaux, there were only two potential attestants (Jacques and Sami) whom I knew well enough to ask for their testimony.

As for my acquaintances in Paris (faculty and students from my Sorbonne days, mostly), I had not remained in touch with them and they were definitely not an option—trying to contact them after so many years, and for this sort of sordid chore of all things, would be nothing short of disgrace.

It was embarrassing enough to ask Jacques and Sami; but ask them I did, and they both handled my request with tact and discretion.

When I spoke with Sami, I said vaguely that I was going to tell him about unsavory private matters: "If any of this bothers you, we can ignore the whole matter—as if nothing has been said. Also, if you think you need a few days to think about this, no problem."

He said, "I have no problem testifying on your behalf, Si Abbassi."

"Thank you," I said.

"Don't mention it. It's the least I can do."

Acting in accordance with Arab custom, he did not look at me during that moment. He kept working as if no words had been exchanged. Framing me in his gaze would have been an act of unspeakable vulgarity.

I also asked Zoé.

Her printed declaration, of which I received a scanned electronic copy, was the longest; and it was not so much a declaration as an apology:

I, Zoé Selma Brahmi, affirm that I am writing this statement in order to address the mendacious accusations leveled against Dr. Tariq Abbassi, my friend and fellow Sorbonne alumnus. First, I would like to state that it would only be fair to begin this testimony with an account of Tariq's role in his family during the years I have known him as a husband to my friend Regina Schmitz and as a father to Shams and Haroon Abbassi.

However, knowing how loath Tariq is to see any aspect of his private life exposed to public scrutiny, I have decided to refrain from such an account.

Having said that, I will start my testimony with Tariq's current struggles in the face of public scrutiny, precisely, since I have witnessed firsthand how traumatic and disruptive it has been for a man of his discretion to find himself subjected to so much exposure. Indeed, to the deeply disruptive disintegration of Tariq's home and his tragic separation from Shams and Haroon is now added the unfathomable emotional cost of slander and character assassination. The apparent purpose of the accusations is to construct the image of a man who has been consistently violent, in word and deed. The reality, however, is that the man who stands accused today of destructive conduct has never expressed himself through violence. In fact, he does not even express himself through anger.

During our long and frequent conversations on relationships, I have often urged him to adopt a less stoically aloof and dignified stance toward the normal frictions of married life, exhorting him to realize that controlled expression of anger is sometimes a healthier alternative to dignified withdrawal into sadness.

Seen from the point of view of a poet, however, the withdrawal and the aloofness make perfect sense in a man of Tariq's sensibility—a sensibility so refined, so exquisitely attuned to the secret beauty of the world!

How can a poet entirely dedicated to the pursuit of beauty, a man of impeccable order in everything that he undertakes, opt for violence and dis-order in the one thing that matters to him most—his own family? Arguments based on such a presumption will never stand up to scrutiny. I am positive that a psychological expert testimony would reveal not a closet monster gone amok, as some would have us believe, but a civil and mild-mannered man of great composure and unflagging responsibility.

In speaking with Tariq, it was painfully obvious to me that the accusa-
tions have led to great suffering. More than once, he told me that he would
even welcome the possibility of an investigation to clear his name.

As if Tariq's reputation needed to be cleared!

But such is the nature of a sensitive conscience that each scurrilous word
thrown at it, however self-defeating in its luridness, is experienced as an
arraignment of its honor. As Tariq Abbassi's closest friend, not only have I
never seen in him a man capable of evil deeds or intent, over the many years
of our friendship, I have come to know him, again and again, as a person of
irreproachable integrity and stoic self-restraint—in short, an infinitely gra-
cious and compassionate human being.

I affirm that the above and foregoing representations are true and correct
to the best of my information, knowledge, and belief.

———

A few days after I had received Zoé's statement, Sami e-mailed me
a scanned copy of his handwritten testimony. And it was only when
I sat down late at night and carefully read his words that I discovered how little I knew about him: he had kept his true self in hiding
through the many years he had worked with me—invisible in the
obscurity of his impenetrable silences.

And now there were these thin scanned traces of the man's
mind: manifested on the screen like dark diagrammatic etchings
on yellowing porcelain, they were telling me more about his true
personality than his voice and physical presence ever had: that jarring dissonance between the crispness of his main text (the actual
statement) and the resentment of his closing note—the anger of
those final digressive sentences was like embers lurking through
thin ash; and it spoke of a dark silent seething deep within him, a
smoldering I would have never suspected in a man of his professional rigor.

He worked hard, fast, long (very long), and all I saw in that was
technical masterfulness, endurance, and exceptional composure.

God, how blind I was to the struggling human being within him:
the rage behind the focused drive, and the furious will to live (and

prevail) against the judgment of a world that had branded him with the mark of the odd marginal, if not worse.

It was all there, in that final note—technically a mistake, an irrational slip in a dispassionate statement; but how revealing it was—this emotional digression: it spoke of the shattered ambitions and the monastic choices of a man who willingly, definitively, in an austere leap of faith, had decided to turn his back on the ideals of the French Dream:

I, Sami Mamlouk, affirm that I have been employed by Mr. Tariq Abbassi as his assistant since 2000, the year I quit my position as tenured primary school teacher.

Since the start of my employment, it has been customary for me to put in an average of ten hours per day, cooking side by side with my employer in the physically and emotionally demanding work conditions of his high-end restaurant, The Cypresses. Considering the many stories that circulate in the restaurant business about the whimsies and eccentricities of the so-called star chefs, it seems to me that impatience, peevishness, or even loss of temper can be considered almost logical corollaries of the psychological strain created by the demands of a chef position. But such has never been the case of Mr. Abbassi, who has always displayed extraordinary self-mastery and level-headedness despite the harsh demands of his position.

It is therefore my greatest pleasure to affirm that during the years I have been in Mr. Abbassi's employ, I have never witnessed him in a state of anger or any state that might be associated with verbal abuse or any other form of violence. Instead, I would describe his overall demeanor in public as one of formal cordiality, with the patrons as well as with his employees.

Finally, I would like to conclude on a personal note. Although I am exceedingly saddened by what is happening to my employer, I am not in the least surprised by the nature of the accusations leveled against him, in particular those pertaining to his alleged violence and his alleged plans to abduct his children and seek haven in Tunisia. As a former civil servant of Arab descent, I underwent a similar trial, although not nearly as painful as my employer's. During my career as a primary school teacher, I experienced the pain and humiliation of being reduced to a cliché by colleagues and superiors alike, ruthless sectarian people who cast aspersions on my character and even accused me of mental illness: their repeated accusations of potential violence and their outrageous allegations about my mental health eventually led me to quit the education system in revulsion.

As a Frenchman, I find it sad to conclude that even today these insidious strategies are still the common lot of the Maghrebi minority in a society where accusations of violence and mental illness are frequently used as a devastating instrument of Arab stigmatization.

I affirm that the above and foregoing representations are true and correct to the best of my information, knowledge, and belief.

———

After I read Sami's statement, I knew our relationship would change.

His digression and the world of suppressed suffering that it had ushered into my conscience: those words had suddenly generated a new common reality (a sharing) between us, and I now felt morally obligated to show him that his second declaration (the testimony within the testimony, as it were) was not lost on me—his tough life choices, the depth of hurt behind his words, his wounded retreat from mainstream society.

Somehow something had to be done—a symbolic gesture—and the fact that I still did not know how that gesture would play out in our workaday relationship did not make thinking about the new situation any easier.

Deep within my heart, though, I was convinced that the time had come for a radical transformation in the way I related to the man who called himself my assistant.

———

The deputy mayor, after one of his interminable business dinners:
  He took me aside and asked me if he might have a word with me.
  I said yes, and we went and stood over by the kitchen door.
  He leaned over and sort of whispered in my direction (although he did not need to), slightly flustered, keeping his eyes fixed on the door, as if he was

about to confess something grave to an almighty presence lurking behind the slats.

He was from Bergerac, a dark-skinned man with curly black hair and dramatically set dark eyes. His close-knit eyebrows and hawkish nose gave him an air of conspiratorial intent.

DM: "Mr. Abbassi, I know these things are highly sensitive to—address in conversation, but I just want to tell you: I have heard of your predicament, and you have all my sympathy. I know how unsettling this—life transition can be. I've been there."

T: "Thank you, sir. That's kind of you."

DM: "You know, I would have gladly done more than that—something in writing. But you know how it is when you're in public office—"

T: "I understand."

DM: "I'm glad you do. Listen, may I address you by your first name?"

T: "Yes, you may."

DM: "Tariq, it's a woman's world out there. I've learned it the hard way, and I must say I'm still learning—day in day out. We've got to stick together on certain issues. But, damn it, beyond these words I'm sharing with you here, there's unfortunately very little I can do to show my—solidarity. And I just want you to know that it really pains me to say that there isn't much I can do. I just wanted you to know that."

I said to him that he had done plenty already through his gesture of solidarity. His unease seemed to have lifted when he shook my hand—looking into my eyes and telling me that I had to carry on, that his thoughts were with me.

Then he left with his guests.

It was around that time that I began to suffer from insomnia.

I sought help from my doctor, thinking that she would prescribe sleeping pills. Instead, she sent me to a psychiatrist and he put me on Prozac.

I was glad that he did not ask too many questions, and relieved when he accepted my declination to undergo therapy.

I was depressed and I knew it—vaguely conscious of the extent of my misery, of a certain urge to nurse myself out of the melancholy.

But the nightmares erupting in the middle of slumber were quite another matter—heart-wrenching bursts of vivid visions from the depths of the unconscious, with a logic and a language all their own, beyond conscious grasp or rational explanation.

The only coping strategy was in and through writing—keeping a precise record of this secret trial of mine:

Somewhere in the south of France:

I am walking down a tree-lined street—sidewalks swelling and gaping with roots bulging between the cracks.

The street and the neighborhood are entirely alien to me—a bit seamy and run-down, but not threatening. Yet the moment is somehow—as if a storm was gathering.

A station wagon stops in the middle of the street: a man, shirt wide open, leans out of the window and asks about a street.

From where I am standing on the sidewalk it is almost impossible to hear him above the infernal din of the engine.

His is the most scarred and bruised car I have ever seen: rusted and scabby-looking in the spots where the paint has peeled off, plastered with tape in a few places to keep the patches of disintegrating metal from falling off.

And yes, I can at last place his face now. It is the taxi driver who barked at me to put away my sandwich when we got into his cab. As we settled into the backseat, Zoé whispered in my ear: "He must be on something."

Of course, I don't know anything about the street he is looking for. All at once, standing on that bumpy unlevel sidewalk, I feel my mind go numb with fear—torn between two equally terrible options: having to admit that I am a stranger in town or giving him fictitious directions, which is exactly what I end up doing. I give him bogus directions and he roars off.

Soon enough, though, I can hear him tearing down the street again, farther up behind me this time—that insane-looking station wagon wheezing in a gritty whine.

I turn left and run toward the first back alley off to the right, but just as I vanish around the corner I catch a glimpse of his car parked across the top of the street behind me, like a roadblock.

I am hoping he has not seen me.

Everything terribly still now—except for the sound of my footfalls, the echo of my frantic breath.

Suddenly, I realize it has gotten dark already.

"Hey!" he shouts.

I stop and turn around: he is standing at the top of the alley now, a very powerful light shining behind him—maybe a klieg or a floodlight.

Then he comes charging—shirt flapping about his chest, the tangle of jet-black hair inhuman and unrecognizable, like a crown of tangled wire haloed in the white light.

I am still standing there, blood pounding in my neck, thinking, "My God, this is going to be terrible."

Then comes the dreadful moment of semi-wakefulness, of panic and disorientation—feeling as if I am about to miss a crucial train that I will never manage to make up for, or fail a fateful test that I will never be able to retake.

Awake with that recurring all-too-familiar sensation of being too unready, too overwhelmed, too frail; and, yes, that terrible sense of mourning myself, my own death—of being both the dead man and the mourner.

She wrote: "There is no limit to human suffering. When one thinks: 'Now I have touched the bottom of the sea—now I can go no deeper,' one does go deeper. And so it is for ever."

The sheer miracle of those notes from the nightmare world: the bravery and the power to express all this in words (however vague and shaky) when you're still so riven and divided—a nameless wedge of pain pushing deeper and deeper within the darkest recesses of the feeling self even as the writing self fumbles for pen and paper in the darkness.

You wake up shaking in a dark and strange room—the Eternal Chamber of Solitude: cold, deep, and unfathomable, like the street of your nightmare—never known before; and you are the Eternal Orphan—a creature of pure primal lack.

The scratch of your pen against the paper, the shaky lines: your only solace in the dead silence of the night.

The fact-finding hearing took place in a musty, file-cabinet–choked room the size of a professor's office.

We were seated in uncomfortable wooden chairs with our lawyers wedged tight between us, facing the judge and the clerk, who sat side by side behind an immense file-cluttered desk that looked like an inherited dining room table.

I could only catch Regina's presence out of the corner of my eye—she seemed vague and distant despite the diminutive size of this phantasmagoric room.

(The only time we had seen each other face to face on that day, for less than a minute, was when we stood by the bench in the atrium.

As soon as her lawyer had seen us standing there together, he came over and asked to have a word with her.

She complied immediately, and that was the last I had seen of her before the hearing.

It is quite a painful thing to talk about the unreality of finding yourself separated from your wife by total strangers: no matter how alienated you feel toward her, the fact of a lawyer's peremptory physical presence between the two of you can be profoundly unnerving.

The judge summons you and you answer the summons, and suddenly you find yourself in a nameless room filled with the sad ghosts of past contentions, with two people sitting between you and the woman you had, till very recently, shared your life with—two experts in the sinister craft of contention rattling off impenetrable formulas in an alien tongue.

Somehow there is something deeply unnatural about such a situation.

It took me a long time to grasp it, but now I think I know why the whole process is so unsettling:

It is the self-inflicted pain that suddenly enters into your life after the summons of the Law—that is, I believe, the most troubling thing about the brutal intrusion of the Justice System into your existence: there is no physical brutality, of course, only the microscopic bureaucratic manipulation of your conscience with the horrid toxic stream of written words they pour into your life, its inevitable aftermath of relentless torment and self-interrogation: the anger, the guilt, the many doubts, the sleepless nights, the endless torture of wondering why and where the two of you went wrong.

This, the self-administered heartache and the unreality that comes in its wake, was what Regina chose to bring into our life—her life, my life, the life of our sons.

But as I said before, after the loss that I inflicted on her, I am in no position to make any judgment on my former spouse.

Silence is respect, and I do owe Regina my silence.

That is why I have chosen not to give her a real presence here, and the outcome of this elision—the blank narrative space in which she dwells—is a place of reverence and deference not oblivion.)

———

Judge Ravenin had very black hair and an ivory face—sallow, expressionless, and stiff; lifeless in its stiffness, as if it was a paper mask tightly glued to her skull.

"Mr. Abbassi," she said, "I suppose you understand that it is not in your interest to take your children out of this country."

That was how she chose to open the hearing, and I remember my first reaction was a sickening tightness in my chest and abdomen.

I also remember thinking, "Is this a warning or a question?"

She had taken me by surprise and here I was, my stomach in a knot, my mind confronted with the burden of an impossible question (or was it a warning?) from this dark woman of power behind her desk.

It turned out that the judge was not really addressing me, for she immediately commenced to introduce the case and then asked my lawyer to present her argument.

I must confess I was relieved that I did not have to respond to the judge's confounding statement, being utterly uncertain about my ability to stand my ground and assume and defend my position—remind her that I was a man with deep professional commitments in my adoptive country, a decent law-abiding immigrant, and a firm believer in shared parenting.

I never had a chance to say any of that—and maybe I would not have been able to: it was as if she had managed, by virtue of that one sentence, to turn me into a powerless bundle of jangled nerves.

Later, when I sat down with my lawyer in the atrium to discuss the outcome of the hearing, I was not at all surprised that she saw no violence whatsoever in the judge's opening words.

And when I asked her why she had not questioned Regina to help steer the hearing in our favor, she looked down for a second and stared (in disappointment, I suppose) at the speckled floor—that dull dark mirror of huge granite slabs, so perfectly polished and jointed they looked like one single layer of stone.

Le Bel said, "You can't do that here—in the French system. It's the judge who does the asking. Everything revolves around the judge here."

The words tumbled out of her mouth fast and disarticulated, like dice rolling down a glass counter, dry and pitiless—the machine-gun admonitions of a gangster defining his turf.

She had lost the polish of her diction.

That was when I managed to pin down the other thing that had always eluded me about her: it was her occasional lapses into the sloppy tone and diction of student conversation.

When she was tired and stressed out, Le Bel regressed to law school.

———

(And so the case was made—for me and against me, in that nameless room where I sat mute and law-observant after all my private rages, witnessing two agents of the Justice System trying to convince another agent that the other party had failed terribly, had committed terrible wrongs, and had to be held accountable for the failure of a marriage and a family.

This is all profoundly repugnant, of course, much more repugnant, I realize, than my words can convey—much more repugnant than I am *willing* to convey. And that is probably why I am forcing myself to omit the details here—it is just too putrid for words.

The less said the better.)

———

The moment when you find yourself outside the room with your lawyer:

You ask all the questions, except the ones you never dare to face.

And your lawyer responds to your queries and shakes your hand and goes about her business among the other black-robed figures and their clients.

Then, at last, you lift your head, forcing your gaze away from the sky-like trompe l'oeil surface of the floor, the dark dull sheen of it—the flecks of quartzite twinkling underneath the polish like remote stars, magnifying the cold depth of the black granite, its fascinating resemblance to interstellar night.

And now, as you begin to walk toward the exit, you discover that your body has become fully conscious of the feeling: your muscles—they have grown so inflexible with the effort of merely sitting quiet in Ravenin's room, as if you have been traveling on a bus for days on end and are barely beginning to take heed of your body in motion again, the sluggish movement of your frame through space.

Simultaneously, like a man awaking at dusk from a too long nap, you begin to realize that all the while you have been cut off from all traces of time, and the light of day, and the sounds of the streets; for now you recognize, with outrage, that the building is indeed deaf and blind—soundproof and entirely windowless.

Even the gigantic glass door that you now push open to exit this massive black box of dark aluminum, granite, and acrylic glass has been darkened to shut out the light.

And as you take your first steps outside, you cannot help but feel it coursing through your bones and your torpid nerves—not quite a sensation; an association, rather, or a thought: with the dull glare of the sky and the clamor of city life suddenly making too many demands on your attention, you feel disoriented and dazed, awkward and unfit—and yes, now that you know what you know, drowned in the implacable presence of the association (or the thought), which has now become as tangible as the rank air of the river before you: a man taking his first steps out of prison.

And to think that it was supposed to be a day like any other day.

You get up in the morning and fold the bedsheets and the blanket and put them down on the air mattress in neatly shingled rectangles—like any other day; you go to the bathroom and you stare at your grayish face in the mirror and it stares right back at you, tired and somewhat surprised; you cover your day-old bristle with shaving foam, pick up the razor, and set about making yourself presentable to the world; you go to the guest room and choose your clothes for the day, stacked with the rest of your garments on the still unopened IKEA boxes with your new furniture in them; and again, like any other day, you feel on your fingertips the wafer-crisp stiffness of the shirt, in the unheated room.

Eventually, you find yourself ready and the moment comes when you step out onto the sidewalk: the sharp tang of the winter morning burning in your nose like alcohol; the gritty scuff of your footsteps that sounds so much like a lazy shuffle on the wet cobblestones no matter how briskly you walk.

And then, unlike any other day, you take a different street—in fact one of those tiny medieval lanes that never see the sun, with their shimmery film of mold on the lower stones along the curb like patches of vaporous green—the same diffuse green that you see on the back of an anole.

Then you start to realize how long you have been deferring this different instant, denying it, like a debt you cannot even begin to imagine redeeming.

And that is when you come to register the deeper changes: the quality of your step—not hesitant and weak-willed necessarily; but certainly stiff, stubborn, and inobedient, in a purely physical way, like a mountain climber's muscles rebelling against the outrage of yet another threshold of height, the frenzied cells seething with their own inner churning rage—pleading for mercy; for something in you, far wiser than consciousness itself, knows that it is simply inhuman to be here, pushing yourself, each step an insult to your kinder gentler nature.

And when you come to the bottom of Quai Richelieu and take the stairs down to the narrow stone bridge and stop for a moment to contemplate the quiet simmer of the Gironde and the aspect of the courthouse beyond—an uncanny onyx-black cube to your eyes—you realize how violently unnatural it is for you to be standing where you are, dazed and awed as you try to take in the inexplicably forbidding aspect of that windowless building; and the jaundiced pallor of those thin clouds over the courthouse, the pregnant swollenness of the river, the false morning silence before you cross over.

———

Le Bel called in person to let me know:

She told me that Ravenin was very generous on visitation rights: I was awarded the entirety of school holidays, pending the final hearing in the fall.

It was her starchy official voice again today, like a radio news reporter reading out an important announcement.

"Also," she said, "the text of Judge Ravenin's ruling makes clear and specific mention of the fact that if she has decided against repatriation of Shams and Haroon, it is in order to provide them with temporary stability. Those were her words: temporary stability. This is going to put us in a very strong position when we fight for shared custody."

On the whole, she thought, it was a good ruling—considering the size of my dossier.

Now she wanted me to think of more material to give her—anything that would boost my image as a "caring, responsible, and *involved* father."

(I was relieved that she did not bring up the statements that I had e-mailed her—I remembered Le Bel's witheringly terse response: "Very, very flimsy," she wrote.

She had made the authors themselves a liability: Zoé's testimony was "overkill, pompous, digressive, and arrogant"; and Sami's "too biased and, yes, sectarian.")

———

I said, "I *am* excited, of course! I just don't know how to deal with my excitement yet. It scares me—in a way."

"Nonsense," Zoé said.

She sounded buoyant and in the mood for sweeping plans.

"The worst thing you could do at this point," she added, "is to start thinking that you'll have to fit the boys into your schedule. They'll sense it right away—and they'll hate it. Between now and Easter, we have plenty of time to think of ways to cut back on your workload. Right now, your number one priority is to bond with your kids. Charm campaign—think of it that way. Isn't it marvelous? Anything else, we'll find a solution—DON'T WORRY!"

———

Two days later it was January 18—a meaningful date since I had met Regina, she being German.

She had the boys call me early in the morning to wish me happy birthday.

After I hung up, I remember thinking that there was not much I was in the mood for in terms of celebration—some music and champagne later after work maybe.

———

I was finishing up in the kitchen that evening when Sami came down to tell me that a lady had barged in on Jacques, made herself at home in the special-guests corner (the Nook, as Jacques called it). She was expecting to be served.

"What?"

"I told her it was well after closing time, but she wouldn't budge!"

"How did she get *in*?"

I did not wait for his reply and went straight to the Nook, and when I saw the alcove draped with a makeshift spray-painted paper curtain, I knew what was happening: it was Zoé, of course (she had not called all day today).

And so with Sami and Jacques standing behind and watching, I decided to play along with her prank—walking back and forth along the curtain and talking to myself in histrionic fashion, wondering who on earth this person was and how dare she appropriate the premises for such outrageous games.

I did not lift up the curtain, which was my way of turning the tables on her—trying to beat her at her own game; instead, I kept up my soliloquy of the outraged boss, till she started giggling behind the curtain.

Then it was her turn to take over, pulling down the curtain and revealing fine foods and drinks beautifully laid out on the table: savory petits fours, canapés, champagne, and a torte—*Altwiener Schokoladentorte*, my favorite and Regina's birthday treat each year.

"So how does it feel to be thirty-nine?" she said, after we cheek kissed, putting her hands on my shoulders and leaning back a little—as if she was taking a probing look at a painting in progress.

"Tired," I was tempted to say, but I knew that would not do—it would be a rude letdown indeed.

"Surprised—endlessly surprised," I said.

I made sure to add a broad smile as I spoke the words.

I would get my present at home she had said, when we left The Cypresses.

And there it was, in full view as soon as we stepped into the apartment—a wonderful present from my greatest friend: my home refurnished—more or less as I imagined it.

Zoé had arranged for an IKEA team to come and turn those dusty boxes into furniture—while I was at work.

"How did you manage to get in?" I asked.

She gave me a steady look of amused mischief, leaning against the kitchen doorframe—the same mock studying look that she flashed me at the restaurant.

My apartment smelled of newness now (some vague redolence of turpentine), and I wondered how I myself smelled to Zoé (those sticky particles of smoke and fat in my hair and on my skin—the rancid reek of a whole day of cooking).

"Simple," she said, with an unusually sharp rise in her voice. "Assistant lets girl into boss's office, girl steals boss's keys, lets IKEA guys in, and hands keys back to assistant. Remember the caller who hung up on you so rudely two days ago?"

Again, the barely delineated deepening of her dimple and the clever twinkle in her eyes: laughing in her own unmistakable way—deep, sustained, inward ripples of mirth.

"I *had* to hang up without a word," she said, in a mock defensive tone. I wanted to talk to Jacques and do some planning with *him*."

She held a small pastry box in her hand: "What's in the box?" I asked.

"*That* is not for you," she replied with a laugh. "Cannelés—from Sami to my father."

We were still standing in the hallway. I was blissfully dumfounded, a bit drunk, and probably looking it.

And Zoé? She was tipsy and spoke and acted with a theatrical verve that showed no signs of letting up.

"Well, what do you think? You can't expect me to sleep on the floor!"

I told her the boys and I were so grateful.

"Wait," she said, "before we get sappy and tearful. Let's take a tour of your renewed home, shall we? See if you like the product."

———

My last written thoughts in bed that night: picturing Zoé in words, as she dropped the curtain. *She* was the greatest of all presents, a rare gift from Providence.

———

Those were the days when I began my acquaintance with Sami.

In a way, our friendship started in the form of a business arrangement, when Zoé suggested he take over all the cooking during the boys' visit.

Zoé and I were sitting in the living room, in the still-stiff, cowhide-smelling armchairs—her feet propped up on the Moroccan leather pouf, a present from me to Regina and one of the few things that she had left behind.

There was a floor lamp in the room, a pseudo–Art Deco pine cupboard in the corner, and a dun rope rug (ghostly substitute for the Egyptian kilim that used to decorate the floor, a gift from my mother to Regina); and yet the room still had an air of forced, untimely emptying about it—like a recently burglarized space.

"You tuck them in bed around eight," she said, "I babysit, and you go down to The Cypresses—do the PR work and help with the closing and everything."

"So, *that*'s the solution?" I said unironically, but with a deep shade of apprehension, which she must have mistaken for skepticism, or worse.

In fact, her plan appeared quite workable, but the parameters were many (and somehow not tangible enough), and I was trying to think my way through them at the moment, while Zoé was obviously a few steps ahead of me—after all, it was her idea and she must have spent some time figuring out its various ramifications.

"Well, it's the solution if you *see* it as one," she said.

I sensed a hint of offense in her voice.

"Oh, I find it a wonderful idea. I just don't know if I'd be able to sell it to Sami—what's good for me isn't necessarily good for *him*. He's certainly hardworking and very reliable, but even with the best of intentions he wouldn't be able to run the kitchen properly on his own. It's maddening work. He would definitely need Fatma—mornings. In the afternoon she works on her own deliveries—*and* she has three kids. I will talk to them, though; but it's going to be a tough sell."

Suddenly, Zoé went dreamy-eyed, gazing into the fireplace—feeling thwarted by circumstances? Hemmed in by my negativity?

It was hard to judge the shift in my friend's mood, but her silence was unnerving: there was a secret quality of peevishness to it, and I did not want her to think me ungrateful—or even half-hearted.

"Also," I said, "I really would like to make a meaningful move toward a friendly relationship with Sami. So I don't want this arrangement to get in the way—turn into a power relations thing. I want to make sure he understands that it's completely up to him to decide, but I also want to tell him that I was going to give him a pay raise anyway—*before* this proposition. I'm treading on tricky ground, as you see. That's why I'm trying to figure out all the parameters."

She said, "Let's hope for the best. In terms of meaningful moves, you could invite him for an informal business lunch one of these Sundays—see what happens."

———

And that was how I began this new chapter with Sami—a random shot at authenticity veiled in the half-pretext of a business lunch.

By the time Zoé had left, every logistical detail was spelled out: I had met with Sami several times to discuss the temporary handover, and Fatma was quite willing to work with him all mornings except Wednesdays.

But those initial talks with Sami were not about business only. I think he knew from the start that I was trying to connect with him on a more significant level.

Today, Sami is far more than a friend: he is my only link to the outside world—the only person that I was able to speak with right after the death of my sons.

And what he did for me in that horrific summer of 2007 was beyond anything I can express in words.

I owe him a lifelong debt of gratitude.

———

Zoé said, "Those statements—they're still on your mind, aren't they?"

We were sitting in the coffer-ceilinged central hall of Bordeaux's railway station. Her train was leaving in fifteen minutes—ample time—yet the bustle of rushing passengers around us made me nervous and I felt her question was untimely, rather irritating in fact.

"What statements?" I said, evasively.

"Come on, you know what I'm talking about. *Regina's* statements."

"Well, you can't expect me to get over a thing like that overnight, can you?"

"No, I don't," she said. "Who would?"

My words must have sounded edgy and defensive. In fact, I was trying to dodge any potentially meaningful exchange at this point— neither the time nor the place was right it seemed to me.

Then she started to say something but checked herself; and suddenly her gaze turned diffuse and indecipherable, lost in the huge neon-lit white tunnel gaping across the hall—the tubular walkway leading down to the ground floor and the platforms.

She was fumbling for something to express, that much I knew—a sort of symbolic statement, maybe—and I had the impression that she was more riled by my evasiveness than by her own fumbling.

She had not looked at me in any particular way, but it was precisely in that abstracted plunge of her gaze down the neon tunnel that I felt the full weight of my friend's impatience—the way a repeat truant absorbs the anger of his teacher before the first word is spoken.

As for me, all I really wanted was simply to prolong the quiet atmosphere of our breakfast at Le Chic Café—to sit peacefully on this aluminum bench and indulge in some more wordless communication.

But Zoé's gaze was remote now, her demeanor chill—something had shifted in her depths, and I could read it on her lips like a warning sign: they were shivery, her lips—indrawn and thin, and I could almost touch the texture of her humor—ruffled to the touch, like crumpled silk.

She said, "Look at all this—the gorgeous facade of this gorgeous train station, the ceiling, the columns. Everything restored to its original splendor, with an extra touch—Art Deco original with a touch of postmodern chic: polished-granite flooring, sleek ad panels, wall-embedded ATMs, high-tech ticket vendors. Affluence and civilization, right? Wine money. Chateaux country. It's so easy to lose track of it, isn't it? In the middle of all this—affluence? But *you*—you know what I'm talking about."

"Honestly, I *don't* know what you're talking about—precisely. Is there anything the matter?"

It was getting late, after all—or was it one of my depression-driven spells of panic? The restaurant calling? My awful fear of parting?

It was probably all of those factors combined, but one thing seemed certain to me: I was somehow in dread of having to deal with something that I was not able to face at this particular moment.

I was not at all prepared for this somber shift in my friend's mood—her grim half-turned face, the glaze in her eyes, and now the switch in her voice. I felt a deeper intensity beneath the forced pertness, but I could not quite put a name to it.

Also, I found the irony in her tone rather condescending—very much unlike the passionate and well-meaning preachiness that I enjoyed in her. Her attitude left me flustered and peeved: Zoé's countenance was as impenetrable as a tight fist—there was no telling where she was taking this next.

Then she said it (almost in an impatient moan at first), and for the first time I thought I saw bitterness in Zoé—bitterness mingled with deep-seated despair: "The stink of the dirt, Tariq. That's what I'm talking about. Dirt mingled with manure. These peasants have it all over them—they reek of it. Don't ever forget that. They were born and raised in the dirt and they'll never rise above it. And they're going to hate and envy anyone who doesn't smell of it. The moment you take this thought for granted, you'll be able to ignore these people once and for all. Trust me, you won't even notice them anymore, much less remember what they've said or written. I'm not saying the thought will allow you to look them straight in the eye and think, Screw you—you're nothing. You *are* already capable of that, because the truth is on your side. What I'm trying to say is, the thought will allow you not to *see* them anymore—a much healthier position than 'screw you.'"

She stood up with a strained smile, without looking at me.

"How about that for anger-management therapy!" she added.

She was not expecting an answer, obviously, and anyway I was too confused by what she was trying to say and express.

I picked up her suitcase and we walked side by side toward the tunnel.

It was only when she settled down into her train seat and began to cry that I knew. That strange incoherent moment on the bench: the angry words were her way of fighting back the tears.

———

(As fate would have it, those few days in Bordeaux were my last opportunity for one-on-one significant sharing with Zoé.

We were not destined to have another meaningful moment until my impromptu Paris visit with the boys in the summer of that year.

To this day, I can only guess at how things went wrong with her after the death of my sons.

I know it will be a while before I can empirically uncover Zoé's reasons—the motives behind the things that she chose or did not choose to do in the aftermath of my sons' passing.

Still, something in me—a voice inherently truthful and reliable coming directly from mother's letter—tells me it was terror that drove her to my mother's doorstep after that terrible summer.

All the satanic, nauseating fabrications that she told her about the "real" cause of her grandsons' demise—a narrative so utterly criminal and devilish in its intricacies that it imposed an altogether new version of reality on my mother and my family, fully exculpating Faisal Brahmi and depicting me as an unstable man who had put Zoé's father at the center of his nonsensical confabulations.

Her web of lies was so elaborate in its complexity that the letter sent by my mother after her visit had nothing to do with the reality of what had really happened. But therein resides the inspiring power of that letter, precisely, in its capacity to express wisdom and survival and truth affirmation within and despite the web itself!

I firmly believe that my mother had come under the same criminal pressure as Zoé, otherwise she would have never accepted her monstrous distortion of the real story.

Unlike Zoé, however, my mother was able to develop a cryptic strategy that allowed her to circumvent the pressure and send me a message of resistance and truth affirmation in and through a letter that presents itself as an unequivocal endorsement of Zoé's dictated narrative.

As for Zoé, I have no doubt whatsoever that she was instructed to distort the truth.

I also firmly believe that she had no knowledge whatsoever of being used by her own father as a key instrument in his devilish design.

After all, the man *was* beyond all suspicion—my numerous references to him in the diary depict a kind and fully trustworthy gentleman!)

———

There were more Sunday brunches with Sami at Le Chic Café that winter.

Typically, he and I would meet there at ten and we would part company around noon, sometimes getting together in the early afternoon for a matinee film and a drink.

———

It would be a mistake to assume that Sami is a passionate person. Still, the more I got to know him, the more I got to discover something quite similar to passion in him: a kind of carefully contained intensity. He had a lot of it, but he always managed to keep his intensity hidden—through a quiet exercise of the will, something akin to spiritual self-mastery. He had an astonishing capacity to be passionately involved with certain ideas and principles without letting the involvement manifest itself as emotional excess of any kind.

Sami was intellectually sharp, mentally focused, in control of his self, and it was always his spontaneous capacity for self-control that struck you most once you got to know him, because that was where he seemed to channel a great deal of his mental powers: keeping his energies from getting scattered.

He was also deeply private, the type of person most people would describe as secretive.

During our conversations, the closest he came to a personal disclosure was when he told me about the end of his only meaningful relationship after he had resigned from his teaching position.

He said, "We were living in two different worlds after that. I was very angry on the inside and she didn't know what was really happening to me—and *in* me. Not that we didn't talk about the horrible conspiracies I had to deal with at work and in society at large, but I think she was not willing to face the uglier complications. Also, at some point she started saying my resignation was a cop-out—'one more escape from reality,' she called it. That did it. I just left our apartment and never looked back."

He was not talkative on the subject of his former life as a teacher and a married man, although I tried on several occasions to get him to open up.

I even used humor once: I said, "I guess I'll never find out what it means to be married to a Frenchwoman."

"I guess you won't," he replied, with a smile, but there was firmness and a sense of finality to his words. "My mother," he added. "She's my only confessor and therapist."

———

Sami was going through the files on his laptop while I watched the cook put about a dozen chickens on the spit rods of the rotisserie.

That redbrick wood-fired rotisserie had an immense lip: it was custom-designed to look like a big fireplace—the only touch of rusticity in a diner of mica furniture, faux black marble, and chrome plate.

Le Chic's idea of cool postmodern decor was actually cold: your gaze seemed to be constantly slipping and bouncing off the sleek streamlined surfaces of the place.

Still, it was one of my favorite eateries in town: the flexible American-style menu was unique in Bordeaux and the service and food were impeccable.

And there was that singular rotisserie in back: it was quite literally a heartwarming change to sit there and contemplate the dance of the flames in the dark concavity of the oven, which was probably the only earth-toned object in the café.

The day Sami showed me his WITNESS activities. The excerpts from my diary are very poor and sketchy, but quite instructive:

Sami is still busy with his files—his Darjeeling getting cold, but he does not seem to mind.

When he is done going through his various directories, he turns his laptop around and places it between us.

Last Sunday he told me that he was going to show me samples from a series of "visual testimony" that he had put together for WITNESS, an online watchdog group on race and discrimination that he wants to create.

(Also: he constantly refers to the visual material as "the visible conscience of our times," and in themselves, the words sound decidedly intriguing—mysterious enough to capture my curiosity, at any rate.)

Sami organized the visual material under two menu items: "Do You Know" and "It Happened."

The "testimony" is arresting with an intense (aggressive?) way of captivating your attention: it is a series of what appear to be pop-up windows with neatly designed statistics, photos, and video clips.

The captions that he created are almost strident—in their colors, their urgency, their pressing appeal to your fundamental humanity, their unsparing sarcasm.

Sami takes me through his photo gallery first—showing me the material in layout form, then clicking on individual pictures and scrolling down to the captions:

There is a picture of illegal immigrants—looking exhausted, angry, and confused. The caption on the photo reads: "Rounded up on the beach and sent straight back home—illegally!" And centered underneath the caption in bright red lettering: "IT HAPPENED IN SETE. "

The fruit pickers of the Southwest—hunkering in the gloomy depths of the nearly roofless ruins that they call home: "Who needs light? Their kids don't like to read! IT HAPPENED IN PYRENEES ORIENTALES. "

The Maghrebi boy in tank top and shorts playing soccer barefoot with bundled socks in the sewage-flooded lane—a corridor of concrete walls and glaring graffiti: "See, he can be very creative playing. He doesn't need a park! IT HAPPENED IN MARSEILLES. "

The African father standing astraddle the doorstep of the building, literally dragged out by the gendarme. His wife and his two daughters on the sidewalk, staring blankly at their furniture—his son still inside the building, holding onto his arm, trying to help: "Can't pay your rent on a meager salary? Try the bridges! IT HAPPENED IN PARIS. "

Sami clicked on the Do-You-Know directory:

More material, and again, the same red letters smoldering with fascinating intensity—"THE FACTS" in bright red centered above each Do-You-Know entry:

"THE FACTS: Do you know that a hugely disproportionate percentage of residents in our inhuman housing projects are ethnic minorities, making the projects not only a racial ghetto but also a de facto concentrationary urban structure?"

"THE FACTS: Do you know that 90% of minority business-school graduates stay on the corporate job-search list for three years before they stop applying and settle definitively into their 'temporary' jobs?"

And so on.

There were also the video clips—Gritty, grainy, consciously amateurish (?) with an intense, gripping quality of happening about them, like reality TV. Scenes of quotidian banality transformed into symbolic battlefields:

The video of the two women, one African French and the other European French.

The African French woman is on the phone first, inquiring: "Did you receive the copy of my pay slip and my bank statement with the dossier?"

A voice on the speaker—an employee in the Office of Social Housing: "Yes." (An aloof yes.)

The African woman, in deliberately inarticulate French: "What are my chances?"

The clerk: "I'm afraid all our vacancies have been filled. You'll have to reapply in two years."

A few seconds later, the European Frenchwoman calls, introduces herself, and makes a very similar inquiry:

"If I send you my dossier in the next few days, will you still consider it?" The OSH clerk: "Sure. We still have vacancies."

There was a video of a Maghrebi couple turned away at the door of a nightclub: filled to capacity, says the surly bouncer. A few moments later, a European-looking French couple is ushered in with a smile and a joke.

Suddenly, in a physical reflex, I lift my head and look around me: it is like stepping out of another time dimension—the pictures on the screen are extremely fast and harsh and strident. Cognitively very demanding.

Still, despite their jarring visual quality and content, they really manage to make you think about ethnic inequalities in France.

I have never stopped to consider the disproportionately high percentage of ethnic minorities in the HLM housing projects.

I never knew that a huge number of minority business graduates have to settle for low-level jobs after six years of studies and a grueling job search.

I never knew that minority employees were systematically excluded from top-level management positions.

I never knew.

But why have I never tried to know?

Tariq: "Pop-ups?"

My question is irrelevant, I guess—its irrelevance only a measure of my amazement.

Sami: "Yes. The visual material and the facts."

He seems to be very satisfied with his work.

S: "I'm trying to take the video material beyond the Net, though. I went to Arte's French headquarters and asked them if they would be interested in broadcasting the videos. I didn't get any further than the information desk. One of their staff came down and spoke with me—he looked at me like I was from outer space. Actually, at some point, the clerk threatened to call the police."

There is a certain fervor in the way he exposes his difficulties—an attitude that many would describe as righteous.

Is there anything unhealthy about this other life of Sami?

It would not be fair of me to judge his work: I am bound by our friendship.

Suffice it to say here that he does not appear to betray any excessive feelings whenever he talks about the work he cares most about. He does not use any intolerant discourse either.

———

Another diary entry written after one of our Sunday conversations—again, poor, boring, and confusing, but highly revealing about Sami's passionate commitment to ethnic equality:

T: "Did you take your work to The League Against Racial Discrimination?"

S: "I did and I offered to design their visual material for them—free of charge, of course. They're totally in cahoots with the system—completely corrupt. I sent them a very long e-mail with samples from my work. No response. A couple of days later, I got harassed by a cop outside my apartment—supposedly because of the way my car was parked. Then my computer kept crashing for no reason—for days on end. The League takes such pathetic pride in being basically in collusion with the system. They can't even imagine changing the rules of the system, the way it works. They're totally out of touch with the younger generation of Maghrebis. Take me, for example: my idea of Frenchness, of belonging, of militancy, the right course of action in the struggle—my world vision runs counter to everything they represent, which is integration into French society based on the way the rules are currently written by the Euro French. Militant, aggressive pressure on the collective conscience isn't on their agenda. "

S: "You can never make the legal apparatus change if you're working from inside a system based on hate and exclusion. Meaningful change never happens from inside and it is always rejected by 'the insiders.'"

All this is happening over brunch in the heart of ultra conservative Bordeaux—Sami eating very intermittently, without apparent appetite, sipping at his orange juice with his usual imperturbable composure and understated style.

No apparent agitation on his face, no angry expression of extremist beliefs: the clinical detachment, the contemplative calm with which he is saying all this is admirable—he might have been a dentist discussing the ill effects of tartar and how to deal with them.

And his face: it might "take some getting used to, " as Zoé once put it, but I remember that the first time I saw Sami's face I found it profound and powerful: his grayish-brown skin wrapped up so tight around his face, you could actually see the ridgelines of his zygomatic bones pushing against the skin, delineated in a darker shade of ivory. The knuckles on his long reedy fingers—same shade of ivory. Extraordinarily thin, "skeletal" fingers.

Sami is extremely thin and I never dared ask him the terrible question: eating disorder? Bone and nerve—shrunken down to the bare essentials: the mere sight of him reminds you, almost unavoidably, of a body baked dry; and even though my bond to Sami is very strong, it is true that you have to get used to him before you can put away his appearance once and for all—and deal with the great, pure essence of the man himself.

Last thoughts before sleep:

Why can we not have our own great creative American Melting Pot? Why are we so poor at seeking, cultivating, and optimizing difference?

Is it in the nature of Europe to make people withdraw further and further within instead of seeking to connect and recombine and recreate with the other? Become more and more desperately entrenched, rabid, extreme, pitiless? Lonely?

This new form of insular being (if Foucault were alive today, he would probably call it The New Confinement): the future Great War of Europe— totally unpredictable (but seemingly normal), volatile individuals nursing a huge grudge against "The System." In total isolation—not many social/ community "connections."

Bergman's Silence *comes to mind—insular beings cooped up in their radical islands of utterly untranslatable thoughts and longings.*

It was a winter of strange inner transformations—filled with feelings that I had been unwilling to confront for some time.

In the weeks and months that followed Sami's demonstrations, I would often find myself wondering if I really had it in me to face the full implications of the facts that he had made me witness.

It was all the more difficult to confront this new awareness (the fact of hate and discrimination in general, not just ethnic discrimination) that the themes of his "visual testimony" were ultimately quite related to the reality of rejection that I was facing as a struggling Arab poet in France—and now as a man wrongly accused of committing heinous deeds in his own home.

The respite of the ruling was just that ultimately: a temporary reprieve from the deepening sense of loss and alienation that was beginning to take hold within me after Regina's flight. Sami's work forced me to view my own private tribulations within the bigger context of race relations and discrimination in France.

He was able to put his finger on a long-ignored nameless nerve of pain buried deep inside me—something that I had always relegated to the recesses of denial: the power of discrimination to make people like me feel hurt and excluded.

I was as much in resistance as I was in awe: my friend's capacity to stand alone and affirm his vision, however painful and unpleasant for most people, was quite admirable.

After all, the man was nine years my junior—a virtual stranger who was now lecturing me on the sinister (and mostly invisible) underpinnings of racial discrimination and social exclusion.

———

One day I asked him if he would be interested in watching the movie *Festen*: I sent him an e-mail with the link to Le CinéAccro's website: "*Check out synopsis (link below). Could go and watch it this Sunday, if you'd like.*"

After the film, we walked down to Jardin Public—going in through the small gate off Avenue de Verdun.

The Cedar Walk—that was what Regina and I used to call this end of the park. We would bring Shams here to bike along the quiet dirt trails under the fir trees.

I asked Sami if he did not mind entering the park on this side and he seemed a bit surprised at the question.

"Not at all," he said.

I always liked the sensation of coolness in the shadow of the huge Lebanon cedars—it felt as if the trees themselves were capable of producing a breeze of their own making.

"I love the smell and the freshness here in the summer. It has been a while," I told him.

He just nodded and I said, "It's funny, though, the way some scents can stay with you—and the impressions and the people you associate with them: they come bursting in on you in one instant, like fragrance from a pop-up greeting card."

Sami laughed, and I thought I knew why.

"Those down-home pop-up cards," I said. "The scented ones, you know. The kind your aunt sends you from the country right after Ramadan."

He kept chuckling.

Suddenly, for no reason at all, I thought of how little difference there was between the color of his skin and the blanket of needles below—those tones of wear and weather.

"I know," he replied. "I thought, 'Pine-scented pop-up cards? I wonder how many people here would know what he's talking about!'"

We came out of the shade of the cedars and into the soft glare of the sun with the trail forking on either side of the big central lawn.

I asked him if he would like to go for a drink at Le Pavillon.

He said he preferred to walk and I agreed: it was an unusually beautiful day for February.

An extremely thin-haired blond woman in a teal sweat suit and phosphorescent pink running shoes stood on the lawn curb. She was calling an invisible dog named Neo.

"Come here, Neo," she kept saying, "*come.*"

After a while, we went to sit on a bench by the rose bushes where the flagstone path rose up gradually along the lawn, leveling off at the top of the knoll by the belle époque Rotunda.

Farther down before us, in the middle of the lawn, where the hillock bottomed out in a hollow the size of a basketball court, there was a fire-eater and his girlfriend, who was juggling with orange tennis balls.

"The Christian of the Jardin," Sami said as we watched them.

Almost immediately he noticed that I did not understand and added, "Christian—the twin brother in the movie? He was breathing fire, wasn't he? Giving his old man hell in the middle of his birthday party. Great timing."

"You mean the director's timing or the character's?"

"Both, I guess. It's amazing how much everybody hates whistle-blowers. I think what's probably almost as dreadful as the father having repeatedly raped the twins is the way the guests go into denial mode—and the twins' horrible mother making that speech about how Christian basically fantasized his father's abuse. There's nothing worse than collective denial. Sometimes I think it's as unjustifiable as the crime itself."

"I see what you mean. The strategies of denial can be horrifically complex and confusing, and it's always the individual victim who gets saddled with the collective guilt. Like that creepy scene in the cellar where his father tells him how he's spitting in his family's face and hurting everyone."

"Powerful scene—and creepy indeed. You know, I kept thinking, 'Is the bastard going to make a pass at his son?'"

I told him that for me the criminal father was more than just an embodiment of insane abuse. He was an embodiment of radical evil.

"I'm actually going to write on that topic," I said. "I'm trying to find the most radical embodiment of evil then I'll attempt to encapsulate it in a novel—a sort of devilish parable. A mix of kitschy romance, Gothic mystery novel, and morality tale."

"And what would the most radical embodiment of evil be?"

"The senseless murder of children."

"Is that what your novel is going to be about?"

"Yes. Not very pleasant, I admit, but highly necessary. Would you like to read the outline I made? It's only a few pages."

"Yes, of course, I would love to."

"I'll e-mail you a copy."

Sami kept studying the fire-eater as we spoke.

"God," he said with a hint of amusement in his voice, "this guy is breathing fire all over the damn lawn! I thought this place is actually monitored by *guards*. Is there nobody who can tweak his ear and remind him of the old saying?"

"What saying?"

"If you play with fire…You know?"

"I know, I know," I said vaguely, and stood up.

We went on walking around the lawn facing west, leaving the box hedges and the fin de siècle limestone statues behind us to the right—the flowerbeds, mulched and exuding a smell of rot and vinegar.

"Funny," Sami said, "there aren't too many people out here for a sunny Sunday."

I said, "I think I can live with that. Let's not speak too soon, though. Wait till we get to the carousel down there."

———

There was indeed quite a crowd down by the carousel as we took the downward-sloping flagstone path along the landscaped hillock then swung to the right on the tarmac path that flanked the second lawn, walking past the carousel, leaving the crowd behind us and heading toward the Chartrons gate.

On our way out, I told Sami that I had forgotten how beautiful the Jardin was and he agreed.

The hum of late-afternoon traffic around the Quartier des Chartrons seeping in through the pine trees like the muffled sound of surf in the distance. Somewhat depressingly, I remembered life out there, as I always did when leaving a peaceful place—the terrible stubborn obligations of the real world.

Then it dawned on me that I had never taken my sons to the park by myself.

"I'll bring the boys out here more often," I said, speaking to myself, halfway between a reproach and a resolution.

―――

There were many more tormented nights that winter, but as time passed, I got much better at controlling both the anxiety and the panic attacks with writing, alcohol, and drugs.

I also grew less dependent on the calls with Zoé, and I think Sami had a lot to do with that: my new awareness that I now had a reliable friend in town gave me much courage and comfort.

Then, one day, it was the first stirrings of spring—and Easter looming, and the joyful anticipation of a reunion with my sons.

In my mood of buoyant expectation, I found it easy to tune into the nascent energies of nature—the fevered sap rising in the trees, the first green frenzy of budding, the mating madness in the air.

The promise of change.

―――

Today I spoke with S and J at The Cypresses:

I'm leaving after tomorrow, I told them. Said I wanted to put in a full Saturday with them.

I suggested we sit down together after closing time—have a drink and deal with last questions.

It's strange, though, how it feels the instant I take off my uniform: like a parting ceremony, complete with intangible nostalgic twinges.

Steps in a vaguely sad ritual—from one step to another, I feel it, in slow and solemn sequence—the way you walk side by side with somebody you will not see in a long time—to the platform, the airport terminal, the car loaded up and ready.

I push through the kitchen door and walk toward the back tables in the big room: Jacques sitting in the Nook—his hands clasped atop the white table-cloth he has spread for tomorrow's patrons.

He does not notice me at first—looking down into the small oil lamp on the table, as if he's inspecting the wick or something. I sense a certain tension in him.

I walk over toward him and he swings around in his chair, turning it at a slight angle to the table.

I tell him that Sami will join us in a minute.

He just nods, tipping back his head a little—his neatly trimmed designer stubble like pencil shading in the soft light.

I sit down and wait with him.

Then Sami comes over walking between the tables—the bottle of whisky dangling between his index and middle fingers, and the three lowball glasses in his cupped hand, like bunched cellophane wrap.

J [after his second drink]: "Let me get something off my chest: the Guide Michelin inspector shows up at 11:45 a.m. Tuesday. What do we do?"

He looks back and forth several times between me and S—wincing and grimacing and wringing his hands in mock panic: "What's a man to do?"

T: "Put valium in his aperitif?"

We all burst out laughing. (Jacques has a name for the various people who inspect us: "Gastro-inquisitors.")

The Scotch is coursing warmly through our veins and now that we have dealt with final details, we can allow ourselves to sit back, think of the worst, and laugh about it.

T: "Well, well, what can we do? How about: the chef is sick and he's got solid replacement in the kitchen. We're ready—that's the only thing that matters. We're always in a state of readiness. Full readiness is our normal everyday state. We don't have to worry about a thing. They've done it before: they tried to trip us up—on food, service, decor, atmosphere. They've tried us and never found us wanting. Several years on, we're still among the best."

I put down my glass and smile at Sami.

———

The travel agent told me that she could not book me on the morning flight to Düsseldorf. It was one of their busiest lines, "Because of the Strasbourg layover," she explained. "The European Parliament people, you know?"

And so it was the afternoon flight, which meant that I would have to overnight at a hotel in Düsseldorf and head back to the airport to meet my sons the morning after.

———

On the bus—riding into Düsseldorf:

When she booked my hotel room she assured me that it was "within convenient distance of the airport—they provide a special shuttle service."

She never specified how convenient.

It is in fact a cramped and winding thirty-kilometer "shuttle" from the agricultural countryside to the outskirts of the city.

Riding under driving rain most of the time—the monotonous swish of that country rain, the sad drone of the shuttle bus.

Halfway through the ride:

Something strange has just happened. Epiphanic? It kept my eyes riveted to the window of the minibus—in silent wonder.

We are driving through farmland when the sky over the wheat fields clears up somewhat, turns a sickly yellow toward the west with the sun shining through the dark clouds in shifting patches of sepia-toned grayish yellow.

Suddenly, a bright rainbow comes through the clouds, rising above the gray billows rolling in from the east.

Just above the horizon line, underneath the rainbow, a twisted monolith of alabaster clouds rising up and detaching from the pale-yellow mass: it reminds me of an enormous penis-shaped stalagmite Regina and I had once seen in a cave in Colorado during our honeymoon.

The gorgeous rainbow, the miraculous beauty of this fleecy pillar shooting up out of nowhere, the memory of Regina and I in America: bittersweet thoughts on how much time has passed since the beginning of our story—sitting here in this rolling droning transiting capsule, torn between the scattered times and places:

Memories of the American West and the ravishing depth of our love-making in the tent under the star-studded skies of America—the poetry, the abandon, and the sheer lavishness of those grand skies.

Thinking: how sadly fitting—to find myself feeling bittersweet and "deep" when and where I least expect to be, trundling along on this nameless black strip of road between two of the shallowest transitory places imaginable—an airport and a one-night hotel!

My face in the rain-distorted mirror of the window—shifting dark-gray blur.

Those scalloped fringes of stripped treetops peeping over the hills, like grimy lace trim plastered across the horizon line.

She drew back the tent flap to let in the moonlight that night, outside Glacier Park. The rustle of the stream behind the trees, the extinguished fire still hissing in the pit.

And Regina straddling me, sliding up and down—her hair spread out across her dark shoulders, like a curtain of silver thread.

I want to make you happy, she whispered, I want to make you happy. I want to make the past go away forever, until there's nothing left but a blank virgin page of pure future.

———

I cut myself shaving the morning after.

I put my fingers to my throat and brought them up under my nose: the blood on them was dark and thick and smelled like rust from a dank bathroom pipe.

I remember calling down and asking for something to stop the bleeding, to which the receptionist replied with a skeptical and apparently bemused "Hmm."

I suppose her skepticism was not altogether unjustified: I must have called out of nervousness—and attention-craving, because the moment she stepped into my room and took a look at me she seemed more irritated than relieved.

She gave me the small kit and left without a word.

And even with her gone now and me sitting down to write, I could not get the thought of the cut out of my mind: for some reason, I kept thinking that the excessive blood flow had to do with the overheated room (the air in it so dry it made my pants crackle with static).

Sitting here—between the mushroom desk lamp, the maple-leaf crystal ashtray, the B-movie and porno-channel flyers—obsessing about the bleeding starting again.

And this unbearable heart-clenching aloneness—the vicious suddenness of it, its crippling hold over all of me. Poor, unmoored me—faceless, anonymous, disconsolate, cut off.

———

Our meeting at the Air France terminal was, as I had feared, a heartbreaking failure:

Shams and Haroon were simply not prepared for me, for being alone in my company. Haroon's reaction and his terror spreading to Shams.

After the last hugs and kisses, as soon as we began to walk toward the counter, he ripped his hand from mine and turned around and took a few steps away from me—sobbing and calling after his mother with his back turned to me.

My gesture was no consolation: going straight down on my knees—a wan smile on my face, my throat parched and my lips dry as I tried to speak, fumbling for whatever words of consolation I could put together.

Small comfort: the next thing I knew, he was running toward his mother, leaving me there on my knees amid the flustered passengers milling around the counter.

I must have looked foolishly clumsy—a shameless menace to my children and an embarrassment to the others, who must have all felt like unwilling witnesses in this mortifying scene of domestic dysfunction.

Poor, brave, little Shams, though: he stood by me, holding my hand vaguely, his body at an odd angle to mine—strained by the burden of his own tears, his face twisted with the effort of containing his disconsolation, his hand tight and clammy.

Haroon buried his face between Regina's legs, bawling something incomprehensible.

———

And so it was both a relief and an embarrassment to find Zoé at home, waiting for me and my two distressed sons.

The instant we stepped into the apartment, I knew why she had insisted on being there.

"I have a long way to go before I can achieve some semblance of fatherhood," I told her as we settled down after dinner. The boys were in their pajamas and quiet at last, sitting in Zoé's lap.

I said, "Not even the duty-free chocolate helped. Haroon actually slapped it out of my hand when I offered him some."

I did not want to sound plaintive or reproachful saying those words, so I casually and playfully slid off my armchair and knelt down before him, making a clownish face: "Do you realize, young man, what *that* has done to your dad—your dad who loves you so much? Do you want to know how much I love you? Let's say from here all the way to the sun and back! Is that enough for you?"

He only gave me a sulky cringe in reply with his eyes fixed on my face. He was still trying to come to terms with me, the man who had brought him back to what had become another home so suddenly.

I turned to Shams and asked him, "How about you, son?"

He gave me a weak smile and said, "Great."

I held their hands and tried to put as much wonder into my voice as I could, speaking softly and slowly: "Do you, boys, have any idea what marvelous things we're going to do with Zoé, before your mom comes to take you back to *Grossmama*'s house? Tell them, Zoé."

"I need the pictures first," she said. "Pictures speak louder than words. Bring me that kite—it's on their bunk bed."

I gave her the package and she immediately turned it over to the instructions side with the boys still sitting on her lap.

Underneath the assembly instructions panel, there was the picture of a blissful-looking boy flying a kite on a sun-drenched beach.

"You see this boy?" Zoé said. "He's as happy as can be, isn't he? Well, soon enough, you'll be doing the same thing. You know Biarritz, right? We'll go there and run ourselves breathless on the beach. We'll kick ball, fly this kite, and eat Nutella crepe. Tell me, how would you like to go to the beach?"

She was addressing Haroon, who actually turned his head slightly and looked up at her with a tired smile.

Her words were not lost on Shams either: "When are we going?" he said with a broad smile.

"Oh soon, soon, my little one," Zoé said. "We'll be there faster than you can say Nooooo-ooooo-ooooo-ooooo-TELLA!"

The three of us laughed, and Zoé went on: "Now, tell me boys, do you like treasure hunting?"

Haroon, with his usual frown: "What is *that*?"

Shams: "It's pirates—when they go looking for gold, don't you know?"

"I didn't *know*," Haroon said—irritated, his voice gruff and tired and already tinged with that note of abstraction that creeps into the words of children when they begin to drift on the edge of sleep.

"And when are we going?" he wanted to know.

I said, "This coming Saturday. We'll take one of those scenic riverboats and there'll be many boys and girls like you and two clowns who'll tell you all kinds of funny stories about treasure hunting. Then you'll land on an island and go on your own treasure hunt."

"That's nice," Haroon said—a bit grudgingly, like a hard-to-please customer.

Shams: "Of course, it is. What do you think?"

"And the Jardin Public," I went on, "and the puppet theater in the Rotunda—and all the other things we'll be doing together! It's going to be tremendous fun, boys!"

———

Then it was bedtime and Haroon's anguish in the half-dark of their room, and the three of us holding his hand as he lay on his back in the lower bunk, moaning low, stopping long enough to utter his brother's name—over and over, like an invocation.

Of all the horrid events of the day, those last moments in bed were the worst: having to witness this impenetrable fog of estrangement rising between my son and me. The air of confusion about his eyebrows, tight knit beneath the tangle of his hair; the jugulars straining; the nervous darting of his eyes—animated by a glower of anxious mistrust.

Haroon was in great anguish and misery and I was confused and saddened beyond words, even though I tried desperately to project tenderness and composure—struggling to show him that I very much wanted to reach out to him and know in what part of his being he ached.

But all my efforts were of no avail: my own fatigue and emotional confusion were starting to take their toll, and my capacity to project equanimity was beginning to crumble under the oppressive weight of his grief. And so now the only thing that I could think of to alleviate his sorrow was to seize on his one solitary word, Shams, and turn it into my own invocation in song—an improvised tune that I began to hum to my son, hoping that the words would speak to his suffering.

I began to chant in a deep soft voice: "Sha-ams, Ha-roon, Da-ddy—three boys together, three boys forever."

Then it was Zoé and Shams's turn to join in the chant, singing in shaky unison. We kept at it for a while, our impromptu lullaby, until he went to sleep, his face perfectly peaceful.

———

After Shams had gone to sleep in his turn, Zoé and I sat down and talked at length—planning for the coming days.

Then it was my turn to go to bed: now that the many shocks of the trip were absorbed, the impressions taken in, the faces and places assimilated, my mind was in a haze and the prospect of being alone in bed with my diary loomed like a refuge and a consolation.

But the unreality of the day lay heavy on my heart, and so I had to sit at my desk first and do what I had always done when I was uncertain or confused: I leafed back through the diary, trying to get a sound grasp of the events as they appeared in the labyrinthine mosaics of my words.

In a way, that backward look was the closest that I came to seizing the full implications of what had happened to me over the last few months: how far I had come into my nightmarish journey and the strange uncharted terrain stretching ahead—the still unmapped future that I had to craft day in day out with my sons.

And there was Zoé of course: the role that she was willing to play in spite of all the risks.

My friend was very much aware that she was putting herself at the mercy of cruel neighborly gossip—and second-guessing, too, from friends and family.

I did not know what her parents thought of this visit, but I was almost certain that many complex factors must have gone into her decision to come down to Bordeaux and help me turn the boys' stay into a genuine new start for the three of us.

———

Their last afternoon in Jardin Public:

It was the afternoon that sealed my belief in them, in us, and in the certitude of their trust.

At first it was just another sunny day in the park—a day of scooters, soccer, and playful tussling on the grass.

And then there came a moment unlike any other: the shadows were long and deep on the lawn, the sunlight red between the treetops. I stood and watched the carousel—leaning against a sycamore tree with Haroon by my side and his brother bobbing up and down on the white-and-gold horse, coming and going with the other children.

I will never forget the joyful expectation in his eyes every time his horse would come galloping around and he would begin to face us: the way he kept his gaze fixed on mine, the way he looked back at me just as the horse whirled past, smiling broadly, holding onto the brass pole and leaning back a little.

Permanence, I thought, in that brief timeless stretch of time—that is what his eyes are telling me: I want you to be permanently there for me. I felt the tender, imperative quality of his injunction in every fiber of my being, in the sudden unexplainable awakening of my soul, in the excited rhythm of my heart absorbing every second in this magical eternal moment.

Later, when the Jardin was all but empty, we left our scooters propped up against the curb by the Rotunda and we ran down toward that deep hollow in the middle of the central green where the lawn swept down to its lowest point—the early evening sky over our heads like an inverted bowl of China blue, the grass already exhaling that deliciously cool breath when the sun goes down and the dew starts descending.

I kept telling them we had to go, but Shams insisted we "hang around some more."

So we went and sat by the statues, with the sky darkening, our shadows gone by now.

He wanted some more of the magic although he knew that he had already left his mark on the day and on the whole visit.

He snuggled up to me on the bench (his alabaster face flushed with our run, his onyx eyes giddy with life); and then he lay his head across my lap and gave me another broad smile—his neck in repose, his upper teeth shining between his lips like a row of perfectly rounded-out white pebbles.

I am not sure if Haroon knew that it was their last day, but I was certain Shams did—they were leaving tomorrow and he knew it; and in his own way, he was putting all the final words into those seconds of tenderness, that smile he was giving me as a security against the parting and the loneliness to come: he felt strong and ready, we both knew it, ready to start over in a new life crafted by the three of us.

Shams knew all this all along, without a single word exchanged between us. He knew everything even as he rode around on his gilded white horse and kept his eyes on me, until the inevitable moment when he had to follow the sweep of the carousel and shift the line of his gaze.

That night, at bedtime, I told them about Tunisia—and the things we would be doing differently this year when we got there.

Then I kissed them good-night and stood up and crept out—leaving the door ajar behind me, the way they always wanted it.

The day after, they were gone—their going as unreal as their coming.

Regina and her brother came to pick them up, and the second their taxi slipped out of my lane into the early morning traffic on Rue Esprit des Lois, I knew that their departure would leave me in the same state of loss and disorientation that I had felt on the night of their disappearance. At the same time, I was feeling something different within me as I stood on the sidewalk and watched them go: a new sense of elated expectation—the hope that I had something to look forward to.

The South: through an act of imaginary projection in which loss and hope converged on that sidewalk, I began to believe that by going down to Tunisia in the summer I would allow myself to work my way up the stream of time with the greatest of ease, traveling back to the days just before exile, when my future life in Europe was still a blank page and I had all the power to fill it as freely and as beautifully as I wished.

Something in me was dreaming of a new beginning.

South '07

"**D**ad," Shams shouted as I took a picture of Haroon, "take a picture of the sun! It's so *low*—like a tomato!"

His face framed by the oval rim of the porthole: eyes wide open in wonder, head bobbing with excitement—this endless capacity for amazement that I was beginning to discover in him, so much unlike Haroon's understated manner.

I asked him to sit back and let me film it: it was just about to disappear below the horizon line—an intense crimson sphere with a rim of orange, nestled in the thinnest membrane of cirrus clouds, like a blood-smeared egg yolk.

Haroon was amused by the concept of the tomato—slumped in the seat, chin resting on his chest, eyes fixed on the net, chuckling to himself in his unusually low husky voice: "Like a tomato? Why not like—like a ketchup!"

———

Later, after nightfall, we took a terrifying buffeting over Andorra—tail winds and turbulence.

Mercifully, the boys slept through the agitation.

A vicious gust of wind threw the Tunis Air flight attendant off-balance, flung her headfirst against the restroom door.

She stood back up immediately, straightened out her uniform, and turned around somewhat robotically to face us with a strained artificial grin.

———

Descending into Carthage.

I found myself restless and confused, as usual: that loss of mental bearings that is not quite fear but a murky mix of panic and expectation and out-of-place alienation—as when you return (after too many years) to a cherished face that has been growing older by the day in your absence, stranger and more remote.

And to think that I had done this so often before, that it should be second nature to me by now.

And in many ways, going back home was the quintessential second-nature experience of sameness and predictability—same anticipated descent on the city, same mind vista, same visual fragments projected in mental space, over and over: the abyssal stretch of sea leading into the bay of Carthage—gray and furrowed in the shadow of its eucalyptus cliffs, like a sheet of rough-hammered lead; the sweltering hell of Tunis and its insane through traffic; the Tunis Sud expressway and the last coastward road—our eastward drive into Rades after the last exit.

Still, there was always that frail, naked sensation of being in strange unexplored country: like an ex-convict after a long period of confinement—having to take his first steps on the outside within the unmitigated chaos of a rough and indifferent city; having to learn from scratch how to be there in the chaos and navigate it, and negotiate it, and not be invaded by it.

(Strange and confused thoughts—these weak words on "sameness" and "unexplored country."

Still, in their own muddled, sentimentalistic and pathetically self-important way, the words are instructive—despite the strangeness, the confusion, the weakness.

There is perhaps one more thing that needs to be added to these reflections—a further contribution to the strangeness, the confusion, the weakness—one last thought on images of home and their power to defy time itself:

I have known Tunisia in so many ways that I can remember—at springtime and in the Indian summer; in late fall and in the dead of winter, when the leaves on the orange trees are a glossy jungle green and the fruits ripe and incandescent, hanging like lanterns in the dark density of their foliage.

Yet in my imagination Tunisia has always been a scene of summer nights; a blurry scene maybe, but one that is rife with a mad jumble of summer impressions—ecstatic garden fragrances at nightfall, the timeless memories of my first sailing pleasures, late-night dinners by the seaside.

The wistful mind always everywhere warping and weaving effortlessly between here and there, now and then—as if the totality of time-space was one single glowing thread of presentness suspended in a black eternity.)

———

Outside customs I spotted three of my siblings waiting for us, standing bravely by the gate—Nour, Kareem, and Mourad, who looked quite the dignified patriarch with his graying hair, his perfect bronzed skin, and his brooding solemn air.

Khayyam, Nour's husband, was there too.

The initial show of high spirits was brittle, as I had anticipated—the moment they crowded around the boys, their joy quickly gave way to a melodramatic mood of verbal tiptoeing and embarrassed, half-hearted gestures.

They were not capable of interacting with them in the usual clownish playful manner: there was something ominous in the air between us—heavy yet impalpable, electric and volatile.

I was already beginning to dread this visit—the uneasy sense that things were going to be even more difficult this time around.

I saw the looming complications in Mourad's attitude already— the all-too-obvious, all-too-rehearsed cold-shouldered arrogance only a ruse to mask his chronic feeling of deep embarrassment in my presence (of shame almost), his incapacity to deal with me as a different but equal man.

Already his eyes were beginning to betray that deep-seated nervousness—as if he regretted being here, as if his presence here was part of an obligation that he hated to fulfill.

Apparently speaking for the family, he told Shams right away that if his mother were here with us, "our joy would be complete."

I remember turning around at his words—staring at him—and him ignoring my gaze, bending over Haroon to cheek kiss him.

Nour tried to smooth things over, holding my arm and asking us all to get out of here: "Come on everybody," she said, "your mother's waiting and these boys need some dinner! Let's go!"

She took Haroon by the hand and spoke to me as we walked toward the exit: "Don't worry," she said, "I'll ride with you in his car—I can handle him. Your sister stayed behind with Lamia and Mouna—they're helping mother with dinner. Khaleel couldn't make it either—he had to drive his father down to Sousa—but he's dining with us."

Kareem, who had insisted on pushing our cart, left us standing next to Mourad's SUV and went back to his car with Khayyam. (Mourad, meanwhile, kept walking a few steps behind us in silence—a deliberate theatrical step, head slightly bent—the patriarch.)

Not once did he address me.

Something was amiss, I knew it, and as we pulled out of the parking deck, I began to wonder how much talking there had been about my situation; how long it would be before the questions would start coming out in the open; how much of the blame I would be made to bear for initiating the hated procedure—the nameless thing that was breaking up my young frail family.

Mourad leaned out of the window, validated his parking ticket, and drove us out of the parking area. We were only a few ramps away from the beltway now—the chaos of Tunis traffic.

Thinking:

Behind the initial warmth of our reunion and the chatty small talk with the boys, I could sense my siblings' private anxiety about this ugly domestic meltdown—a catastrophe witnessed from far away but lived closely and secretly within the most intimate depths of their being.

To them, the ugliness was far more than a battle between Regina and me: it was something much more personal and intimate—something that had erupted from the hidden recesses of their darkest memories, down where the bristling creatures of the past lurked.

Mourad leaned slightly forward as he drove, tense and latently aggressive—shaking his head slightly at regular intervals, as if he was constantly deploring everything about drivers and driving.

The beautiful blue of my brother's eyes was lost in the shadow of his chronic frown, the deep-copper shades of his splendidly tanned skin appeared grainy and dull in the yellow light of the Gambetta-Rades Freeway.

Silence.

———

I turned around and smiled at Shams and Haroon in the backseat—they snuggled limply on either side of Nour, leaning into her.

"So how does it feel to be back?" I asked them.

"Good," they said.

"And getting better," Nour added. "Tomorrow morning, we'll pump up the raft and I'll take you to the beach. You know what you'll have for breakfast?"

"Ice cream!" Shams interjected, teasing her.

"Not on my watch! Oh no, you won't have ice cream in the morning. You're going to eat one of your favorite treats: figs and bomboloni. You'll pick the figs yourself and Haroon will put them in the basket and wash them under the garden tap, just like last year. It's going to be a lot of fun!"

Haroon said, "Let's go to the beach *now!*"

"To the beach right now?" my eldest sister replied. "Does that voice of yours sound like a beach voice? It's the voice of a boy who needs to eat his dinner and get a good night's sleep."

Shams was amused at the idea of a beach voice: "A beach voice, are you?" he slurred.

Mourad took the Rades exit off the freeway and we glided down the causeway across the marshland east of Mount Boukorneen—the Two-Horn Mountain, hulking in sea mist like a colossal gray tent pitched hastily on two poles.

My brother took another turn at the traffic light and headed for the underpass.

There was a full bright moon behind us over the ridgeline east of Boukorneen.

I remembered how I once fibbed to Zoé about August Macke's painting of the Two-Horn, telling her that he had done it from the roof of mother's colonial house.

Mother:

I found her sitting in the swing chair beneath the mulberry tree.

And I thought, "Oh God, here I am again—standing before her with my own offspring; unable, once again, to stop the wave of inner trembling that seemed to dwarf and drown every other sensation, rising from a dark and mysterious place within me."

She adjusted her shoulder wrap mechanically—the only woman I knew who could pass for Maria Callas: the same regal air, the same prominent nose, the same slant in the corner of her proud eyes; and the undefeated almost unwrinkled slender neck that made her appear taller than her real height somehow.

My nervousness every time I stood before her: I was never able to fathom the source of this unease, except that it felt like being in the presence of something highly cherished but very fragile, something that you wanted to hold tight but were afraid to shatter the moment you held it, because you never knew how close you were meant to hold it before you reached the shattering point.

(*The power of place,* I wrote of her that very night.

Seconds before I stand and face her under the mulberry tree, as I open her gate and take the first steps onto her courtyard, a swarm of impressions come rushing into my mind all at once—remembering without having to recollect and reconstruct, nor even imagine or project.

Those first seconds—so dense, almost unbearable, with raw remembrance, instantaneous recall:

It is body-memory taking over, as it always does whenever I enter mother's home; or maybe it is the idea *of embodied memory, like the ghostly reality of phantom feeling—traces of sensation that remain long after a member is gone: the unmistakable pull under my feet of the century-old cratered brick floor tiles of her courtyard, perfectly tiered and solidly embedded in the ground—their jagged pocks, which I visualize in that instant with so much magnified power, filling up with shiny rainwater after a late-summer shower; and their natural chaotic motifs of marbled patterns in slate blue and ocher and orange madder that I used to take so much unspoken pleasure in seeing darken and deepen and come to colorful life as I hosed the courtyard cool just before teatime, with the sun slipping behind the dogwood tree and the sky turning into an endless dome of cyan blue.*

How can a place come to occupy the center of a man's secret being so much—to "mean" so much in his memory—that his mind's eye can picture, in a fraction of time, every hidden fragment of it in magnified vision?)

"Well," she said, "here you are at last," as if she had been waiting under the tree much longer than she had expected.

Her dark eyes sparkled with minuscule amber reflections from a string of small decoration lights hanging in the low branches of the tree.

We cheek kissed and she immediately turned to face the boys.

Shams and Haroon stepped forward and she bent over them and hugged and kissed them.

She took one step back to contemplate them, saying "*Mash'Allah*" with a broad smile on her face.

My sons stood motionless before her—in awe of the woman who was no longer a word or an idea now but the living incarnation of their grandmother from Tunisia: Assia Jaafari—*Oummi* Assia to them, the mother of their father.

Her interactions with the boys were always marked by that awkward but respectful protocol of tacit communication that the three of them managed to observe with astonishing consistency: the meaningful smiles they would use to make up for the opacity of words; the gestures and countergestures; the gifts and countergifts; the solid mutual trust encoded in their physical gravitation around one another.

Using the language of the unspoken, mother smiled again and ushered the boys toward the swing chair and the mist-cool earthen jug of lemonade on the table, the plate of homemade anise cookies.

They sat next to her and I pulled over one of the chairs and sat by her side after I had greeted Latifa and the rest of my relatives—my sister Heend and her husband Khaleel, my sisters-in-law Lamia and Mouna.

Shams wanted to see the fig tree.

I interpreted for mother.

She leaned closer toward him and addressed him with a steady smile: "Oh, it is so dark now," her voice artificially deep for dramatic effect, the way one tells about darkness in a fairy tale. "Tomorrow, my darling boy, tomorrow I'll take you on a full tour of the garden: the fig tree, the grape arbor, the tomato vines. You'll help me fix the tomato trellis, won't you? You'll choose the reeds and hand them to me?"

I interpreted and Shams was pleased—his sweaty hair plastered to his white forehead in pointy tufts like black feathers, the lemonade cup wedged between his spindly thighs.

"And what do *I* do?" Haroon asked, offended.

"You and I," I said. "We will be handling the wire and pincers—*somebody* has to take care of that very important task, don't you think? That's you and me, son."

Nour said, "I'm taking them to the beach tomorrow morning. Then they'll eat figs and bomboloni and play around in the garden. Latifa will show them the turtle she found in the lettuce patch."

We were all seated around mother's swing chair, now that the couples, following some natural impulse, had finally paired off after a silly chair shuffling frenzy that left no room for spontaneity: Lamia with Mourad, Mouna with Kareem, Nour with Khayyam, Heend with Khaleel.

They came as couples, leaving their children at home. Was it a deliberate choice? I wondered.

To me, my sudden apartness seemed both ridiculous and excessively artificial: sitting by mother, I felt unnecessarily separate from them—overexposed in my singleness and in my single-fatherhood, like a man sitting under the gaze of a jury or a committee.

———

I tried to limit my field of vision, keeping my gaze focused on mother—leaning forward in my chair, feeling a bit stiff and awkward, as if I was not quite ready to face the others yet.

I began with the crucial opening questions: asking about her vast reading interests, her brothers and their families, the garden.

First conversation with mother—the deep, grave, solitary center of our family—amid the waves of overlapping garden scents borne on the sluggish breeze: the sweet aroma of basil in its terracotta pots flanking the swing chair; the waves of subtle fragrance from the jasmine bush that she herself had trained to grow evenly along the stone arch of her nail-studded Moorish door.

First sensory images of her place: not so much perceived as intuited, apprehended through pure instinct—a subconscious extension of my deepest, most intimate senses.

Mother spoke at length and I listened carefully—sitting squarely outside the tight semicircle formed by the couples, a loose link in the family chain.

When mother and I were done talking about her life and activities, it was Lamia's turn to address me with the usual announcement: the ritual visit to their farmhouse in Mornag—inviting me and my sons to the annual family cookout, throwing fitful sideways glances in Mourad's direction as she spoke.

"Of course, everybody else is invited," she added, unnecessarily it seemed to me. "As you all know, ours is an open house—and we're always happy to have you. We'll barbecue in the afternoon and the kids can swim and play together. It's going to be a simple, mellow get-together."

"Wonderful," Nour chimed in with a broad smile. "Get ready for the raid of the *Radesi*!"

I asked the three other couples, "You're all coming, right?"

It was the men who spoke—with that proud (and somewhat artificial) diffidence of a Tunisian male accepting your invitation: a certain ritual coyness that is at bottom purely rhetorical.

Through all this, Mourad sat in godlike statuesque silence—we were all to pay him homage, of course, and he took it for granted that we should acknowledge his importance as head of the family.

———

After a quick buffet dinner, we chatted about small things until the conversation began to falter and it was time for the three of us to go up to the rooftop studio.

With Haroon half-asleep in my arms, I thanked them for the dinner and wished them all good night.

Shams and I went behind the house and took the stairs out back. (The railing was overgrown with honeysuckle and bougainvillea—I made a mental note to trim them in the morning.)

The studio was perfectly tidy and clean, but very warm despite the feeble breeze blowing through the open windows.

Haroon was fully asleep by now and I laid him in the double bed and went back down the stairs to get our luggage.

That was when I saw mother again—a dark-gray silhouette in the moonlight—standing at the bottom of the stairs, holding up something in her hand.

"Your slippers," she said, firmly and audibly.

"Oh yes," I replied, rushing down the stairs, feeling flustered and apologetic for some reason, as if I had just left them behind and had every reason to apologize for putting her through so much trouble.

With the same firm resonance in her voice she said, "I dug them up this morning—thought you might need them."

"Of course," I said, and took them from her.

She just turned around and walked off without a word—leaving me there to watch her slip into the slanted shadow of her colonial house, past the black sprawling mass of the fig tree, the rustle of her footfalls on the shingle path amplified in the silence of the night.

Holding the butter-soft shlaka of yellow Moroccan leather in my hand: feeling strangely, inexplicably irritated at myself for letting her get away with this final gesture, this furtive moment of codependence that she had deliberately planned for her own amusement; irritated for not reminding her that I did *not* need her slippers, that I had *stopped* needing them long ago.

Feeling all the more upset for reminding myself how self-defeating and ridiculously trivial it would be to remind her of anything whatsoever. After all, such small acts of care were her only way of affirming her natural right to claim me as her son—her favorite.

———

Both boys were asleep now and I was too excited and too full of impressions to go to bed.

I put on my shlaka and went out on the tiled terrace, which took up almost half the roof.

Nothing much had changed in the layout of the place since last year: the geranium creepers in their planters along the wrought-iron railing—their fluorescent-pink flowers bright and vivid even under the weak light; the rope hammock and the pear-shaped pots of succulents; the corner where I wrote—its weather-grayed rustic table and its bench, made from two storm-felled pine trees processed in the local lumber yard and crafted in Kareem's joinery workshop.

The table corner: where I loved to sit after a long day of sailing, enjoying the gentle rush of the sea breeze in the last moments of daylight—typing and thinking, in that last hour of crisp blue light when all the glare was gone out of the sky; that peaceful stretch of strange Mediterranean luminescence between sundown and nightfall, just before the sultriness of the evening began to descend on everything and everyone.

The sweat on my face had dried into a salty film. I needed a shower.

But it was tempting to linger on the terrace without a purpose, relishing these minutes of stillness and marveling at the sudden, miraculous proximity of the sea—just a few houses away, a few strides.

After showering, I sat at the pine table and wrote in my diary.

———

Sometime around dawn, I had a vivid dream that woke me up shortly before the call to prayer.

I sat up in the couch with my back propped against the armrest—I was dripping with sweat, my mind alarmed and restless.

My first impulse was to write down the dream, but I decided to check on Shams and Haroon first.

They were both sound asleep—their hair soaking wet, their faces beaded with sweat.

Dehydration, I thought, but then immediately dismissed the possibility—they had had plenty of fluids last night.

I remembered Nour's promise: she will come up with Latifa and take the boys to the beach. Then I will go down for a quiet breakfast with mother while the morning is still fresh and cool.

I sat down on the couch and began to write.

———

Back from the beach, the boys showered and breakfasted in the garden.

Then we worked with mother, patching up her tomato trellis, until Mourad and Lamia came to pick us up.

After he exited the causeway, Mourad took the Boukorneen turnoff and headed west across the overpass toward Mornag.

Lamia sat between my sons in the backseat, her arms around their shoulders.

First look at the valley of Mornag from the overpass:

The rough shaggy aspect of this country under the blinding glare of the summer sun—like a gigantic patch rug in progress: the diminutive dirt-road-partitioned fields of wheat, barley, and oats; the patches of uncropped soil and withered weeds like scab on the dun expanses of the valley; and Wad Milian—a shadow of its rain-swollen winter self, winding northward into the plain of Siliana, like a barely begun monogram of dull silver thread.

It was not even noon yet and the fields shimmered and baked in the African sun. And the ridgeline in the distance, west of the Two-Horn—dull-colored, liquid and chimerical in the heat haze, like uncertain drawings on a trembling sheet of cellophane.

Sitting next to him in silence as the country trembled outside the air-conditioned haven of his car. My mind awash with disconnected memories rushing in all at once—remembering our weekend visits out here when many of these fields were still father's, remembering the many sensorial impressions that I had associated with this country in childhood and adolescence: the hoarse rustle of dry corn leaves in the searing summer sun; the glazed feel of the cornstalks that we used as toy swords—hard and smooth as bamboo reeds when we stripped them of their brittle, dried-out leaf sheaths; the sheer power of the land in heat pressing against your body (your flesh) with its suffocating urgency—claiming every second of your attention, every bit of your fighting spirit.

The burning persistence of that age-old madness possessing the earth (the ancient spirits of the fields raging about us—precious land cunningly acquired by the Phoenicians, forcefully by the Romans, then the Arabs, the Turks, the Spaniards, the French); madness this country had never bequeathed me, for better or worse—that headlong capacity for frenzied, decisive action that I had always admired in my compatriots.

We drove on amid the fields, taking a country road now, and I kept watching the land in silence—absorbing Mourad's somber mood even as I tried to resist it. (At the airport, Nour had told me that it was a drought year and that Mourad was very unhappy with the crops.)

Again, feeling (in sensorial memory) the land's presence, remembering: the power of its reflected sunlight with its stunning capacity to dazzle your eyes and blind you to shade and color, to subject you to the incessant urgent presence of the heat and the dazzle, making it impossible for you to even think of the lavish gifts of this country during the other seasons: snails creeping up the trees after the showers of March; huge green lizards sunning on the whitewashed walls; the pomegranates of October glowing on their branches like glazed porcelain; the turtles we used to pick up in father's orchard (Mourad's now).

All traces of green evaporated, it seemed, out of the sun-crazed earth, baked into a trembling shimmering canvas of depthless desiccation: a patch-work of bristling stubbly fields, withered pastures, and tobacco-brown weeds.

Then, all at once, we were in orchard country—vast peach and citrus-fruit plantations fenced behind the perfectly lined up columnar cypress trees with the lower part of their trunks meticulously exposed and whitewashed to look like a straight row of snow-white logs or piles.

This is Mourad and Lamia's world—a world of overachieving, success-crazed "businessman farmers," as they are pejoratively called in the area; a universe of pure performance, of who gets the best deal out of the dealers who come to appraise the fruit long before it is ripe, who will manage to pocket the biggest check, who is fastest at tackling the pests, who is sending his children to American universities—or getting them started in business or buying them land of their own.

Men who lounge together around the swimming pool with a certain strained theatrical ease—who cook out together, smoke together, drink together, but never learn to trust one another or share anything of significance.

Nothing had changed in their home: their always perfectly rejuvenated gravel driveway with the elaborate Andalusian fountain humming freshly before their house; the unfailingly, perfectly trimmed box hedge on either side of the driveway, forming perfect parallel lines along the driveway, a perfect omega circle around the fountain.

Mourad parked his car as he always did: across from the fountain (headlights facing the box hedge. Visitors are actually systematically warned—well, reminded—not to park their cars any other way here).

I got out of the SUV and into the blinding sun—with that same Carthage Airport sensation of loss and disorientation, of fading, of "Do I really belong here?"

I stood there forcing myself to linger and admire their alabaster fountain in the middle of this vast gravel circle—as a first visitor would, and for no other reason than to get away from my own thoughts for a moment.

What followed after those first instants by the fountain was, I believe, a series of carefully choreographed steps that culminated in a monumental failure.

I was full of misgivings right from the start, standing in their dusky air-conditioned hallway and staring blankly at Lamia as she told me that I would need a pair of swim shorts.

My eyes struggling to adjust to the dimness, my mind to the strangeness of her words: "Excuse me?" I said, stupidly, like a cornered schoolboy stalling for time before his teacher.

She just looked past me at my brother with a timid nervous expression on her face, half smile half wince.

"Well, we could sit and relax by the pool," Mourad explained with a hint of impatience in his voice, as if he was annoyed at having to clarify his intentions.

"So we're not taking the sacred, time-honored tour of the orchard?" I felt tempted to throw the obvious question at him, but then I thought better of it.

I followed their live-in housekeeper, Soumaya, to the guestroom and waited in the corridor while she went into the master bedroom to get me a pair of shorts.

Lamia had already taken my sons to the bathroom—no questions asked. It was understood that they were going to be in the care of the lady of the house—any other arrangement would have been unthinkable.

———

"Let's hit the Jacuzzi," he said, and did not wait for my reply, walking ahead of me toward the corner pergola behind the row of slender cypress trees.

Lamia was standing with the boys by the "baby pool," as they called it, daubing them with sunscreen while they wriggled in excited anticipation.

My sister-in-law's white skin was bright as marble against the cherry-red of her bikini.

I followed Mourad and left them behind me, out of my line of sight.

And I began to think of the irony of my brother's choice—having to sit at close quarters with a man he had constantly sought to avoid.

Their Jacuzzi was built with alabaster surround and coping stones to match the swimming pool.

We sat opposite each other in the water and he said, "No one will disturb us here. We'll be able to talk," looking away with a frown as he spoke—as if he found the act of explaining in itself demeaning.

He went on without a pause or a preamble: "As you know," he said, "we've all been following the—evolving situation between you and Regina; and we've been very concerned about all of you, about the well-being of your boys."

Then he fell silent, his eyes still averted from mine.

Somehow I was expecting something qualitatively different from "concern"—a simple but emotionally significant "How have you been?"

That was when the thought occurred to me, for the first time, that my brother had never asked me about my affairs—about how I was faring in life, quite simply.

Over the years, he had systematically avoided the possibility of any emotional bond between us—anything that might put us on an equal emotional footing.

Our relational failure, I was convinced, came down to his fear and avoidance of that most dreaded situation: the possibility of us developing any form of brotherly bonding—the mere idea froze his blood.

And now I was sitting with him in the agitated water, seeing all this in one flash, for the first time, and I thought, "A problem—that's what I am to him right now—an embarrassing problem forced upon him by circumstances and the imperatives of his position in the family."

Finally, I decided to speak: "The children are doing fine," I said. "I have a lot of catching up to do, but we're doing fine."

"I know. That's why we think that you need to put their best interests first—do everything possible to give them the stability they need."

I found it strange that he would speak of himself in the plural, and I decided to let him know: "When you say 'we,'" I frowned at him, "you mean—"

"I mean Heend and us. She did share some of your conversations with mother. She suggested that we all sit down and talk things over."

"You mean it was mother—"

"Yes. It was mother's idea."

He still had his arms crossed against his chest, and it was hard for him to keep his body from bobbing slightly, which made him look restless.

I remember ironizing inwardly: so it *is* the "we" of the majority then.

Still, I hoped that he would switch to the first person now that I had dropped my hint—he owed me this much.

"And what was the outcome of—the meeting?" I asked.

"We all agreed that it would be best if you both—started to work on bringing the situation back to normal," he said, looking away again.

I tried to follow his gaze, to imagine what he was seeing and with what eyes he was seeing it: he was looking at the saw palmetto in its gigantic pot—the teeth on its petioles neatly curved and crooked at the tip, like rose thorns.

My irritation was mingled with pity: deep down, behind all the subterfuge and the stiff mannerisms, there was in him a fragile need to hide—from his visceral prudishness, his deep-buried fear of intimacy.

When I responded there was both nervousness and exasperation in my tone: "I suppose Heend must have told you already. It was Regina who deserted our home. The breakup was *her* idea. She made sure to leave a note on her way out. She seems to think that we didn't have any normalcy to begin with. It was clear that she wanted to—*frame* the situation in such a way as to force my hand. That was how my lawyer saw it, too. There weren't many alternatives: it was file first or get hurt."

There was a sudden spark of anticipation in his eyes: now that I had started to justify my choice in such shaky terms, he saw my nervousness as an opportunity to make his case more aggressively.

He pointed in the direction of the pool: "Look at *them*, though. Consider *them*. *Theirs* is the real hurt—the hurt that must be heeded first."

I knew he meant my sons, even though they were not within sight.

Their excited cries, their splashing sounds—they seemed sadly remote and anonymous somehow, like buzz track in a film.

All at once, I felt a nameless weariness descend upon me—a sudden, disconsolate sagging of the will—and for the first time in my life, I realized that I was old and uninnocent.

My eyes stung with sweat and my legs felt far away from me, as if they were a vague idea.

My brother was going to press his argument, and I knew that I had to endure it.

"Their ultimate joy," he added, "is to see their parents *not* separated. To keep that from happening, I would accept any sacrifice. I would swallow my pride, set aside all considerations of who's right and who's wrong, and beg her forgiveness—do my utmost to bring her back. And this isn't just me talking, Tariq."

Looking down into the churning water, I told him that I would think about it: a short quick sentence snapping loudly and abruptly in the middle of his last words, but my tone was withdrawn and abstracted and I think this sudden inertia must have flustered him more than the interruption itself.

"You mean you'll think about bringing Regina back?" he asked, looking confused and a bit foolish, like a man who had missed a step going down the stairs.

"The whole thing," I said, averting my eyes from his, vacantly studying the palmetto, "including the possibility of asking Regina to return to Bordeaux."

It must have been easy for Mourad to perceive this sudden inertia as surliness on my part. In fact, there was no room in my words for any form of hostility—at least I did not feel disposed toward hostility at the moment. I just wanted our conversation to be over.

But the conversation was far from over for my brother, whose agitation had grown more noticeable: "Everybody here, especially mother—we just think you've turned your back too radically on—who you are, as a Tunisian. Your own history, your past. I talked about this at length with Khaleel—the need for a man to look back and sort things out. He is of the same—"

"There isn't much to look back on, sadly. Democracy activist gets defeated, democracy activist chooses self-imposed exile. Sad and simple. You won we lost. Democratic activism is crushed, tyranny rules. End of story."

"Tariq, I will ignore your libelous comment about '*you*'—about '*us*' being tyrannical, because you are in my home—my guest. *We*, as you call us, are the only party that has a real vision for this country. *We* are the only party that has accepted to take on the messy, painful task of building it up, step by step, stone by stone, school by school, and hospital by hospital. This I will not debate with you here, because it is *not* the purpose of our conversation, which is a personal—family conversation."

Now he was looking squarely at me, his eyes cold and hard.

"What I'm trying to do here is—*relay* a message that the entire family would like you to consider. Think about it, that's all. The simple story you're talking about in such sarcastic terms—your own personal life among us here—has nothing to do with *us* against *them*, or *loss* against *gain*. It's about reconnecting with your past, Tariq, with who you *are*, fundamentally, as an individual. To consider the benefit of looking back a little bit on your past and trying to get back in touch with people who were so significant to you before you left for France. And I don't mean the political—the activists. Mother had a long conversation with Heend and Khaleel about this lately. There are so many great people here who would love to get back in touch with you. Take Thouraya, for example, I'm sure she would love—"

"Listen," I said, interrupting him once again, "these things that you're trying to discuss in a totally surreal moment like this, as if they were—negotiation points or something. These are very deeply intimate, personal matters. Things that can't be rushed, that I need to think through *on my own*. These are matters that I don't wish to discuss with anybody *before* I have sorted them out personally, *on my own*. The day *will* come when I will look back, as you put it, and think about my past and my political comrades here. That day has not come yet, because I am busy with other vital matters. I have always said this, over and over; you just don't know because we never really talk. Heend and Thouraya know this. When the time is right for me, I will do—"

"All right," he said. "All right. I *have* done my duty. I have conveyed the position of the family, and I guess—"

"Yes, you guessed right. I *did* get the message. I *will* think about the position of the family on the matter of my separation. You can tell them that."

Suddenly, as if he had just remembered something he had neglected for too long, Mourad stood up—as abruptly and as mechanically as when he had brought me here.

"Then I guess I should see about that grill. Would you like to give me a hand?"

"In a minute," I said, without looking up.

———

Thoughts on the Jacuzzi moment:

The odd thing is that my sudden weariness (a sagging of the will, perhaps?) had no palpable connection with the problem as Mourad (and the rest of the family) sees it.

All at once, it seemed, I was in the somber grip of something beyond my mental control, beyond the objective urgency of the moment itself, with its quandaries and its hoped-for solutions; a sense of the death of something, I suppose—a nameless feeling of loss that had, within seconds, thrown me back to those winter days when I was mourning my own tattered self back in Bordeaux.

It is as if I was discovering for the first time, in feeling more than in thought, how uncompromisingly rigid and willful my grief is: like a creature in hibernation—no tolerance for any awakening.

He said it was not just him talking: a hint at mother—the ultimate manipulative ploy.

Not that I am, from a rational point of view, insensitive to his plea. After all, by acting as mouthpiece for the family, he has decided to take on a thankless and touchy task—only to see his plea come to nothing.

The case was thrown out by the brother who is supposed to show him obedience, dismissed before it was even debated.

I am sure that is how he interpreted my stance when he suddenly decided to stand up and leave: he had failed to get things done with the man who, once again, was acting as the problematic younger brother—the one who can only stand up to him through stubborn resistance.

There is evidently a great deal at stake in terms of Mourad's self-image, and I have a feeling that the self-proclaimed patriarch in him is bound to feel spurned—and turn up the heat on me: more resentful silences; more deliberate noninterest; more refusal to acknowledge my life choices and my interests.

Salah el Moncef

Still, for all the damage that had been done and the oppressiveness to come, I am convinced that I cannot envision anything other than confrontation—confronting him with firm opposition (a self-preservation reflex): defending my life choices and what I consider to be a sound and solid truth—the fact that I do not owe Mourad a real discussion, and not solely because of a need to shield the privacy of my pains past and present and my private coming-to-terms with them.

The other, darker, truth is my conviction that I have never really counted with Mourad. Beyond the mutually hypocritical pleasantries, the perfunctory gestures, and the vacuous rituals, there is the solid, stubborn, unsaid certainty that when it comes right down to it, the brother who decided to take a gamble on literary and philosophical pursuits as the purpose of a lifetime never amounted to much in his eyes.

After all, am I not considered (perhaps by everyone's reckoning except Heend's—maybe mother's, too) as the one family member who made the wrong historical choice? I was the one who chose to go to Europe, accepting to settle for less in a country that has no intention to grant me my "fair share"—as a philosopher and a poet. Poetry-Philosophy: insubstantial gifts and bounties of the mind with which, I admit, I am constantly hoping (secretly, ardently, incommensurately) to prove my value to the family—"make them see" that the pain and the exile were all "worth it" in the end.

The loathsome position/task of having to justify my lot, my existential path— and not even to myself either, but to the Mourad within me: wondering whether there is still something in my art and in my intellect "worth" fighting for, "worth" expecting, "worth" offering.

And the crippling power of it all hitting me here, in their house of all places—their overstated guestroom: it is as if I am just beginning to discover (just now, here, in the sizzling heat of my South—my own inner South) that my whole life in France has been built around the quick kernel of this expecting—even (perhaps especially) after the fading of my prospects for an academic career. In my most secret volitional core, I am quite simply (and naïvely?) hoping for a bright residue, a leftover from the ashes of my academic failure; and, in my vision of my evolution into a more genuine meaningful human being, poetry-philosophy seems to be that last saving gift for which I

*want to be remembered—my final proof to the world and the ultimate sub-
stance of authentic being after the defeat of activism here and the failure of my
Sorbonne aspirations there; after the vanishing of all the phantoms of false
hope; after the disappearance of my tormented body.*

Poetry, philosophy as the last lot.

*Sitting in that huge tub of churning water just a few hours ago, I found
myself thinking (in those bottomless minutes of self-doubt) that I have chosen
a life of pain and thankless toil from the start, and the thought of a fate
without gift and reward after the pain and the toil was disorienting and dis-
consoling beyond words: here I was, again, in yet another cold-sweat moment
of loss and unmooring—trying to console myself and realizing how little I
had to show for all my toil.*

*Back to Mourad: he has never been a compassionate brother, not even an emo-
tional one; and that is perhaps the most unsettling thing about his argument
on compromise and responsible thinking.*

*He is not even willing to deal with the fact that it was Regina who had
left; that considering her assessment of our marriage, there was little I could
do to create any climate of compromise and responsibility.*

*I do realize, as I read the above, that my words are whiny and shrill and
self-serving.*

*But, self-serving or not, there is no avoiding the telling: to be true to the
flaws and failures and feelings of the moment; to express them, with whatever
primitive tools, in the full depth and darkness of their clumsy groping.*

In the late afternoon my family converged on the Andalusian fountain and all at once everyone was gathered in the backyard, including all my nieces and nephews and their friends: the atmosphere
on Mourad and Lamia's lawn was like the grounds of a cozy, joyous
carnival.

As usual, I spoke to all but did not have a real conversation with
anyone.

It was a typical family reunion, in sum, with its excited buzz and its many interruptions—so many indeed that I gave up trying to converse in any significant way.

Kareem and my brothers-in-law were busy helping Mourad with the barbecue, shuttling between the grill and the veranda table, bringing in grilled meat and corn on the cob.

I was the guest of honor and giving me any work was out of the question. So I found myself drifting between two clusters of chatter (the teenagers and their mothers), exchanging greetings and pleasantries and small talk, while my children basked in the limelight—almost literally tossed back and forth between the women and their offspring: hugged, teased, kissed by the women and their help; entertained by the youths with all sorts of songs and tricks.

There was constant laughter and excitement every time they found themselves in the middle of either group.

Language was the ultimate entertainment: whether it was songs or words and expressions, my nieces and nephews, who spoke French, kept addressing Shams and Haroon in French even as they tried to coach them in Arabic—the boys' mispronunciations never failed to draw uproarious laughter. The teenagers always found ways to come up with witty, creative interpretations of the mistakes.

Kareem put down a plate of grilled corn and grinned at me: "Hot work!" he said. "I'll be with you in a minute."

The tables on the veranda were covered with a stunning array of colorful salads and side dishes—everything was very beautifully done by the women of the family and their help: kefteji, tastira, sharmoolah, tabbouleh, grilled-vegetable salad, various plates of tajeen, cucumber salad, a variety of koftas, mozzarella-and-tomato salad, hummus, and baba ghannoush.

"We're almost finished—for now," he said over his shoulder, walking off toward the grill—an athletic man with Moorish hair, broad shoulders, and the brisk and expansive gait of men born to lead and get things done.

Kareem: the Moor, as mother used to tease him, because of his hair and skin color—the only member of the family who could boast an Afro in his teens.

He ceased to be the Moor to her long ago, though. Tireless student of philosophy; successful joiner and designer; authoritative restorer; father to Young Kareem and Zayd; husband to aloof and flapper-looking Mouna, who had never liked mother.

(Heend's lapidary explanation of the tension between the two women: "She keeps telling him that he got emotionally shortchanged as a kid, you see. And by who? Mother, of course! Who else?")

———

I saw Heend break away from the group of women and walk in my direction, and I remembered when she had breezed into the house a moment ago, waltzing toward the kitchen with a bowl in her hands and telling me that I was going home with them after the cookout.

My sweet younger sister. She was loveliness incarnate: the smiling emerald eyes, the honey skin, the dark-blond fire of her curly hair—everything about her spoke of hope and health, of boundless vigor and the power to put pain behind her.

Heend acted in a manner quite typical of her when she took me aside and spoke to me—without preamble, as if what she was about to say was the conclusion of a daylong conversation: "Eeeverything will be all right," she said, in a nursery-rhyme-like singsong, tapping me on the shoulder.

She paused and looked into my eyes, tilting her head to one side: "We'll talk later." She mouthed the words after a meaningful silence.

Then it was mother's turn to come over, holding a plate of shish kebab and tomato salad.

When I took the plate from her, she gave me a piece of warm tabouna bread, and to my surprise, she did it in a slightly histrionic way, like a trick—a magician producing bread from her wide sleeve with sleight-of-hand grace.

It was nearing sundown and Soumaya was still busy around the tabouna cob oven while the men worked the grill a few feet away from her, with the peach orchard stretching out in all directions behind them; and the pale-lavender squarish mass of Mount Ressas in the distance, towering over the darkening valley like a stone-age axhead, its ridgeline serrated and deep-red in the afterglow.

"Short night, long day," mother said (a cryptic reference to my sleepless night but also an indication that she had been briefed on my strenuous fruitless conversation with Mourad).

She wore an off-white embroidered satin blouse and shalwar, a purple raw-silk shoulder wrap, and her pearl-drop earrings.

"Any plans for this evening?" she asked, making a quick sweep with her eyes from me to Heend.

Heend said, "We're taking them away from you, mother. Our turn to pamper these boys. We'll take this fellow to the Neptune and get him to sit down and unwind. We'll go down to the jetty and watch the bay where you used to take us. And the promenade in Marsa. And the coffeehouse in Sidi Bou. By the time we're through with him, he'll come back to you so spoiled you won't know what to do with him."

Mother nodded with a smile, looking down: "Nice," she said.

She remained silent for an instant then looked up and off into the distance: "There is so much of life's promise for you, my children. The road ahead is bright and sunny."

She said this to no one in particular, as if she was expressing a universal truth about all younger people, but I had a feeling that she was addressing me—one of the many roundabout coded consolations that she was fond of sending my way.

———

Driving back through the valley and up the causeway toward Cape Carthage:

Barren marshland stretching on either side of the one-way road between Rades and La Goulette ferry dock—monotonous flatness of scrub and salty earth.

Looking out the left backseat window: the last hint of color after sunset, a blush of faded crimson on the western horizon.

And the red-hot Mediterranean moon above the slender line of asphalt stretching out before us like a licorice strip rolled out to infinity: always unreal and implausible that eternal age-old moon— in its fairy-tale incandescence, the hard-to-believe glossed-over glibness of its persimmon orange.

"I thought Ahmed was going back home with you," I said.

Khaleel replied but I did not hear him and when I asked again, Heend turned around to face me: "He was, but then Nour asked me if he could stay over with Young Nour and Adel. We thought it would do him good to be with his cousins. They actually don't get to see each other much."

I said, "It's amazing, they've all grown so big so fast—except for your charming preteen prince."

"Isn't he cute, though?" she said, turning to face the road.

After a moment, she asked me if I had made arrangements to visit with everyone.

"You don't want to miff anybody, you know."

"That's right. I spoke with each and everyone of them before we left. I'll be seeing Kareem and Mouna next—in Korbous."

"That is *wonderful!*" she exclaimed, turning toward Khaleel as if the words had come from him.

The conspiratorial irony in Heend's voice was palpable: "Downtime in Mouna's own inherited vacation home. *Some* people are lucky."

———

In La Goulette, we took the ferry across the sound, got off at Nouvelle Goulette, and drove toward Bourguiba Avenue, the starting point of the fabled Tunis Nord coastal route.

Traffic was slow as usual: we crawled past the Spanish Fortress, the Historic District, the Casino, and the ubiquitous Indian fig vendors on La Goulette Road.

"*Heendee* by the cartload," I spoke to myself, recalling the rich vanilla flavor of the local Indian figs.

"*Heendee?*" Shams asked.

"There," I pointed outside the window in explanation. "*Heendee* in Tunisian means something like 'Indian fruit.'"

"Why *Indian* fruit?" Shams wanted to know.

Haroon replied first: "Because they're made by *Indians*, don't you know?"

A brief silence, then Shams again: "Dad, are they—"

"Actually," I said, repressing laughter, "the word is probably a simple reference to India, maybe because the look of the fruit and its taste are so exotic."

Heend turned around again and looked at the boys with a bright, playful smile in her eyes: "Also, boys, whenever you eat *heendee*, you need to remember my name: Heend. Heend means 'India,' no less!"

She turned around and addressed Khaleel: "As great as *Heend* and as sweet as *Heendee*, right? *Right?*"

He shook his head, chuckling: "Self-promoter," he said.

"Ungallant man," she joked back. "If you weren't driving, I'd poke you in the ribs."

More chuckles from Khaleel: "She would, too," he retorted, looking at me in the rearview mirror above his head.

———

Heend and Khaleel owned a marvelous Liberty house perched on a hill overlooking the Punic Harbor.

By the time we reached Carthage Byrsa and drove into their lane, the boys were already fast asleep, slumped against me.

Heend turned around to address me: "I made all the necessary arrangements: diapers, pajamas, clothes, swimming shorts. Your boys are all set."

Their domestic Souad would babysit for me tonight, she added.

Khaleel said, "Any clothes you need, feel free to dig into the wardrobe. There's a toiletry bag in the guest bathroom. I bought you some stuff this morning—razor, socks, T-shirts, and underwear. It's all in your room."

The two of us carried the boys in our arms, and Heend opened the gate and the front door for us.

Souad was waiting inside.

———

Before we left I told her to keep the door ajar and the upstairs corridor lights on.

"They're afraid of the dark," I explained, nervously and unnecessarily.

She smiled and nodded, with a touch of good-humored impatience, as if she was indulging the whim of a spoiled child.

I gave her an envelope with some money in it then it was off to the Neptune.

———

Champagne aperitif at the Neptune:

Heavenly state of drugged fuzziness in my head—the blissful alchemy of alcohol. Everything and everyone wrapped up in cotton wool—the clang and clatter of the world mercifully remote and filtered; the clashing colors of existence toned down like the hushed shades of a rainbow bleeding out, leaching softly into the sky before it fades away.

Heend [in a singsong]: "Loosen up, brother!"

Tariq [laughing]: "Loosen up. A typical Heend statement. Right out of the blue."

And we did "loosen up," of course—over seafood in the restaurant then mint tea and sheesha pipes in the Turkish café upstairs.

In other words, we talked a great deal—freely, unguardedly; and I found it heartwarming to be talking (reminiscing mostly) without a specific purpose or "agenda."

When we got back to their house, we sat in the living room balcony.

It was late in the night and the Punic Harbor below was as still as a circle of black glass—neon lights reflected in it like icy dragonfly wings; and farther off beyond the pier, looming above the bay to the north, there was the northern tip of the cape, its tinselly lights like constellated stars—the places and their magical echoes: Sidi Bou Sa'eed, El Marsa, Gammart, Raou-waad.

After a short silence, Heend acknowledged the cape's magical presence with one sweeping wave of her hand: "We'll have a piece of all that tomorrow. We'll dine and drink tea up in Sidi Bou then we'll go clubbing at El Barraka. I'm inviting somebody very special—don't ask me who. I'll tell you tomorrow—before I invite the...person."

Khaleel kept laughing softly through her words—putting his fingertips to his forehead and shaking his head in mock disbelief.

I sat between them, laughing, too, thinking: here I am, drifting in a sweet fog of weed and wine, looking out over the Harbor and the Bay, feeling the salt touch of the air wrapped up around my body like a second skin. The cape towering over the Bay like an immense dark log in a dark fireplace, twinkling and smoldering here and there.

Looking at things and listening to sounds and words that seemed to come to me from far away, filtered through a strange haze of the mind—a miraculous illusion of inwardness, of all this coming straight from within me like an ideal emanation from my own transported soul.

Everything about all this, I reflected, is so pacifying—this suspended moment out on the balcony—and somehow the peace and the acceptance seemed to include Heend's last words as well.

I thought it was only fitting that I should react with humorous submissiveness—my protest a purely rhetorical gesture:

T: "Let me tell you, sister, you've never been good at slowing down, have you?"

K [chiming in with a chuckle]: "And not at pulling any punches either."

H [to K]: "What? What are you laughing at? You're supposed to be in on this!"

K [laughing]: "I'm not, and I've never been—right from the start."

T [to H]: "All right, have it your way. I don't see what difference a few hours will make, but I'm not going to ask about this mystery 'person' of yours."

Khaleel excused himself just when Heend started to ask me if my own separation had made me think of mother and father—"The Big Unsaid," as we both called it.

He told us he had a long day tomorrow. Heend remained seated.

He kissed her and she told him she would not be long.

I had a feeling that this moment was planned by the two of them—a brother-sister heart-to-heart.

I said good night to Khaleel, remained seated.

T: "It's interesting that you mention their split. Actually, I never really thought of them. Maybe I'm like the rest of us—not wanting to face The Big Unsaid, out of shame, I suppose."

H: "Shame. That's a strong word."

In fact, H was secretly testing my loyalty to womanhood, as usual—she always did it as if she was broaching the subject for the first time, every time; as if she did not know what I thought of father's bigamy.

Maybe it was the sudden shift in the conversation, but I was beginning to feel a tad irritated all of a sudden.

T: "You know how I feel about father. I don't need to waste any thinking on him. What he did was shameful, we both agree on that. Plus, he's a man who spent a very significant part of his life with a woman he never had the courage or decency to marry, because to him she always remained the secretary, until the day he died."

H: "Yes, but think of what mother did—or didn't do."

T: "Sure, she could have divorced him—technically, legally, strategically. Whatever. But I think it would have been highly destabilizing, at any point in our lives—to see mother do it, rip the family apart. That was her thinking through all those years, I'm sure, and she does deserve credit for it, I think. She was in a terrible spot."

I must have sounded edgy saying this, and she had probably sensed my nervousness.

She told me that she had *been thinking, unlike me. Pondering our parents' influence on us, the influence of their failure. Heend was tentative all of a sudden—it was not like her. My immediate impression was that she was trying to defuse any potential irritation on my part. I felt it would be a letdown not to keep the discussion going.*

H [laughing nervously]: "What the hell, we're old enough to trash them, don't you think? That's what it means to be a grown-up, right? Let's trash them: you tell me everything you find wrong with them, and I tell you *... next summer!"*

I laughed—as nervously as my sister.

T: "You're a total master at building trust through subtle manipulation, do you know that?"

H: "Speaking of which, don't you think mother has always, you know, kind of used *her situation with father? I mean, that's what I've been trying to say all along—without having the nerve to say it!"*

T: "Oh, no. Do you really want to get onto this topic?"

H: "Oh, yes. That's what I meant by 'talking' this afternoon. But I don't want to force your hand either."

T: "No, you're not forcing my hand at all. It's just... anyway, what was the question again?"

We both laughed.

H: "All joking aside, Tariq, your separation got me thinking—in a big way."

T: "Me too. But I actually didn't do a lot of thinking about our parents—over the last few months, that is. Mother. Well, I don't know. I guess she did have a tendency to use her pain strategically at times—to get us to take her side. I hesitate to call it using, though. I don't believe it was that exactly, because her humiliation was real. And *constant. What bothers me more than any potential manipulation, though, is the extent to which we were actually affected by the humiliation. I think over the years her humiliation sort of rubbed off on all of us—in a silent, creepy way.* That's *what gave her the moral clout. She didn't have to do or say much to win us over to her side."*

H: "The Big Unsaid, right?"

T: "That's right. And the result was... I don't know. I'm not sure I have the right words for this. Actually, the result was two things, it seems to me: I think the big problem was that mother's pain eventually became ours and we spent an important part of our lives licking our wounds by proxy. So we weren't really able to develop any sense of emotional support—for one another. The other thing was that we spent most of our time avoiding one another, really—out of a sense of shared humiliation, I think."

We went on talking and I had another drink. After a while, I began to feel slightly drunk and talked out.

Heend's voice was getting hoarse, too. She said it was time for her to go to bed.

When I kissed her good night, she told me that she had put out clothes and underwear for me and the boys. She told me to sleep in and not worry about getting up for the little ones. Souad always came in very early. She would fix breakfast for them and keep them busy.

I sat alone on the balcony for a moment and then I went upstairs and into one of the guestrooms—checking on the boys.

Then back to the balcony.

My muscles were stiff and sore—tired but sleepless.

Still, it was the loveliest thing to be standing barefoot here, partaking of this moment in the heart of Carthage: the sea air filled with the perfume of Heend's jasmine and passion flower bushes; the first stirrings of the roosters echoing across the hills of Salambo; the distant staccato of the cables ticking against the masts of the sailboats by the pier; the sweet acacias, their clouds of canary-yellow flowers coming to life in the early light.

The sun was not fully above the point of Korbous on the eastern flank of the bay, but its reflections were visible in the water beyond the Harbor and the canal—long strokes of garnet red on a still sheet of silver gray.

The entire rangeland southwest of Korbous still veiled in sea mist—all the way to the foothills of the Two-Horn.

On the opposite side of the bay, Sidi Bou Sa'eed facing the sun: perched high atop the cape, its whitewashed neo-Moorish houses a deep copper.

With its eastern versant patchy and mottled below the tree line, cape Carthage looked like a giant animal's forepaw from here—a mangy limb stretched into the sea.

Heend has another name for it: she calls it The Eggplant. That is how one sees it from the lowest point of the bay, from Rades or Ez-zahra.

Back inside, with the window closed, the air in the house was full of that peculiar soothing warmth—warmth exuding from bodies united in peaceful sleep, under the same roof.

Writing all this from the quiet of my temporary bed—sleep coming at long last. Peace to us all. Peace to all the ghosts.

———

I slept uneasily and woke up to guilty feelings in the guestroom—the thought that I was neglecting my sons and making them feel left out.

They were shouting and screeching and laughing in the garden—sounds of water splashing, falling on big leaves in deep drumlike thuds, and Heend's excited voice egging them on.

I decided then and there that I was going to take them down to the pier for pizza. Later in the afternoon we could go to Odeon Hill and the Roman Villa—I would show them the mosaics of the athletes and the hunting scenes, the view on Rades and the Two-Horn across the bay.

I opened the blinds and saw Heend standing on the lawn, dressed in shorts and a sequined turquoise halter top, sprinkling them with a hose as they screamed and jumped by the trumpet tree.

"Go for it, go!" she was saying. "Grab the big diamonds!"

I knew the trick, a childhood favorite: with her thumb, she squeezed the water out of the hose into a forty-five-degree gush and sent it spurting upward in the sunlight like an arc of crumbling crystal, raining down in big iridescent beads.

"Old habits die hard," I shouted down, and regretted it immediately—the pain in my head made me wince.

She turned around and looked up at me. Shams stepped forward, took the hose from her hand, and tried to raise an arc of his own.

"Good morning," she said, squinting up at me. "We just got back from the beach. There's croissant and coffee in the kitchen."

———

It was one of those mild but uncomfortable conflict situations that sometimes arise when people spend time together:

"Why pizza on the pier?" Heend wanted to know. "Souad cooked her okra stew."

Souad was playing Mikado with the boys at the kitchen table—I knew that she was listening.

"I know," I replied a bit sheepishly, "I love it—"

"I'm not saying you don't like it, mind you."

I was not sure how to take her response. I just paused, hoping that I was not offending anybody.

At the same time, I felt quite tempted to tell her that I was not saying that she was saying that I did not like Souad's okra stew.

This conversation, I thought, is going to turn completely silly: we're splitting hairs, and Khaleel is standing between us, tired from a long day's work and as much at a loss as I am.

His southern eyes were blank, and I could see from his expression how he felt about my idea.

I said, "Forget it. Really, I mean it. I just wanted to spend some time—"

Heend interrupted me again—out of nervousness, I assumed: "No, it's a great idea, really. I see your point. We *will* take the boys out: have some pizza and lemonade, sit in the shade like in the old days with mother. Watch the boats. We can do that and come back for a nap. We'll take the binoculars."

She looked at Khaleel and that was when I realized that I was being insensitive: she was thinking of her husband, of course. He was tired and in need of a shower and some rest.

I tried not to let my embarrassment show through my last-ditch effort—my desperate attempt to save the moment from misunderstanding: "Great, then," I said with strained cheer. "It's Souad's okra stew. What more could we hope for? We'll have ice cream at the pier later, after lunch."

———

Haroon was watching Khaleel over his melon plate and laughing: my brother-in-law was falling asleep at the table—his eyes rolling up and his head lolling sideways, his fruit untouched.

"Don't mess with my warrior," Heend admonished them playfully.

She leaned toward him and put her hand gently on his shoulder: "Khaleel," she whispered in her lush contralto, "why don't you go lie down?"

He mumbled an excuse, stood up, and staggered off to the couch.

When we got to the pier, the sky was covered with a translucent tinfoil layer of haze. The heat had eased up and a certain windless silence fell over everything.

We sat down on the bench with our sorbet cups and I spoke to Shams and Haroon by my side, but I was also speaking to myself, to the child within me: "You see what's happened to the sky and what it's doing to the surface of the sea? I call it sleepy weather, boys."

The water before us was an immense unruffled sheet of shifting shades of gray and silver, and I told the boys that by late afternoon it was going to look dark gray and even more quiet, like a gigantic lake.

"Like Steinhuder Meer!" Shams exclaimed.

"Oh, *much* more beautiful," I said.

"The pebbles will look like moldy ostrich eggs," Heend said, abruptly, with a no-nonsense frown that was meant to be comical. But she drew a blank and I had to jump in with an explanation.

"Well, Aunt Heend means that the water is going to be dark, and when you stand in it and look down at your feet, the big round white pebbles won't look so bright anymore—and the specks of algae on them will turn really dark, just like mold."

Heend laughed: "Now we've really lost them."

"We? *You're* the one who sidetracked them—*and* me."

Then Haroon spoke out—to no one in particular, looking at the sea with all the intensity of his wide grave eyes: "It's really beautiful out here," he said, a statement that resonated with so much depth of meaning—the words sounding like a call to order, a command not to spoil this precious moment.

I took my cue from him: "That's it, son," I said, still looking at the bay. "The beauty of it all—that's the only thing that counts. The color of the sea and the stillness of the water make this place so beautiful that even when you look at it later, say at six o'clock, just before dinnertime, in your best Aunt Heend clothes—looking at it like that, you feel tempted to…tempted to…tempted to do what? Can you tell me?"

I looked at the boys and gave them a broad grin.

"We'll go for another swim!" Shams said.

"Are we going to do that?" Haroon asked, smiling and frowning at the same time.

"Yes!" I said. "We will—the way we used to when mother would bring us up here to visit with the wife of the Lebanese ambassador."

It was Heend's turn to explain now: "That was long ago, when *we* were kids—some of us just like you, boys. The maid and the cook used to bring us down here late in the afternoon for a swim—even when it looked like rain. It's probably going to rain tonight, judging from the look of the sky. You know, boys, one of the kids farted in the water once—and we heard it. We saw it bubble up. It wasn't one of *our* kids. It was *their* kid. We don't fart in the water—not *us!*"

"A water fart, eh?" Shams said with a grin. "It can't be too bad."

We laughed and I said, "You're right. It wasn't bad. And neither was the boy who broke wind. He was actually their eldest—so the discharge was really big, *and* you could see it!"

The boys laughed again.

Heend said, "That was Nour's joke, remember?"

I explained to the boys: "Your aunt Nour was treading water next to the boy who did it. It came out in these big bubbles, you see, and so she swam away from him. 'I know where *that* came from!' she said."

"Among us," Heend said, "we started calling him Liquid Fart—even though we liked him a lot. He was stuck with that bubbly fart somehow."

"Water Fart," I reminded her. "What was his real name, you remember?"

She chuckled: "I don't know. Lost in the mists of time."

I showed them an albatross perched on a wooden pile by the ice cream booth, on the Sidi Bou Sa'eed end of the pier—the only space where the handful of vendors and their white-and-blue concession stands were allowed. Otherwise, it was all pleasure boats.

Shams wanted to walk up to the albatross.

Heend told him, "Don't even try, young man. You go anywhere near him, and he'll take off in a wink. Plus, it's so much more beautiful from afar, don't you think?"

And it was truly as Heend said it was: this snapshot instant of oily stillness in the slate-and-silver sea, when even the moored boats had ceased to rock and groan, and the becalmed sails in the hazy distance had turned into blunt dagger blades.

That albatross resting on his weathered, barnacled pile: it would have been a shame indeed to mar the moment with sound or motion, even the flapping of a bird's wings.

After the nap:

We would take a streetcar, I had told Heend in the garden.

Odeon Hill was just one stop down the line, I had said.

She put down her watering can and frowned at me—I could not tell if it was a frown of reproach or confusion: "Khaleel will be up any minute. We could all have tea then go together, don't you think?"

"No, thanks, really. We need to be getting along if we want to catch a swim later. It's just a question of timing."

In fact, I wanted to be alone with my sons for a while, and so the three of us set out for the trolley stop with Haroon riding piggyback.

The boys got quite excited about the streetcars' graffiti floral motifs, spray-painted on the occasion of the Carthage festival ("SPIRIT OF WOODSTOCK," was written above the doors and windows in Day-Glo letters).

"You haven't seen the *other* streetcars," I told them as we sat by the window, "the ones we used to ride when *we* were kids. They looked like saloons on wheels, really: they were all made of lacquered wood and black wrought iron and had gorgeous woodwork inside. At the end of the streetcar, on the last coach, you had a small balcony with wrought-iron railing where only adults were allowed to sit. Well, I remember standing on that balcony with Oummi once. I'll never forget it: she took me by the hand and I stood there looking back with the streetcar trundling along, watching as it went up and down between the wooded hills. It was thick with trees and there were huge thick vines and creeper plants with huge flowers all over the trees. It was like riding through the jungle on a roller coaster!"

"Can we go there now?" Shams asked. "Can we go, Dad—*please?*"

"We can't," I said, genuinely disappointed myself. "Those were the old streetcars, son, the streetcars of *my* childhood. Today nobody cares to preserve those things. They're just gone."

———

The boys were probably expecting to see a full villa: they looked disappointed when I pointed uphill to what was left of the original construction.

We started at the bottom with the Roman bathhouse and the different chambers. I explained again that what they were seeing were remnants of very old buildings and that ruins were just like this structure before their eyes—scattered bare-bone traces from a bygone age.

What was left of the large bathhouse was a chest-high perimeter of neatly preserved stone walls and a warren of stone partitions and basins and conduits within them.

The outer wall was too rugged for the boys, and I had to climb on top of it first and help both of them up.

We stood there looking down into the remains of the building, and I began to tell them as much as I knew about the conduits, the basins, the troughs, and the hot and cold rooms.

Then Shams came up with the notion that it was a labyrinth: "Like the botanical garden in Köln," he said, "except this one is made of stones."

Haroon's eyes lit up, and the fancy of the labyrinth, for them and for me, bested all talk about the rich and powerful Romans bathing. I knew what I had to do: one at a time, I lowered them onto the floor and told them once more not to move any stones.

"Climbing allowed?" Haroon asked.

"Yes," I replied, "but be extra careful. I'll tell you when *not* to climb, okay?"

Immediately, Shams began to test his regained freedom: he climbed on top of a diminished partition wall running across the entire building from where I stood: it reminded me of those ancient farm walls in the Northwest around Tabarka.

My son stood facing me down there on that spine-like line of ancient rock, and he seemed so remote and reduced and small, holding out his arms crosswise for balance, like a ropedancer.

Shams flashed me a wide grin, lifting his eyebrows with comical mischief—as if what he had just done was a private prank to be shared by the two of us only; as if he knew as much as I did that Tunisia was perhaps the only country on earth that would lavish on him the joy of a perfectly licit late-afternoon caper amid the ruins of a Roman bath.

Farther down behind him: the tips of the columnar cypresses poking out over the hillside like miniature spires, and the dead-still silver sweep of the bay beyond, with the Two-Horn and the foothills to the east like faded etchings on a pewter plate.

———

They ran around and played hide-and-seek in their stone labyrinth, and I kept an eye on them and took the time to think of what Heend had told me before lunch.

"Surprised?" she had asked.

"Oh yes. Definitely. But I have nothing against the idea. The only thing is…whew. Thouraya. I mean, it's been such a long time. We haven't really seen much of each other in all these years—just quick and shallow conversations here and there. Small talk, basically, nothing much."

"Precisely," she said. "The idea now is that you're getting together to do some catching up—that's all. After all, neither of you expects this to be binding in *any* way. It's not a *date*, for heaven's sake: former lovers drift apart, former lovers meet as friends to chat and reminisce in a totally commitment-free setting. I don't see anything wrong with *that!*"

"Neither do I, as I said. It's just that the timing seems—sort of weird. Awkward, in a way. I don't know how to put it."

"You don't *have* to put it—that's the point. You're not finding the words because you're not used to the idea. Trust me. You'll see: just let yourself gradually get into the friend-meets-friend mode, and you'll see. In a few hours from now, you'll feel perfectly comfortable with the prospect of a cozy old-friends type of evening with Thouraya—and *us*. Trust me, brother, and trust the way this old world works."

And so she had made the call and Thouraya was "thrilled."

"That was the word she used. She didn't sound the least bit hesitant or self-conscious. You see?"

In fact, for all my apparent skepticism, I was not nearly as unenthusiastic as I sounded, and by now I was rather excited at the prospect of an evening with a woman that had meant so much to me in my college days: the shaky Tunis years, when I used to hole up in my apartment for days on end, with my diary—and Sartre and Camus; and Dostoevsky and Ma'arri and Ibn 'Arabi; and all the others who were much more real to me than the so-called reality around me, the reality that life in Tunisia had given me.

Later there was Nietzsche, too: she had introduced me to him in my third year at university—a "philosopher of healing and intuitive power," she had called him.

In our senior year, Thouraya had taken to calling him "the samurai of philosophy."

———

"Come, let's check out the villa," I shouted to the boys.

"I curled up and hid in the stone tub over there," Shams told me, breathless and flushed.

"You *look* like you did," I said, dusting his clothes.

"It was so cooold!" he shrieked, "How could they stand it in there, the Romans?"

"They filled it up with hot water—that's how they could stand it."

I helped Haroon up over the wall and he rode piggyback as we took the uphill path toward the villa.

———

The boys and I kept going up, with the dusty path snaking downward behind us through the field of skeletal ruins, sloping gently all the way down to the bottom of Odeon Hill, vanishing into the green rim of the bay and its chaotic bursts of colorful vegetation—anarchic, unpatterned, and undesigned growths of acacia, oleander, and mimosa, wild honeysuckle and hibiscus and passion flower.

Now we were up on the court of mosaics, as they called it here—a rectangular tennis-court-sized space surrounded on three sides by what was left of the villa: the tile-roofed gallery with its marvelously intact Phoenician columns.

My sons went straight to the mosaics.

"What's this?" Haroon asked.

It was the "scene of pugilism," as we were often told on our various school trips to Carthage.

"Boxing," I said.

"Boxing?"

"It's a sport," Shams said, "where two men fight with gloves on a stage."

"A ring," I corrected him. "It's called a ring, not a stage. You know, boys, I actually first saw this scene in my fourth-grade history book. I remember when I first came up here with my class and saw this: I was very excited and I told the teacher about it. She was not impressed—and I was disappointed that she wasn't. Somehow I thought it was such a big deal, like I was privy to a secret that set me apart from the rest of my classmates."

———

(I still have her words with me, written on the back of the photo, dated November 9: "Today is my birthday—and I'm not celebrating it with you. I know it's over, and it's probably for the best. I just thought you might be in need of a few sweet words in lonely Paris. You know, I think that love is even more beautiful in memory. Remember me as well as I remember you."

It is a picture of her at the beach, a cove not far from Carthage called La Baie des Singes.

Around her neck a string of red coral beads—almost the same red as the ruffled lace trim on the straps and neckline of the black swimsuit.

The necklace was a present from me.

I called her the Mermaid of the South Seas when I took the photograph.

She was indeed the picture of exotic beauty—with her glowing golden brown skin and honey Yemeni eyes, her wavy chestnut hair and sensual body.

My first love.)

———

The guard who had greeted us at the entrance down below showed up mysteriously as we were about to leave. He stepped out from behind another colonnade and came over with a reed basket in his hand.

He handed me a round, still-warm loaf of fried bread, and although he did not say that he was selling it, I knew it would be inappropriate not to give him some money in exchange for his act of kindness.

I paid him and broke the loaf for the four of us, and the sweet tang of sourdough rose out of the crust, mixing with the peaty aroma of charred semolina.

Shams wanted to know what it was.

"It's a very yummy variety of local country bread—baked in a big earthen pan with a little bit of olive oil. It's very tasty—you'll love it."

I gave a piece to the guard—a wiry dark-brown man in his fifties with a snow-white shirt, yellow straw hat, and sunglasses from the seventies.

He thanked me and put down his basket on the capital of a broken marble column behind him.

The man asked me if I lived in Europe and I nodded.

Then he was silent for a moment, looking at the sea down below, his eyes indecipherable behind the gun-metal-blue mirror of the glasses.

The guard was still looking at the bay when he spoke: "And now you have come this far, with your offspring—for this bread right here, in your homeland, and the oil in the bread. Remember the old saying? 'Sons of the oil and the bread.'"

———

Down at the bay, the three of us went for a swim followed by a sit-down, as Heend and I used to call it.

I explained to my sons how the two of us used to do it when we were teenagers—lounging in shallow water, groping around for flat skipping stones (ancient worn-down pottery shards), then standing up and tossing them across the sea. We would keep score by counting the highest number of skips.

That was when Shams came over to snuggle up, I remember, while I was still explaining, and the thought occurred to me for the first time that our flesh had never touched before this moment.

All at once, I felt a certain crowding in my heart, and for some inexplicable reason I began to imagine our sit-down in the lazy surf from Souad's point of view (Souad who was sitting alone on dry sand and with so much serenity, as if in meditation—the random heap of clothes by her side, the beach towels neatly stacked in the basket).

I did not know if she was looking at us, yet I could not help feeling exposed to her judgment—a clumsy out-of-place father who did not know what to do with the affections of his progeny.

Then there came the saving recollection: I remembered that moment when we all cuddled together at sundown on a park bench in Bordeaux, and I knew the only reaction that made sense at this point was to sit still and wordless for as long as the boys wanted it.

And it was right then that it happened, in the exact instant when I chose to respect their wish and observe their silence: the feeling, for the first time since our separation, that there might be a real chance for the three of us after all; that it was actually within my power now, beginning with this timeless minute, to forge and shape that chance and grant my sons a space of happiness for us to fill with *our* words, *our* gestures, *our* rituals, *our* memories.

The future—that was what I thought about as I sat there with my sons, the beginning of a meaningful future made by the three of us.

———

Heend fixed her gaze on Khaleel for a few awkward seconds before she spoke, addressing nobody in particular: "I don't know what I would have done without him—my special man. I would have probably turned into a horrible witch. I don't know…he made me so tender inside."

She sighed and looked down at the street through the bay window.

"Such are the laws of attraction," she added. "They're weird, impenetrable."

Khaleel smiled and reached out across the table to caress her shoulder: "I just let you get tipsy once in a while—that's my secret."

I winked at Thouraya opposite me: "All right," I said, "we're the free-floating singles at this table. We can still slip out of here quietly, before things get too mushy—leave these two lovebirds reminiscing in their romantic alcove. For heaven's sake, this is just the aperitif. We're talking about how relationships change, wilt, and *die*. All of a sudden, we've got Miss Eternal Love here waxing sentimental. Next thing, she'll be talking about their first *date*!"

"No, you're not leaving," Heend retorted, and for a second I thought she had taken my banter seriously. But then she gave me a playful sideways smile and said, "The praise to my man was just a parenthesis. As for our first date, well, the adrenaline rush was certainly quite unbelievable, but I wouldn't exactly call it romantic. My last session with him: that was our first date, if you can believe it. Before that session even began, I told him I wanted to terminate therapy. We went out for tea at the neighborhood café, we talked about his replacement, and then he had to run back to the office. As far as I'm concerned, our romance started on the couch, as it were."

Khaleel grinned at Thouraya next to him: "You didn't hear it from her."

"I told you it's going to get hot and heavy," I said to Thouraya. I was still surprised at Heend's sudden sentimentalism and I decided to go on teasing her about it: "Never mind, sister. I'm just giving you a hard time. It's called comic relief—the prudish man's refuge when things get too intense."

Thouraya laughed quietly as I spoke: "It's never boring when the two of you get together, that's for sure."

She wore a black wraparound silk dress with a print motif of red poppies, a pearl choker and matching earrings. Her hair was done in a ballet bun.

Khaleel began to say something to Thouraya about sibling complicity, and I allowed my eyes to briefly drift away from her spellbinding presence—looking out the window as my brother-in-law spoke, imagining the darkening bay beyond the street, the twinkling cruise ships scattered across the sea.

Thouraya had always been a powerful, mesmerizing woman—profound and mysterious, magnetically attractive in the ease and swiftness of her comportment.

She was driven by a deep-running power that never failed to leave you ambivalent and somewhat clueless about her manner and her motives: there was the Thouraya who had that certain something—a compelling quality of endless energy expressed as infectious passion, decisiveness and ease of action; and then there was the Thouraya of the cold silent rages—that fundamental anger that she was so good at suppressing and camouflaging and that always left you suspecting a sinister sense of ruthlessness buried deep within her.

Thouraya:

The woman in herself, the woman and me.

Even in those few seconds of detachment from the conversation, I could not help but compare, once again—her situation, my situation: the slightly uncomfortable fit of my clothes, borrowed from another man's wardrobe; the sleep-starved look on my face; the heft of my solemn disposition and my silent broody moods.

I imagined myself through her eyes for a painful instant: wondering why she had once loved me in the first place; what thoughts she had associated with my presence just a while ago when the four of us had met on that parking lot by the roadside café, at the bottom of the cobbled Moorish street that would take us high up to the breezy slopes and terraces of Sidi Bou Sa'eed—the narrow jasmine-choked lanes, the hubbub of the scorpion vendors and the nougat hawkers, the toy-camel craftsmen and the rug merchants, the spell-casters and the mappers of the future.

What had she been thinking all along? Of me and how far I had wandered off from the promise of my student years? Of us? Of what we used to be? Of what we might have been?

This velvet-voiced moth of a woman, this summer-night apparition—with her fresh trail of night scent, her almond eyes and their flawless lines of kohl, her silver-dust eye shadow.

I must have looked weary and vanquished in her eyes—a man of pent-up will and stalled hopes.

Thouraya must have read my mind, and in her own way she tried to reach out to me, by bringing the conversation back to failing relationships:

She began to tell us how breakups within interracial European couples were different from other separations.

"A crucial difference," she said, "is the unusual amount of stress that an Arab man is likely to deal with *before* the relationship begins to fall apart. From the start, Arab men in Europe find themselves in a totally different situation than women: they're immediately seen as the vehicle of Arab culture and its values. They're perceived as a threat by the host society. That puts them under tremendous pressure and the strain ends up spilling over into their relationship. When there is a separation the consequences can be disastrous, as the Arab man finds himself really cut off from society."

Heend looked at Khaleel: "You know, this reminds me of Amina," she said to him.

"I don't think Thouraya knows Amina."

"She's a former colleague of Khaleel's—a researcher now," Heend told Thouraya. "She moved to Paris with her husband a few years ago."

Khaleel started to tell us about Amina's research on domestic violence among Maghrebi couples in France.

"She told us she was shocked at first. She found out that the women were very protective of their husbands, even though they trusted her fully on confidentiality. They didn't necessarily justify or downplay the violence, but they were pretty maternal about their men. It was quite incomprehensible to her that they wouldn't even express anger or resentment. And then, one day, she had a major breakthrough."

She was interviewing a married university professor, he said, trying to get her to talk about her marriage: "The professor got angry and started lecturing Amina. She basically told her, Amina, that she didn't get it. The real issue was not the men's violence, she told her. Arab men in France were trapped—*that* was the real problem; caught in an invisible crossfire—and nobody was talking about it. It was amazing: the professor basically told her to shift the entire focus of her research."

Maghrebi men were getting hell from the European French—men and women alike, and not just because of the usual racism. The really intolerable "pressure factor" was the fear and rigidity of the French. To them, the North African male was a fundamental menace—not because of his potential ambitions, or even his supposed violence, but because of the position for which he had been chosen by society from the outset: sinister custodian of an antagonistic religion and value system.

"She explained to Amina that a Maghrebi woman never had to put up with that sort of pressure," Khaleel said. "That was the defining moment for her. At that point she was able to identify the cause of the women's resistance. She had to rethink everything she was doing with them. The men had to be directly included in the counseling—listening to their pain, providing them with a constructive outlet for rage and resentment, identifying with them the invisible pressures and oppositions from French society; all that secret banal violence on a daily basis—the kind that can make a normal person insane beyond recognition. She told me there was no significant research on the subject of hate-related stress among Maghrebi men—not in France and not in Europe. So she basically decided to *create* the subject."

"It's stunning that they're not doing anything about it," Thouraya said in a low voice, as if she was muttering an angry resolution to herself.

My words overlapped hers when I spoke: "And how is it coming along? The research, I mean."

"She is very prolific. They like her a lot here," Heend answered. "Right, Khaleel?"

"Very much. Her papers, her articles, her graduate workshops. The Americans are also very interested in what she's doing—for obvious reasons. She publishes and speaks there a lot. It's an interesting approach—derived from the specific reality of what she's witnessing. She was in fact taking a big risk, in terms of her career: she was trained in psychiatry, and her observations were taking her beyond the field—to a sort of interdisciplinary psychiatry, if you will, a mix of therapy, anthropology, sociology. Totally new approach."

Secretly, I was glad that the conversation had once again turned in a different direction—I was in no mood to discuss breakups, mine or anyone else's.

Thouraya seemed a tad irritated, though.

Later, she took me aside and asked me if I would like to get together with her on "the situation over there."

I accepted without hesitation.

———

After mint tea:

Outside 'Aaliah Café, we took the flagstone steps down toward Kheiriddine Lane, Khaleel and Thouraya walking a few steps ahead of us.

There was heat lightning on the horizon and the air was muggy.

In jest I told Heend that I was glad the conversation had meandered away from my marriage: "I managed not to get dragged into a discussion on Maghrebi men and domestic violence—got away with my own history of private rage."

As soon as I spoke the words, I found myself wondering, once again, if she was going to misread the self-deprecating humor in what I had said.

Heend's retort was swift and painfully bitter. Her voice had an edge to it as she spoke—the words inexplicably cold all of a sudden, and forbidding and machine-gun snappish: "I know another one who got away too—and he was not the raging kind either. The Ghost of Rades."

I felt thrown off and shut out by this shift in her mood, the sudden sadness and anger in her voice. She had spoken the words as if she was addressing a total stranger—someone who had never known "The Ghost."

Heend's rages against our father never failed to affect me with a terrible sense of helplessness: they always took me back to those dark times and places, when I was too young and confused to alleviate her hurt, her mutilated pride.

And so when I responded to her words, it was for the two of us that I pleaded. I stopped, two steps below her, and turned around and addressed my sister—but I was not able to look directly at her: "Come now, sister," I said.

She took one step down to face me up close, leaning over me with a frown of disbelief, as if I had just committed a terrible act of rudeness: "Come now *what?*"

Under the yellow lamplight, her face was beaded with sweat, unnaturally sharp-angled: "There are far worse things than rage, don't you think? Think of the man who walked away from us—abandoning the family just days before I was born. He did more devastation than the worst physical bully. Don't you think?" she repeated, staring down at me with that unrelenting bitter look in her eyes.

I could not help feeling targeted, as if I was a reincarnation of the man who had never been there for her.

I remained silent, my eyes slightly lowered, averted from her gaze.

"What's a poor girl to do?" she hummed in a vague singsong. "April 14. Mother said he didn't even send flowers to the clinic. That's how I'll always remember my birthday—the flowerless day. He didn't show up for months, she said—too busy working with his cronies on how to repudiate his wife the old-fashioned way, cheat her out of her lawful alimony. But you men don't want to hear any of this—it's just not in your *nature* to want to hear such things. How silly and tasteless of me to bring it up—on such a lovely evening."

"Heend, listen to me. *Forget* him, quite simply. He is *not* worth your memories! Just forget him. Flush him out of your system! Look at what life has *lavished* on you: a great husband, a wonderful son—and oodles of time for your writing. Forget him, please!"

She looked away from me, down toward the crowded lane below: "We don't want to keep them waiting, do we? Speaking of writing, I have to give you my story before you leave. Don't forget to e-mail me some feedback."

"Sister, have I ever forgotten?"

She turned her face toward me and spoke softly: "Never, bless you. You're as steady as a rock."

My second date with Thouraya:

Shortly before I left, I told my sons I was going to the beach and they seemed sad that I was not taking them with me. I told them we would all go to Sidi Bou Sa'eed later for bomboloni—a guilty parental trade-off.

By the time my taxi pulled over before the gate, they both looked quietly forlorn—standing by their aunt under the apple tree, staring up at me with wide apprehensive eyes, and I felt that I had to say it again, with histrionic cheer in my voice this time: "It's only a few hours, boys. Before you know it, I'll be right back here, on this lawn—telling you to get ready for your treat."

Shams nodded (a weak, unconvinced nod) and Haroon looked down and frowned, grinding the ball of his foot into the grass.

Heend stood behind them, her hands on their shoulders. With her eyes, she motioned me to go.

I kissed them good-bye and left.

When we got to the Carthage-Marsa Route, I asked the taxi driver to take the old cliff road to Gammarth: "Hotel Mouradi," I told him. "That cute cove I still stubbornly call La Baie des Singes."

He turned almost all the way around and informed me with a conspiratorial smile that most people of our generation still called it that. "Some habits are just too nice to give up," he added as he turned back around to face the road.

It had rained in the early hours, and the dark-green hills and hollows of the country below were slowly coming to life under the sun. The veil of lifting mist made them look soft and indefinite, like a spongy mass of amorphous matter pushed out overnight by the sea. The mercury-and-hematite stillness of the water, the phantom silhouette of the Two-Horn beyond—tin-sheet flat and unreal in the haze.

The air inside was thick and heady—a mix of cheap air freshener and new Sky leather. My limbs were sore and my head was still throbbing from last night's noise and smoke and music and dance frenzy at El Barraka.

But the morning felt full of promise and the misty, Indian-summer laziness of it had put me in a mood of buoyant expectancy: somewhere down there by the cove, a beautiful woman was waiting for me on a quiet beach, its sand sugar-white and fresh and crisp from a night of summer rain.

———

I found Thouraya on the completely empty private beach of the Mouradi, sprawled in a lounge chair underneath a thatched parasol.

She sat facing the sea and did not notice me coming through the swimming pool gate behind her.

"Same old spot?" I felt like saying as I approached her, but I thought better of it. Too sentimental.

Instead, I crept up on the woman who had once been my lover, stepped under the parasol, and stood over her with a broad smile on my face.

Thouraya looked a little startled seeing me there by the empty lounge chair alongside hers. She sat up with her legs astraddle the chair and said good morning.

The top of her swimsuit (bright red) showed through the sheer halter she wore.

I had to bend my head slightly to keep it from touching the ribs of the parasol (standing there with my shoulders hunched, looking down at her, taking her in—the hay barn smell of the thatching; summer scent of stacked-up hay).

Thouraya said, "You must think I'm crazy dragging you all the way out here so early."

"I love this place," I said, "especially at this time of day. I had a good night's sleep, considering. Turned in at three and slept straight through."

"Good heavens! Some things never change. In bed at three and up at what? Seven?"

She swung her right leg over to this side and sat on the edge, smiling up at me: "Isn't the weather lovely today? Like a fall morning."

I sat down on the chair opposite Thouraya, our knees almost touching, looking away from her to take in the bay: the lazy surf lapping the sand, the beach looking as I had anticipated it—rain-pocked and white and still untrodden.

"They don't, do they?" I said, as I turned to face her.

"What?" she asked with a genuinely mystified frown.

"Change," I replied, smiling into her eyes.

Without smiling, she leaned forward with her face.

I leaned closer toward her and our lips locked halfway, right above our knees.

———

Lounging after our first swim:

Thouraya said, "We love talking behind your back, don't we? In answer to your question: yes, we did discuss your situation— extensively. Every time I got back home from your sister's place, I would sit down for a moment and reflect—wondering what to do. Write you a letter, maybe—trash all those terrible people and tell you how weak they are, deep down. I'm not always a nice girl, you know. I *can* think and say and write all kinds of devastating things. Thinking all those terrible thoughts and ruminating all kinds of terrible words that I wanted to write was bad enough, but sitting there and not knowing what to do with the thoughts and the words was far worse."

I was lying on my side with my knees protruding over the edge of the chair—looking at my lover's face so close across from mine, her left cheek cradled in the bundled-up shorts: "Oh yes," I joked, "you're a *bad* girl—very bad."

Gentle breeze wafting off the sea, fragrant heat rising from the baking sand, terry-cloth tepid and soft under our bodies.

Thouraya said, "I have to admit I'm still at a loss even now. Last night—I mean, I'm still at a loss for words. What to say. How to say it. To say or not to say. Last night I wanted you to express your *feelings* about what happened—as opposed to being analytical about it and all—but then I thought it over later on my way home and I realized I wasn't so sure anymore. Maybe talking about terrible people and terrible events only exacerbates the pain we associate with them."

She sighed.

I turned over and sat up with my shoulders against the back of the chair.

Gazing into the horizon: by now the sun had chased away every trace of mist from the sea and was burning fiercely above our thatched patch of shade—making the sand shiny and bright, turning the horizon where the sea met the sky into one single concavity of the deepest blue, like an immense seamless ultramarine sheet swelling outward in the breeze.

Last night. Of course, she *had* been thinking about last night—my precariously cheerful mood and my evasive tactics. Shocked and unsettled at the sight of me. Not liking the sudden reality of finding herself face to face with a man whose life was falling apart; having to put herself in a position of helpless empathy with a soon-to-be divorce whose existence was turning into a space of confinement and victimhood, controlled by cold and calculating and sadistic people.

I looked about me and let my gaze wander around the by now busy beach, realizing at once how mentally cut off from the other bathers I had been all along, as if the two of us had been interacting in a vacuum.

And yet beyond our patch of shade, it was just another day at the beach: those clusters and pairs of sand and sunshine lovers sparsely scattered around us—their world seemed blissfully innocent in its placid banality, its ordinary commonplaceness.

"It's so nice down here at the bay—never gets too crowded," I said, once again trying to shift the conversation away from me.

"Oh—of course it is," she replied, sounding tentative and thrown off.

Silence.

"Sorry," I said, "I was trying to be evasive—once again."

She let go of my hand, turned over slightly, and propped herself up on her elbow, looking at me long and deep, her cheeks flushed from the heat.

She said, "Last night—may I actually tell you this? I'm not sure if I should."

"Sure you may."

"Well, last night, I wanted so much to say what I had been meaning to tell you all along—all these months."

There was another short uncomfortable silence. Then she sat on the edge of her chair and addressed me again, leaning forward and speaking in a whisper almost, her face so close to mine that I could see the amber starburst around her pupils: "It's going to be an uphill struggle for you from here on out, Tariq. That's what I really wanted to say and was not sure I *should* say it. Now that you don't have the legitimate image—the image of someone who fits even if he doesn't belong. Now that you don't live with a European woman and you're separated from your children. Well, you'll be facing all the others *alone* now, and you'll be discovering an altogether different side of their nature—something much harder, harsher, darker; something you'll have to learn to inoculate and harden yourself against."

"And what makes you assume this?" I asked her in a neutral tone, even though I did not feel like interrupting her.

Suddenly, I felt hungry, and had an intensely vivid picture of food in my mind: I visualized grilled swordfish and carrot torshi with lemon on the side.

They're all out here, I thought, and the pool is at its emptiest. Now is the time to head for the poolside grill, order our barbecue lunch for midday, and settle down for the afternoon in a cool and shady place.

"I don't know," Thouraya said, "it's more intuitive feeling than assumption, I guess. Intuition. A man in your condition, a man of your *identity*, is bound to face serious pressures in France—no matter how successful he is; in fact, *especially* if he's successful. An Arab woman there faces tough conditions, too, of course, but it's different. The unrelenting low-key strategic violence is something she's very unlikely to face—certainly not when she enjoys the legitimacy of motherhood."

Thouraya turned around for a few seconds, as if she had just remembered that she was expecting someone at this precise moment, her gorgeous hair swinging above her knees like a massive tangle of silk thread.

Then she turned back to me and went on: "You may not have to face the violence openly, but I think you need to be aware that the pernicious extent of that particular violence, the deep-running reach of its viciousness, is always proportional to its invisibility—its microscopic subtlety, sometimes even its technicality."

"That particular violence?" I asked, just as she spoke again, my voice mingling with hers.

"Yes," she said, "the one that's aimed at isolating you, Tariq. Confining you inside a category: Lone Angry Arab Male. You won't *see* it, but you'll *feel* it—in your trial to begin with. The lawyers, the judges, the witnesses, the social workers, the child psychologists, the educators: neutral assessments, opinion, expertise, testimony, right? Wrong. In reality, everybody involved in the trial will be all issuing pronouncements on your person *as* an Arab man—your Arab body, your Arab soul, your Arab origins, your Arab behavior. Sooner or later, you're bound to realize that you've entered a world where you're observed closer than ever before—judged, tested, tried; *and* made to feel excluded and singled out, *marked*, quite simply."

Thouraya paused again and reached out to me, caressed my chest with her fingertips, leaning so close that I felt completely penetrated by the sea-and-sand scent of her skin (redolence of salt and ferny marshland).

She kept her fingertips wandering around my heart and rested her chin on my shoulder, speaking softly behind my ear: "Do you see now? Why I'm in a bind? The moment I saw you, I knew you were weary—your pain entered my entire being all at once, like a wave. And the longer I sat with you, the more I became convinced the time was for words of healing and softness—not sickness. But something in me wanted to tell you the painful truth as I saw it, and that something was unyielding—a nagging moral obligation, you might say."

———

(Thouraya never let feelings get in the way of unmitigated honesty, and I had always admired that quality of tough, hard-nosed candor in her as much as I had dreaded it.

I have revisited her remarks often since, and I must confess that it took me a long time to find illumination in them: those words uttered on the sun-drenched beach of La Baie des Singes—so much out of place when they were spoken that they seemed too detached from any tangible reality, too distant from the world of tangible consequences.

And yet when all is said and done, Thouraya's words of tough healing have taught me more about the banal face of evil than any document I know.)

———

Poolside with Thouraya:
When I woke up in the lounge chair, our side of the pool was in the shade and the sun was going down behind the western wing of the hotel. The sky above the beach was navy blue.

Woke up but still lying on my side with my back to Thouraya reading close by (I could hear her turning the pages of a book or a magazine, feel her absorption). Secretly watching and observing the world from my chair, secretly enjoying the fact that to her I was still asleep and unreachable.

Only a handful of people scattered around the swimming pool area and on the lawn now, our side completely empty. The place had a quiet and strangely fascinating feeling of desertion about it, a certain sense of unreality, too, as if it was all going to warp into another time dimension any second now: deserted grill area with no one around it; rustle of lazy surf crashing on hard sand, pulling back with a sigh; palm fronds nodding above the lawn in the totally vacant grill area by the beach gate; old-fashioned tin pipes of the showers like upside-down, excessively long and disproportionate J s; dull unperturbed mercury-and-indigo gloss of the swimming pool; flagstone paths in the lawn like flat embedded fossil bones, all traces of wet hurried feet gone.

Thouraya had thrown a towel over me in my sleep. It felt good dwelling in this moment of sweet sadness without a name—curled up in the fetal position with my back turned to her, knowing that I could amaze myself with the sight of my lover at any moment just by turning around.

Still lying on my side. Still and so close to the lawn. Almost level with the ground. Watching the sky deepen, listening to the soothing whispers of the sea.

Then I rolled over and lay on my back, looking up at her out of the corner of my eye.

She was sitting up and at an angle to me, her legs straddling the chair. Reading a novel, The Box of Sour Crystals.

Tariq: "Intriguing."

Thouraya: Looking down at me with a question mark in her eyes.

T: "The title. Who's the writer?"

She handed me the book, told me it was a first-time novelist from Alexandria.

Th: "The opening is slow and microscopic and yet intensely gripping. The narrator is a woman, and pretty soon you find out that she is this elegant, classy old lady from the Turkish aristocracy who has outlived four husbands—all of them having died violently at different points in her incredibly rich and tormented life. Four lives. The novel is in four parts—one part for each marriage."

I was a little clumsy handing back her book, trying to keep my index finger between the pages where she had left off. She told me not to worry—just put it down.

T: "Ah, your flawless photographic memory. How could I forget?"

Th [flirtatious smile]: "Child of a lesser god, I forgive you."

Th lifts her legs up one at time, slides down the pad a little and sits like a rower in the drive phase, pulling her thighs up against her chest and throwing her wiry arms around her shins. Chin resting on her knees, she smiles slantwise at me—the smile of a woman with a beautiful secret.

Th tells me more about the novel: the Egyptian author begins with an extremely slow and detailed description of the box. The scrollwork on its lid; its ivory inlay; its wood grain; the velvet padding inside; the compartments and their stories; the chips of sandalwood that she puts in the diamond compartment; the pellets of ambergris among the pearls. The description goes on and on. Then the old lady starts to tell about her favorite "crystals," as she calls them (the breathtaking gemstones in the jewels she had received from her various husbands); how she got into the habit of putting them to her lips, absorbing the feel and memory of each individual stone (she does have quite a few of them, as it turns out, stones and memories). The aristocrat from Alexandria spends page after page telling us about the aura and vibrations of each precious stone and how they speak to her body and her soul in their own different ways—their memory running through different parts of her skin, her bones, and her organs. The various feelings and moods (and weather!) they evoke in her.

I lay there silent, looking up and smiling at her with admiration—lust also, a great deal of it.

Her mind had merged with my thoughts and my desire in that instant. I could feel it in the triumphant sensual flutter of her eyes.

At some point I told my lover that I had to leave: "My boys are expecting me up there. I'm taking them to Sidi Bou for bomboloni. Maybe we'll catch the brass band up on the square."

Th: "They're on every evening till mid-September."

T: "The kids love it—the musicians' outfits, the monkey, the whole racket."

Th: "Shall we meet there? I mean on the square—round about eight?"

T: "Yes. The boys will go back down with Heend. I'll just hang around till eight."

Then I ask her the *question: "Where will we go?"*

"Surprise." That was all she said.

———

Up in Sidi Bou:

We ate bomboloni with Heend and we played and laughed and lounged around the main square until it was time for the boys to go to bed.

Before I sent my sons on their way down with their aunt, I bought the three of them jasmine garlands and put them around their necks.

I kissed them good night by the parking lot and went back up to the square and loitered alone in the alleys for a while.

The moon was already up and the beautiful lights were on in the doorways of the gift shops and the Moorish houses.

My night with Thouraya had begun.

———

She wore flat leather sandals and a traditional silk outfit: off-white Turkish blouse and baggy bright-green shalwar pants.

Thouraya's face was bronzed and burnished, her hair done up in a loose bun. Two coral drops dangled from her ears like holly.

I told her that she looked great and she gave me a smile.

"How about a drink somewhere with a terrace?" she asked.

It was hard to tell, but Thouraya had a hint of something unusual in her voice. Thrill? Nervousness? Impatience?

"'Aaliah Café?" I suggested with a smile.

"'Aaliah it is," she replied.

———

I was in a state of total fusion with Thouraya and enjoyed partaking of her playful mood as she assumed a role specially created for the evening: master puppeteer and custodian of a special secret.

I said, "Why don't we stay a little longer. I want to take another guess."

She laughed and signaled to the waiter for the check, and I kept teasing her about not wanting to leave: "You know, I'll never tire of loafing around here—the moon-flooded view on the bay, the night jasmine, the sea breeze. Not to mention the lemonade. I want *more* lemonade! I'm dying of thirst!"

"Think of it this way," she countered, "you will not be leaving Sidi Bou, in a way. You'll be carrying it on the inside for the rest of the evening—all the way into your dreams. Actually, you'll have the whole town at your feet, as it were."

More puzzled-looking histrionics from me, more laughter from Thouraya.

"Are we going up?" I asked her, trying to sound as stupid as possible.

"Yes. We're going all the way up. And we're *staying* up, too, for some time—way above everything, in a little bubble of moonlight."

"Hey," I said, "have pity on me. This is getting too tricky for my poor little head."

"But there *is* no trickery. You know me. I mean what I say and I say what I mean. We're just staying in a place high up, where we can see it all and have it all—without being *in* it. The whole bay. What's so tricky about that?"

Then it suddenly hit me that the place she had been mysteriously hinting at was right here, just outside Sidi Bou—the highest and most solitary point in the cape.

"Thouraya," I whispered between surmise and disbelief, "you *are* kidding me, aren't you?"

"No I'm not," she whispered back with a smile, but there was earnestness and breathless excitement in her tone.

"Al-Khayyam?"

She nodded.

"The Blue Suite?"

She nodded again.

I leaned across the table and kissed her.

We were in the Blue Suite only once (a goodbye gift from Thouraya), the night before I left the homeland and plunged into my French exile.

———

Together in the Blue Suite:

The room still very much the same—same redolence of myrrh and honeycomb; bakhnoug tapestry above the antique brass bed; mother-of-pearl inlay furniture in the alcove.

The multiple temporal folds and layers of this place, the dizzying play of its many mirror effects, and the fractal geometry of its ceramics. Its ineffable spirit of scandal and secrecy penetrating your soul as you stand under the amber light of the Andalusian chandelier with the woman you once loved in this very suite before you vanished into your chosen exile.

Impatient already to slip out of your too-warm shoes and feel the sweet chill of the ceramic tiles beneath your feet.

I stood barefoot before Thouraya and reached out to unbutton her blouse, but she stopped me and said there was one more thing that she wanted to tell me.

"Another guessing game?" I said, laughing.

She shook her head with a smile: "No more guessing games. I went to a beauty salon right after I dropped you off. The boss. She's this epic, matriarchal type of woman. Your quintessential old-school beautician: the old-fashioned sequined caftan, the silver anklet complete with charms, the huge Berber earrings, the harkous and henna tattoos all over her body. The woman is a walking anthropology museum. I told her what I wanted in detail, and *where* I wanted it."

"Aha, the plot thickens!"

Thouraya took me by the hand and I followed her and sat next to her on the edge of the bed.

She began to tell her tale with a certain theatrical exaggeration in gesture, voice, and idiom, and I knew that this was funny histrionic Thouraya taking over—my lover at her iconoclastic best, displaying her brilliant gift for working-class humor, subversive mimicry, and irreverent theatrical performance: "She had these two front teeth sticking out like a pair of blanched almonds, and she chewed her Arabic gum with a constant click, just like in those Egyptian movies from the fifties. She had a totally fascinating way of jawing and smacking gum at the same time; you could actually see her stretching the gum *inside* her mouth and making those little air pockets that went click click click under her teeth. I'm telling you, she was straight out of an Egyptian movie. And her name? You know what it was? Her name?"

I just shook my head, convulsed with laughter.

"Dabbabya. That was her name, I swear. The Tank.[2] Stop laughing, man. This is facts—my anthropology field report. I'm not kidding here. This is living history, my friend. What's the point in my reporting to you if all this precious information is going to be lost in laughter?"

She was saying all this with a straight face, which made her story even funnier, and ever so vivid and pictorial.

"Anyway," she went on, "I told her what I wanted, right? So she looks me over from head to toe, sizing me up. Then she says: 'Men, men, men. We'd do *anything* to please their eyes, wouldn't we?' She was so cocky—in a seen-it-all kind of way. And so I tell her, 'What makes you so sure I'm doing this for a man?' She looks at me with this dirty conspiratorial smile and says, 'I see.' Then she adds, 'You know, I'm a lot less old-fashioned than you think. I could tell you stories.' She was a tricky one, but in an endearing sort of way. So now I *had* to tell her: 'I'm taking him for a stroll through my garden,' I said. She laughed, with those huge *miswak*-whitened teeth of hers: 'It's going to be a gorgeous stroll,' she said, 'that's for sure.'"

And now Thouraya was done telling the story of the beautician.

---

[2]In Arabic, *dabbaba* means military tank.

She stood up and threw her head back, pulling the chopstick out of her bun with an ambiguous sigh—an expression of resigned weariness? The dark flames of that marbled hair spilling out in tongues of muted blonde and hazel, walnut and sepia.

There was one single croak from the hinge of the alcove window behind us—breeze coming through the dormer overhead and stealing back out into the sultry Mediterranean night. A solitary note in the sudden silence of this room full of age-old traces and signs and symbols.

Thouraya sighed again, and this time the wordless utterance did sound like a note of resignation—so much at odds with the dark fire of her hair, the redolence of sea salt and baking sand wafting from her body like a sweet secret scent hidden beneath her skin.

"Now we can lift the veil," she said. "There's nothing more to tell."

She stepped back a little, closed her eyes, and unbuttoned the blouse. And when she spread it open, her gift was all at once revealed before my eyes, to love and admire—a breathtaking scene in shades of henna and black harkous tattooed on Thouraya's chest from the collarbones down. The sketch was so arresting in its sudden surreal revelation that all I could do was whisper one senseless empty word to fill my staggered silence—a croak, like a dry leaf crumpled in your fist: "Tattooist?"

"Yes," she whispered, "she has her own tattoo artist in the salon—a woman."

Thouraya did not move—her head still thrown back a little, her chest thrust forward, and her arms stretched out behind her.

It was a contrasted scene both in style and expression: the seafloor motif was almost perfectly mimetic, and the fantasy sea ferns and anemones tattooed across her flanks and belly were brilliantly executed to convey the mild-swaying rhythms of sea depths.

But it was the russet-and-sepia-toned sketch on her chest that kept me riveted—a hybrid creature with a woman's head and a horse's body. The mixed being was depicted in the middle of Thouraya's bosom with its head slightly above breast level as it rode an out-of-scale cresting wave that started just below my lover's clavicles.

And the fascinating expression on the face of that centaurian creation: a countenance darkened with experience and profundity; her demeanor not exactly defeated, but certainly bruised. Yet the hurt in her eyes did not diminish the intensity of her proud martial posture as she rode the wave with an air of triumph, her muscular chest thrust out and her forelegs pushing forward through the foaming water.

With her eyes still closed, Thouraya said, "When the tattooist was finished, Dabbabya walked in to take a look at the masterpiece. She asked me if I was a water sign and drew a blank. Then she asked me when my birthday was. It turned out I *was* a water sign, whatever that meant. She said it made perfect sense that I chose the seafarer's tattoo, as she called it."

I eased myself off the edge of the bed, knelt down before her, and started admiring the sea ferns on her belly. Thouraya gave a startled laugh when she felt the touch of my lips.

The tattoo on her skin had a fascinating scent—a mix of damascene rose, fireplace ash, and crushed walnut leaves, and when I closed my eyes, it did feel as if I was in a garden.

I heard the rustle of her shirt falling to the floor, opened my eyes, and looked up. As if by miracle, there was a XXXL joint and a lighter in Thouraya's hand: "Let's light up," she whispered mischievously. "Then I'll lie down and let you *really* discover my garden."

We smoked and lay down together. We loved each other and talked well into the night. Then there came a time when her voice trailed off and she fell asleep, and I got out of bed and went to sit in the alcove, looking outside the open window at the bay down below with the bone-bright moon lowering in the west. Cold solitary moon.

Looking down at the lights around the bay, I was far from "having the whole town at my feet," as she had said, a lifetime ago; in fact, I could not have felt more cut off—from Sidi Bou and its magic, from the Cape, from Thouraya herself.

Of course, I knew from the start that there was no future for us as a couple, but I was already missing her. I was far away on another cold continent of solitude already, bereft of both the woman and her memory—the poetry of her words, the magic of her garden.

I was already missing everyone and everything—those unmistakable intimations of doom penetrating my soul like a cold exhalation from the sea: the anticipation of those desolate moments of recollection on the flight back to Bordeaux, when I would find myself, as usual, contemplating the already fading traces of my days in Tunisia—those moments when I would be a witness to the gradual disappearance of my memories of Tunisia; feeling them disintegrate in the wake of that plane, as it were—moment by moment, impression by impression, word by word. Accepting the disintegration of every retrospective thought of the homeland rather than having to grapple with the awful truth: the dreadful fact that I was utterly powerless to remedy the immitigable frailty of the faces and the places—their helplessness in the face of time and its terrible sadistic trickery. How precarious it was in the fickle hands of history—the full comforting solidness of the things and the people that I had known and loved so well (the names and the families and the towns, the sights and the scenes, the smells, the tastes, the colors). As I sat and brooded in the alcove after those precious moments with my lover, I was almost forcing myself to see (envision) them all vanishing already (the faces, the places, the names, the things and their sensations); gone in the hurtling swoon of an instant, like cloud-pictures in a windy sky, like trickling drops on a foggy window; gone as I begin (in my mind already) to project myself into another country, another border, another life.

Don't know what I am writing—confused words.

Sad, tired, running out of hotel stationery.

Must not feel guilty, though, it's good to write in confusion. Proof of bravery.

The day after my tryst with Thouraya in Sidi Bou Sa'eed, I went back home with the boys in a taxi. (Just before I took leave of Heend and Khaleel, I called mother to let her know that we were coming. Kareem was waiting for us, she told me: "He drove all the way up from Korbous," she added, sounding emphatic and enthusiastic, like a telemarketer talking up the exceptional advantages of an exclusive service.)

I saw my lover a few more times that summer, between visits to my siblings.

On two occasions she reminded me that I needed time to decide where I wanted to go from here.

She never brought up the past or the future, and the last time that I saw her, two days before we flew back to Bordeaux, she gave me *The Box of Sour Crystals.*

———

Nour was there too, and the three of them were playing rummy under the mulberry tree.

Mother sat opposite my brother and my sister, leaning forward in the swing chair, her bare feet on the brick floor.

My niece Young Nour was daydreaming on the house steps, and when mother saw the three of us walk in through the gate she put her hand down, stood up, and spoke to her.

Young Nour climbed up to the threshold on all fours, leaned into the doorway, and called Latifa.

Mother kept following us with her eyes as we walked toward them, contemplating us with that peculiar expression on her face—an ambiguous semblance of ironic distance that anyone unfamiliar with her could easily mistake for arrogance or disrespect.

I greeted them and she began to fix her gaze on me as soon as I sat down: "We've just had tea," mother said with a sigh—as if she was owning up to an insurmountable weakness of character.

"You did right!" I answered her. "After all, we *are* late."

"Do your boys know they're staying over at Nour and Khayyam's house while you're visiting your brother?"

"Yes, we talked about it on our way here. They love it at their aunt's place. Ahmed is there too."

Mother told Latifa to bring us lemonade and cookies. Then, as if she needed an instant to refocus her thoughts, she looked down before her for a split second and turned her gaze toward me again. She had fine glowing skin and the subtly rouged full lips and impeccably dyed hair made my mother look much younger.

"I suppose you haven't eaten mittaouma in a long time," she said to me in the direct, random, and somewhat awkward manner with which she addressed everyone.

"No I haven't," I replied, and I immediately laughed—a big hearty laugh, as if I had suddenly caught her playing a naughty prank on someone.

The boys went over to sit by her side and she leaned toward them and put her arms around them and kissed them: "*Mash'Allah,*" she said in praise of God's providence. "*Mash'Allah* for these two sweet angels—Allah's most bountiful gift to you and us."

"So let met guess," I went on teasing her. "Let me do some supposing of my own. If I'm not mistaken, what you're telling me is to be a good son and make time for you, and in exchange—"

"Make time for *all* the *Radesi!*" Nour interrupted with a burst of nervous laughter.

I said, "Rades and the *Radesi* are up next, of course—right after Korbous. After all, I've got a lot of catching up to do with *this* brilliant young lady here—and her equally brilliant brother."

Young Nour smiled with a self-deprecating flutter in her eyes. Sitting on the stairs with her elbows on her knees and her chin resting on the cusp of her joined hands. Young Nour's hair and her amber eyes reminded you of a princess from ancient Egypt.

My niece said, "I'll make my special samsa. Just let me know when you'll be heading back up here."

I turned to address my sister again: "Samsa, eh? And I guess you taught your brilliant daughter that secret technique for the perfect stuffing, right?"

Nour gave me a broad smile in response and her daughter rattled off the family secret: "I roast the sesame seeds—no unroasted sesame, that's for one. Then I let them sit for a while. I don't crush them before they cool off completely. Plus, another secret—*my* secret. I use roasted hazelnut *powder*—and *brown* sugar. Oh, one more thing—*my* own personal touch also: sometimes I use filo instead of warka leaves."

"Oh no," I said to Young Nour, laughing, "don't you come to study in France. You'd put me out of business, I swear. All right, then, I'll sample your filo samsa; maybe I can do it in my restaurant—unless you got it patented already."

"Nour," mother said to me, "has earned her name: she is the light of her parents' life. She wants to follow in her father's footsteps—pharmacy."

Young Nour told me, "I also want to earn a degree in acupuncture. I'll have to wait and see, though. I still don't know if you have to be in medical school first. We'll look into it in the fall."

I said, "That's going to be a cinch, girl—with *your* kind of potential and your wonderful, supportive parents!"

"We do the best we can—and the rest is up to her," Nour said, earnest and inward-looking.

———

"Shall we?" Kareem said, as soon as I put down my cup. He smiled, but I knew that he was getting nervous. We had to go while it was still light out—the road to Korbous was extremely treacherous in the dark.

I nodded and went upstairs to get my things.

———

Mother stood behind the white iron gate of her house and smiled at us: "Kareem and Tariq driving down to the cape, just like in the old days," she said.

There was a certain familiar tone in her voice—fondness mixed with melancholy. In fact, she spoke the words as if they were wishful, chimerical dreams.

There were two white shafts reflected in those big sad brown eyes—two iron bars, and even though Nour was standing farther behind our mother, hiding behind her, I knew that my sister was on the verge of tears. I had to keep the moment from slipping into tearful nostalgia: "You're not going to trick me into fishing, are you?" I said, looking at my brother.

"No, I'm not," he answered with a strained laugh. "You haven't held a fishing line in your hands in years—I'd have to give you a refresher course. Imagine the embarrassment!"

Now we were all laughing, after a fashion, and I felt that the moment had been saved from sentimentalism.

Again, I told mother that I would be seeing her soon, and we were on our way.

———

When we got on the coastal road to Korbous (Road 23), Kareem asked me how I was going to take care of the boys when I got back to Bordeaux.

He sounded like a busy doctor concluding a routine checkup.

I told him this time it was going to be much easier than in the spring: "I'm going to be with them all the time."

"How do you mean?" he asked me with a frown, eyes on the road— the most beautiful and the deadliest in the country: nothing between you and the blue abyss to the east but that flimsy traffic barrier.

"Summer vacation," I answered. "Between July 14 and early September, Bordeaux is virtually deserted. Anybody with any money to spend heads out to the coast. For most businesses like us, it actually becomes more costly to stay open than to close shop."

"Strange," he said absentmindedly, his voice flat, his eyes fully on the road.

I just let him drive.

To our right, the craggy mountainous country was a pinkish pale green in the afterglow—the smoky green of sparse Mediterranean brush; and to our left, there was the massive sheer cliff that formed the eastern face of the Korbous Cape with the darkening ink-blue of the bay at its bottom, gathered into a ruffled strip of snow-white froth shimmering on the puckered hem of the shoreline.

I thought of mother and could not help but conclude that the old days were no longer what they used to be. I was feeling rather apprehensive about this visit. Kareem was definitely different from Mourad (like Heend, he was warm and laid-back, and we had had many shared experiences growing up together), but now there was his recently discovered religious fervor to contend with—my brother's bizarre metamorphosis into a strict practicing Muslim.

I'll just have to wait and see, I thought, as we approached Korbous.

———

Sunlight was all but gone from the surrounding hills when we drove into town.

Kareem and Mouna's recently inherited summer home was a small two-story Liberty house on the town square overlooking Korbous's tiny fishing harbor. Mostly recreational, the harbor stood at the end of the only other paved road in town, a steeply inclined street that branched from Road 23 like the stem of a Y, plunging down to a cove that was evenly divided between a pier and a very well-kept sand-and-shingle beach.

Mouna came down to greet us as soon as we stepped into the house.

My relation to Kareem's wife was devoid of any form of meaningful interaction: beyond her outward appearance and the shallow performances dictated by custom and familial obligations, I knew nothing about the woman.

She wore pearl jewelry, was very subtly made up, and had no veil on, revealing the Greek contours of her delightful boyish face. And there was, of course, her hairdo—an interesting mix between pageboy and flapper—which had not failed to surprise and delight me when I saw her during our Rades get-together.

———

I had not had much of a conversation with my nephews: Young Kareem and Zayd had left (rather rudely, I thought) right after the appetizers and the usual exchange of empty, depressing pleasantries and small talk.

Their mother had given me a stiff apologetic smile as they stomped off to their rooms: "The boys have to get back to their RPG pals next door. They're in the middle of a Prophecy game."

And now it was the three of us on their vast beautifully decorated upstairs terrace. Down below the cove was dark except for the misty purple glow of rope lights around the swim raft, the fitful phosphorescent signals from the beacon buoys. The wide open sea beyond was pitch black.

My brother spoke first: "You've been very much on our minds lately, brother, you know that?"

"Yes, I do."

Mouna looked down and nodded gravely.

The huge plate of couscous was still untouched. Our Berber couscous bowls still empty before us on the bamboo place mats.

Kareem kept looking at me as he spoke, his gaze earnest but not cold: "You know, I've mulled your situation over for some time. It was painful. My younger brother deprived of his children and falsely accused of domestic violence—and there is nothing I can do about it. I could not even write you a letter—I wouldn't even know how to *begin* it. You know me, Tariq. I've never been one to linger on feelings and introspections and self-analysis—all that sort of stuff. I've never been good at talking or writing about feelings. But in case you're curious about how I felt and how I still *feel* about this mess, just ask Mouna. *She*'ll tell you."

Mouna started to say something, but my brother cut her short with a raised hand and a frown. He did not even look at her.

"What I *can* talk about, though, is far more powerful *and* empowering than all the words of feeling, or analysis, or whatever. It's something completely different, and it comes straight from my heart; a pure act of giving from me to you. What I want to talk to you about is faith, Tariq. This is what I *can* do now; what I must share with you here—my duty as a Muslim. To tell you that faith can give you far more empowerment and support than any feelings you might get from me or from your own existential self-analysis and your writing and your thinking. Because sooner or later, there comes a point in a man's life when he must seek refuge in the only source that really helps: faith."

Kareem broke off and looked the other way, obviously put off by the bewildered look on my face. He remained silent for a few seconds, still not looking at me. Then he resumed his lecture: "Listen, Tariq, a year can bring an awful lot of change in a man's life, and the man talking to you tonight is a changed man. Let me tell you how it happened—the day I decided to turn to my Maker for guidance and help. Well, it was one of those sad gray days, when you wake up and take a long hard look at the world around you. And you know what *I* saw on that day? I saw fear, brother. It just hit me in my chest like a sledgehammer: fear, I realized, is the force that drives all these people around me—including *me*. Fear of losing my business; losing my fingers to the machines I use every day; losing my money and my standing—my wife, my children, my life. Fear, fear, fear. That's all I saw in that terrible moment. And then I realized how unrelenting and how terrible, and how *universal* the fact of fear is: you can see it written all over the faces you meet, all over the places you go. Then it just happened, and what a glorious thing it was. Suddenly, in an instant, it dawned on me: the question and the answer at the same time. What if I surrendered all my fears to Him who controls the whole universe? And you know what I saw in that short moment? By Allah, I saw all my fears vanish—no more doubt and terror. It was instantaneous. From that moment on, I knew what I had to do."

He stopped and appeared to stare into the circle of white tablecloth underneath the jasmine wreath centerpiece—rocking his torso ever so gently, like a preaching imam swaying to the rhythms of some mysterious inner music.

"And," I said, "do you—"

"Do I what?" he asked, startled, addressing Mouna, as if the surprise question had actually come from her. "Do I pray and observe the five pillars of Islam? You bet I do—every moment of my life, and you'd be..."

He broke off again and chose to elaborate on another point in his carefully prepared lecture: "Oh brother," he said, "if only you knew how easy it is to take that step and change your existence completely, opt for an altogether new world vision—move on to a place where the very idea of fear is banished."

Actually, I had wanted to ask him if the rest of his family had gotten serious about religion, too. My intention was not to be rude or disruptive. I was just curious about the potential lifestyle adjustments for everyone in this household, especially Mouna.

Mouna. She sat in complete silence during the entire lecture. I wondered how much she agreed with Kareem's newfound beliefs.

And what was going to become of her wardrobe, her hairdo, her physical appearance? Did she really know?

And the boys' RPG passion?

I wondered how the situation was going to develop for Mouna and the boys if he decided to get even more serious about his religion.

Meanwhile, Kareem kept on sermonizing about the main theme of the evening: fear and faith.

The candlelight shone in fitful pale highlights on the lines and ridges of his beautiful African face.

Suddenly, I was beginning to feel rather desperate and, yes, quite trapped—as trapped as a man with four flat tires on a deserted country road.

I thought, "Oh God, here I am sitting at the same table with my favorite brother and all I want to do is vanish."

Oddly enough, though, throughout Kareem's tedious reflections on his transformation (and on the need for everyone to experience the same inner revolution), I never gave up hope. I kept thinking that sooner or later he was going to start addressing me as a mature and equal human being and not as some sort of potential spiritual customer.

Well, that moment never came. As long as I was unwilling to get down on my knees and experience the same life-changing revelation that he had, I was *not* his equal; I was not worth inquiring about, sharing with, or even accepting.

"You know," he went on, "when I saw you at the airport—a father standing alone with his kids and no supportive wife by his side—my heart was filled with grief. And it wasn't just because of what I had heard—the terrible accusations that you had to endure. It was also because of what I was witnessing right before my eyes: the changes that had come over you. I was face to face with a man, my own brother, who was trapped, caged in his fear. That's when I began to pray for you, brother. I prayed to Allah that he might help you free yourself of your fear, and even as I prayed I was resolved to share my own experience with you."

Then, all at once, Mouna began to weep (very quietly) into her napkin, suppressing her sobs, her shoulders heaving gently: "Your brother suffered so much," she said to me.

Kareem raised his hand again, without even looking at his wife: "I suffered nothing. My suffering pales in comparison with what he has had to endure and *will* go on enduring at the hands of those ruthless people."

He fixed his eyes on me again and said, "Tariq, you are my brother, my own flesh and blood. I'd do anything for you, because this is what Islam *ordains*: to preserve the sacred 'bond of the womb' between siblings—'*seelat al-rahim.*' But I also need you to help me help you. And the best way you can help is by easing my conscience: I don't want to think of you as a lonely man living in an alien, alienating country, a man who has to face those unspeakable people every single day—all alone, a fragile *individual.*"

He was getting straight to the heart of the matter, like an eagle that had zeroed in on its prey and was ready to swoop down.

And Mouna—the brilliantly timed words that she managed to slip in: "You still have strong ties to your country."

"Ties to your country." Thouraya, of course. From where they stood, going back to Bordeaux with my former flame would be the perfect arrangement.

I looked down and started rapping on the table with my fingers. I was deeply disappointed.

That was when Kareem decided that it was time to stop, that it was now time to call the help and ask her to warm up the cold couscous.

"We've talked too much," he interjected. "Let's eat now and worry about the future later."

My brother was intimidated by my dismay, and when he proposed the outing to Qassar, his voice was artificially cordial and understated: "Come with me to Qassar," he said, a touch beseechingly. "Let's talk about the future, precisely. Tomorrow at the break of dawn. There's so much I want to tell you—so many truths that are going to help renew your life. It's not the old days anymore, I know, and you and I won't fool ourselves trying to pretend nothing has changed between us. But I'm sure it'll be the onset of a new day—for *you*."

———

With the blade of the oar, I kept pushing and maneuvering the cooler and the backpack toward the bow until they were neatly wedged between the hull and the hood.

I heard behind me the voice of my brother at the tiller, invoking God's help—his prayer like an echo from a pit: *Allahu anta almusta'aan, bism Illeh tawakkaltou 'ala Allah.*

And off we went, churning out of the harbor ahead of the fishermen, hugging the coast along the northeastern flank of the hills to our right—the half-naked hills of Korbous reflected in the purple sea in ocher streaks. High above the town square behind us, the dome of the sanctuary was snow-white even in the first sunrays, seamless and pure as a giant egg carefully set down on the hilltop. On the opposite side of the bay, the Spanish fortress was already bright and visible on the point of Jabbar.

———

When we entered the buoyage area, Kareem killed the engine and we rowed the rest of the way toward the shallows.

Then he anchored and we stood up and took off our windbreakers, stripping down to our swim trunks.

I crammed the clothes into the backpack and handed it to him as he swung himself out of the boat and turned around knee-deep in water with his hands thrust out toward me.

I handed him the backpack and he slung it across his shoulders and asked me to pass the cooler.

"I got it," I said.

I picked up the cooler and stood in the boat for a few seconds, contemplating the beauty of the cove—its handful of stilted huts and its pristine sands nestled between the two massive pillars of crag plunging from the cliff into the sea.

There was a careened skiff off to the right by the shore, just beyond the tidemark. Dry sea muck was spread out thin like a blackish paste over the wrinkled sand this side of the sugar-white beach.

We stood there side by side for a second, knee-deep in water, motionless. The sun was an unbroken shaft of ember-red blazing across the still sea.

I felt that I had to tell him about Thouraya right away, as if last night's conversation had not been interrupted.

I kept my gaze fixed on the shore as we sloshed through the shallows toward the beach with the sun already warm in our backs, glinting off the rippling water: "You people need to get over the whole Thouraya thing. She's a very independent-minded career woman. She cherishes her freedom more than anything or anybody. That was clearly understood between the two of us *before* we spent the night together."

"I don't know anything about Thouraya," he lied, looking straight ahead.

Snubbed with one single arrogant sentence.

Still, I felt that my words of admonition were some kind of vindication—one-sided and a bit petty, but satisfying nonetheless. I felt I had made it clear to Kareem that even though I was not as good with words as he was, I was perfectly capable of drawing a line in the sand when I saw encroachment.

"Come and pray with me first, Tariq. Let's put everything behind us and turn to God. There'll be time for the other things later."

Pray with me? I wanted to tell him. To what purpose? An agnostic has nothing to bring into *this* prayer—and ever since our student days, you have known and *accepted* me as an agnostic!

I did not say anything, of course, knowing full well that any form of opposition would only upset him further, and so I chose to submit and join in his prayer.

———

Self-contained, pacified, and powerful: that was how Kareem stood as he led the morning prayer.

He was, in short, everything I was struggling to become: a man who was capable of tapping into an inner source of strength and plenitude completely detached from any worldly being, no matter how powerful!

Was that why I wept? Was I mourning my own lack of inner resources, and certainty, and rootedness? Or was it the death of something between us that made me shed those tears?

As I bowed and knelt down with him, pressing my forehead against the sand, I found myself thinking of the flimsiness of my intellectual and artistic existence compared to Kareem's spiritual certitudes; remembering those long-forgotten words from a book my brother now cherished more than any given person or thing in our world: "*Ya laytani kountou touraba.*"

"*Would that I were dust!*"

As for Kareem, his voice was echoing with something altogether different as he recited the words of *Sourat al-Tariq*. The Sourat of the Nightly Visitant:

> "*By the heaven and the nightly visitant!*
> *Would that you knew who the nightly visitant is!*
> *It is the star of piercing brightness.*"

———

He said, "You say you're an agnostic, and because of that the Europeans see you differently? As someone who is secular and moderate—one of them, basically."

We were sitting on the narrow stairs of his hut and my neck was already beginning to ache from looking up and listening to my brother pontificate on the threshold of his fishing refuge. I stood up and took two steps back in the sand, facing him.

He looked down for a moment and paused, thinking, gathering momentum. When he looked back at me, his beautiful Moorish face appeared disappointed, or maybe saddened: "Your beliefs are completely irrelevant to them, Tariq. You could shout your secularism from the rooftops among the Christians of France; you could show it in the way you talk and walk, in your dress code, and your lifestyle. 'People, see me, hear me: I'm so happy that I'm *not* a practicing, mosque-going, Qur'an-packing Arab. Free at last! I'm now just a regular, average, totally invisible citizen of modern France—secular, agnostic, Republican.' But the problem is, French people, Europeans in general, don't *expect* you to be invisible; they don't *expect* you to be neutral. They want you to take sides, precisely, and be a Muslim *for* them. The last thing they want you to do is blur the boundaries. And you know why they don't want you to do that? It's because by blurring the boundaries, you're going to strip them of the one thing they need: a legitimate reason to build their entire existence around hating you, keeping you indefinitely detained even as you dwell in their midst and share in the fundamentals of their existence."

He was sitting cross-legged on a thin mat that he had spread across the threshold. His shorts were still damp from our swim.

The gap between my brother's athletic outward appearance and his preacher's poise and language was uncanny: it was hard for me to process the sight of him meandering in these long arguments, like a Sufi in a trance; and this new habit of his—rocking his upper body to some inaccessible inner rhythm—more than annoyed me, it now made me feel sad beyond expression. It was as if his nervous system was in the grip of a condition that I was just beginning to discover in him.

Kareem said, "I can sort of understand—the temptation for an Arab to go out of his way to exhibit his faithlessness in a land of Christians, especially a country as racist as France. It must indeed be very tempting to many—denying their religion and living in hope that someday those people, of their own accord, will say, 'Great, boy, you've done really well. You've earned your right to belong here and be one of us—unlike those Arabs of the *other* kind who are still stubbornly holding on to their roots.' Vain hope! In fact, the Europeans' thinking couldn't be more different; because whenever you endeavor to present yourself to them as a man who professes no religion, you're certain to get in a bind. They'll tell you, tacitly of course, 'Yes, granted you are a man of no religion. But are you an *Arab* man of no religion or a *European* man of no religion?' And how are you going to counter *that* sort of bigotry, *that* brand of torture? And this creepy madness that's going to eat its way into your soul is all *unspoken*: you'll see it in their insidious snubbing, their flabby handshaking, their cowardly backstabbing—but never in their *words*, written or spoken. For you, as a single man up there, that kind of secret psychological warfare is going to be very—corrosive. That's why I fear for you, brother: the invisible disease that'll creep like a fog from their scheming minds into the deepest, most hidden recesses of your existence. That's why I'm saying a new life with an Arab sister will be for you a sanctuary. Together, you'll be a sanctuary for—"

I had to interrupt him and put a quick comment in, although I must confess that, torso swaying or no, I was deeply fascinated by this extremely clever sermon posing as an intellectual argument. My interruption was shaky, lacking in conviction, and clichéd, but I felt

I had to remind him of his shockingly skewed vision of France and French people: "Funny," I said, "you make it all sound like a 'devilish' plot. Believe me, you don't have to fear for me being at the center of so much concerted action. People in France are a lot busier with their own lives than you think, brother. To hear you talk you'd think my having to act like an Arab—whatever *that* means—is a matter of life or death for them. I must say I find your view of French people both naïve and terribly unjust."

And based on so little direct knowledge of the French, I could have added, but I did not want to hurt his feelings.

"Talk about naivety! You have a dangerously unquestioning attitude toward the fundamentally negative core of the European mind, Tariq. And to think that you taught me more about philosophy and critical thinking than all my professors put together."

"Oh, come on. You know you have more intellectual gift than I—intellect *and* fiery eloquence; the Jaafari kind."

But he went on with his stupefying monologue as if he had not heard my words: "A man in your position," my brother said, "cannot afford to underestimate the power of negativity. You permanently need to keep in mind the power of organized hate to unify people, to help them define themselves, both as individuals and as a country, by excluding the non-European other. A man who pretends to ignore that basic aspect of the European mind will do so at his own risk. The awakening could be pretty terrible for you, Tariq. That's the painful reality I'm trying to make you see: the fact that you're probably still incapable of grasping the dark and ugly side of your life as a stranger in a land of exile. Plus, I want you to know that I'm not articulating this reality to dishearten you. Quite the contrary: my aim is to strengthen you against the ruthlessness of your enemies. You know the saying: 'Listen to the words that make you cry, not the words that make you laugh.'"

"And what's the remedy against the painful reality," I interjected, "if I don't want to be hurt by the horrible powers you describe? Building a French-free sanctuary with a Tunisian woman? Is that the solution? I must say I'm rather disappointed at the harshness of your judgment. I'm also disappointed on behalf of all the French people I know who have been simply wonderful. I mean, you've seen Zoé, for heaven's sake. She's a great woman. I'd do—"

"Tariq, my brother," he interrupted, standing up with the mat in his hand. He pivoted, tossed it behind him inside the cabin, and stepped down. "I have never uttered nor will I ever utter one single word of doubt about Zoé. She's Tunisian and Muslim. That makes her—"

"*Humane*," I almost shouted, "very humane. I'm sure you'll agree, right? At the end of the day, what she means to me has nothing to do with her beliefs—Jewish, Christian, Muslim, Buddhist. What difference does it make? Zoé is ultimately a *French*woman who happens to be amazingly, miraculously humane. I don't know what I would have done without her in those first days of.... Plus, just so you know, Zoé's mother is Christian. And so officially she was raised in a—"

"You don't have to explain anything, Tariq. You don't. I do respect your friend greatly. I hosted her in my home before and I will continue to do so—treat her as your friend. But how about the others? After all, it's *them* I'm talking about! The countless others who don't like who you are and what you stand for—not even the sound of your name."

Impatiently, I asked him to tell me again—about the solution, the "sanctuary": "So, the solution," I said, "what is it? Can you tell me now? Did you speak with Mourad?"

I knew where he was going with this all along, of course, but I found myself taking some sort of dubious delight in pushing him—getting him to spell things out once more for me.

Yet as soon as my words were spoken, I began to regret the irritation and strident sarcasm in my voice, feeling a pang of remorse at my tone even as I fired those questions at him. After all, this was Kareem: however unexpectedly overbearing and manipulative he had been, I knew that he loved me dearly, and I felt that it was my duty as a younger brother to show some understanding for his motives, however strange they were. The thought of my suffering was sheer torment for him. There was nothing manipulative about his suffering!

He said it again, gruff-voiced and weary this time, as if he was already beginning to give up on me: "As I said, the solution would be a new life with one of your sisters in the faith." After a few seconds of hesitation, he added that he had had a long discussion with Mourad: "It wasn't easy, but I did win *him* over. Your conscience is your guide," he added, as he went behind the hut to pick up the plastic crates.

He sounded both high-handed and self-satisfied saying those closing words.

Kareem: "Oh, I understand. I see your point. They do have the laws and the democratic institutions. I'm not questioning that. *What I'm saying is, even though those high and noble places are quite visible and quite undeniable as great achievements of civilization, they're not where the* real *battlefield is. The battlefield is your dirty one-on-one struggle against the countless wicked creatures who will do nothing* but *bypass the laws and the institutions in their small, daily private dealings with you: those dreadfully banal unrecorded confrontations when you have to face them and do business with them and be confronted with their insidious tactics—*day in day out. *Or worse still, those moments when you turn your back to them and they start working on you, conspiring against you in the shadows. Tell me, how are you going to fight that sort of unwitnessed, unrecorded injustice? What court is going to hear you? What advocate is going to defend you or purvey your voice?"*

We were walking toward the beach down the familiar sandy path—that gentle sloping ridge at the hook-shaped tip of the eastern bluff; heading for the rocky shallows where Kareem had laid his octopus pots two days ago.

It was a day of sirocco, and the dry southerly wind was now beginning to ruffle the surface of the sea and whip back the crests of the little morning waves, blowing so low and steady over the water that all you saw from above were the shifting patches of shudders and wrinkles across the water, like the random patterns stirred up by schools of sardines when they travel on the surface. The foam on the wave crests was of the purest, starkest white and the surface an immaculate infinity of indigo.

Walking between the ferns, down the path we had taken countless times together—as kids, teenagers, young men—in our "rock-fishing" days.

But now there was not even the remembrance to talk about. It was all a ghostly parody of those days—and that was the worst sting of all. In some deep, damp, and disconsolate place within us, we both knew that the very recollection was going to be forever polluted in our minds, that there was no longer any room for even a vaguely nostalgic conversation, however perfunctory or shallow.

That unspoken knowledge was stalking us every step of the way, in this ravishing scene; and yes, I thought, it is irrevocably killing something in us that has been hallowed by time itself—something meaningful and beautiful and precious.

It certainly did kill something in me.

———

The day after, Kareem dropped me off at our mother's house. Significantly, he did not come in with me, and so the last time that I saw him in her garden was during the get-together she mysteriously billed as "the send-off party."

He looked at me only once that evening in Rades, with a slow smile that lit up his fine Moorish features. I knew the meaning of that smile, of course: it was the pitying smile of the righteous man, the pacified man, the man who had finally found his place in the universe.

There were no words spoken that night except for our final good-bye with its vacuous gestures and wishes. We both knew that from here on out there would be nothing but mutual disappointment between the two of us, and the knowledge pained us both.

As I stood by the gate and watched him drive away in the late afternoon, I had a sudden flashback—a snapshot memory of him from years ago, when I was in my late teens: we were watching Hitchcock's *The Birds* at home with Heend.

There was a scene in the film that terrified me—the sight of the hero's former lover sprawled before her front porch with her eyes gouged out by the crazed birds.

Kareem had immediately absorbed my pain, like a blotter absorbing an ink stain. Then he blurted out this hilarious line: "I'll never see birds with the same eyes again!" he said in mock despair.

The three of us burst out in uproarious laughter, our tension gone in an instant.

Kareem was that kind of man. When we were young men, it was always so uplifting and exciting to hear him say, "Let's grab a bottle of whisky and hit the cliffs. It's rock-fishing time!"

Now I hardly knew what kind of man the *future* Kareem was going to be—the kind of thinker he was going to turn himself into. At this moment, though, one thing was clear in my mind: things between us would never be the same again—not the fellowship of the sea, not the unspoken support, not the rugged camaraderie.

He had become a sort of slave to a system of thought that he cherished much more than our shared memories. Now everything and everyone had to fit within the confines of that system or drop into oblivion.

———

(I still remember us rowing out to sea just before sundown as we headed back to Korbous. Once beyond the buoyage area, my brother cranked the engine and we began to pick up speed. Feeling the dry *t'rabi* breeze on my face, contemplating the snow-white furrow of the wake: for an instant, it did feel "like in the old days," as mother had said.

But the words that came from my brother in that moment were decidedly new and unsettling in their newness, uttered like mechanical pronouncements in an alien, confusing tongue: "Oh brother," he said, raising his voice over the din of the engine, "so much trouble all around us, and yet the remedy is within everyone's reach. Whatever you decide, Tariq, do not forget to seek guidance from God. Let God be your first recourse, always. The moment you decide to turn to Him for guidance, you'll see mountains of trouble crumble in an instant.")

———

Nour came to greet me as I walked through the gate: "We're taking the boys to the promenade in a horse buggy, but don't tell them!"

She looked at my sons furtively and laughed. They were eating watermelon under the mulberry tree.

"We're doing it in style," she said. "The day you got back from Carthage, I went and talked to Boubakkar—the carter, you know."

"Oh yes, I know *him*. And so what are you all up to *now*?" I added as I hugged the boys and greeted mother.

"Romantic magic," mother interjected mysteriously with a giggle.

Nour's face lit up with a naughty smile: "Boubakkar is diversifying," she explained. "He's now in the horse-buggy rental business—for weddings *and* romantic outings. His words. He said 'romantic'—"

"And circumcisions!" mother added.

We all burst out laughing at that last addition, and I simply thought, "What a relief. What a wonderful change from Kareem's silly manipulative pontifications."

———

Later, Boubakkar and his son came and parked their elegant buggy by the gate. I went out to greet them and converse with Boubakkar.

"I'm going to let Muhammad here handle the buggy," he said. "He's good with the horses, and he'll let your boys try their hands at it if they feel like it."

Then it was the boys' turn to be brought out by my sister for their "surprise," with Latifa and mother standing behind the gate, and Haroon saying it was "like a story horse," and Shams so excited and jumping: "Can I drive? Please, Dad? Will you let me drive?"

Then he started to balance himself on the running board, and I told him to climb down: "Please, no acting on your own, son! Let Muhammad *instruct* you. He'll show you the ropes. You're all going with him and I'm staying here with Oummi. I want you boys to mind Muhammad and be on your best behavior, promise?"

"Promise," they both said.

———

"And did you dice the garlic?" mother asks.

"Everything is ready," Latifa says, a tad impatient.

"It's not quite the same when you press it—the garlic."

She says these words for my benefit, with her eyes closed. She does not rise from the swing chair.

There is an age-old rust-colored gash in the mulberry trunk just behind her head—the broken bark raised and twisted like a scabby welt, with the long-dry trickle of sap still marked in a dark solidified drip trail frozen in the middle of the cleft.

The shadows in the garden are long, the brick tiles cooling under my bare feet, the stillness uncanny now that the boys are gone.

It is all too tempting to sit in this jasmine scented peace and not do anything but smell the plants come to life again, their sweet perfumes borne on the sea breeze. But the mutton-neck broth has to cook for more than an hour, she says, and the bed of rice and bread chunks on which it was to be poured out had to be prepared separately and placed in a serving plate.

I say, "All right, Latifa prepared the ingredients and you'll mix and cook, but I get to break up the bread chunks for the fatta while I hang around in the kitchen. I can't stand being idle, you know me."

Mother answers with her eyes still closed: "No, you won't," she says in an out-of-tune singsong, "not as long as I'm mistress of this house. After all, you are our guest of honor, our stellar philosopher-poet—and I want to give you the royal treatment."

"But I am not a king," I protest, sheepishly. And suddenly (irrationally, stupidly), I want to scream it in her face: "Just a man. I am just a miserably flawed man, who has tried again and again—and failed every time he tried; a desperate man who would be infinitely happier if he managed to take one last gamble on his stupid bumbling self."

Instead, I say, "You're getting carried away, mother. That's not like you."
This strange shift in my mood, like mud stirred at the bottom of a pond.

Right now I know what I need: Thouraya's weed—help myself feel freer, lighter, more detached. And so I just stand up abruptly and tell her that I will catch up with her in the kitchen—in a couple of minutes.

Mother opens her eyes and looks up at me—both hurt and confused, but she manages to nod in consent.

I just turn around and walk off toward the stairs behind her house.

After my terrace smoke: by the time I begin to think of facing mother again, I am feeling detached and aloof—in the best way possible, as when, in a moment of self-transcendence, you manage to view the network of human affairs at once with benevolence and knowing distance, like an artist contemplating the luminescent lines and links of a string drawing.

I go back into her house through the kitchen veranda. She has thrown the kitchen door wide open and the air all around the veranda is warm and tender with the brass-and-chives redolence of fried garlic.

(Memory flash as I stand on her sunset-gilded veranda: noontime in the cold damp winter days—back from school and stomping through the garden with the straps of my schoolbag chafing my shoulders. Looking up toward the smell and the kitchen clatter—the frosty condensation on the window panes; the numbing chill in my nose and my fists dug deep into my pockets; the thought of coming in from the cold—standing among the steaming pots and the rising smells and noises of lunchtime; my siblings bustling in the kitchen around mother, as usual, their school stories floating pell-mell in the spice-saturated air.)

Now the sun's waning mirror-play on the copper pans on her walls. And as I stand in the middle of mother's kitchen, I have enough time to glimpse the rounded fireplace in the eastern corner of her living room—the garnet sunray refracted above the wood box as through a prism, slanting across the peacock-tail bouquet of dried thistles in their green vase, the ash of last winter's fires (flattened across the hearth), the soot-streaked bricks in the back.

Mother's winter corner.

She steps back in from the bathroom and shuts the door behind her, the ray shrinking into a crimson spot on the door panel.

With no particular intention in her voice, she says, "You missed the fry-up."

"Well, I'm right here for the rest of it, am I not?"

I utter the words in a semi-whisper, with a chastised smile on my lips, looking outside her door—toward the tomato trellis by the stairs, the vines in the gathering twilight like tattered sheets of ink-blue silk dripping with clots of poppy red.

(It isn't "sorry," but the whisper is the closest thing to an apology that I can think of at the moment.)

"Actually," I add, "there was a moment there when I felt a bit overwhelmed by the excitement—the carriage and all. I guess I just wanted to be alone with my thoughts for a minute."

Mercifully, tactfully, she changes the subject back to the cooking: "Have you tried putting in the cardamom and the myrrh with the onion—right when you pour in the broth water? And the sprinkle of vinegar comes in last, over the fatta—before you lay out the meat."

All this is hardly a lecture, of course: just a well-rehearsed ritual of playful teasing; and her coy and indirect way of fishing for compliments.

How can I not indulge her?

So I laugh and tell her what she wants to hear, responding as I always have, many times before, in some sort of exaggerated comical-histrionic outburst of exasperation, which is also a mock admission of my utter inferiority: "I've said it before, mother. My mittaouma will never, ever be as good as yours. Never!"

She just stirs the broth and laughs in her deep, resonant way, still looking into the pot—too flattered to turn around.

Somehow it feels so naturally easy here—to be standing, hovering above time and matter, as it were, in this clement, plentiful haze of nowhere, leaning with *my shoulder against her door jamb—standing at the fuzzy borderline between the steamy kitchen and the awakening freshness of the sea night in her garden.*

The kitchen is darkening in the twilight, and it is becoming hard to make out her features. Still, I can easily feel my way toward some of her physical discomfort—the turquoise satin djellaba, darkened to silver, already sticking to her arms and between her shoulder blades; the stray locks of hair plastered to her forehead and her temples; the hard-to-breathe air, heavy with floating fat and oil particles—the vaguely tripe-like odor of half-raw mutton meat.

But then I also know the moment will come when she will call in Latifa and ask her to run a bath. And she will go to the bathroom and come out fresh and perfumed, sit under the mulberry tree with a sigh of contentment, a sprig of jasmine in her hand.

Then she will ask Latifa to set the table for dinner.

———

The two of us are having desert together under the tree, after my sisters have taken the children to bed.

Heend is spending the night at Nour's. She serves us coffee and samsa before they leave.

There is also a platter of fruit on the table: cantaloupe wedges, pieces of watermelon, figs, peach slices, and Indian figs.

Mother asks them to sit down with us.

"No, we can't," Nour says. "Honest, mother, we have to do a lot of chatting of our own, don't you know? We're going to put our heads together and revolutionize the world of relationships—and we've got just this one night to do it!"

And so they leave as they have come—joking and giggling; and just after they shut the gate, Nour puts her face between the bars and tell us to be good and not go to bed too late: "We're coming to pick you up really early. Like the old days, mother. Breakfast on the beach: coffee, toast, honey, and everything. At sunrise. The boys will run around with their cousins like wild horses. Exactly at sunrise. It's going to be a lot of fun!"

They are still laughing as they turn the corner, around the acacia tree and along mother's fence—the fence that was dipping each year closer to the sidewalk: she will not hear talk of setting it straight again.

"And lose this gorgeous curtain of honeysuckle and wisteria? Never!"

———

"Faith," mother says. "More of it, less of it. Who's counting? And who's to say—how much of it a person actually has, and how he's putting it into action. But you can't blame him, can you? He's just discovering something larger than life and all its actors within himself, like a new country. He needs to go all the way before he can find the right measure of spiritual fervor."

"I'm not blaming him, mother."

"I know you're not. The way I see it, some people may express their faith non-religiously, through their deeds, while others do it through prayer. Some may even carry it on the inside, in silent contemplation. Who's to say which is the higher spiritual path?"

———

I tell her that I need to check on the boys: "I'll be back in a minute."

I do take the time to smoke some more, though, out on the terrace.

From where I am standing, I can see her in fragments, sitting in silence under the tiny tree lights: that Persian hair in which she takes so much pride, oiled and combed into a tight bun, glancing with a dull sheen, like a leather flying cap; that sunny Nigerian gown, like a huge pumpkin flower draped about her waist and legs, flaring in a circle of golden light all around her invisible feet.

I cannot help wondering: how long it took her to tame her inner rages, to reach the state of quietude that allows her to sit like this, quiet and at peace in her garden.

Then I find myself caught in another tangle of remembrance—thinking of how I grew up in her house as a child and teenager: responsible and compromise-minded beyond my years; incessantly haunted by that look of tormented waiting in her sad, skittish eyes (the torture of always expecting someone she both dreads and cherishes—the rusty buzz of her doorbell, the late-night ring of her telephone, the dreadful knock that never came—the impossible visit of the man who, with each passing day, was becoming a total stranger to her).

Standing above her on the terrace, I find it easy now, rewarding, and mercifully "pain-free" to imagine and give substance to the countenance of this woman, sitting under her tree on a breezy summer night: the poise and peace on her dimpled face no longer rehearsed—the composure of a woman who has harrowed the fiery stretches of her own secret hell.

Her own new country.

———

It was a bittersweet "send-off bash"—quite odd, in a semi-hypocritical unspoken way.

My siblings, their spouses, their children and their friends all came, but they had this unnerving way of showing up and leaving at different times.

They were like delegations—coming to display some vague and shaky sense of allegiance.

The shallowness of our conversations was awfully depressing, but also quite understandable. After all, my siblings and their friends were saying good bye to a man whose life had undergone a traumatizing transformation.

To my intensely conservative upper-middle-class siblings and their spouses, the complications of my situation must have appeared terrifying—and deeply depressing.

Before she left with Khaleel and their son Ahmad, Heend told me that she would pick us up tomorrow. She handed me a USB stick: "There's lots of junk on it. Don't read it—too embarrassing."

"So why are you giving it to me?" I teased.

"Oh, come on, don't be such an arrogant rogue," she said, with real irritation in her voice.

I did not blame her for the tone, though. I knew the cryptic fear lurking behind the irritation only all too well. Her words were not uttered in anger. It was nervousness—the kind that we all suffered from. Fear of separation expressed as extreme irritation. The peevish words were Heend's secret tears.

"What's the title of the story?" I asked.

"A Tree with a Dream." Be tough, please, but don't forget that it's only a first draft. It's still very, very rough. Plus, I'm not a style-obsessed *artist* like you. I just don't have the patience for that. I guess I just enjoy telling stories—that's it."

———

I saved Heend's story on my desktop later that same night, but I never got around to reading it.

I opened the file and read it when I moved to Brittany, though, revisiting it several times since:

A Tree with a Dream

We were putting our school things into our bags with the mechanical sullenness of yet another cold school morning when Ahmed started calling.

"Amina, Amina, come see what I've got for you!"

As far as Amina was concerned, whatever he's got for her was worth opening the window for.

("For heaven's sake, Amina, can't you wait till we're out in the *garden*, with our *coats* on?")

But not Amina. Ever since she had lost her leg on that paddle boat in the Louisiana bayou, she developed a bizarre addiction to Ahmed's monstrosities. Actually, it always seemed to me there was more to their relationship than just the mechanical bond of addictive need—something more consistent, almost systematically principled, a sort of unspoken pact sealed in tender agreement. Fueled by her irresistible charm, Ahmed's twisted fantasy was constantly driven by the wildest schemes. He would sit for hours under the red ant- and termite-infested pomegranate trees, pondering over something new he would have for Amina, while his tea bubbled away on its ashen embers, evaporating into hellish pitch. There, amid the intoxicating fumes of terminal caramel and carbonized weed, Ahmed's ecstatic labor would yield the most gruesome conceptions: things that never failed to light Amina's eyes with a spark of malicious joy.

With a mixture of hedonistic appetite and experimental rigor, she would help him put a scarab on stilts by taping its legs to evenly cut straws. Then they would sit and contemplate the dance of the scarab, its overwhelmed motor system choking with the drunkenness of unaccustomed heights. They would put a lettuce leaf at the end of a strip of mica thickly daubed with super glue and watch a slug inch toward the goal with increasing slowness till it lay completely flat and still in its fatal ripples of solidified jelly. They would observe it for days slumping into the stupors of dehydration and famine. Some Sunday afternoons you would find them munching red ant pralines under the pomegranate trees. One day in advance Ahmed would put a wok under the pomegranate trees and pour honey into it. By Sunday afternoon there would be thick lines of industrious, anal ants heading systematically to perdition. Then Amina would come and watch Ahmed start the fire. He would pick up the wok, left hand on his hip, and tip it with a dramatic flourish for her to see. Holding the wok over the fire, he would throw in a bar of butter to break the mass of honey. As soon as the mixture started sizzling, he would start stirring with a wooden spatula, till it broke up into amorphous clumps of red ants prematurely fossilized in half-charred candy.

Those were some of the ways my sister started relating to the living world after she lost her leg to that Cajun alligator. It was in the summer before I started going to high school. I remember Mother crying on the phone when I came in. She was talking to Grandmother, who lived in Alexandria, Egypt.

"He said he can't make a strong case against the state. All the experts he consulted told him it had *never* happened before. They *never* attack unless they feel threatened—plus, he said the guard *saw* her lean over and poke it with a *stick*. [Pause. Sobs.] He said he'll see to it that the state takes care of the expenses the policy doesn't cover. I told him I will *not* have her [pause, more sobs] carry anything synthetic in her body and be barren for the rest of her life."

Later that evening, she told us more about this American attorney, Mr. James Ehrlich. She said he could not understand how she was going to act against her daughter's will and disfigure her for the rest of her life, forcing on her an outrageous stick instead of a state-of-the-art prosthesis. When it was obvious that all his scientific-aesthetic arguments were wasted on her, when he realized there was no way he could convince her that there was no link whatsoever between synthetic material and the fertility of her daughter—that, as a matter of fact, the best way to make sure the young woman got *inseminated* in the first place was to supplement her fertility with the decent likeness of a leg—he let Amina talk to her. With tears in her eyes, Mother told us how our mutilated sister cried and moaned and begged her to let her have a more credible version of her vanished limb. First, she didn't even know how to *discuss* it with her. But as the painful conversation dragged on, as she felt her resolve waver under the weight of our sister's tortured entreaties, she *ordered* her to arm herself with the memory of her ancestress and namesake Amina Bayram, who had to wear the painted egg of a swallow for a left eye and was still so beautiful she managed to win the heart of a Mongolian prince. Now the attorney was back on the phone, telling Mother that since she decided to go for wood, he would suggest something from South Carolina, his native state. A very distinguished type of wood. It was so tough the legendary Andrew Jackson, a man who lived constantly in the eye of a hurricane, was nicknamed after it. And, by the way, while she was talking to Amina he had made a few calls. A museum in New York could get an artist from San Francisco to carve and paint Amina's leg. We would split 50 percent of all exhibit and reproduction rights with the artist; the other half would go to the museum. When/if she outgrew the leg, though, she would have to "donate" it to the museum. She told him she would check with the family first. She'd call him back tomorrow. Then she called Grandmother, who was thoroughly scandalized that she would even *think* of settling for hickory. No matter how presidential it was, a hickory leg could *never* equal the bludgeon of her ancestor, the great Barbarossa II of Algiers! As to the carvings of this artist, they could not compare with what the wild hand of *History* had carved, painted, and bas-reliefed into a bludgeon that had faced the furious claws of polar bears, the copper padlocks of thrice-bewitched Indonesian coffers, the hermetic skulls of ambitious Dutchmen—flying, sailing, and otherwise transported...With such a leg Amina would conquer the New York museum *and* the Smithsonian! She was going to send her brother to New Orleans right away, with the future leg.

The day after, Uncle Yunis called Father. The director of the orthopedics division said he was washing his hands of the whole thing. Now he could perfectly understand how the attorney could handle all this craziness—otherwise how could he *be* an attorney; but what he was asking *him* to do was not only an affront to his humanity, it was also professionally devastating. Considering the gravity of the situation, however, the board of trustees would consider renting him clinical space, surgical equipment, and paramedical staff—provided he took care of hiring the services of an orthopedist with a valid license issued or approved by the National Medical Association. Just a moment ago, Mr. Ehrlich had his secretary contact the major TV networks to see if they could broadcast an emergency ad/announcement. Since CNN had covered Amina's story, they agreed to run the ad. He'd let us know as soon as they found somebody.

When Father was done briefing us, Muhammad switched to CNN. Hours later, I was struggling to keep up with the "grownups." Coffee, chocolate, candy—nothing could keep me awake. In the morning Mother woke me for breakfast. Uncle Yunis and Mr. Ehrlich had found a doctor. Amina's doctor was a Navaho American who told Uncle Yunis that he believed in a certain spiritual continuity between the human body and the organic realm in general—although he didn't really say if he believed in the relation between chronic barrenness and the partial synthecization of the body. Anyway, she was now assured once and for all. Thank God, now she knew her poor little child was in good hands. She'd be back with us as soon as she was done with rehabilitation.

As it turned out, rehabilitation started rather vigorously for Amina—at least by Uncle Yunis's standards. Later, he told Mother how impressed he was by the first signs of her recovery. Shortly after the operation, when he asked her what she wished for a convalescence present, she told him she had heard in the news that the guards finally found the alligator. He had slowly choked to death on a fragment of her tibia. She wanted to have him for a suitcase. Although he knew he could not refuse the sacred wish of a convalescent, secretly he had to admit that his little niece's was a rather odd (not to mention embarrassing) convalescence present. You know how it is, Mariam—had she asked for it in Egypt, it would have been a *totally* different matter. But in a country where people are religiously fussy about their zoological patrimony... Much to his delight, when he could finally get himself to *confess* Amina's wish to the Navaho doctor, the latter answered his concerns with the acquired eloquence of Anglo-Saxon lawyers. Amina's wish was not only a legitimate consumer *right* in a free country, his brother, an herbal pharmacist, would gladly help her *fulfill* that right. Except for gutting the alligator and using his brain for the tanning, his brother was capable of preserving him in as natural a state as possible—thanks to an express-embalming technique he had learned in a colloquium of Native American pharmacologists at Chichén Itzá, in Yucatán. But when the three of them went to claim the suitcase-to-be, the park officials told them they'd have to wait a few hours before they could *buy* it at auction. For hours he had to battle all sorts of potential owners: peculiar collectors of the Hitchcockian bachelor type, bloodthirsty sensationalists of the X-rated type, traumatized Vietnam War veterans, angelic environmentalists. Finally, he managed to save the alligator from his last opponent, the sales manager of a particularly aggressive company specializing in the manufacture of sadomasochistic paraphernalia. While America's private

consciousness was still high on the media hype, they were trying to market the first-rate fetishistic value of Amina's accident
by processing the animal into luxury scourges, whips, handcuffs,
anklets, and amulets—each item coming with a picturesque narrative presenting the historical background of the artifact.

As long as she was in New Orleans, Amina's accident was, in a
way, an abstract *event*. It was only when she came back that I started
living the full extent of her pain and the profound change that
came with it. Every night she woke up in a swelter, holding her leg
and screaming. One night, as we stood motionless around her bed,
we saw Father cry for the first time. He was sitting on the edge of
the bed with his hand on her head, his face blank, his chin dripping with tears. That was when she asked Mother to let her sleep
in my room. It took her many days before she could manage her
nightmares. For a long time I would wake up with a start and find
her sitting in bed, her hands clutching her leg, her face distorted
with agony. Those were the most painful moments for me—when
I saw her mutilated, disfigured, slipping away from me with only
the frail light of a lamp and the vague contours of a rug between
us. And the stubborn stillness of the night still ringing with her
scream. Then one night, when I could not choke my fear any longer, I went to her and buried my face in her hair—as much to hug
her and soothe her as to be hugged and soothed by her. Choking
on my own tears, my chest still pounding, I held on to her firmly—
as if to keep her from drifting. With an eloquence born of despair,
I told her that together we could chase away the horrors inhabiting
the night, together we could people the darkness with fistfuls of
star dust and talk the hours of despair into broad daylight—if only
she would open up and tell me.

Since that night, we would lie together in bed, hand in hand. She
told me how as soon as she went to sleep her leg started *getting* all
kinds of things—like people who get stuff in their eyes all the time,
you know. She just could not help it. All day long she kept thinking
of it for hours, telling herself that it was just a piece of dead wood.
Every night, she would go on and on reminding herself that she was
sleeping under a roof, that her leg was really nothing more than a

piece of *dead* wood lying on a mattress, tucked safely under a blanket. But the nightmares came every night, and every night she found herself somewhere outdoors. When her leg was green it was snails. She could *feel* them sliding up her leg ever so slowly. The tickle was unbearable. In the middle of the dreams she kept telling herself she had to shake them off. But she just *could not* get her leg to come off the ground. It was as if it had roots. When her leg was cracked and dry it was termites. She felt them *everywhere* drilling their way into the scabby cracks, then into the muscles and the bones. It was like thousands and thousands of long, hot needles driven in at the same time...As her voice started drifting into a sleepy drone, I would lie there holding her hand in the stillness. I had developed a special sensitivity to her dreams in my sleep. With the first twitches I would sit up and shake her.

One night, after I woke her, she lay on her back, smiling. It was the first time I had seen her smile since she came back from New Orleans.

"I was wearing a gas mask and there was a *huge* can of pesticide next to me. So I started fumigating the hell out of them. It felt so *good*. You should've seen the bastards. They were all over the place. Dead—perfectly *dead*."

Amina leaned back on the sill, window wide open and blinds flapping back and forth.

"He said this time it's really—"

"God, Amina, how about closing that window *first!*"

When I leaned over to hook the blinds, he was still looking up, his weathered tuft of canary feathers like a dissolving wisp of sulfur smoke stealing between the endless creases of his stark white turban.

After breakfast, we found him waiting for us in the courtyard. Amina was hard at his heels, her wooden leg stomping with a thud when it went between the cobbles.

"See there?" He pointed in the direction of the peach tree. All I could see was the pitchfork standing upside down like a candelabra next to the tree. Amina must have seen it first, because she went hopping along even when Ahmed stood behind. I came closer too, and there it was, hanging at the end of a silver branch propped on the prongs of the pitchfork. Ahmed stood close by.

"I saw it this morning. I thought, first thing let's keep that branch propped. Then I stepped out of the mulch and recited the prayer of thanksgiving right here on the dirt. But what I still can't figure out is how on earth the branch didn't snap with the night frost and all. This thing is *bigger* than a mango!"

As he rattled on we stood there completely still, our eyes riveted on this twist in the order of things, this winter chimera, this unbelievable peach of January. There was something about it both crippling and enchanting as it hung among the maroon twigs speckled with scabby spots where the leaves had come off in the fall. Its fuzz was so bristly in the crisp cold it shone like a translucent film of silver haze over the burgundy blush. Like a sleepwalker, Amina stepped up to the pitchfork, holding onto the handle, her leg sinking into the mulch and wet dirt. She too had a deep flush I had never seen so intense on her amber skin. She leaned over the fruit, her face coming close, her nostrils twitching.

"By God this peach is mine. I swear it's all mine." Saying it she sounded both wistful and resolute, as if she were whispering a tender, secret vow to someone hiding close by.

"Of *course* it is!" said Ahmed. "Go tell Mrs. Mariam, now. Tell her the peach tree's had a dream."

"What?" I was awake at last, suddenly wanting to know what all this was about.

"Yes, sir. Trees dream all the time. But, with luck, a *good* dream happens only once in a thousand years."

That day we didn't go to school. All day long Father and Mother were on the phone. Being the farmer's daughter she was, Mother wanted to call Aunt Najia first—before she went on the air. She wanted "our tree" to get an announcement in *The Voice of Nature*, Aunt Najia's program. At once Aunt Najia decided to reschedule everything she had prepared for this morning. Through the receiver you could hear the frantic buzz of her voice. She thought the best way to rearrange the program was to make it sound like a casual spur-of-the-moment call. Aunt Najia would run it as a spontaneous interview where Mother would basically try to sound casually entertaining, anecdotal. Yes, entertaining, casual, and anecdotal are the words. Keep this in mind: most of the listeners are farmers, taxi drivers, and janitors. Nothing factual, drily formal—or informative, for that matter. Just keep feeding them all that folksy stuff.

I positioned myself on the staircase, at what I thought was the middle point between my room and the living room. I sat there with my face stuck in the balustrade, watching Mother all tensed up on the couch while Aunt Najia's velvet voice cooed through the open door upstairs. Everybody else was sitting around Mother.

"This morning I received a *very* special call from a *very* special listener. It was my sister who wanted to share a *fabulous* event with me—something that happened *right* in her garden. When she told me the whole story I was simply *dumb*founded. I said, you know, Mariam—you *have* to share this with our listeners. You can*not* avoid it. Well, after some hesitation, she agreed and that was that. So I decided to reschedule today's program and let my sister tell you about this *unique* story. She'll be calling us right after this. Stay tuned for the story of the year—sorry, the story of the *millennium!*"

After the song and the commercials, Mother called in. She did most of the talking, Aunt Najia directing her occasionally with a few questions. She started talking about the dreamlife of trees. She said Grandfather used to tell many stories about the beliefs of Berber peasants. One day in the winter, when he was inspecting the orchard with Ahmed, the Berber supervisor, he saw a midgety almond on a twig. That was when Ahmed told him about the dreams of trees. He said the tree had had a bad dream—a dream that had yielded an abortive fruit. If you saw the abortive fruit and didn't nip it off immediately, you could see a great deal of misfortune for not easing the misery of the tree. And indeed the tree had good reason to feel miserable. Because it was the first in many of its kind and line to have a chance to do boundless good. Somewhere in the bowels of the earth, it seems, it was written that at the close of one thousand years in the life of a particular line of fruit tree, it befell only *one* tree to bear the dream of good luck and prosperity. Toward that goal, all the trees in the line would sacrifice their summer yield and go barren and leafless for an entire year, so that the chosen tree could keep all their sap and juices for itself to nurse its dream in the dead of winter. For all this sacrifice, nursing the winter dream is no easy matter, because somewhere in the bowels of the earth it is also written that, in order for the dream of the chosen tree to come to full fruition, it had to clash with the bad dreams of 999 descendants of other lines. Even the most exhaustive family tree analysis could not predict with *the faintest degree of probability* the time or place of such a rare fruit. Legend had it that for many years Ramses II spent sleepless, frustrated nights with a top-secret committee of Berber sages hopelessly trying to find out if any felicitous dream was due on his land during his lifetime. If Ramses II had chosen to trouble his sleep about a good dream for so many years, it was certainly worth his trouble, because whoever was lucky enough to spot the winter fruit in their orchard would see bonanza crops burst around them within a radius of 999 kilometers from the one-kilometer epicenter of the dream. The epicenter, a real agricultural orgy zone, was fated to bubble with indefinite fertility for one thousand years. The first person to touch the fruit would trigger an irreversible process of instantaneous growth, perennial foliation, and chronic fruitfulness all through the epicenter. Anything planted or sowed would grow almost immediately to vertiginous proportions, yielding again minutes after it was harvested or picked—on and on, relentlessly, for one thousand years, as long as there were pickers and harvesters. It was slightly different within the remaining 999-kilometer radius, where you could only grow the crops and trees of the area. And those were only the *direct* effects of the dream. The *side* effects would fan out from those who ate or touched the fruit, those who came into primary contact with them in *any* way, and those who directly or indirectly came into contact with the latter, down to one thousand persons. These individuals were called the "secondary carriers." They could spread the side effects of the dream through a line of 999 tertiary carriers, each of whom would carry the side effects to 999 people. From the eaters of the winter fruit a flood of good luck and prosperity would spread like a happy plague—the more they traveled and came into contact with other people, the more good luck and prosperity would spread around them: terminal cancers unexplainably terminated, doomed bridges suspending the fatal call of gravitation for a few crucial seconds, sagging shares rising to undreamed of heights...And those were just a few of the happenings she could think of—things that any infected person could cause without even *trying*. Obviously, the people who came into contact with the peach in a primary, secondary primary, and even millenary primary way could do much more than that...

As Mother went on listing the countless gradations and nuances of good luck and prosperity that came with the millenary infection, I saw Father stand up, almost jump past her, and fly up the stairs past me. What he should have predicted when Mother was rehearsing with Aunt Najia had finally dawned on him! I heard him speaking on the phone.

"This is the minister of defense. I'd like to speak to General Nadhir."

When he got through to General Nadhir he gave him his code name and asked him to send a company, a communications team, and a switchboard.

Mother was still on the phone, talking to Grandmother this time, when we heard Amina cry out. For a split second we stood dead still. From very far, it seemed, I could hear Mother's sharp, excited voice drop to a hoarse drawl.

"I'll call you later, Mother. All right? I'll call you later."

Then the twelve of us ran out to the garden to see all the trees in the orchard covered with leaves, their branches sagging with clusters of fruit. Amina stood next to a sapling.

"It's growing, it's growing!" she shouted. She had nipped a twig off a quince tree and was watching it grow by the second.

Father was the first to come to his senses. Now he knew that it was all true, that he had not called General Nadhir in vain, that his daughter was really the blessed carrier of a millenary plague of good luck and prosperity. Slowly, he walked up to her as the tree rose in the sallow January light, its first burgeons shining in their silver fuzz like minuscule buttons of satin. He knelt down before her and, with a trembling voice, asked her to touch his head. As soon as we got over the excitement of hugging, and kissing, and mutual touching, Father called the officer in charge of security. He had him place four guards around the tree.

The calling frenzy started even before the switchboard was installed. While Father was making invitation calls upstairs (the president, some family members, friends, and colleagues), Mother wanted to make sure *her* family flew in as soon as possible. She called Aunt Fatma in Ankara, knowing that if she called her first she would spare herself many other calls. Aunt Fatma's husband had his own airplane. They were going to pick up Grandmother and Uncle Yunis on their way. Then it was London. She could join Uncle Ali in his office. Then it was Uncle Salem in Scotland and Uncle Omar in Malaga. With those calls, she knew the "family that matters" wouldn't miss the event. I had never seen her talk with so much excitement. When she was done with the last call she said Grandmother was so enthusiastic she swore she would bring with her the lock of Josephine Bonaparte's hair. (It was a death-bed gift—or a plea for secrecy, she never knew—from her grand-father, Admiral Mourad Bayram, as he lay hopelessly besieged by the deadly swelters of Sudanese malaria.) We would burn it in the living room and with its smoke confound the global Evil Eye, which would soon be fully focused on our house.

Meanwhile, a commotion of apocalyptic proportions was raging outside. The troops, who, by now, had fully encircled our mansion, were pushing and threatening the onlookers who wanted to venture too close to the palisade. The news was spreading so fast. Amina and I grabbed Father's binoculars and ran to one of the balconies. Amina was the first to spot Mr. Ben Jaffar. She pointed in his direction and I zoomed in on him. He was still in his pajamas, and I saw a cellular phone in the pocket of his dressing-gown. He was busy checking a shrub with tiny clusters of what looked like small, tough dates. I had never seen a coffee shrub before, and it was only when I saw him crush the berries that I understood. Mr. Ben Jaffar was the biggest coffee importer in the country. Then he dialed a number and, wedging the phone between his shoulder and his cheekbone, he went on talking and picking the berries, which were replaced by new ones almost instantaneously. I gave the binoculars to Amina and went to the other end of the balcony. Beyond the thick circle of soldiers and armored cars I could see the crowd rushing with hysterical restlessness from one spot to another. As soon as a twig started growing there would be a roar of jubilation, the crowd would rush and form a huge circle, cheering, and then climaxing into chaotic tumult when the tree sprang up in their midst. All the streets were now choking in green. Then someone came up with the crazy idea. When they ran out of dirt surface they started throwing seeds and sticking green twigs into the deeper cracks of the bitumen. That's when the soldiers started getting very nervous. The situation was getting rapidly out of hand, and so far they had no orders except to protect our mansion. I saw an officer run through the gate. General Nadhir was inside. Then, shortly after he came out, I heard the evacuation order on the megaphones.

But the crowd was thoroughly intoxicated by the wonders of its creative drive, the new gushes of green now bursting in the middle of the bitumen, cracking the cobbled alleys and the driveways, overturning cars and palisades. It was not before they started moving on the trees with the tanks and firing rounds in the air that the soldiers could get the area cleared out. When the neighborhood was quiet again we heard the drone of a helicopter. It was the president.

It was not the only helicopter to have flown over our neighborhood that day. Most networks were covering the story. After lunch, Najib and Sami took the TV down to the game room (the communications team took over the TV room and the living area was already crowded with Father's guests) and we watched the news. The reports were already overwhelming. Almost every major TV network had its special show with its special guests: food industry experts, political analysts, military strategists, stock-exchange wizards, top executives of major airlines, EU ministers of agriculture, botanical geneticists. They were all speculating on the global impact of the event. All refuted vehemently the objectivity of this Ali Babaesque act of charlatanism—a piece of media vaudeville mounted by the Tunisian government to boost a sagging tourist industry and speed up ratification of the free-trade agreement still under consideration in Brussels. Still, despite worldwide agreement to deny the reality of our peach, despite all the nervous attempts to downplay the knock-on effects of the event through the frantic use of what a French propagandologist called "media counterevents"—despite all this, the president and the members of his cabinet kept constantly going back and forth between the living room and the TV room to confirm to the mighty men and women of this world that this peach story was truly a lie. One by one or in groups, our government officials would rush into the TV room, tell the same story, and come back with a new one.

In the meantime, Mother's family were arriving grouplet by grouplet, escorted by the Presidential Guards. Much to our surprise, Grandmother and her group, who didn't have to rely on commercial flights, were the last to arrive. She said she had *virtually* turned the house upside down and still could not find the lock. The only place left was the chest down in the cellar. When Hikmat and Fatma started worrying about its being late and all that, she told the servants to take the chest to the airport and load it into the airplane! Now we had to find the lock and burn it in the living room, and then she would proceed to the slicing of the peach. Father had two servants bring the chest from the truck. It was the sarcophagus of an unidentified Pharaoh princess—a convalescence present from the head of the Cairo Institute of Egyptology.

While the peach waited on a silver plate in the dining hall, we all stood there in the living room for what seemed like endless minutes, watching the children as they rummaged through the dusty chest. ("Let *them* look for it, Mariam. Don't you know their hands are guided by the angels? If they don't find it nobody will.")

It was Amina who found it in a small scallop-shaped mother-of-pearl box. Grandmother ordered the lock dipped in rose water and brought along with an incense burner. With religious pomp, Ahmed brought the lock and the incense burner on a tray of burnished copper. It was now late in the evening and the events of the day were reeling in my head like pictures whirling in the wind. When Grandmother ordered us on our knees, I suddenly felt a painful longing to lie down and let myself drift off to sleep. Kneeling there among this unbelievable congregation of an occasion, this human concoction born of faith and hard-headedness, the truth burst on me that one day I could wake up in a dark and lonely room with the unbearable burden of time lying on my soul like Grandmother's gaping chest. I looked up. Grandmother lifted the carved lid of the incense burner, threw in the lock, and spun it around three times. While the smell of charred bone filled the air of the living room, her voice cracked the stillness like a whip.

"God preserve us from the evil of those who tie the knots, the tracers of patterns in the sand! And now, to the dining hall!"

But Grandmother could not start slicing the peach yet. The secretary general of the United Nations wanted to speak to Father. When he came back with a transcription of the phone call, we were all standing around the dining hall table. Today, the Security Council had met in an emergency session. It had unanimously voted in favor of declaring Tunisia a "No-Access Zone." Financial experts were predicting the worst. All the major stock markets were already bubbling with the riotous fever of this peach of discord. In a matter of hours Tunisia had become the thumping nerve of a global hysteria. For the first time in history stock markets the world over were running round the clock. Literally every single minute in the life of this blasted peach had witnessed the birth of the wildest fantasies. Sharkish real estate wizards were rigging a virtual sale of huge tracts of Tunisian desert to wealthy Italians in quest of eternal youth. Unscrupulous speculators were destabilizing stock market indices, announcing all kinds of airy deals and dirt-cheap shipments, ranging from popped-on-the-cob corn to coffee roasted and flavored in the pod. Maoist nostalgics, vegetarian gurus, antimilitaristic save-the-whalers, and the Indian Association of Active and Dormant Fakirs had formed an across-borders coalition and were fanning the dying flame of protest in the hearts of sixty-eighters long converted to yuppyism and the new world order. Now they were hailing the advent of the *agri-cultural* revolution. In Worms, Germany, an underground coalition of millenarians and historical materialists had come out of the closet ("the times" being "ripe," as they put it), announcing the historical, economic, and spiritual necessity of a Lufthansa-sponsored mass pilgrimage to the "Land of Rebirth." All these crazy collective whims were creating the wildest air traffic patterns in the history of commercial aviation. On account of free competition and the dictates of supply and demand, the flights that weren't directed to our part of the world had suffered nauseating slumps into the bottomless pockets of devaluation.

He *must* realize, the secretary general went on, that if this situation goes on unchecked, it would automatically lead to a devaluation of the concept of wealth in general and, in the long run, the very concept of peaceful cohabitation between the social classes in the Free World. If the situation was not monitored by a multinational force, it could truly degenerate into what some countries were already calling the "Green *Blitzkrieg*." And, as a matter of fact, he was calling to tell him precisely about *that*. Considering the irrefutable fact that this peach business was taking a rather sour turn, the Security Council had also voted an emergency resolution putting it under UN control and banning any forms of contact with it. Consequently, and in view of the application of the resolution, he should expect a multinational force to begin evacuating the area located within the troubled one thousand–kilometer radius—namely, the Protected Zone designated by the declaration.

But Father, who by now knew more about the unimpeachable edicts of fate than the secretary general himself, told him he could identify with his dilemma all too well, having spent his life hunting down the hysterical rhetoric of false political prophets, the chimerical hopes of mock-green revolutions, and the bloody promises of genuine-red ones. Still, there was nothing that could be done about the sad irony of this terrible truth: whether this peach incident was a deplorably happy event or a happily deplorable one, it all depended on where you happened to be when the Green Lottery started cranking its numbers. What's more, as with all things chancy, the peach had now picked up a momentum of its own, and there was nothing he could do about that. That said, he had yet to inform him of the saddest of all ironies. His call had come too late. We had already eaten the peach. It seemed that this tragic event had been inscribed in the womb of time, and that nothing on earth could ever erase it.

We are not good at saying good-bye: that was what my mother and my siblings told me at different points during the send-off party, each in their own individual way.

Of course I knew that it was not evasiveness: severe fear of separation was a weakness that we all had in common. It was a legitimate excuse to which I related.

Still, I was disappointed that it was Heend alone who ended up saddled with the task of driving us to the airport.

Later that night, I kept telling myself that was how it had always been, that we all shared this intense fear of parting. And yet I could not dispel the nagging thought that my new circumstances provided ample justification for a departure from custom—an exceptional show of solidarity. The bitter self-pity that came with the thought rankled. It kept me awake all night.

And so it was Heend and the three of us, after all.

When we got to the terminal, she hugged and kissed my boys.

Then she turned to me: "Well, this is it," she said. "Let's say good-bye right here. Walk away and don't look back, Tariq. Please."

My sister's voice was desiccated and shaky, her face twisted with pain. I kissed her in silence and walked away.

North '07

*L*ove is a fool's pursuit, even when it is happy.
  Sooner or later, there comes a point in your life when the thought starts stirring in your mind and you begin to realize how much illusory belief goes into love, to understand that once upon a time—in the fairyland beginning, when you were still under the sway of its magic and mystery—you always found all sorts of clever and creative subterfuges to help you avoid this self-evident truth: the fact that love is ultimately nothing but a tapestry of illusions woven in the flimsy yarn of your self-centered fancies and fabrications, a side-effect of your own egotistical desire for self-transformation and rebirth—that giddy, long-forgotten belief in the miracle of a new beginning.

So what do you do when you wake up one day and find out that you are a victim of the side-effect?

If you are lucky, you will be able to pick up a pen, open your notebook, and embark on a meditation that begins with these words: "Love is a fool's pursuit, even when it is happy."

———

Looking back on the summer of 2007, I realize it was pure selfishness that compelled me to put the boys in my car and undertake the trip from Biarritz to Paris.

It was late August, and the mad chemistry of longing and lust was coursing through my whole being—my body, my memory, my dreams.

The lust and the longing: they felt rejuvenating and heart-quickening in spite of a vaguely guilty awareness of my infinite egotism, in spite of the humiliating one-sidedness of my fantasies. The random faces I met in town or at the beach: fancying their eyes locking with mine in a spark of wished-for meaning, picturing (in my vanity) a wildly romantic immediacy of attraction.

But the attraction was never there, and Biarritz gradually began to turn into a secret theater of humiliation in which I suffered from the combination of two terribly disharmonious forces: lust and lovelessness.

Thouraya had awakened a new spirit in me, and I welcomed it in the same way a sick man brightens up to the prospect of an unexpected recovery.

Still, deep down I knew very well that my expectations about meeting a woman in Biarritz were ultimately illusory, and the unrealistic fantasies that I built around those expectations ended up acting like a persistent force of uncertainty and self-doubt within me. Beneath the life-affirming drive of my desire, I sensed the sapping pull of diffidence the way a seasoned seaman intuits the silent force of an undercurrent: under the scrutinizing gaze of my conscience, in my deepest moments of self-searching, I came face to face with the power of my insecurity and the limitations imposed by reality.

That was how Biarritz grew oppressive to me.

Selfishly, I asked my sons, who loved Biarritz, if they fancied a trip to Paris.

They said yes.

Selfishly, I called Zoé and invited myself.

She accepted my self-invitation.

Before she hung up, my friend told me about a Billie Holiday sound-alike contest at the American Bar on Place de la Contrescarpe: "I went there on opening night," she said.

"How was it?" I asked.

"Very good! Would you like me to buy a ticket for you? It's actually a sort of table reservation voucher that you can purchase in advance."

"Great," I said. "That would be lovely. We'll settle up when I get there."

"Are you driving up here?"

"Yes. I'll have to head back on the twenty-ninth—of August. Regina will fly into Bordeaux. She's picking them up the day after. I'm going to call Sami and let him know: we'll open a couple of days later than usual this year."

"A vacation extension! *He's* going to be happy. By the way, when you get here don't even *think* of parking your car near the Panthéon—traffic has gotten crazy around here. Your best bet would be to skirt the Panthéon and head for the parking area by Place d'Italie. You can take a taxi from there."

———

That summer:

It seemed everyone in the city was romancing—kissing, eating out, strolling in the gardens and in the parks.

And amid all that romancing I did remember Zoé's admonition, of course: "Lock your heart and throw away the key," she had said. Still, I found it impossible to turn totally inward, to achieve a measure of self-contained peace—tame the fires of ego with some kind of neutral attitude toward the world of the others (all those lust-driven tourists exploring the town with so much joyous abandon).

It was a strange failure whose root cause I still have not been able to identify: to be not only obsessed by my own aloneness, but by the togetherness of others, too—those lucky fellow humans swarming around me in coupled constellations, conjoined in pairs of body and soul.

And the sheer sexual heat of them: every body radiating those intense energies of conjunction like a halo of health, power, and triumph. (Romance, the magical rites of togetherness, the pain of being an envious spectator in the shadows.)

That sense of being deprived of the beauty of fusion with a loved one is my most marking recollection from the second day of our visit—the day of Zoé's departure. The sexual longings inside me: they represented a wistful shift in my mood, my inner being; a certain giving in to primal desire that did indeed feel like the beginning of a rebirth.

And it was not lust only (this much I know), but something far richer: an aggregate of feelings both complex and confusing—as vague as the soft contours of the moon on a foggy night, when you cannot tell if it is the familiar luminary you are looking at or a mystifying silver smear in the sky.

The nameless alchemy of those bodies simply had that certain power of cryptic appeal—to stir and move me into a state of obsession beyond any conscious explanation. The effect they had on me was so profound that I found it impossible to tell myself if it was something in me or in the others—those transient tourist lovers who had come to be united (by chance or by design) under the same sky.

———

(There. As you stop and start reading what you have just written—your own retrospective reflections on the page—you realize, in the very act of beginning to write about love, how doomed the entire enterprise is, from the start; bogged down in the mushy excesses of the speaking tongue—that rambling swollenness of the verbal flow, that unbearable air of turgidity rising from the words as they begin to spill from your pen.

As soon as you start putting your thoughts about love in writing—these bizarre backward words of self-indulgence—you realize that one does not get better at reflecting about love as one "opens up," as one "self-analyzes" in and through the written word.

And the cause of the incapacity?

Possessive attachment. If love has come to hold so much tyrannical sway over our souls, our volitions, our bodies, it is because we have allowed all of its innate anarchy, its indefinite energies, to converge into one single purpose of the will: to *own*—the insane illusion that *having* someone is the highest expression of our being, the best hope in store for us.

And yet it has to be done somehow—the talk about love and its maze of illusions.

To accept, then, the reality of being tangled and trapped in its web again, as a witness this time—to succumb, once again, to the attraction of those words that you once lavished on love in your diary: the labyrinths of long-forgotten lines that you revisit and relive; the arabesques of your heedlessly naïve, totally unabashed mawkishness unfolding before your eyes, flourish by dim flourish.

The sweet, fevered sentimentalism—words and feelings that you never imagined revisiting in this way; the cloying redolence of those days rising from your diary page after page, like cheap perfume from a scented greeting card.)

———

The day I met her:

I first saw Annaelle on Place de la Contrescarpe, outside Zoé's apartment.

It was late afternoon and we were buying fruit on our way to Jardin des Plantes.

She was sampling an apricot at one of the food stalls and I found her intensely appealing right from the start. But it was she who approached us first, standing over Haroon with a small bunch of grapes proffered in her hand.

When he refused her offer, she decided to squat very close opposite him, plucking one grape and holding it out with a broad smile.

"Go ahead," I said, just as she asked him about his name.

"Haroon," he said to the tall, slender stranger without taking her grape.

"Would you like a grape?" I told my son.

Then to her: "I think he understood 'Go ahead and tell her your name.'"

To my ear, the words that I had just uttered sounded instantaneously silly and trivial—the awkward, artificial posturing of a man stalling for time.

Without shifting her weight, she directed her gaze toward me just as I spoke, her cheeks slightly flushed, her hand resting on the padded armrest of the stroller.

The gaze from her green-blue eyes was arresting, but it is the fluid movement in the arch of her curved eyebrows that lingers most vividly in my memory of our first encounter—their wavelike rise and fall punctuating a fascinating look that seemed to waver between outright mirth and veiled mischief.

And the expression of those slightly slanted dimples when she smiled: was it wry, rebellious, jocular?

It was impossible to decipher the meaning of it, of her, but that barely visible slant in her cheeks made the look she cast upon you daring if not deep— hauntingly open-ended, like a hanging sentence in your memory, a vaguely promising phrase that you have not managed to finish and put behind you.

———

She asked me if I was going to Jardin des Plantes, standing back up after Haroon had accepted her grape, putting the paper sack of fruit in her backpack.

Now I was even more at a loss for words and she had picked up on my confusion: "I know, I'm psychic—it takes some getting used to."

She laughed—an understated, aspirated, hesitant laugh, as if she feared offending me with a more frank outburst: "I'm just kidding. Actually, I overheard you talking to your sons. I'm going there, too."

———

I learned about Rue Gracieuse from her.

First, she told me the street had no name; then when I looked at her, she laughed a bit nervously: "No, that's not true. That was the first time I came here. I thought the street was just that—nameless; but the plaque is actually right where it belongs at the top of the street. You'll see it when we get there."

It was a very narrow cobblestone alley, sometimes not much wider than two paces.

"You must think I'm a shallow trivial person," she said.

"Why would I?"

"Well, here I am quipping again for no reason—not letting you get even with me on that first joke. Truth be told, it's only nervousness."

I smiled and looked at her as I went on pushing the stroller: "Why would you—why nervousness?"

"Approaching people isn't my forte to begin with. You know, barging in on you like that—not letting you put a word in edgewise."

"Oh, *that's* no problem at all—I'm not much of a talker anyway. Say, is this going to get narrower—and more ornate? Maybe I'm experiencing some sort of optical illusion here!"

I was talking about the tiny street, which seemed to be getting even tighter. Its stone walls were now decked with ivy, moss, and wolf lichen, with dwarf ferns in the gaps between the stones.

And it was perhaps more than just perceptual distortion, for the walls truly felt as if they were closing in on us with the blue sky above us looking remote and unlikely, like a tear in a canvas tent. Then there was the darkness and the downward slant of Rue Gracieuse. It felt as if we were descending into a cave.

"Are you sure this place can accommodate a rickshaw like ours?"

Her expression was suspended between a smile and a frown now—an unsteady frown, one might say.

"I'm the one who's kidding this time," I went on. "Actually, I love this alley. I never thought a place like this existed in this neighborhood. The gateways and the tiny courtyards—"

"And the vegetation on the walls."

"And the vegetation on the walls, yes. With a little bit of imagination, this could be a backstreet in Saint Emilion."

I wanted to keep the conversation going, so I started to tell her about the smell of Rue Gracieuse: a mix of moist clay and wine-cellar walls, I said.

Annaelle half-looked at me with a smile and a skeptical hitch in her eyebrows: "Mossy," she just said, sounding curt and perfunctory—as if, now that she had made the effort of approaching us, she either wanted to be passive or left alone.

Also, I thought I knew now about the movements of those eyebrows: she must use them to punctuate the nuances of her thoughts, the way you use shadow to emphasize color. And so they kept rising and falling as she spoke, their angle changing with amazing fluidity and variation, shifting with the inner motions of her moods.

The glistening cobblestone pavement plunged downward before us, tapering around the bend, like the tail of an armadillo.

Then, all of a sudden, we were out on Rue Monge and in the full glare of the summer light, a stone's throw from Jardin des Plantes—the dazzle of the sun like a flash, almost electric blue. Back in the bustle of downtown life.

"So that was Nameless Lane," I said.

She laughed—a nervous burst of laughter that made her shake a little with her head bent forward, like a suppressed sneeze.

———

I was hot and pushing uphill on the sun-drenched stretch of old cobbled sidewalk. The water from the hydrants running down invitingly along the curbstones on either side of the street. The still fierce sun gliding above the treetops. The haven of the garden was not far and I was looking forward to a pleasant lounge on one of the shady benches by the Reptile Pavilion.

I began to tell her about the feeling that this neighborhood always gave me: a sense of promise—seeing the spiked black iron fence and anticipating all the wonders inside the garden, its endless capacity to surprise and enchant you.

"When I come down here, I always feel like a kid on his way to the circus," I said.

She laughed and said, "You feel your feet getting itchy—that's what I get when I start approaching Le Jardin. It's such a beautiful escape from the noise and grinding pace of the city. It's like another country altogether!"

Slowly, the strap of her black bra started slipping out from underneath the cap sleeve of her lavender blouse, inching toward the sharp angle of her shoulder.

As we entered Jardin des Plantes, the air felt fresh and misty within the narrow gateway, redolent of wet clay and broken mushrooms.

The cobblestones leveled off and it was easier pushing the stroller.

The boys' mood shifted all of a sudden: despite their mild bafflement at the presence of the mysterious woman who had suddenly become a member of our party, they were excited and already fidgeting in their seats.

When we got to the little square off the Rotunda, I stopped and let them wriggle out of the stroller: "Roam around, boys, the garden is yours!"

Haroon went straight toward the seesaw by the bronze hippopotamus, but Shams kept standing by the carriage, squinting up at me, his gaze suddenly less frank than I had discovered lately. He was curious about Annaelle but still too shy to scrutinize her: "Are we still going to the bear pit, Dad?"

"Of course we are. Run along now! Say hi to the turtles."

———

We sat on a bench by the playground and she brought up the Sheb Jamaal concert again—on our way to the garden, she had seen his concert posters and told me that she was going.

"When is the concert?"

"Tomorrow. He's singing in Oberkampf. I can get you a ticket—if you're available."

She spoke fast and kept looking at Shams climbing up the life-size hippopotamus.

Before I knew it, I found myself accepting: "I don't know much about rai music, but maybe it's time I checked it out."

"You don't listen to rai?"

There was neither disappointment nor surprise in her voice.

"Well, I listen to Billie Holiday an awful lot. I minored in English *for* her, practically. When it comes to Arab music, I guess you could say I'm more of a classicist. I listen a lot to Oum Kalthoum, Asmahan and Farid also—the old-timers. Although I *am* fond of Najib Alwi, come to think of it. He's very much of a—new-wave musician, you know. He actually makes his own lutes—gives them all those sharp and crisp effects in the upper register; and the bluesy expansiveness of the lower notes. And there's Souad Nassay too. She's very good."

"I don't know either of them. It sounds like I have some learning to do."

"Me too. I can show you some of their stuff—Alwi and Nassay. About tomorrow night, shall we make it concert *and* dinner? I know a great Lebanese place on Place de la République."

"Sounds good."

The enthusiasm was decidedly understated—but not artificially coy, I thought.

She kept her eyes fixed on the boys by the huge animal sculptures as we spoke, but only as an excuse to avoid looking at me, I thought. Out of shyness? Or was she simply just like me—still tottering about in a transitory state of beautiful confusion, loitering between the still-virtual and the soon-to-be-actual?

Beyond the lawn that bordered the tiny playground: the limestone-trimmed red-brick Rotunda with its lovely Art Deco windows, its perfectly manicured lawn, its giant turtles lumbering sheepishly around a sandstone basin sunk into the bottle-green grass like a saucer of sherry.

My eyes were back on the boys. Contemplating them with a pang of guilt, I came to my senses and realized the obvious: only Shams was actually playing.

Haroon just stood by with a helpless look on his face, his eyes riveted on Shams; while his older brother squatted on top of the snarling hippopotamus, his feet firmly planted on the animal's bulging eyes, his arms thrown around its impressive snout, looking at me with triumph in his eyes.

"Haroon, my son," I said, as I stood up.

The words shook him out of his brooding expression, that fixation on Shams's ascent.

He turned to face me and I took his hand and pointed at the life-size copper bear: "He's positioned on all fours, waiting nicely and quietly. He's probably dying for company, don't you think?"

"Oh yes," he said and smiled, to my guilty relief.

The verdigris-mottled bear—his back worn smooth and toffee brown by decades of riding. I had to keep holding Haroon as he sat on top of him; that bear was just too broad to be comfortably straddled by my son.

He found the moment quite enjoyable all the same, holding on to my arm with his hot hands, the sudden height putting an expression of excitement in those big wide honey eyes.

"Oum Kalthoum," she said. "She's unique. The Star of the Levant."

"You know quite a bit about Arab culture. I'm—"

"How much did I say? Am I acting pretentious?"

There was a mix of ironic distance and excessive defensiveness in her tone. I did not like that. Then again, maybe I was just nervous, still trying to get my head around the out-of-the-blue, too-beautiful-to-be-true charms of this magical woman.

"You're right," I said, "I was just assuming."

"Sorry, I didn't mean to be abrupt. I was just thinking out loud—wondering if I was monopolizing the conversation. You assumed right, though. My best friends are Moroccan and Algerian. I have so much ... I don't know. I have a profound affinity with Arab culture. It completes my existence so much. I've felt this way ever since I was a child, too. I'm sure I was an Arab in another lifetime. Actually, I can even say Star of the Levant in Arabic: *Kaoukab al-Sharq*."

"It's amazing! Your pronunciation is *perfect*, Annaelle!"

"Oh, I don't know about *that*."

"Honest, it *is*."

We were now sitting by the taller flowers: chrysanthemums, foam-flowers, and dahlias—the maze of narrow aisles halfway between the Rotunda and the Mexican Greenhouse.

Our bench had a name, too: Le Centaure—printed on the cast-iron side in raised white letters.

I had taken out our food and offered to share it with her, she threw her fruit in with ours in return, and we laid everything out picnic style on the stroller.

Soon a murder of crows arrayed in a semicircle began to hop around us with hungry eyes—their sleek necks darting back and forth incessantly as they invested the grassy side of the flowerbeds and part of the gravel path where we were sitting.

Then Haroon began to toss some of the fruit—grapes and apricots.

For some inexplicable reason, I found their mechanical hunger and their pushiness deeply detestable: the way they went about it—savagely tearing at the fruit, their heads shaking frantically. And the eyes of those who were left out of the feeding frenzy were even worse—they were crazed, those eyes, driven by a sort of tortured inordinate greed.

"Whatever made you do that, young man?" I asked my son.

"To keep them away, Dad. That's their share right there on the grass, and this is *our* place here."

I asked him, "Do you think they'll understand your thinking? Keep to the lawn?"

"Of course. Look at them. They're clever."

Shams was staring at the crows in deep thought: "Oh yes, they are. That's why they'll be *back*—for more. You keep giving, they keep coming back. That's just how they *are*."

———

Shortly before sundown, we left our picnic perch and began walking toward the big central path—the one that starts at the Rotunda square, dividing the Menagerie side in two.

We strolled through the bamboo grove for a while then turned left in the direction of the Mexican Greenhouse and the Winter Garden, walking down the shingle path with the boys before us and, on either side, the chest-high cactus dahlias—their slender-stemmed flowers radiating around us in bursts of pink and purple and canary yellow, like colorful starfish.

The scent of clay and cut grass rising from the earth on the moist air; the cry of the peacocks in the evening hush; traffic along the Seine like a sea hum in the distance off to the north.

The garden's most enchanted hour; but soon we would have to go and leave the place to its night silence.

———

Eventually the boys grew definitively tired: they climbed back into the carriage and we pushed on over the rise between the Winter Garden and the Mexican Greenhouse, heading for the east gate on Rue Buffon.

I saw the sign outside the greenhouse and I said, "My favorite flowers," talking to myself.

"Which?" she asked.

"See the sign there? There's an orchid show in the Winter Garden."

"I know. It's a gorgeous show. Of course they're closed by now, but we really need to go sometime soon. It's beautiful."

We stood up there for a moment on top of the hill overlooking the Rotunda side, surveying the part of the garden where we had sat a while ago. The sun was going down behind the enclosure and the trees by the west gate. The bench where we had had our dinner was invisible behind the ruffled bluish-green shag of the bamboo grove. In the gathering darkness, the flowerbeds and benches that were visible down there appeared like a scene from a gigantic cyclorama, concave and unreal and much farther away than they actually were.

The Mexican Greenhouse was empty and silent, its massive structure of square iron-framed panes glowing over the west door in diffuse shades of purple.

"We really have to go." The imperative, emphatic quality of her interjection was beautifully promising.

The instant she uttered those words, it was as if an intangible hand had suddenly shaken me out of a deep dream, and then I began to realize that this woman was real, that there was a tangible possibility of something meaningful happening between us.

We exchanged e-mail addresses and phone numbers outside the gate.

When she turned and walked away I was still standing there and I think she had sensed that I was curious as to why she was going in the opposite direction.

Just as she reached the edge of the sidewalk and was about to cross the street, she turned around briskly and addressed me, leaning slightly forward as she spoke: "Normally, I should be walking back with you, boys, but I'm meeting a friend. I actually live two blocks up the street from where you're staying. I'm a neighborhood girl!"

Then she blew the boys a kiss and was gone.

We arrived home late from the garden, and as soon as I got the boys into their pajamas, I called Babysitter Express.

My sons settling down before their cartoon—their faces tired in the bluish glare of the screen, their lips ringed with a neon-pink ice cream halo (strawberry—their favorite flavor at Di Angelo's).

Babysitter Express was very expensive but excellent with a highly reliable staff.

There was a brief silence when I asked the dispatcher: "Would it be possible to be serviced by the same young lady as last year? She gets along very well with the boys."

She spoke just as I was about to rephrase my request: "I'm checking our reservation records, sir. Here it is. It was last summer, sir?"

"Yes."

"You were serviced by Samia."

"That's correct."

"Our reservation book shows that she won't be engaged for another week. But I'll need to get in touch with her first—see if she's in town. I'll get back to you momentarily."

"Thank you very much. Let me give you my cell—"

"I've got it displayed here, sir. I'll get back to you shortly. We'll take care of this."

And so she did: by the time the boys were tucked in bed, she had Samia booked for the entire duration of our visit—"night shift indefinite," as she put it.

August 29 was Samia's last day with us. We were leaving the day after.

The babysitter was going to cost a fortune and I had not informed the boys about her yet.

Still, there was no doubt in my mind that night: my arrangement with Samia would work to everybody's satisfaction. The boys were going to be in good hands and even though the young woman's nighttime babysitting might run longer than usual, she was going to make a lot of money.

And as far as I was concerned, Babysitter Express afforded me the priceless benefit of guilt-free certainty: it was the best agency in town—my children were going to get the best of care. I just had to explicitly instruct Samia to take them out as often as possible: the marionette shows and the children's theater in Jardin du Luxembourg, the belle époque carousel, the Tuileries carnival.

The night was hot and humid as I stood on Zoé's balcony, but it felt good to be out here in the dark amid the shadows of her plants, feeling the cool tiles under my bare feet, listening to the random sounds and short-lived stories of Rue Mouffetard.

The accordionist outside the Verlaine was playing a bittersweet waltz, "Mon Amant de Saint Jean."

I was smoking weed, listening to the night, dreaming about tomorrow.

———

The morning was muggy and the sky over the rooftops was covered with a film of translucent gray, like a thin layer of fat.

We were having breakfast with Samia and I excused myself to take Annaelle's call out on the balcony.

She told me that we were in luck: her Algerian friend Amal knew one of the promoters and they had called him last night: exchanging her ticket and buying two new ones was a cinch. Amal was going to take care of everything.

I thanked her and said, "How about a thank you lunch?"

Silence.

"I mean in honor of your friend—for her act of kindness. Somewhere close by, you know. Maybe Le Verlaine?"

"That's—"

She checked herself and there was another silence.

Was I being pushy?

I felt that I had been pushy and was immediately disgusted at myself, regretting my hasty invitation. The terra-cotta Buddha sitting on top of the old wooden milk pail next to Zoé's geranium planter: he had long water spots across his lower belly. I made a mental note to clean him up later.

"I think it's a wonderful idea," she said. "I'm sure Amal will be able to make it. I was just thinking maybe you'd like to spend some time with the boys."

"Thanks, that's very thoughtful of you. You know, we've been spending a lot of quality time together lately—in Tunisia and Biarritz. They have a wonderful babysitter here. They like her a lot."

"I'm really glad of that. I just—don't want to impose."

"You're not imposing, Annaelle—not in the least."

———

I called Le Verlaine and booked a table for three.

Then I spent the rest of the morning going over various logistical details with Samia and loafing around with my sons. But my mind was far away and in my imagination I was already meandering up the street to Le Verlaine, anticipating the moment when I would meet this new woman who was so full of magic and mystery.

I did not feel the least bit guilty about my secret fantasies of escape: the instinctive man in me was showing signs of rejuvenation that I had not felt in years.

———

The waiter ushered me to a table on the terrace.

We were not meeting for another twenty minutes, so I ordered a kir royal and sat down.

The flagstone sidewalk terrace was almost as wide as a courtyard here, and it smelled of acacia flowers and a fresh sprinkling: the geraniums bright and beautiful in their wooden planters; the accordion player pouring out a soulful rendering of "Cuesta Abajo" at the curb, swaying in his canvas stool, his right shoulder always just about to brush the menu board.

By the time the two women showed up, I was tipsy and in a very pleasant mood.

Annaelle's friend looked impressive: her bosom was immense and her lower body shaped like that of a huge mermaid, the powerful thighs so closely pressed together in her white bellbottom satin pants that she appeared to be wearing an extremely tight ankle-length skirt.

Amal's long, thick platinum blond hair was mesmerizingly implausible against her brown Berber face, glistening in stark bangs above those beautifully kohled eyes. Surreal apparition—a blond, white-clad pharaoh princess wobbling along on a pair of golden stiletto slippers.

The two women had not spotted me yet and they appeared tentative, somewhat alarmed—standing in the middle of the street before the accordionist, looking down in the direction that I had come from.

When I stood up and waved to them from the table, Amal let out a shrill cry and immediately checked herself, putting a heavily jeweled hand over her mouth. Then, assuming a more composed expression, she took a stride forward with a firm step and hopped onto the sidewalk. Amal was stunningly agile and had excellent balance for a woman of her girth.

The two women were discussing blondes and the stupidity of blonde jokes:

Annaelle's voice was low-register and melodious—a very erotic cooing voice: "Blondes," she said, addressing Amal. "I like your blonde joke. It's deep—a great way to make fun of anti-blonde prejudice. Take Grace Kelly for example. She was very elegant, very beautiful, but also extremely smart and articulate. As I said, our society puts so much pressure. Women are *so* pressured, and the demands that are put on us are highly contradictory. Nowadays a European woman is supposed to be innocent *and* seductive; beautiful *and* 'modest,' as they say; financially independent but not too threatening to her partner's ego. Damned if you do, damned if you don't. Add to that the collective obsession with looks and fashion: cosmetic surgery, makeup, designer clothes. That's way too much pressure for today's average working woman. It's as if the whole culture is trying to condition women to feel insecure about their choices."

She fell silent, tossed her head back with an ironic laugh; and when she looked at Amal next to her, she was smiling with those wide imponderable eyes—her face flushed, her bangs beautifully disarranged: "Look at me, I'm spouting off again."

Amal was looking into Annaelle's eyes with a proud smile as she replied: "Powerful words, Annaelle! You're as smart and articulate as Grace Kelly."

"That's because I've got auburn hair," Annaelle retorted.

The three of us laughed at her clever quip.

The waiter came over to clear our entrée plates—carpaccio de coquilles Saint-Jacques.

We waited silently as he refilled our glasses and picked up the plates.

When he left, Amal leaned daintily across the table with a sweet conspiratorial expression on her face: "Enter 'the Arab Mind,'" she said to me. "The knight in shining armor. The answer to all our problems."

I thought that her statement was random and completely incomprehensible, but I tried to be as polite as possible: "So you're saying—"

"*I'm* not saying. *She* is—my very dear friend here. She thinks Europe has a lot to learn from Arab culture! The lecture she just gave you: I heard it so many times. She won me over to her side long ago. I'm always finishing Annaelle's sentences—even when she's not around!"

Amal kept smiling as she addressed me, her four-ringed hand on Annaelle's alabaster shoulder—the bright Tuareg silver sunk into the flesh of her fingers like inlay; the dazzling scarlet of her stiletto fingernails.

Annaelle looked down before her and smiled, taking her friend's playfulness with good humor.

Down by the sidewalk, sitting next to the menu board in the stifling heat, swaying to the rippling echoes of his music, the accordionist played on bravely and passionately over the general din of the eaters, putting a lot of verve into his performance—his revenge on our indifference, I thought.

There was another shift in Annaelle's hard-to-decipher gaze, and suddenly I found it difficult to decide whether it was an inner sensation of pain that had darkened her expression all at once or simply the gravity of her thoughts: "Well, yes, it *is* about lessons ultimately. Every culture needs to learn a lesson every now and then. Our European culture *could* use a lesson from Arab culture. Call it a civilization lesson. Arabs are capable of great tolerance for the flaws of human nature. They're capable of facing those flaws in themselves and in other people without feeling at all diminished or inferior or angry. Arabs are so good at managing imperfection. Here we've become so frantically attached to our petty little consumers' lives, so obsessed with the false dream of a perfect life."

Amal looked at me with a twinkle in her black eyes: "Whew!"

She asked me rhetorically, "Would you please tell her? Arabs aren't what they used to be—the way she knew them in her childhood?" Then to Annaelle: "It's just that—how can I put it? I don't want you to end up being disappointed, my dear little sister."

(It was an intellectual cliché, of course, a hackneyed, condescending argument I had heard all too often before; one that never failed to infuriate me—this reference to some sort of Arab "innocence" the better to lament the supposed decline of European culture.

But today I was a man in love and there were many things that I was willing to take from Annaelle. I was hanging on every word she said as if she was singing in a strange and deeply alluring tongue— sounds my mind could inhabit on its own terms, people with new meaning of my own creation.)

———

We parted company with Amal on the north side of Place de la Contrescarpe, right behind the church, by the tiny pale gate of the yard.

Having said good-bye, Annaelle and I walked through the gate toward the iron bench in back.

But Amal was not through exiting yet.

Like someone with a deliberate intent to surprise, she said, "Hey! You two stay out of trouble."

We both turned around and saw her standing there behind the gate in all her surreal mesmerizing beauty, a gorgeous platinum-blond siren in white satin, wagging her silver-studded finger and smiling with those big black byzantine eyes.

And now there was silence between us again, but it was the pacifying hush of the early afternoon hours: the pigeons hopping across the basalt cobblestones—hunting and pecking in the pocks and between the cracks; the drowsy air so still you could hear their beaks tapping the stone with a dull click—and every now and then the low choking sound, half coo half gulp.

Above us, the unrelentingly dull flat translucent sky like an unbroken sheet of fluffed-up wool hanging just above our heads, its downward push unrelenting.

"I was dull, wasn't I?" she asked.

"You were—"

She went on speaking through my words, with a smile that was almost rueful: "You'll never see me get on my high horse again, though—now that you know where I stand on the issue of gender equality. Maybe I'm the kind of woman who is too serious about first impressions—too much solemnity and all. I guess I just wanted to impress you."

"You were wonderful company," I managed to slip in.

Annaelle laughed and lowered her head, looking up at me with a slanted gaze, her ravishingly flirtatious alexandrite eyes locking with mine: "Thanks. But still, you mustn't think of me as—Joan of Arc or something."

"I know you're not, but it's great to have ideals that set you apart from the passive majority—*and* to feel strongly about them. 'The man who lives by his ideals is the man who is alive'—something like that."

"That's beautiful. But how about women?"

"No—"

I laughed, even though the look in her eyes was serious.

I said, "Those weren't my words—not all of them, I mean."

All at once, I realized the conversation was threatening to slip into a ridiculous misunderstanding, and that was probably why I found it funny—this unexpected twist in the scene and the script, and so I laughed again: "Sorry," I said, "let me try and sort this out before it gets out of control. I'm just laughing at my total lack of clarity. I was actually quoting Cervantes—about the man who lives by his ideals. In fact, I'm not even sure I got the quote right—I mean the wording of it. In short, I managed to mangle the moment. Didn't I tell you? I'm not much of a talker."

She was still looking at me and her face was still serious and expressionless.

I went on, painfully self-conscious and careful, apologetic almost: "Well, he certainly forgot women. I could not agree more. Think of Joan of Arc, precisely: she wouldn't agree with him all the way now, would she?"

"No she wouldn't."

———

After a while, I told her that I had to get back home: "Believe me, I would love to stay, but I need to head back home and get some writing done."

"What do you write?"

She slipped back into her lighthearted mood in the same way one slips into a fresh shirt, swiftly and magically and confusingly, and it was with both relief and awe that I saw her brighten up and shed her grave expression so quickly.

"What do I write? Let's see: passing thoughts that need to be developed into something more profound and elaborate, random reflections, fragments, contemplations, questions. Sometimes if I'm lucky I even manage to bag a poem or two."

"So now you've got to run back while it's all still fresh in your memory? Reflect on all this before it tumbles into a black hole? Is that what you're going to do? Freeze-frame everything?"

"Wow, Annaelle, you sound so—curious all of a sudden, in a nice flattering way. But it's not as big as you think, really. It's just semi-random writing, most of the time. Nothing much."

"Well, I *am* curious—of course. *All* women are supposed to be curious, didn't you know? Plus, I'm Gemini. That makes me *particularly* curious. So are you going to satisfy my curiosity and tell me about it tonight?"

"Tell you about what?"

I enjoyed acting coy and she enjoyed acting persistent: "Come on," she said, "you know what. What you've written, that's what. What you *will* have written, actually."

"There's really nothing to tell. Really. Plus, it's bad luck to talk about your writing, didn't *you* know?"

"Hmm. First, that sounds like an all too glib cop-out. Second, how is anybody going to find out about your ideas if you don't actually *tell* them?"

"But that's the whole point of being a writer, you see: you don't *tell* anybody about your writings—they just *stumble* on them, if they're lucky."

"You make it sound like a lottery—for the lucky few."

"But it *is*. You'd be amazed how many great books were discovered by chance."

———

(On my way back to Zoé's:

They've probably left by now, I thought, with guilt-free relief and joy.

And I can see it so clearly now—that moment—as I read those pages written after parting company with her; revisit both the moment and the pages in their full sentimental credulity, their naïve beauty and their utter blamelessness: no feelings of guilt about being disburdened of my sons by Samia, no feelings of guilt about not really wanting to write during those precious hours that remained before our evening out together.

There was no sense of culpability whatsoever as I took those few steps to the apartment, with everything around me so strangely revealed, every movement so decelerated and pacified. It was all like an extremely magnified, extremely slow scene from a film.

Everything so new and so significant—so resolved and fitting.

It was (is) what I am seeing, reading, and writing right now about my other self, the other beautifully maudlin and silly and sappy and love-struck man—joyfully spilling his blood and guts on the page, instants after that precious moment in the churchyard:

The strange, impossible-to-explain sense of detachment, of walking down a different street altogether, in a different city; of knowing vaguely that you are on your way to a new, still undiscovered place—as you stand for a few very long seconds before the door of the building, beautifully conscious of this dizzy new world unfolding within and about you; beautifully conscious of the task ahead—to commence unpacking these tightly clustered constellations of brand-new things, brand-new impressions, and brand-new feelings that have come to you from your brand-new world, your brand-new self—yes, to unpack it and write it all into clarified sense and sensation, new meanings and new feelings that you are yet to untangle, explain to yourself in many long hours of the deepest pondering.

And you feel, in your new state of grace, that you have at last earned the right to take the time to linger here/now and wonder, and imagine the beauty and excitement of the task to come as you stand before the monumental dark-green door of Zoé's building with its huge wrought-iron frames around the two rectangular frosted-glass panels, their symmetrical grids rising up like two gigantic, slender-stemmed candelabra—these beautiful grids that you see with so much poetic newness now, and these panels behind them that light up at night with a warm glow, like a massive sheet of illuminated wax. You know that these new things you see are all here for you to own in your new mind, subjected as they are to the reach of your new gaze, the grasp of your new hands, the dominion of your new thoughts and words; you know that what is left for you to do now is to push your wonderment one step further—open the door and take the wide, time-worn granite stairs up to the place, the home you are still unaware will be the scene of your children's undoing; you know that it is perfectly legitimate to take your time and stop at the bottom of the stairs and contemplate the age-old dilapidated staircase and the persistence of beauty amid the ruin—the gorgeously carved pine-cone mass capping the cast-iron newel, the eye-captivating surreal fascination of the jaundice-hued stair walls with their lichen-like patches and patterns of peeled-off paint and mildew stains and rust patches, the chandeliers hanging from their thick rusty chains like immense censers.

Then the moment comes when you find yourself standing before the other dark-green door, the one you will eventually unlock and push open just after you're done taking in the vertiginous tangle of rococo carving on the breast-shaped pewter doorbell, the low transom like a mother-of-pearl fan, and, arching above you like the lid of an age-old chest, this tattered stair ceiling dyed in random patterns of rusty water spots and mold, oddly left unrestored and unpainted ever since you have known the place and given it room in your memory.

And now you find yourself within at last, standing in the middle of the living room, your children rushing to meet you—flushed and clumsy from their play, grabby and loud and eager to drag you into a playful scuffle.

But you resist them firmly, right from the start, dismissing them out of hand and telling them that you want to rest.

And the young woman tells you that she intends to take them out anyway.

So you take out your wallet and give her the money, relieved at her words, her solid sense of responsible initiative: for taxi fare and expenses, you tell her.

Then you go to Zoé's study, without even a polite transition—not even a playful word to your children.

And you lie down with your head propped against the armrest of the little floral-pattern couch, trying to sort it all out in your mind, your memory—this beautiful throb of excitement that is happening in you, building up momentum in the vast expanses of your heart, pouring out of your soul pure and straight and crystal clear, like an upward gush of spring water.)

———

She looked heavenly in the bottle-green moiré shalwar pants, the cream silk tank top. Her dun rope sneakers were bought for the occasion, I guessed—the creases in the middle were still crisp.

"You look great," I said to her.

"Please don't. I can't take a compliment."

"Duly noted," I replied, noticing that she had the same wide-eyed expression I had seen on her face as she stood stranded-looking in the middle of the street with Amal.

"Which way are we going?" she asked, perhaps with a sudden touch of apprehension in her voice—it was impossible to tell with any measure of certainty.

"I was thinking maybe we could head for Quai Saint-Bernard, cross over, and take a stroll along Port de Plaisance—possibly catch a taxi to Canal Saint-Martin, if you feel like more walking."

"Beautiful. And where's the restaurant?"

"Very close by. I mean close to the canal—just off Place de la République. After dinner, we'll take a taxi to Oberkampf."

She nodded with what appeared to be a strained smile.

It occurred to me then that the wide-eyed look was most likely not simple excitement: she was on something this evening, I was certain of it (just weed, I hoped).

We went down to the Seine through Rue Buffon, and we ferried over to the other side from Quai Saint-Bernard, with the sun slanting down over the river—the clouds scattered enough for the sunlight to come through and throw a burst of lavender dashes and purple smudges across the horizon; the soft glow from the burnished arches of Austerlitz Bridge reflected in long stippled streaks across the water. Behind us, the southbound traffic along the bank sounded weakly sibilant in the distance, like the whisper of small waves.

It felt good and peaceful to be able to once again feel the soothing sugar-cane-and-iris scent of Annaelle's perfume, to be able to imagine the rustle of her hair against the silk fabric of that boyish tank top. Wandering together with her, my mind racing forward to Port de Plaisance already; already at midpoint between this magical sunset river and the walled-in, below-street-level meanders of narrow canals awaiting us—the strip of quiet waterways stretching north of Place de la République like an assemblage of thin ribbons lined up together by a hasty hand.

The air was still sluggish, hot, and heavy. Yet the seconds unfolded slowly and gently as our ferry chugged along (even the river seemed to have slowed and quieted down for the evening).

With the soft light of our fairy-tale sky shining so kindly above us, the moment felt as chimerical as a flash from a friar's lantern; and yet it was also charged with the nameless promise of a beautiful dream, a projection as sweet as this endless procession of shadows and reflections shimmering in the twisted mirror of the Seine.

When we got to Canal Saint-Martin, we took one of those below-street-level rusty iron stairs that led straight to the embankments and the waterways.

About halfway down Quai de Jemmapes, she asked me if we could take a rest on one of the locks. (Unlike the stairs, the iron structures were painted a neat mint green and spanned the canal at regular intervals along the cobblestone embankment, like footbridges over the oil-still water).

So we stopped and climbed on top of a lock, and the instant we stood next to each other—side by side, leaning against the thin rail—I thought we were going to kiss.

The thick arch of the trees formed a dark canopy overhead and I could barely make out her expression; but what I managed to intuit in that first second above the canal was in fact a deliberate feeling of distance coming from her, something that one might easily interpret as whimsical irony or capricious cunning—nothing resembling the fevered impulsiveness that precedes a first kiss.

The air was intensely muggy and the thick foliage over our heads felt like a ceiling of black rags. I stood there with my gaze trapped in the dull luster of those illegible alexandrite eyes.

Unavoidably, it felt like being in a tunnel standing there by her side—the erotic charge of the place was almost unbearable.

She broke the spell by asking me a question: "Any thoughts?" she said, bafflingly matter-of-fact.

"This spot is beautiful beyond all thoughts and words."

"No, I mean any thoughts you *wrote*."

"I see. You really want to know, don't you?"

"Oh yes."

"Well, I've been writing about things that seem to happen by pure chance and lead to an entire concatenation of events that changes a person's life completely. Things that spring up out of nowhere. Then they lead to other things that happen in quick succession—on and on, like a fireworks. Then, all of a sudden, life is no longer the same. There it is—my bad boy confession. I've been toying with fireworks—the pyrotechnics of fate, if you will."

"I don't believe in chance, you know. Everything happens for a reason and there is predetermination behind every significant event. But right now we're talking about you. I mean, could you be more specific?"

"I can't—not now, at any rate. It's still too personal—too subjective. It's also very messy and blurry, so you can't really call it writing at this point in time. Nothing that can be viewed as relevant communication. The only thing that counts is *re*writing. It's all about rewriting."

"I understand."

"Are you hungry?"

"A little, yes."

"Shall we get going?"

"All right."

I started toward the embankment, but she stayed behind and spoke to me again from where she stood: "Well, obviously, you're no stranger to the art of fireworks. You know that they all must have a climax—something in the very nature of their progression, right? The buildup then the grand finale?"

I had already turned around at Annaelle's first words, trying to look into her eyes as straight and as long as I could. It was impossible to read any meaning in her eyes or to discern a tone on her face. But I was stunned just the same: she had her retort ready seconds after I had spoken, and I found that both confusing and compelling.

I just laughed.

"Yours has been building up," she added. "Well, just before you write your climax tomorrow, maybe you'd like to check with me. I'm sure I can throw in a suggestion or two."

Her figure was all but silhouette by now and for some reason the darkness had made her cooing velvet voice even more erotic. But her tone was palpably cocky and provocative—an attitude that invited resistance.

I laughed again in order to veil my amazement and stall for time. "Deal," I said, businesslike. "I'll call you when I get to the grand finale." "You don't have to. I'll *be* there."

———

Annaelle and I walked along the canal for a few minutes.

Then we headed for Rue Jemmapes where we took a taxi to the restaurant.

The evening was sticky and it was a relief to be sitting in the air-conditioned bubble of the car, watching the night streets flashing by like scenes from a silent film.

When we arrived at Oberkampf, the quarter was already crackling with life and light. Traffic was so dense that we decided to get out two blocks before the concert hall.

When we got to the building, I tried to sound as cheerful and casual as I could when I spoke to her: "I wonder if I could sneak around the corner of this building and have a very special smoke."

"What an exquisitely wicked idea! You've just sold me, bad boy."

We smoked in the back lane and when it was time to go inside, I went to line up at the beer stand.

I said I would catch up with her and she told me to look for her in the orchestra seating section.

———

The architectural cachet of the building was very well preserved: everything consistently Art Deco in the lobby as well as in the concert hall—the only thing that was not Art Deco were the very high-tech psychedelic lights strobing and flashing across the equipment-studded stage.

A few men were busy onstage with last-minute sound and lighting testing.

The hall was humming and vibrating with the restless, kaleidoscopic carnival energy of the crowd—music lovers of all ages, colors, and styles.

I walked slowly down the aisle with our drinks, looking for Annaelle.

It was not long before I spotted her (we had excellent seats, in the middle rows of the orchestra section, by the aisle—she was sitting in mine and had her clutch bag across the aisle seat).

The last instrument tester had just put down the *darbouka* drum and left. The stage darkened and went still, the house lights dimmed, and the last stragglers were rushing to their seats.

Then there was the band strutting onstage one by one and the crowd roaring in crescendo, wave after rolling wave, from the balconies all the way down to the outer edge of the orchestra pit.

And now only one position was left empty, under the round bluish beam of the spotlight—the pale lute on its stand, metamorphosed with uncanny luminescence into a strange abstract sculpture. And the crowd chanting in two pounding thrusts: "JA-MAL! JA-MAL! JA-MAL!"

And the front man stepping at last into his light under the crashing shout-out, his voice booming as he shouted into the clip-on microphone: "HELLO, PARIS!"

The strident screams and whistles and cheers echoed all around us like one single wave crashing.

He goes on, his powerful voice riding over the collective ecstasy: "Now, whoever said a guy from Marseilles can't get a warm welcome in this town? They're lying, right? RIGHT?"

More resounding cheers.

As the collective excitement begins to die down, his voice drops into a beautiful baritone croon: "And just to prove they're lying, we're gonna start with a Marseilles song, how about—"

And the crowd goes into a frenzy again, and she turns her face toward me—eyes wide open with joy: she shouts a few words to me but I cannot make them out.

I lean closer to Annaelle and I can hear her say it again: "Leela fee Marseilles." The opening song—"One Night in Marseilles."

He raises his hand, laughing—his teeth like steel splinters under the black mustache, almost as bright as the thick silver chain dangling across his black-T-shirted chest: "We're gonna start with a

Marseilles song and you're gonna show me how much you love it. Are you gonna show me?"

YEEEEES!

"Boy, I loooove this town! All right, guys, hit it!"

The first thing I remember about Jamaal's music is the quality of his percussion: its foundation was quite traditional—the ordinary *doum tak* beat (nothing particularly novel, like Nassay's experiments with Caribbean percussion); but the razor-thin sharpness of the *darbouka* was something completely novel to me—an admirably sustained high pitch that pierced through the supplications of the Algerian violin, the arpeggios of the violas, and the keen of the *'nahii* flute:

> *Sitting in a barroom by myself,*
> *Lonely in a lonely corner,*
> *Nursing my wounds and my drink—*
> *Drowning my sorrows in my cups,*
> *My love-loss and my bitter rout.*
> *Oh, how often I mourned that night;*
> *How often I cursed and I cried—*
> *Swearing off love*
> *And its vain and foolish ways.*
> *But little did I know:*
> *Your eyes were waiting,*
> *Waiting patiently—*
> *In the cold, cold crowd.*
> *You kissed my bleeding heart*
> *With their light,*
> *And I arose from my ruins,*
> *Reborn and ready for you.*
>
> > *Leela, leela fee Marseilles,*
> > *It was one solitary love-dart:*
> > *You hit a proud lion, and*
> > *Your aim was truer than the hand of fate;*
> > *And now I'm all adrift in your love—*
> > *The gorgeous blue of your loving eyes—*

> *A willing prisoner of your sweet sorcerous ways,*
> *A ship heaving between the furious waves of the sea.*

Just before he wrapped up the refrain, Jamaal picked up his lute without turning around and launched into the solo.

I was already beginning to realize why Nolwenn was so enthusiastic about him.

The sound of his instrument as he picked and strummed it, his gracefully choreographed body: besides the quality of his lyrics and singing, Jamaal as musician and dancer had truly enchanting stage presence.

His lute was tuned up in such a way as to give each note a rich, reedy twang—a sound fundamentally alien to the traditional registers and textures of the instrument; and the quality of his finger vibrato and slide play both lengthened and twisted his notes beyond the duration of the basic tone of the traditional lute, giving them a stunning flexibility of range, sound, and texture.

It was a moment of awe-inspiring discovery from the start—and amid all the beauty of it, there were only two visual impressions that I retained with utter clarity (and that I was later to record in my diary), throbbing on either side of me in discontinuous movement, like two shimmering holograms: Annaelle—stepping out onto the aisle, motioning me to come along, then breaking into dance, her uplifted arms moving in oriental-dance undulations (the rings of sweat under her armpits, the sweet mossy scent of her sweat); and, to my left, the monumental, gape-mouthed face of a tall brawny Tunisian man with a boxer's nose and deep shadowy pockmarks like awl notches on a wax face, a face twisted by the shrillest coloratura scream possible: " *'AWOUD! 'AWOUD! BJEH RABBI 'AWOUD!'* " ("Again! Again! In the name of the Lord, again!")

The sight of her all at once bewitched by the music: her slender boyish body swaying in the shifting metallic beams of the lights hurled around us with stroboscopic speed; her auburn hair flailing like a ragged banner in the wind. That was the greatest revelation of all—the sudden spectacle of all this monumental electric energy pouring out of her; her immediate, miraculous power to summon all these stunning faculties of motion and emotion that she both possessed and was possessed by.

———

She pointed toward the unmistakable silhouette of her friend Amal, standing three or four rows down from us, dancing by her own aisle seat; the athletic figure of a man next to her (I waved to Amal and wondered if the man was her boyfriend).

By and by the music trailed off into silence and Jamaal waited for the crowd to quiet down. Then he raised his hand and whispered to the audience in a theatrical sigh of longing: "Maouwaaaaal."

The only accompaniment were one viola and the Algerian violin, hushed into a low, almost inaudible lament for the singer's Mawwal—the percussion section silent, and the wind section too, except for the deep velvet drone of the *'nahii* (the fabled deep keen of the Arab flute).

The Maouwal, a sort of prelude to an important song, is a softly accompanied, almost purely vocal virtuoso act; the artist's expression of his solitary voice, its exalted loneliness before the night (the lament to the night is the central feature of Mawwal). Everyone understood the significance of the moment and the crowd fell completely silent as Jamaal began to chant his vocal variations around the two traditional lines of the Maouwal:

> *Yah leelee, yah leelee, yah leel!*
> *Yah 'eenee yah 'eenee yah 'een!*

He goes on improvising on those two lines for a few delightful minutes; and when he's done, the *darbouka* springs into action first with a flurry of high crisp raps, followed by the rest of the orchestra and the rousing applause.

And now Jamaal begins to sing again:

Why should the river smile to me
As I sail slow and hug the bank?
The river is riled, roiled, and wrinkled—
Not even a hint of a smile on its face:
After all, isn't my story the saddest of all?
Sad as the clang of doom itself:
The tale of lost love and shattered dreams;
Of the water-bearer who fills and fills
His water cans and never,
Ever saves a single drop
For his dry and withered lips.
    Why should the river smile to me
    As I sail slow and hug the bank?

Again, Jamaal picks up his lute and begins to riff with his awesome depth of tone and breadth of register, the flights of his beautifully long vibratos—twisted and twirled like origami floating in weightless void; and the crowd sighing together at each one of them with an ecstatic, swooning AAAAAHHHHH…

A lovely, sad poem of love loss that has us all swaying and singing along on the refrain—the theater all aflicker with the shifting glow of dozens of lit cell phones swinging in the dark like frantic fireflies.

And as he works his way toward the closing lines, Jamaal lowers his voice to a weary, raspy, and slightly broken baritone—coming back to the figure of the lone artist soaring painfully but beautifully above his suffering:

Mountains upon mountains of forbidding
Has fate raised between you and me,
But I am no eagle and no angel and cannot soar.
So here I am, adrift and lost
Down the river of time
And bittersweet remembrance—
Wailing and weeping on my lute,
Mourning the false promise of your eyes,
Your love sighs under the raven wings of the night,

The lush and glorious gardens
Of your treacherous heart.
    Why should the river smile to me
    As I sail slow and hug the bank?

———

After the concert, the two of us went over and chatted with Amal and her boyfriend for a while. We went out together, walked a few blocks down the street, and parted ways with them at the subway entrance.

Then Annaelle and I took a taxi, and it was only when we settled into the backseat that I had a chance to look into her eyes for the first time tonight: they were still brimming with excitement.

She sighed and asked me what I thought of the concert.

"I loved it. It was a great discovery. You know, the river song—"

"Yah Khaaynah."

"Yes. It reminded me of an Egyptian song I used to be very fond of when I was a teenager. I haven't heard that song in years. I must say it was quite an experience. On one level, he's very much of a classicist, but every now and then, he just hits you with a flash of pure iconoclasm—touches of jazz fusion and rock you'd never imagine hearing in Arab music."

"I know, he's a genius. I only know his lyrics from the French translations, though. Sometimes the stuff doesn't seem to make a whole lot of sense in translation. Do you think—"

"His lyrics are really great. I don't think any translation could ever do them justice. We could go over the stuff together, if you'd like—compare the translations with the original lyrics."

"That'd be nice," Annaelle said, and she leaned back and started looking out the window with a dreamy smile.

———

The taxi dropped us next to a backstreet off Rue du Cardinal Lemoine, a walled alley similar to Rue Garcieuse.

I told her that I would like to walk her home. I could hear my voice bounce off the thick stonewall and tumble down the tunnel of the confined street—as soon as they were spoken, those words sounded like an utterance that did not belong to me.

She walked by my side for a moment, but when we came to where the street began to curve, vanishing into the shadows of Rue Descartes, she stopped and swung around on her heels to face me.

It was late and the backstreets were utterly silent. Her statuesque skin was a pale shade of ocher under the yellow streetlamp: "Thanks for walking me this far. Shall we have croissants at Papa's tomorrow morning? Around ten or so?"

I smiled and said, "Tomorrow?"

She returned my smile, but Annaelle's features looked tired. Her lips were dry and the shadows along her dimples deep: "In a few hours. I stand corrected." She looked into my eyes with deeply moving earnestness and said, "It's good to know that, isn't it?"

As she uttered those words, there was once again the same feeling of dissolving reality within me, like our first minutes in the garden yesterday—the baffling impression that this was not at all happening in material space; only now there was the added realization that Annaelle had so much beauty manifested in her at once, and so profoundly that it was almost impossible to stand still and bear this moment, grasp it in all its dazzling shades and colors—the breathtaking beauty of her, of us suspended here above time and space, between the echoing walls of this deserted street in Paris.

The night air was soft and cool and charged with dew, and for some utterly inexplicable reason, I felt the moment and the place were appropriate this time around: I leaned forward in an attempt to kiss her, but she put her hand across my chest, gently, and dragged it down a mere fraction of a second.

It was our first touch.

She said, "Croissants later. And orchids—loads of them."

Annaelle was nearly breathless as she spoke—I could see the blood pounding beneath her jaw line, the sinews around her neck tightening.

Her eyes were getting restless. I knew I had to go.

So I started to retreat, theatrically, comically—trying to look like a courtier making his deferential backward exit before a queen.

She chuckled quietly and held out her arms in parallel lines, like a traffic officer: "Keep backing out like that—you'll be able to clear that mean, bristly lamppost in two seconds."

"Sweet dreams," I whispered.

She just smiled.

———

Later, toward dawn, I awoke from a strange rambling dream:

I am making out with Thouraya on the couch in my Rades studio—haltingly, awkwardly, almost reluctantly.

She is wearing a very short skirt and no underwear and feels totally not in the mood.

I am not sure if she has begun to sense my half-heartedness, but she, too, is painfully unresponsive; and when she speaks to me, her voice is broken, bitter, and openly hostile—the voice of an aggressive drinker in her cups: "I haven't shaved them in weeks," she says.

With my cheek pressed against her bosom, I look up into her sad eyes, not knowing what to say. I can feel all her sadness deep inside me, as if it is my own.

But she interprets my silence as stupidity: "I'm talking about my legs, genius—not my eyebrows."

Suddenly, the phone rings and I pick it up with relief.

It is the French woman—the one who kissed me last night on our way back from the theater. She looked like Audrey Hepburn, but she would not get off her bicycle as we kissed, and I still have a vivid memory of my lower body pressed against the cold, gnarly metal.

Now the French woman is saying that she loves me, and I suddenly feel moved, dreaming furtively with her—of escape, of random walks along deserted beaches.

"A new beginning," she says, "a new life. We owe it to ourselves."

After I hang up, I tell Thouraya I have a situation that I need to deal with: "My father-in-law is very sick. He's downstairs in my mother's house. I have to run down and see what I can do."

Instead, I find myself walking across the main hall of the Sorbonne with a group of students, complaining about the stupidity of not allowing Catholics to proselytize.

We are all heading to a theology lecture and as we walk out of the main building and into the annex across the court, I realize that the stones of the annex are moldy and crumbly, the age-old doorframe termite-infested with chunks of rotten wood coming off.

Inside, in a neon-lit corridor, a half-bald, dark-bearded man meets me outside his office, telling me that the photocopies are almost ready.

Then, all at once, the urge grips me in my groin like a nettle sting: I have to run out and relieve myself.

I dash out of the annex, and discover that it is snowing heavily outside— a swarm of thin, wind-driven artificial snowflakes blowing across the court, some sort of volatile Styrofoam-like material.

"Not again!" I shout, as I find myself standing in the middle of a familiar path (the one I take with my family on our Sunday walks along the Gironde). "Oh God, please, *not this climate shit* again! *The hell with it, I'm going behind a bush* right this moment. *I don't care!"*

There is laughter behind me and I turn around in midstride: I see a very big black-bearded South Asian-looking man snickering.

He is walking with a group of business executive types (suited western men, all of them), but the man himself is dressed casually: a navy-blue jacket and matching slacks, a pink shirt and a gray silk scarf.

They have overheard me and they're still laughing.

In a big booming voice, he tells me to stop talking nonsense. His teeth are like pebbles of white marble.

I decide to ignore him and walk away, until I reach the spot that I have always only half noticed during our long Sunday walks—the roofless, ivy-covered shed-like structure off to the left. Now, in my frenzied urgency, it strikes me as the most appropriate place—a makeshift outhouse.

I step inside the shed (only the doorframe is left intact) and unzip in the middle of the half-stripped ruin, standing over a pile of rubble—shattered bricks and mortar and tiling.

Now, someone else walks right in and stands very close behind me.

I turn around and see another South Asian man—face to face this time. He is younger than the bearded one, his face thin and his eyes very sad.

I decide to hold in my pee at once and begin to study his terribly sad countenance: he is carrying a large yellow notepad with mysterious, neatly written and spaced-out entries.

Standing there with my penis in my hand, I am not at all shocked by the intrusion. Instead, I end up craning my neck further, trying to decipher the entries in the notepad.

His face remains completely blank even as he addresses me: "I'm trying to keep track of all the hopeless bathrooms in the wild," he says. "You'd be surprised how much work it is."

If having faith in new beginnings means a headlong plunge into unknown waters, then that was how it happened for me the morning after—the dash to Jardin des Plantes with Annaelle and the innocent redeeming belief that I was ready for a new start.

I was not able to go back to sleep after my incoherent dream and so I ended up going to the balcony several times to stand in the cool air—smoking, thinking, trying not to feel that I was waiting for the morning.

Eventually, the day dawned and it was cloudy and sulfurous, leaden and unusually warm with tall billowy rainclouds looming over the rooftops of the quarter, appearing strangely yellowish, like desert clouds before a sandstorm.

Earlier on, I had seen the first throbs of the storm from the balcony, flashing in fitful flickers of pale light reverberated high above the horizon line—in one instant, the tricorn slate rooftops would light up with a glossy deep-purple sheen; followed by a second of fully impenetrable darkness before everything fell back into place.

The peculiarly unmitigated quality of that false darkness had reminded me of a dream I once had: I was blind in the dream, and

I had no sense of depth, no mind-picture of anything around me. The suffocating panic was overwhelming—it felt like being fully immersed in tar with my eyes wide open.

———

I began to sweat already walking the short stretch between Zoé's building and Papa's, the café on the street corner opposite the fountain.

Luckily, I decided to skirt the thick multitude of shoppers and loafers that milled around the stands on the marketplace—working my way through the crowd on Zoé's sidewalk then taking a wide turn on the outer edge of the throng toward the fountain and the café across.

All the businesses around the square had their awnings rolled out.

When I got to Papa's, I went in to take a look, but she was not there. I stepped back outside and waited on the terrace.

I just sat there and tried to empty my mind. Eyes fixed on the outer rim of the fountain to the left—the random patterns of white water tumbling down into the basin, the patches of verdigris, the pigeons hopping on and off the base.

I suppose it was a sort of private wager with myself—trying to focus on how long I could sit motionless, thought-free. A playful attempt to trick time.

Eventually, she did appear where I guessed she would—on the outer edge of the crowd and within my line of sight—but I did not get to see her entire body before she came up around the fountain.

I smiled and addressed her as she drew near me: "You took the same detour as me. What a great nose! You must have been a blood-hound in another lifetime. An Arab bloodhound?"

She stopped and stood over the table, laughing with her head thrown back, the same way she had laughed at her hair joke yesterday.

Today she wore a snow-white drop waist dress with a bright print pattern of scarlet tulip buds and a pair of flat thong sandals. That was all she wore—along with an agate neck ring and a dusty-green buckskin pouch slung over her shoulder.

She was ravishing and it took all my pride and will power to refrain from looking at her too directly, to deny her spellbinding power over me in those painful first seconds as I tried to remain in playful, casual verbal intercourse with her.

And I was also thinking of the coming rainstorm—and what was to become of our walk in the garden, as if calling it off now would make her vanish into thin air.

Unlike me, however, Annaelle did not appear to be concerned about any of those somber considerations.

She sat down and leaned across the table and started matching wits with me, staring straight into my eyes with a frown of mock toughness: "I guess you know what they say about where all roads lead. I walked up to your building thinking maybe I'd run into you, found the square too crowded and skirted it altogether, detouring toward the fountain instead—exactly like you, mister."

———

Annaelle and I did not go back to last night. We just sat there and watched the fountain, had our croissants and café au lait, talked fitfully about orchids.

The sky kept rumbling with remote but tangibly threatening thunder.

I was quite worried about the impending rainstorm and at some point told her so: "I hate to interrupt our cozy lounge here, but we probably need to run along, don't you think? Before it starts pouring, you know."

She said, "I wouldn't worry about that at all. Actually, it's good luck to walk in the rain, didn't you know? It's cleansing—spiritually cleansing. I love doing it in the summer."

I just looked at her, without any particular expression on my face.

She returned my gaze and spoke again, blushing a little: "What? Are you actually—concerned about us walking in the rain? It's very warm and muggy, and it would actually do us a lot of good."

She did not say "afraid," and her words did not sound at all like a challenge.

"It *is* good luck," she added with a smile that was meant to reassure me.

I smiled in return and I told her, "One thing *I* know, I did a lot of *swimming* under the rain in Tunisia, and I can testify that it's a lot of fun—in the summer, of course. But I never tried walking in the rain. It looks like I'm going to find out soon enough, though."

Eventually, we stood up and left Papa's.

We skirted the square and the market crowd altogether and walked in the direction of Rue Gracieuse.

Long before we got to the alley, though, the thick clouds ripped open all at once and the rain came pouring down. Rue Gracieuse was not in sight yet and we were already soaking wet.

Annaelle put her hand on my elbow. The streets suddenly began to appear eerily deserted and she must have mistaken my Tunisian prejudice against walking in the rain for lack of resolve or discouragement.

In fact, I was very much in the mood for experimentation and certainly not discouraged. It was also hot and the rain felt warm and rather pleasant in this sultry weather.

And there was Annaelle's touch of course: the heedless power that touch had given me as we plunged forward through the thread curtains of rain! An act of pure poetry—perhaps her way of telling me that in the end, the grave and purposeful judgment of those who had decided to desert the streets did not matter in the eyes of two people embarked on a poetic journey to Orchidland.

In a matter of minutes, the sidewalks were churning and sizzling with jumping craters of white foam as the rain kept coming down in huge drops—runoff already flowing down the middle of the slanted street in thin sheets like liquid glass. The driving deluge was flailing hard against the awnings of the shops and the cafés, the deserted doorways of the townhouses, the parked cars in the empty alleys; bearing down on the city in thick sheets that whipped the slate roofs and rose on the updraft in long spectral wisps of spray.

By the time we got to Rue Gracieuse, Annaelle's dress was soaked through, sticking to her slender frame like a blood-smeared sheet. Her hair was slicked back in one straight tassel down the nape of her neck.

I ran and took shelter under one of the porches and she followed me. My need to look at her was physically unendurable—to take all of her magical presence into me, like a long breath of fresh morning air, a hungry drag of star shine and memories.

As we stood in our temporary shelter, with the water sloshing and rippling down the cobblestone street, I noticed that her breasts were not as small as I had imagined.

I just could not help it: trying not to think of last night's rejection, I lay my hand on her hair—ran the tip of my fingers through it.

It was soft as silk.

"Annaelle," I said.

She gave me a wry smile: "I know. The curls are pure artifice. What did you expect? Conditioner and elbow grease. All it takes is a bit of rain, and poof! Back to the old straight hair. Your basic European hair."

"Your hair is *gorgeous*, Annaelle—like everything else about you. You look like a real—nymph with your hair like this."

"Compliments—again?"

She still had the ironic smile on her face.

Rainwater dripped from her chin and she looked marble cold even though her face was flushed.

"Sorry," I said, "I just couldn't help it."

"Never mind. On a more practical note, I believe we have a mission to carry out, right? Or are we just going to—hang out here?"

Annaelle's face had once again undergone one of those sudden shifts as she spoke, her eyes brightening up with a playful, naughty smile.

"Annaelle," I said "you're soaked all over and—"

"Tariq, dear, do you want us to stop *here?* We've come more than halfway already! I'm feeling *great*—and we're not cold. This rain is actually a *blessing* in this suffocating heat. Don't you think?"

She did not say "quit," but this time her words did sound like a dare.

And that was when it happened: something in me just opened up at once and I lost all hesitation. I was ready to take the plunge.

"You're on," I said to her. "Show me how fast you can run!"

We both dashed out into the rain, and starting from that moment the sensory world became a shifting mosaic of fleeting perceptions without depth or material substance—flying impressions whizzing by on either side of us like fragments from a blurry film, all the way to the Winter Garden.

When we entered Jardin des Plantes, we slowed down a bit and as we ran up the rise toward the Winter Garden, she asked me to wait. She wanted to take off her sandals.

"My thong notches are killing me," she said.

Farther downhill by the Rotunda, the dark tangle of the magnolia grove shook like heavy drapery as the pounding rain ripped and lashed in the canopy, lifting up from the treetops in long gray plumes of spray.

We ran on up the ramp and dashed through the west door into the mossy, humid warmth of the Winter Garden.

For all I knew, the place was completely deserted.

She kept on running, eventually settling into an easy jog, and I just followed her—past the first pots and planters of orchids, neatly arranged on long, age-old tables that looked like workbenches and butcher counters.

Farther to the right, behind the usual row of potted tropical plants, the rain rapped at the oblong bluish glass panels of the greenhouse, with the water coming down from the eaves like chunks of icicles.

I said, not without irony, "Is this how it's supposed to be?"

She stopped for an instant with her face half turned toward me. Her cheeks were flushed pink, but her eyes looked ice-cold and driven: "What is?" she asked me, sounding impatient, almost disappointed.

"I mean the tour. Are we going to *run* through the show like this?"

I must have sounded rude or whiny to her ears, because she went right back to jogging: "Yes. The first time around, yes."

Annaelle's dress flapped around her hips and thighs with a wet sound. She kept going and I went on running close behind her.

We rushed past the tropical pond toward the south wing of the greenhouse, then we came to a skywalk and she stopped.

"This is so beautiful!" I gasped.

"Come," she said, "let's get up there. It does get better."

The skywalk started with a banistered spiral staircase of galvanized steel. From where I stood, I could see at the top of the stairs a circular structure made of teak planking that looked like a small garden deck or the terrace of a tree house.

From the bottom of the staircase all the way up and around the deck, the skywalk was festonned with lush tropical vines. And on the deck surface, lined up side by side against the glistening leafy curtain of the vines, there were round pots overflowing with creeping orchids artfully draped over the deep-green leaves behind them—their sensuous, bright petals bursting with color.

I stood still at the top of the stairs: it was more than one single heart could take in an instant like this. And the sight of her walking over to the opposite end of the deck before my eyes—sashaying *for* my eyes, like a strange rite of courtship in dance.

Annaelle craned her neck and stood on the balls of her feet, like a dancer, and then she swung around to face me with her eyes closed and her arms held out crosswise: "Now you may," she said.

And I did. With adoration, with playful butterfly-stroke tenderness, with mad longing, melting together with her into one single being, one single drop of thumping hot blood—like one of her scarlet tulip buds in their ocean of whiteness.

And the thick summer rain all hail and hammers on the ceiling of our iron-veined glass dome, our sanctuary of an hour: this place of escape so suddenly, so unbelievably stolen from the indifferent life of the city; far-flung and withdrawn from the hectic flux of time, given to me fully and freely, all at once—mine to take, by will or by chance or by providence or whatever force of giving that had put me here in this magical place, with this magical woman.

———

When the rain began to let up, we left the greenhouse and headed back through the alleys, following a different route than the one we had taken on our way down to the garden.

The backstreets were still deserted and the smooth round cobblestones were cool and shiny as metal, rainwater still trickling downhill between them.

The mortared back walls of the old apartment buildings, thoroughly soaked with rainwater, were unrecognizable: in their metamorphosed state, they made the buildings look strangely anonymous, like giant cardboard boxes thrown together at random, odd angles.

It was like walking through a city without a name, where space itself had to be claimed back and redefined, gained from the tides of oblivion.

(A believer: I suppose that was how I felt and acted on that morning.

I must have simply, blindly, ineffably believed in the fated nature of the moment—the predestined force of the days and the hours that had led up to that walk with Annaelle in an anonymous rainwashed street in Paris.

I also believed in the woman herself and in the beautiful gift that she had made of our garden outing.

And isn't it the power of belief that makes love what it is in our imagination—an event inextricably tangled with fate? Having faith in the fantasy that it—love—was all destined to happen to us from the start, that it was all written in the tangled womb of the universe from the instant we drew our first breath.)

She was still barefoot and I was about to ask her if she felt all right walking without shoes. But then I remembered her telling me just moments ago how walking barefoot under a summer rain was one of the most poetic things she could possibly think of.

I walked by her side in silence, admiring her beautiful feet, noticing with wonderment that she had six toes on her left foot.

We decided to go to a hotel and get a room.

I suggested Hotel du Cardinal and we joked about our lack of luggage: "We don't have a credible, bona fide bourgeois suitcase," I said. "We'll look exquisitely suspicious."

"Don't worry about that," Annaelle retorted. "I'll conjure up a suitcase for us right now. I have a friend who has a shop right around the corner. I'll buy us T-shirts and shorts—*and* a bag! You get us something to eat."

I bought cherries, rosé, and savory petits fours and waited for her in the alley where the taxi had dropped us off last night.

The hotel was housed in an impeccably renovated eighteenth-century townhouse and had the distinctive *passage cocher* entrance with a beautiful door, a vaulted gateway, and a small but elegant courtyard inside.

When we were within the gateway, I told Annaelle that I needed to call Samia.

I leaned against the wall of the passage and watched her walk up to the front desk—she had either bought or borrowed a miniscule potato-shaped rolling suitcase and was actually pulling it behind her, its tiny rollers clicking between the cobblestones.

I dialed Samia's number and waited.

The passage where I stood was rather dim—only a feeble light from the lamp dangling on a thick black chain. The courtyard looked much brighter by contrast, and farther away than it actually was—the lush green shrubbery against the bright walls and the white marble fountain with its single jet of water gushing upward;

the potted saw palmettos in the corners, their fronds nodding like black tinfoil feathers in the rain.

I asked Samia if everything was all right.

She said that everything was fine: "I had to order lunch, though. We could not—"

"I know. What a downpour!"

I smiled and looked at the rain falling into the courtyard, thinking that I was referring to something we had in common even though I was living this rain in a way that she could not even begin to imagine.

"Now it's raining again," she said.

"So it is," I replied.

There was a sudden urge to share my secret with her, immediately followed by the pained awareness that I would only spoil the poetry of the moment if I told her that I was watching the same rain in the same neighborhood—so close yet so far: the rain that was pattering on the balustrades of the courtyard balconies, shaking the palmetto fronds, whispering in the potted plants, rapping secretively on the window panes; the rain that I was going to listen to from the shelter of a room with my lover in just a few minutes.

I did not tell her anything, of course. She said that if the rain kept up, they would play games in the apartment and watch cartoons later.

———

We ate and drank in our temporary shelter, a cozy courtyard-level room. We smoked and made love.

And the rain kept falling—soft and steady now, echoing with a faint hiss in the hedge outside our window.

The courtyard was like a well of sibilant reverberations. I imagined the plants and the palms nodding softly as I lay in bed with her, and I remembered the Arabic word for the hissing sounds of the rain: *khareer*.

———

Oh God, how I believed.

———

That night, after I put the boys to bed, I spent many hours on the balcony thinking and writing.

I remembered the time that I had spent with my sons in Biarritz after our return from Tunisia—days that seemed so removed from what I was beginning to experience now, a dark stretch of time when I found myself full of unfulfilled desire and in a panic at the prospect of a life without a meaningful relationship.

And now there was this woman and me and the thought, full of excited anticipation, that things were looking up, that I was at last beginning to see the light.

The rain stopped a while ago. Then the sky began to clear up.

And now the night is slipping into the ethereal predawn hour—the air turning cool and crisp; the moon over the rooftops.

Our first real conversation today in the hotel room:

The beautiful resonance of her voice filled the room with soft echoes of dreamy poetry. As she lay on her side and spoke with her eyes closed, her skin, her whole body had metamorphosed in the bluish-gray twilight of our room—sublimated into something both magical and impalpable; even her scent had shifted (a rarefied redolence of roses and broken grass) now that she had allowed herself to relax by my side.

As Annaelle grew introspective in our temporary bed, fully sincere and trusting, there was only one thought racing in my mind: to ease her sorrow— eradicate all the scarred stories of drug abuse that she confided to me with so much pained candor.

Kneeling beside Annaelle, with my face bent near to her, I began to kiss her whole body: "I believe in you—everything you were, are, and will be. I believe in us and in every thread of time in which our destiny was spun, in the circumstances that have made us exist, come together, and emerge resurrected from the dead blank emptiness that was the before. I believe in our power to write our new page, our new story; to exist above everything and everyone, above chance and circumstance (and even time itself).

"As we dwell in the precious now (every second of this eternal now that we inhabit), I want you to witness it unfold, our story, because this is what I am doing, with my lips and my fingertips: I am erasing all the pain that was and writing everything that is and will be. Do you feel the traces of my lips and my fingertips? They are the trail in the sand—our path in the desert that you love so much, even more than I do. There is a moment during the day when the sun begins to descend behind the dunes and the hollow curves in the sand turn dark and deep, and the dune ridges shift to a color that is neither drab silver nor bluish-gray, but both—a color beyond perception or comprehension. Your skin, my love, has now turned into that moment of beautiful indefinite fading, and it has grown more beautiful than any color the sands have ever given."

Words of weak sentimentalism, and yet those were the exact words that I so deeply, so achingly wanted to say while I caressed Annaelle's body.

But I never uttered them, simply because I had feared, the moment I had felt them form in my mind, that they would no doubt fall flat the instant they were spoken.

Words that I was now revisiting once again in my memory, sitting on Zoé's balcony; and they were making me, once again, weak and sentimental yet filled with undefined intimations of peace and giving and abandon: to let my rigid "I" melt and flow unconditionally into this world of new feelings that had just been revealed to me through her—a new world created through the magical powers of our chemistry.

(And now, after all the words—past and present—have been written, after all the retrospective pondering, you still find yourself face to face with the inescapable truth that words and thoughts can never fathom the full reality of what happened in those last days of summer.

All these interminable words, past and present: you ultimately have to admit that they are no more than ghostly substitutes for the ineffable substance of those days of abandon and serene resolve; those precious moments when, weak sentimentalism or no, you felt assured that you could rise above yourself, buoyed by the heroic and innocent belief that those first words of confession from Annaelle about her addictions—the sound of her most private sorrows echoing in your rented room—were more than a tragic secret confided to you; they signified a once-in-a-lifetime gift you swore to keep locked in your bosom, cherishing it like the beat of your own heart.)

———

Our last days together were beautiful and carefree. Even the sweltering heat and humidity were no more than a vague, remote irritant that had no place in the world of esthetic bliss we had managed to create together.

The only time that I sensed some difference between us was the day after our hotel room tryst, when I suggested we go to the Cardinal once again. Annaelle flatly rejected my proposition, telling me that she did not feel comfortable going there on a regular basis.

It was around sundown and we were lounging together on the lawn in Arènes de Lutèce. The heat was starting to ease off, and the evening scents of the garden were beginning to rise into the humid air. The hour was suffused with that peculiar feeling of quietude that never failed to envelop the city at the end of a hot summer day.

The sky off to the west was streaked with contrails that reflected the last blush of sunset—some of them were loose and fleecy-looking in the afterglow, like scattered cloud puffs.

She also told me (perhaps to change the subject or to deflect the awkwardness of the moment) that I had probably never been in the Arènes at night.

"Of course not," I said.

Annaelle was studying the contrails as she spoke: "I'll take you there. No, wait, wait. What am I saying? I'll *bring* you here, but it'll be like going somewhere else altogether. It beats trysting in an anonymous hotel room hands down."

I was beginning to understand.

I said, "That sounds like a great idea, but how are you going to get us inside?"

She raised her eyebrows and gave me a playful, mischievous smile: "Don't you worry about it. That's *my* job. After all, I'm a nymph, remember? Everything is possible with a nymph. I suppose you know that by now."

———

It did not take me long to understand the full significance of Annaelle's words.

In her own mysterious way, she was telling me that this city was filled with small unknown spaces of intimacy for us to appropriate—places of beauty that we could call our own and invest with our imagination. It was as if, together with her (*through* her) I was beginning to turn into a being that I had never been able to become on my own. I was beginning to acquire a virtue that I had never suspected existed in me: the power of improvisation.

And so I just let Annaelle guide me, allowing myself to discover with her all these new "lovers' rites," as she called them—rituals of togetherness that I saw as the first symbols of my rebirth: she taught me to cavort around Jardin du Luxembourg and laze on the lawns and sneak behind the arbors with her for long passionate kisses, like a teenager with time on his hands; she taught me to hug and caress and whisper love words under the bridges and along the canals in the long, silent night hours; she taught me the art of sharing the stories locked inside my head—stories about my private thoughts and secret uncertainties in those brittle first moments with her, stories about the slowing of the flow of time during a cherished moment, stories about the infinite peace and beauty of scattered impressions coming together like drops of seawater crystallizing into salt; she taught me to speak to her about the miraculous alchemy and all-but-impossible odds of meaningful attractions.

As I witnessed the transforming power of Annaelle's presence in my life, I gradually came to understand why she did not think it necessary for us to "get a room," as she once wittily put it: there was so much of this endlessly festive, blessed city that was simply there, given for us to marvel at and to cherish. In those few days, she managed to show me in so many unspoken ways how to unveil and explore things and places in myself that I never even knew existed.

Those were also the days when I came to realize, once and for all, that I was now ready to reinvent myself and my attitude toward the world. In embracing the improvised mode of existence that she had created for us, I was stunned to find out that I had enough power of belief in me to do these quirky new things that were ours amid all those anonymous strangers—the transient tourists—with their bodies and their motions, their private wills and motives, their gazes and theirs guesses; amid all those perceived fields and forces of hostile otherness that had always inspired mistrust and fear in me—beings, things, energies, and volitions that I had always considered fundamentally irreconcilable with what I was.

For all I knew, those projected fields and forces of hostility had disappeared from my life forever.

As if by miracle, in accepting to live from one day to the next, I became enthralled with the fancy that there was only Annaelle and I in this world of utter unpredictability that she had managed to create out of nothing. Together we were floating through the most exquisite universe of esthetic detachment: a space of our own, indeed, marvelously labyrinthine and indefinite; and so much more intense and enchanted than I had ever thought imaginable—a space where everything was indeed possible.

West '08

*A*lways *the same walk—same pace, same stops, same duration:*
Up *the jetty opposite the Croisic fish market on the headland—standing*
at the head of the jetty for a while with the pleasure harbor and the sailboats
behind you at the bottom of the bay—gazing into the horizontal depth of the
sea, filling your eyes with the limitlessness of it;

then it's back down the jetty and on toward the one-lane country route to
your right, walking due north along the grassy shoulder of the road, past the
oyster nursery in the cove down below, its barnacle-studded rocks dark and
dull at low tide, like shapeless furry lumps jutting out of the graphite muck;

past the snow-white, gingerbread-trimmed belle époque mansion ensconced
amid the pines beyond the road—the only visible trauma center construction
from here, historic flagship building of an institution that you have pledged,
along with all the other "residents," to embrace as your "Community" (which it
is in many ways—your only home since you left that Paris hospital in the fall);

finally, there comes the high point of the walk: with the city limit sign of
Le Croisic receding behind you along with the tall wrought-iron fence of the
Community and all sense of place and space marks, you leave the route and
take the snug, hardly noticeable side road to the right (no more than a tortu-
ous pebble path, actually, choked with sand drift and sedge and salt-seared
ferns, sweet flags and cattails and rushes);

and your feet and the rest of you know: you are almost out among the dunes
now—and the gray weathered wooden bench by the path (where you will sit to
face the hazy expanse of the sea) is just a few steps away after the last rise.

Before long, you find yourself on the bench, no more than an arm's length away from the twenty-five-year-old man who has been your semiofficial guardian since you were transferred from Paris (trim-bodied, clean-shaven, neat-ponytailed Sylvain—seated at the end of the bench and always somewhat uneasily, as if he were about to stand up any moment and walk off; the bevel of the outer slat cutting across his buttocks, his back half-turned to you).

Ignoring his rudeness, with your mind fully intent on making the most of these last moments of open space, you allow your gaze to travel across the flat infinity of the Atlantic—the great slate-gray expanse stretching to the point where the sea fuses into the gauzy rim of the livid sky.

About an hour after leaving the center (the so-called Community), I stood up and began to walk back toward the complex, with Sylvain following close behind me.

Sylvain was not a police employee, but his guardianship—Dr. Cohen's grudging concession to the Justice System—did carry a great deal of authority: the man's cold mechanical presence during these daily walks was part of a set of court-ordered security precautions that had to be provided by the center. (The cripplingly complex battery of institutional measures set in motion to regiment a man who loses sovereignty over his own choices become even more complex and restrictive once that man is branded as suicidal.)

Within the protective microcosm of "The Community," however, everyone tried hard to be polite and caring about the brand, with the staff going to great lengths to avoid any reference to the forbidden word: "security."

"Guided Social Activity": that was the concept created by Dr. Cohen to define what I did with Sylvain every day from two to three, the same term with which her staff coordinator tagged museum tours and the outreach activities organized by nonprofits here or in town.

This particular trauma center is, after all, an institution that proudly bills itself as "holistic" and "alternative." A pilot project of national significance, it is the only Level-II trauma center in Europe that boasts three separate buildings housing each of the three divisions that make it possible for the center to provide definitive care for all types of trauma: Neurology/Neuropsychiatry, Rehabilitation, and Psychiatry—the latter being the flagship division, a nationally renowned service headed by Dr. Cohen in the historic building visible from the road.

I remember once briefly discussing the matter of my transfer with Dr. Cohen: she told me then that the head of the trauma center in Paris had made a good decision by sending me to Le Croisic instead of Lille. The Centre de la Mémoire in Lille was excellent, she explained, but the personnel in the psychiatry and neuropsychiatry divisions here were better equipped to deal with a case that might require hypnotherapy.

———

I was transferred in the late fall of 2007, and my first day here started with both distress and triumph.

The initial signs of distress emerged during my first "work meeting" with Dr. Clémence Cohen and Dr. Pierre Masson from neuropsychiatry, the center's leading expert in clinical hypnosis. Both doctors opened the meeting by referring to my initial work with the neurorehabilitation psychologists in Paris and the "challenges" that "we" were going to face here in reconstructing the events that had led to my traumatic injury on August 30.

I was shocked and shaken when they told me that their primary therapeutic goal, along with the work of rehabilitation, was to help me "recapture the real events" that occurred in the night between August 29 and August 30.

In other words, I was now confronted with two doctors who were proposing to resume where the Paris doctors had left off! They were offering to base my entire therapy on "real events" that had nothing to do with my recollections of that night in Paris: those memories roiling my mind day and night were the only empirically valid truth, I knew it with certainty, and yet I could not help but feel deeply shaken and discouraged.

I was also terrified.

Rereading my copious diary notes on that first encounter, I realize how violently upset I was (due to my impairments, the exchange among us took place in written form on my laptop):

Dr. Cohen: "Initial neurorehabilitation and occupational therapy work is going well, and so is speech-language pathology. We need to build on the progress that was achieved in Paris. Our focus in the weeks ahead will be on helping you recapture the real events that took place—in order to be well prepared for our work on your loss and the grief process that will ensue when the reality of your loss begins to sink in. The confabulation that you experienced while working with our colleagues in Paris is to be expected due to the effects of trauma."

Tariq: "Listen, we've been over this before. I told the doctors in Paris: facts are facts and there is no denying them—regardless of the number of people who are doing the denying. I may be in a state of shock, but I am fully capable of recalling what I saw in Zoé's apartment a few hours before my injury—that is an empirical fact. Your mission as doctors is not to elide or curtail or delete or redact. My sons were in Paris in those dreadful hours; I was in Paris in those dreadful hours! That is what I experienced empirically; that is what I recollected when I emerged from my coma; that is what I recollect now; that is what I will always recollect. You seem to be aware that I did see Commissaire Collin a few days after waking from my coma. He was the second person I spoke with from outside the hospital, after Sami. We only spoke briefly and already one of the psychiatrists had to interfere: he warned him that I was not ready to be questioned. Then there was the report that your colleagues sent to the prosecutor and the decision to suspend the investigation. You know all this, of course. What you don't know (or seem to ignore) is the crucial fact that I immediately recognized the commissaire at the Paris center: the instant I saw Collin I knew exactly who he was—I had an immediate recollection of the functions that he had performed the night my sons died. I told your colleagues in rehabilitation—the team in Paris. I explicitly told them who he was in full detail. I cannot even begin to fathom the atrocity of what the medical staff in Paris did: how can they even mention an 'accident' when I never left Paris in my car that night?"

Dr. Masson: "Mr. Abbassi, based on information obtained from your computer files, we can develop a very helpful reconstructive memory approach.

Luckily, we have learned that you were researching and planning a novel that features events strikingly similar to the murder scenario you related to our colleagues in Paris, and the deposition procedure at the Prefecture. The rehabilitation staff at the Paris center found a number of files and the outline of a novel in progress."

T: "Great. That's just great. The great big investigative breakthrough! It's nothing new, Doctor. They told me the exact same thing in Paris. They said the police made copies of my computer and my disks and even my note-books and text messages before they gave my belongings to the staff. Listen, this meeting has just started and we're already talking in circles. In fact, not only is this conversation going nowhere, it's making me tired and exasperated. I keep saying that the empirical facts conveyed to a human being by his sense perceptions are the only credible, undeniable reality that exists, and you keep referring to some completely senseless theory about a novel in progress whose content remained in my head and that I somehow managed to extend to my experience in the real world. So we are never going to be able to find a working agreement—this harassment has to stop right now. We have to stop talking about the most horrible night of my life RIGHT NOW! Right after these words."

And they both stopped, miraculously. The mendacious, outrageous version of reality on which they premised the meeting was immediately set aside and Dr. Masson began to speak about hypnotherapy and the possibilities it provided in cases of amnesia.

Speaking with them today I felt weak, sad, and confused; but there was a certain desperate power in my words—the power of conviction in and by the truth of my story. Somehow that power must have impinged upon Dr. Cohen and Dr. Masson. They immediately stopped referring to the "accident," and they both indicated that they were committed to helping me "elucidate" the truth.

August 29-30:

Looking back on those decisive hours, trying to grasp the quantity and quality of my recollections, I am stunned at the extraordinary nature of what happened the instant that I saw Commissaire Collin at the Paris trauma center, a few days after I awoke from my coma. While most of what took place between the evening of August 29 and the early hours of August 30 remained blurry and confused in my conscious thoughts, what occurred

between the moment I was confronted with the awful reality of my sons'
deaths and the moment of my injury was within recall. The recollections
were certainly distorted and raw-video-like and nightmarish, but their exis-
tence in my mind as a narrative totality was intelligible from the outset
and, yes, structurally/sequentially cohesive in its odd otherworldly way: my
discovery of Shams and Haroon's dead bodies in the early hours of August
30; the rash doomed visit to the morgue ordered by Collin; my subsequent
detention at the Prefecture on Quai de Gesvres and the consequences that
followed from it.

As I try to come to terms with the fateful concatenation of those horrid events,
I realize that the existence of my memory as a cognitive whole (its presence in my
mind as a visual-mental entity*) is an eerie mixture of clarity and distortion.*
Shortly after I awoke from my coma, I was able to recollect significant details of
my detention, my suicide attempt, and even the intervention of the paramedics.
However, even as I write these words, I realize that the form *(or "format"?) in*
which my recollections come back to me appears to be rather strange—an eerie
unsettling mixture of both extreme focus and extreme distortion, like a surreal
collage from a jumbled dream: sometimes I will remember my Prefecture cell as a
sleek space with rounded out edges punctuated by protruding dark-gray cement
or concrete structures (rounded out, too); and at other times, it will appear in my
memory as an oppressively low, earth-toned room in a Saharan mud house not
unlike the one where I once vacationed with Regina in the Tunisian desert.

After those initial written exchanges and the firm position that I took
on the truthfulness of my version of the events, Dr. Cohen and Dr.
Masson changed their attitude toward me completely: starting from
that day, they ceased to challenge my narrative and the empirical
facts on which it was founded.

My work relationship with the two doctors and the rest of the
hospital staff has been excellent since. Dr. Cohen's help with CGD in
the early phases of the treatment was properly miraculous, and the
results of Dr. Masson's hypnotherapy efforts were brilliant: thanks to
his work, I was able to recall the totality of the events that I had not
recorded in my diary between the evening of August 29 and the early
hours of August 30.

However, I do have some regrets about my initial victory here: in those first days at the center (a period of fear, withdrawal, and confusion), I did not know of the existence of the powerful, highly organized group of criminal individuals behind the murder of my sons— their reach and terrifying capacity to exercise considerable influence over individuals and institutions alike. When I spoke with the two doctors, I did not have the slightest inkling that they had come under the same diabolical pressure as their colleagues at the Paris trauma center.

Also, during that initial phase, I kept thinking of Collin, on and off—wondering what *he* would think of my account of those last hours in Paris. I was still rather stunned at the immediate recognition when I had met him right after my coma—the astoundingly cohesive sequence of recollections that the encounter had triggered.

It was not until the late spring of 2008 that I was able to speak with him.

Writing a sort of summary of my recollections on the tragic events was one of the most important things that I had decided to do here soon after my first meeting with Dr. Cohen and Dr. Masson. That choice turned out to be a highly empowering antidote against the confusing information that had come my way from both institutions.

The decision to record my reality in the diary and analyze it scrupulously—almost moment by moment—was immensely helpful in allaying the dreadful sensation that I was witnessing my self-sovereign mind gradually divested of its powers as an independent entity—its precious contents disintegrating day by day, fading into the insane world around me. Excerpts:

What happened—the hell of that night and the terrible concatenation of events that followed in its wake:

Shortly after my sons' death, Collin had taken me into custody with the intention of questioning and deposing me. Although extremely sick, I was locked up in a holding cell at the Prefecture on Quai de Gesvres.

Collin's decision had an immediate devastating effect on me: left ailing and isolated in a dark and oppressive space, I succumbed to great panic and tried to dash my brains out on the cell door in order to escape my despair.

Instead of escaping, I ended up in the transcendent dimension of near-death experience—the state of heightened otherworldly consciousness that comes with it. I was able to witness the horrid aftermath of my suicide attempt from The Other Side—the hectic intervention of the paramedics, the operating room and ICU.

When I emerged from ICU and the inferno of cerebral monitoring, I had to contend with the physical, psychological, and neurological consequences of my brain injury: motor skill impairment, dysarthria, and dissociative amnesia, to name but a few of the complications that I now had to contend with.

It was fall and Collin and the investigators were barred from questioning me: even though I had regained full consciousness, I was all but crippled by shock, severe panic attacks, and a disorienting sense of not being able at times to conceptualize my identity, define my ego boundaries, or recognize my face in a mirror.

Collin spoke with me only once at the hospital, in the presence of medical staff: I do not know if it was natural dislike or his smoldering irritation at the delays in the investigation, but it was obvious to me from the start that he held me in contempt—no trace of empathy whatsoever on that tough chiseled face, not even perfunctory professional politeness.

The pressure on Collin and the fevered climate of emergency and frustration in those autumn days only further exacerbated existing tensions between the commissaire and Dr. Cohen. Evidently, I was partially exposed to the heat of those bureaucratic power struggles—even in my state I was able to sense the complex power games and the stakes involved.

Collin and his colleagues simply wanted to question me and their attitude toward my case was squarely no-nonsense in its brutal directness: like any hospitalized suspect, I was fit to be interviewed the moment I regained consciousness.

The doctors were dismayed by Collin, but he had a warrant. He ignored the medical staff's demurs and started questioning me—kept at it for a while even though it was obvious that I was in no condition to properly respond to his questions.

The only positive development that emerged from that first encounter with the commissaire: I was able to recognize the man instantaneously. I knew the role that he had played during those fateful hours before my suicide attempt—although in my minimally responsive post-comatose state I found it impossible to fully determine what was happening to me, I was capable of remembering the man.

Ironically, the deadening medications coursing through my body had an unhoped-for assuaging effect in those Paris days: the emerging facts about my narrative and the crushing irrevocability of its tragic culmination, the sinister procession of alien terrifying faces that had entered my life so suddenly in the wake of the tragedy, the inexpressible anonymous rooms and spaces reeking of sickness and sadness and life-or-death struggles—thanks to the sedatives all these nauseating realities of my new life of dispossession and marginal subsistence were metamorphosed into vague and virtual threats, like a distant accumulation of storm clouds looming on the horizon, something probable but still safely hypothetical, a contingent catastrophe that might or might not happen to a fictional character in a yet-to-be-written story.

Amid all this turmoil, Dr. Cohen's plea for an "alternative approach" to my case was viewed favorably by the Parisian doctors: the head of the Croisic center was able to secure backing from her Paris colleagues. Dr. Raimbaud, head of the psychiatric ward in Paris, addressed a copy of my transfer referral to the prosecutor, and by late fall I began preparations for the move to Brittany.

———

When I arrived here I was nothing but pure biological being in a way: unable to reflect without the assistance of a computer, unable to cook, unable to dream, I was reduced to the fundamental elements of physical existence.

I could not even begin to imagine a possible way out of this state of loss and confusion that had shattered my sense of self and brought my existence to a standstill. Here I was, exiled in a remote unknown town, obliged to interact with all these remote unknown others, obliged to learn the excruciating details of what I had done through a psychiatrist whom I had just met, too drugged and too dazed to grasp the full extent of my downfall and destitution (as if the somber twists and turns of the tragedy that had taken place in the summer were the pattern of another man's wretched story, a lurid impossible-to-believe tale of sorrow that I was called upon to contemplate with critical distance).

Along with the labor of recollection, I also had to deal with the arduous process of adjusting to "communal life"—accepting and getting used to the collective character of almost every activity in the Community, from meals to workshop participation to exercise and "outreach events."

My initial reaction to these activities was a combination of mechanical passivity, confusion, and fear. I would mindlessly go along with the other residents for a while, only to withdraw into a sudden tangled state of panic that is quite impossible to render in words or thoughts: an indefinite complex of mental overload and flight reflex followed by some form of stupor—a peculiar type of fatigue that would literally send me wandering off into a nothingness of the mind, an erasure of the senses; and I would end up loitering in the loneliest, most random places—a nondescript corner, a deserted corridor, an out-of-the-way alcove, a broom closet or maintenance room (once Sylvain had to come down to the kitchen and quite literally pick me up—the cooks wanted to start preparing dinner and I was huddled up by the walk-in freezer).

Sometime after the kitchen incident, I got into the habit of stealing away and taking refuge in the men's dormitory:

Once inside my room (my one symbol of private inner space), I would allow myself to let go of my fears—lying down in bed and curling up in the fetal position, or huddling up in a blanket by the picture window.

The hours would pass by without leaving any measurable trace of their passing: time was only the shifting shades of sky color in that window, the cold blinking stars on a clear night, the whine of the winter wind in the treetops, the regular rhythms of Sylvain's machinic appearances.

Those were also the days when I neglected my personal hygiene and physical appearance: the most evident manifestation of my inner sense of inadequacy—plain slovenliness visible to all, exuding from my person like a repellent acrid smell; an embarrassment to everyone else but me.

In the self-image workshop, I worked with a therapist from neighboring Guérande. He had a thin soft beard and called himself a "facial yoga adept." He taught me how to contemplate my face in the mirror while coordinating certain "facial exercises" with "self-reflexive meditation."

He told me that we all needed to learn how to "surpass the negative energies of our less desirable expressions" by affirming "the power of the inner smile"—the subtle messages of self-love we inwardly send to different parts of our body while engaging in "meditative breathing."

It was a "twofold approach," he told me—one that guaranteed "long-lasting healing effects."

He recommended that I do the exercises at different times of the day and one last time before going to bed. He insisted on the double nature of the task—combining meditation with "active physical contemplation" of my face.

I remember the first time I did the exercises on my own:

Sylvain had taken me to a support-group session in one of the second-floor workshop rooms, but I was feeling too listless to participate, and Dr. Gallimard—she introduced herself as Caroline—allowed me to sit at the outer edge of the circle.

At some point, I asked to be excused and went out and shut myself inside the restroom down the corridor.

The turn-of-the-century tiling and bathroom accessories were left intact: the tiny claw-foot cast iron bathtub; the beautiful porcelain-and-brass cross-handle faucets ("HOT"/"COLD" in Gothic script); an original copper-framed mirror above the washbowl.

Ocean wind whipping hard outside: the back garden pond wrinkled like puckered paint; the dead tomato vines whistling in their trellises; the dun-and-russet tufts of fountain grass bending; the savanna-like flat country beyond Rehabilitation—its scatterings of sear yucca leaves like scrap metal, its lone arthritic pines squatting fast in the saw grass and tall ferns.

The face staring back at me was not empty, or weak, or apathetic—or anything that might be associated with the facial expressions of the afflicted: it was more like a lump of matter hastily sculpted into an unfinished look—maybe of deep puzzlement? or anger? or dread?

Maybe. Everything about this face (my face) was hypothetical and tentative and inceptive.

Thinking of what I had learned in the facial yoga workshop, I tried to detect hints of emotion behind this closed countenance. All I was able to discern were the estranging, ungraspable features of a trapped animal still unaccustomed to the confining space of his cage, glowering from a great impenetrable distance of the mind. Even the long stubble on my chin seemed to have an inhuman life of its own—an angry blondish growth of desiccated grass glued to my face.

And the withdrawn, inward pull of my shrunken features—scrunched in somehow, these features, like a dented papier-mâché mask.

Silently, I do part one of the lion face pose—hold my expression and my breath long enough to visualize the movement of my features puckering toward the center of my face.

Then I open my eyes and do lion face, part two.

After three repetitions, I relax my features briefly, close my eyes and contemplate the vacuum of the dark, the dissolution of my gaze into this blissful emptiness even as I follow the inward movement of my breath rushing down toward the depths of my belly.

Now I try to picture, as I breathe, a white wave smoothly gliding forward on the sand then pulling back.

And along with this inner movement of the wave, of my breathing, the smile of recognition, of acknowledgment and gratitude—a nod to the soothing touch of the receding water.

I opened my eyes and began to scrutinize myself: the gaze was still there staring back at me—slightly stranded and out of focus, with a pair of lusterless irises at its pond-green center, like two hazy specks of sunlight in dull water.

The face of hunger, of consuming thoughts, of sleepless go-nowhere ruminations.

I tried to smile once again and was unable to elicit an expression—only a vague twitch around my cheeks.

(My first efforts at self-healing.

Despite all the fumbling attempts, there was always, in those initial days at the Community, the lingering disconcerting thought that none of this was really happening *in* my face, *to* my face; that the secret workings of these healing motions were only operating on some sort of theoretical countenance that I imagined as I closed my eyes.)

———

My initial reaction to Dr. Cohen's work with me:

I do not think it was a consistent resistance strategy; it was not even wariness, for that matter. I must have confronted her with a form of indifference born of fatigue and confusion—a mighty force of silent inertia, like a black hole existing and expressing its force solely in negativity, through its dark power of implosion.

The truth of the matter is that I found Dr. Cohen's presence vaguely pacifying right from the start and at least part of the ineffable feeling of peace that she inspired in me had to do with her endearing appearance: she was wise and poised at fifty and looked very much like Kim Novak.

Our second session took place in her office and she addressed me without hiding behind a persona: Dr. Cohen seemed genuinely pained at the sight of my suffering, and she showed it through the manner in which she spoke—the emphasis she put into her tone, the urgency of her eyes; none of it was strained or theatrical.

She began slowly and deliberately: "I know. You don't want to explore your new environment, you don't want to talk, eat, or do anything except sit down in silence and brace yourself for the next wave of panic. All right, we can skip today's session. No problem. We don't have to talk about why you're here—the chain of events that has brought you here—and we won't talk about the many things we can do together to help you deal with your pain: the panic, the breathing problems, the fatigue, the sleep problems. We'll forget about all that today."

Cohen kept her gaze fixed on me while she spoke. Her eyes felt kind and reassuring, wise and gentle in the way they hovered around my face, knowing but compassionate—eyes that seemed to have had their own share of sorrow.

She wore an off-white blouse and black pants and sat with her legs stretched out and crossed at the ankles, right hand resting easy on her thigh as she used the left one for emphasis. Her black leather chair was placed at an angle before the tall window.

And I remember closing my eyes for a few seconds (a reflex action) as she went on talking in her incongruously raspy smoker's voice—the slow but steady word flow of a speaker who was not expecting a response: "In case you're wondering why we fought against the—people who kept pushing the prosecutor to have you undergo an assessment. Well, the answer is simple: our top priority here is you—*not* their assessment. Helping you regain your strength and your well-being, no matter how long it takes. You will never undergo a forensic screening here. You'll be working with people who are dedicated to the process of healing, not assessing. You can stay here as long as it takes to bring yourself back to wholeness."

She kept making short pauses between those cadenced sentences in order to avoid any risk of cognitive overload, but also in order to convey an impression of calm.

Dr. Cohen kept her eyes fixed on me.

Then she spoke my name: "It's important to keep in mind that you're not alone in your suffering, Mr. Abbassi. There are many residents here who are confronted with extremely complex challenges that are causing them a lot of pain. But they're also learning to conquer pain in order to find their way back to health and happiness, day by day. The Community has so many amazing success stories."

When she was done talking, I failed to realize the session was over. She had to remind me that I was through.

———

Days of bewilderment—a passage in my existence marked by the speechless realization that I was confronted with a totally redefined sense of my thought processes and my outer existence. I did not know it then but the transformation had already begun in the Paris hospital, when I found myself so dependent and confused, but also so fiercely attached to my autonomous judgment. For all my drugged confusion, I knew I was already hard at work trying to assess and decipher the new person that I had become—my relation to the past, my outlook on the future. Even as I found myself processing Collin's towering role and his sinister functions, I became aware that I was going to be laboring with the crumbling residues of damaged memory constructs that I had to rebuild and restore like bombed-out buildings, assembling the material at my disposal slowly and painstakingly—picture by picture, clip by clip, page by page.

My notebooks, my cameras and camcorder tapes, my laptop and external disks with all the files and photos: they were the material receptacles of my identity, and I knew from the start that the sooner I began interrogating them the better.

And there was Sami, of course. My mysterious friend from Bordeaux was the first person that I spoke with—I actually had to do it in writing because of my speech impairment—and he immediately emerged as the only human being that I trusted in this new world I was exploring, an invaluable source of hope and solace through his

unconditional support and his patience pointing out key information about my life before the injury.

Zoé was the third person who was introduced to me by the rehabilitation team in Paris. I was briefed on my former friend's identity
and her role in my life—flashcards patiently designed by the personnel, pictures of the woman and her apartment assembled in a directory bearing her name, selections from our e-mail correspondence.
A rough and hazy collage of who we were, in fragmentary words and
disconnected photos.

Still, for all the knowledge that I now possessed about Zoé
(*because* of it) I kept asking the doctors to deny her access to me,
again and again, notwithstanding her persistent requests. I refused
to face the horrors that I had brought into her life then and I still
do now.

My new relation to the past and its figures:

There they were—onscreen, and on paper. Their stories
unfolding line by line, trace by trace, place by place—in the digital
information displayed on "my" screens, the mushy and conceited
and unbearably solemn scribbles of "my" diary and "my" poetry. I
was now confronted with the task of interrogating all these faces
and places and words—having to process what they meant even
as I struggled with the burden and affliction of my handicaps; to
question those remnants of the past in the same way one revisits
a very significant historic place that one recognizes only in vague
traces and leftovers—an all but erased scene that had turned into
scatterings of ruin, abandoned to wind, weed and weather (skeletal stones and shards of ancient pottery, bits and pieces of dirt-
encrusted mosaics).

Sifting through the rubble of my own secret Carthage.

And secret it was, ultimately, despite my mortifying awareness of
the realities of exposure and public scrutiny—the medical staff's lim-
itless unconditional access to copies of all my documents. In the face
of mounting negative feelings—the accumulated shame and fear
and resentment at the doctors' interference—I managed to develop
very early on an extremely helpful watch-and-wait strategy: I learned

to console myself with the secret knowledge that at the end of the day, the moment would always come when all these horrid people would go back to their meaningless lives; and I would be left alone to commune with the ruins of my vanished life—pausing and reflecting and peering at the debris, but in a different way from them and with a much finer sensibility.

Facing the visual or written remnants of the past by myself and in my own way, I found that I was fully capable of giving them meaningful shape and depth—dusting off the scattered remains of those lives and putting them back together into an emergent totality, breathing significance and density into them.

Disregarding my frail physical and mental condition, I would spend many sleepless hours in intense rumination and self-searching:

Was I capable of tapping into whatever mental and imaginative resources were left in me? To inject sense and structure into this sprawling world of digital and written information that was gradually emerging before my stupefied gaze.

More significantly, was I capable of associating any genuine *feelings* with the information? Despite my frenzied fascination with the leftovers of my past, there was—stubborn and undeniable—the reality of apathy to reckon with: in my new condition, I was quite simply incapable of showing any affect toward any form of stimulus or experience—the second devastating discovery of that late fall of 2007.

Contrary to what most people might have assumed from my stupefied appearance in those days of gradual awakening, the total absence of feeling that I had noticed in myself was intensely painful: the silent sorrow of having to take full cognizance of my metamorphosis into an impaired body and an unfeeling soul—a man deprived of any capacity for emotion, deprived of even the common sensations of guilt and outrage at the spectacle of these guided peeps into what the doctors presented to me as my past.

This shadow-world of words, sounds, and pictures unfolding before my gaze: at first, it was all (now that I have to put a name on it) like successive fragmentary glimpses into the life of another man—very deep, that man, despite the unbearable affectedness and sentimentalism of his prose; plodding under the chosen yoke of stylistic perfection, the grave clouds of solitude, self-pity, and nostalgia.

I *had* no feelings to give to that man (me) and his life, no strength to grow emotional about the devastation he had visited on the people he had once known. Those people were now disincarnate beings on the screen of my laptop and in the pages of my diary—foreign beings calling out to me in an alien tongue that I was powerless to parse and decipher.

Was I capable of breathing genuine meaning into those ghostly residues of existence? Conjuring life from death? Form from the rubble?

———

My session with Dr. Cohen today:

Addressed her for the first time and completely messed things up. (She is a great therapist and a good, good woman—must learn to relate positively to her.)

In her usual informal semi-slangy way, she narrated the story of the man who is always sitting alone on the bench by the central lawn:

She turned halfway around in her swivel chair and said, "You'll see him brooding alone there for hours on end." Pointing toward the window with her thumb. Her chair screeched as she swiveled back around to face me.

"One of my patients calls him 'The Bench Man.' His name is Anthony and his story is quite tragic. He was brought up here a few months ago. Anthony was driving his kids back to their mother's home after a holiday visit with his parents in the Pyrenees. The two children were asleep in their car seats. At some point, he spots one of those roadside store signs you see in the countryside. Anthony decides he needs a pack of cigarettes. Then the store comes up on the left side of the road. There are quite a few cars parked in front of it, so he decides it's perfectly all right to pull over and park on the right *shoulder of that country road. He's thinking he'll only be a minute. No big deal, right? Wrong. As soon as he crosses over to the other side of the road, Anthony sees this big powerful man running out of the shop—a dairy farmer screaming something incomprehensible and dashing across the road*

toward Anthony's car. Only now the car had just gone over the edge of the road and down the cliff—right before the two men's eyes."

She took a long drag on her electronic cigarette and exhaled.

"Anthony forgot to put the handbrake on, and there was no guard-rail along the edge of that mountain road. And now he was literally running for dear life—his children's life—trying to jump after that car, to stop the course of time, to do anything but accept what had just hap-pened. It took all of the farmer's physical and mental strength to literally pull the man back from the brink of death. When he was interviewed on television, the dairy farmer said he thought he had him pinned down, that there was no wiggle room left for Anthony. He said he was used to dealing with rowdy calves, but the fight this *man had put up was something else. Anthony was beyond control: he was intent on terminat-ing his life then and there. In certain circumstances, the will to die can become even more powerful than the will to live."*

Dr. Cohen stopped drawing and her cigarette went off. She held it in her hand like a small flute, looking at it in silence for a moment, as if she was considering its weight or its worth.

Then she said, "In a scuffle where he was held down on the blacktop, Anthony managed to break two of the farmer's ribs. It took four men to subdue him and drag him over to the store. He was booked in Pau and placed on suicide watch, unlike you. The prosecutor wants to charge him with criminal negligence. He's still completely silent, but he doesn't want to kill himself anymore, and I'm convinced that with time and the necessary healing process, he'll pull through all right."

Dr. Cohen leaned over her desk to the left and put her electronic cigarette in a big crystal ashtray—her way of marking another significant shift in the monologue: "I hope you remember this story later, Tariq, when you're by your-self. It's one of the stories that come to my mind when I tell our residents that they'll never be left alone in their grief here."

Then she gave me a handout with a heading titled "Grief and Self-Forgiveness: The First Steps toward Healing."

That was when I addressed her—in words that were unfair, hurtful, and that did not make much sense: "Don't ever mention forgiveness to me again,"

I said. "Just do your job and leave me alone, because that's what I am to you: a job."

———

That man's desperate lunge for his children as they tumbled down in the car: is it not what every parent is expected to do? To stand by one's offspring till the last moment.

But I did not do what was expected of me: I failed to be there, deserting them at the hour of death and beyond. That sad bedrock of cowardice and failure was going to give people from outside the Community (people like Collin) immense moral leverage over me—the leverage of their feelings of righteousness, the leverage of my own guilt.

Take someone like Collin, precisely. Because of the leverage, his most powerful positional advantage would also be his least visible instrument of torture—the power of moral ascendance he had over me (after all, *he* would never fail his children the way I did). That self-validating, empowering feeling of being "the righteous man": it could give him a terrible advantage over me. I could see it in that Paris hospital already, right after my coma: the contempt in his eyes like an icy wind blowing right through me.

To this day I cannot muster the courage to even confront their obituary—as if in refusing to read it, I am giving myself the power to still consider them among the living, to still envision the possibility of a new life with them after the Community.

I am also still unable to open Regina's letter—something about the extent and depth of my ex-wife's suffering has made every thought of her unendurably painful and humiliating.

———

The partial return of my memory—that autonomous capacity to find one's bearings in time, mentally and emotionally—has been slow, painstaking, traumatic, and not without its share of irrationality.

When I began to remember on my own (to carry, as it were, pictures and scenes from my own past within my consciousness), I also began to feel; and with the return of feeling, pain and grief started to set in like the twin shadows of remembrance itself—the dark underbelly of the rain-laden cloud that was my scarred memory.

Grief: it is the wind-and-wave-battered, slippery, craggy islet where I am today—the only home I can fully claim as my own; this isolated dwelling place of the soul that has come to color everything I am—my existence in the world, my body, the air that I breathe, the things that I see.

And the words that flow from my pen:

As I embarked on the recovery process, I knew from the outset that writing was going to be both a measure of my utter hopelessness and a protective reef against its stormy rages and frustrations: it was the first complex mental skill that I was willing to use after surgery, and Cohen encouraged my resumption of writing to the extent that our sessions gradually became a virtual elucidation of my struggle with words and the function that I was going to assign to time and trauma within them.

In the Paris center, when I had begun to gather enough will and strength to think of and envision the act of writing, words were only a murky record of the nearest past—opaque, stifled, and short-sighted, like interrupted glimpses from a courtyard window.

Beyond the indeterminacy of those words, there was also the claustrophobic fear created by their sheer structure—and the vital necessity to pack them in tight and small paragraphs, well-partitioned and amply spaced and rock-solid, like stepping stones in the water.

The terrifying sensation of swarming chaos that big paragraphs give me: to my eye, a large paragraph is like an airport concourse crowded with frantic travelers rushing off insanely in all directions.

The day came when I knew: I was going to be looking further and further back; digging deeper and deeper; searching as far out as I could by interrogating the notebooks, the picture directories, the videos.

And the nightmares.

They were my first palpable inner images of the past. Yet even today they never come in the form of a full, structured story; only intense kaleidoscopic fragments—disjointed impressions in misty gray, radium green, and electric blue; irrepressibly immediate in their urgency, their invasive penetration of my senses with brutal starkness of sound and sight.

(You speak of "palpable inner images," but even so, you are going to have to admit that you are still, to this day, unsure if there is any measure of adequation between the nightmares and what you experienced in reality on that night of August 30. Yet every time those night visions come to visit you—punctual as night itself—they appear to be quite real—shockingly real, ruthlessly real; more real than most things that you experience in the material world.

Not more real in the sense of their believability, their verisimilitude, but of the self-derived power with which they resonate in the labyrinths of your mind—night after crucifying night; the self-validating authority they have gained through their sheer vividness; the fluidity with which they manage to steal into your deepest intimacies, taking over your thought processes with stunning immediacy, like a gallery of shuddering pictures scrolled at maddening speed a fraction of an inch away from your eyes.

And the voices—desperately urgent shouted injunctions or warnings or instructions—funneled with heart-wrenching simultaneity into your ears, like a flood of disconnected audio packets blaring wildly inside your skull.

All this torment invading you in your own bed, in the dead of night.

Always the same night—without the least possibility of ever anticipating the terror from a place outside the dream, of sensing or intuiting (from some providential region of the soul) the first tremors of your nightmare in order to shake yourself out of it. Everything is dead still instead, always. Pitch black of night. Then all at once there comes the onslaught—and the jolt of horror that brings you springing out of bed.

Howling in the darkness, like a burning man.)

It is always voices and sights from the crime scene—same place, same noises: a completely dark narrow naked square space (maybe a landing at the top of a staircase, or a very small hallway). The space is weakly illuminated in fitful frantic flashes of phosphorescent light—from electronic equipment perhaps, maybe cell phones. And the voices, those dreadful sounds—none of them natural, all of them uttered on an SMR system, not in the vicinity of this space to be sure, yet crackling hard inside my ears, both amplified and warped with the effects of sound distortion—and they are all calling my sons' names simultaneously (only they seem to be having the greatest difficulty in pronouncing them, the names).

Or maybe this has nothing to do with us; maybe this is about some other children, because of the nature of the names precisely: I do not recognize them at all—they are completely alien, harsh-sounding names; and yet here I am, standing in this dreadful place—sweating and cramped, crippled with I do not know what terror; thinking, repeating the thought to myself like a prayer: "This has nothing to do with us. Maybe a maintenance team communicating with their transceivers?"

But the voices keep crackling even harder, getting closer—either from the stairs or from an adjacent room.

And now everything that is me begins to sink, because I know who they are now: voices of people communicating with terrible intensity, about the same appalling thing, like a group of surgeons huddled together in an emergency room; forced by the same grinding nervous energy into focusing all their powers on some unspeakably tangled, unspeakably harsh and harrowing enterprise.

Investigators, police officers, crime scene examiners, paramedics—they were all near here somewhere: talking to each other, speaking into their radios or some other equipment, putting certain facts on record—no ordinary talk, no ordinary dialogues, no ordinary information.

And now there is a shift in the texture of the voices: in drawing nearer, they have become much less abstract in their proximity, starkly material and aggressive; manically, inhumanly urgent, too, in their mechanical repetitiveness, their electronic stridency—as if these men were partially robotic beings aiming to occupy my closest space and in the rudest way possible.

It is not at all clear, but the men are apparently giving brief instructions only—or maybe they are just fragments from cut-off sentences. In my ears, though, they crackle like brutal hateful commands—brutal and pronounced with the wrenched gut-level depth of words one utters under great pain or strain:

"TWO MALE CHILDREN—DECEASED"

"WHAT APPEARS TO BE A DEEP GASH IN THE CHEST"

"I WOULD LIKE YOU TO TAKE A SHOT FROM THIS POSITION"

"APPARENTLY A SERRATED BLADE"

"OFFICER, WHEN DO WE STEP IN?"

"I NEED THE COMMISSAIRE'S ORDERS FIRST. WE ARE GOING TO BE HERE A WHILE."

"OFFICER? OFFICER?"

"THIS IS A CRIME SCENE. AS-OF-THIS-INSTANT, IS THAT CLEAR?"

"YOU COME IN WHEN THE PREFECT TELLS THE COMMISSAIRE, WHEN THE COMMISSAIRE TELLS ME, AND WHEN I TELL YOU, IS THAT CLEAR?"

"STAND BY IN THE VICINITY OF THE BUILDING FOR THE TIME BEING. YOU WILL BE GIVEN DUE NOTICE."

Then comes my own screaming: waking to find myself cowering somewhere in the room; my senses gradually starting to return, the real world fading back in like a picture on a screen, inching back into focus—slowly, like tidewater returning; and I hear myself repeating, like an incantation, a prayer: "It's a nightmare. It's a nightmare."

Gasping for air like a man who has narrowly escaped drowning.

———

When people think of a man in grief, they probably imagine someone struggling and stumbling through one single unvarying stretch of darkness.

In fact, the various stages and transitions of grief are more like a plodding climb up the dark stairs of an ancient bell tower—one moment you are outside, standing before the tower in a state of bewildered numbness, and the next you are struggling upward in an oppressive rugged staircase.

As your body and your mind begin to adjust to the strain and darkness of the place, you begin to realize that the simple fact of climbing is gradually beginning to inject something completely new into your sense of being and existing and doing—a feeling of purposefulness and strength and determination slowly emerging, like an atrophied muscle regaining range of motion and strength.

And now you find yourself wondering in amazement, as you begin to feel and watch and admire your regained capacity to climb in spite of the pain: asking yourself how it all happens—the overnight alchemy of life-change; how you have become so suddenly metamorphosed in your capacity for strength and sensation even as you realize that the stairs keep getting steeper and the climb more arduous.

Then, at a certain point, there comes the moment when you begin to realize that other amazing thing: the feeling that the climb has a mysteriously fated quality to it; knowing without a doubt that the stops you make during your painful upward progression are like the predestined stages of a pilgrimage in which you are meant to make a number of ordained stops for retrospective contemplation, for recollection and reflection—more strength and courage to face the rest of it.

There is only one stage in my grief that I feel compelled to write about: a point of convergence in time, in recollection, in thought— a moment in my life that I call the Breaking Point; one step in my climb that I associate deeply with Cohen's guidance and Sami's visits—the way they both helped me realize my pain, grasp it like something I own; the way they helped me work my way out of the dense, downward driven black hole into which my ego was threatening to sink.

Thanks to my therapist and the man who was now the only family I had left, I was able to indulge in that most meager of consolations, the ultimate refuge of the desperate: tearful self-pity.

———

I started to receive visits from Sami at the Community soon after my transfer to Brittany.

From the beginning of my stay in the Paris hospital, and although I did not know it then, he was effectively my only real-life link to the past, to the teeming real world as humans know it beyond the confines of the mental institution.

Above all, he was the only reliable vehicle for the truth.

Before his first visit up here, Zoé and Mourad had dropped by without prior notice.

I did not wish to see them and Dr. Cohen was obliged to turn them away. They called a few days later, and she told them that they had to respect my wish not to see any friends and family members, including my spouse. I was in a state of complicated grief and needed time.

Zoé had deposited my pocket camera at the information desk before they left—told them that she had found it in her apartment but did not say where exactly.

It was the camera that I had with me on my last night with Annaelle. I had bought it for the trip to Tunisia: there are quite a few references to it in my summer diary entries and I have many videos and photos on my disk from it. Did I drop it behind the planter by Zoé's door when I passed out in the landing?

When I began to open its contents, that camera turned out to be the most valuable document of all. I kept it hidden from everyone, including myself. It was not before the beginning of hypnotherapy that I decided to start downloading the files.

I never mentioned the camera to anyone, not even Sami.

My friend's visits here have been different—different from the Paris visits, that is. Those first bleak, nameless visits—they were set up to help me recover who I was after I had refused to speak with Zoé; yet in a strange way, they ended up evolving into a surreal mix of business meetings, clumsy gestures of mourning, and confused attempts at reminiscing.

It was the late fall of 2007 and the future was far from certain: Sami had taken it upon himself to keep the restaurant in business while I was unconscious. Now he wanted to know if it would remain open beyond the first weeks of the vineyard tourism season.

I did not hesitate to turn over management to him. Awkwardly, he had insisted on showing me who he was before I signed the paperwork (he had even brought his employee file from my office).

The paperwork must have been quite complicated, because I recall him coming up to Paris several times—for eleventh-hour signatures and approvals that had to be faxed back to the local authorities.

Ultimately, those fumbling Paris contacts must have been almost as unsettling for him as they were for me—disorienting and conflicted, too, I suppose. Something dark and tangled was struggling within him like a thrashing beast, and you could see it on his face—he was fighting off his own waves of pain and panic.

For many weeks, Sami must have repressed his feeling self completely—the heartbreak, the rage—simply in order to cope for both of us and keep the restaurant from going under.

The day I discovered the truth:

I found Sami in the waiting room on the ground floor of the belle époque mansion.

It was his first visit here and in keeping with Tunisian custom, he brought a basket of fruit—the kind you buy in Bordeaux's specialty food stores.

He was staring at the hardwood floor of that sad barren-looking room, in deep contemplation, apparently, while I stood motionless at the door. Sami had not noticed me as he sat silently in one of the linked potato-chip chairs, brooding with his head down.

Forearms resting on his thighs, hands clasped between his knees with the punchbowl size, arch-handled wicker basket by his foot.

Sami looked lost in his thoughts—quite possibly apprehensive thoughts.

(The windswept, spray-like drizzle outside: clicking and trickling down the tall window panes behind him. The weather today was Breton gray and the trees were all but lost in the mist.

It is frightful how the early morning fog and sea mist can creep into everything here; how high they can rise, too, thick as brushfire smoke at times, erasing everything around: the gentle curves of the flat country, the high shrubs and the tree trunks— only the treetops floating over the blankness like the tattered sails of ghost ships.

The dreariness outside was a perfect representation of what my inner world had turned into.

And this brave, good-hearted friend sitting right here before me, so far away from home on such a dreary day: will I ever be able to reciprocate his generosity with a spark of genuine feeling—a smile of true recognition?

Grief and its stinging thorn of apathy.)

When I finally stepped inside the room, he lifted his head and stood up immediately, grabbing the basket and raising it almost shoulder high.

Then he realized that he had not greeted me yet, gave me a shy self-deprecating smile, and put the basket back down.

Sami held out his hand, and I shook it. Then I leaned forward and we kissed each other's cheeks, like family. It was the first time we cheek kissed.

"This is a very good place, Tariq. You will be happy here. It must be lovely in the summer."

"Dreadful weather. I'm so glad you finally made it up here. Did you find your way all right?"

I looked down at the basket—the vermillion satin bow on the rim was not wet.

"I took a cab," he said.

Then he bent down, grasped the braided handle, lifted up the basket and held it at waist level: "I brought you some fruit," he said, his face flushed.

There was a moment's pause during which he looked hesitant, his eyes unsteady. Sami was probably thinking that he should carry it for me.

Finally, he handed it over and I took it and thanked him for his gift.

But then I ended up putting it down immediately: the basket felt immensely large, heavy, and ridiculously unwieldy.

I suddenly realized that it had been a long time since I had held anything as heavy as Sami's gift.

It was getting well past noon and we were going to have lunch together and then go out for a walk. But we just stood there facing each other in silence, looking confused and clueless, like two men who had just met.

Sami's cheeks were more sunken than ever, his skin the color of a tobacco leaf in the stem drying stage.

He must have felt utterly lost standing here with me, his stoic expression of strained cheer shifting imperceptibly in a number of barely discernible grimaces.

I decided to forget the hassle of this basket for a while and invite him to join me for lunch just to shift his attention away from it: "Would you like to join me for lunch?" I asked, unnecessarily, like a man stalling for time.

Sami nodded with a smile of relief. Then we both bent down (almost simultaneously) to pick up the basket, this immense colorful heap of fruit he had lugged for hours on a coastal train bound northwest for rainy Brittany.

He took one clumsy step back and let me grab the handle.
"Let's go," I said.

———

I don't know what sort of dreadful feeling came over me when we got
to the cafeteria—probably a minor panic attack due to the effort of
having to deal with the basket.

I just found myself unable to withstand the sheer physical sensation of walking through the place with this insane basket in my hand,
amid these people seated at their tables and watching—interrupting
their eating, interrupting their talking in order to watch me.

Suddenly, everything within me (the entire balance of my
inner world) seemed to depend on the basket, and this completely banal dining area setting began to look menacing and
laden with ill omen—maddeningly convoluted and opaque and
crippling. Here I was, standing among thirty or forty seated
people, pretending I was deliberating over where to sit when all
I really wanted to do was get rid of the basket at once, even if I
had to drop it right where I stood.

Then I saw a young woman eating by herself at a round pistachio-
colored plastic table by the salad bar. She looked very lonely.

I walked right up to her and put down the basket before her.
Then I took one step back, not even conscious of what I had just
done; but I do remember being aware of the sudden hush that had
fallen over the room. Now it felt as if they all had stopped eating,
stopped breathing. All eyes were on me—the somber man with the
incomprehensible basketful of glistening colors.

I, too, must have felt trapped in the silence: I don't know how
long I stood there by that table, but I clearly recall the sensation
of being mesmerized, like an animal caught in the headlights of a
car—and time stretching and stretching, in this vacuum of unnatural stillness.

Then, in a matter of seconds, everything changed. Dr. Cohen,
who was eating at the staff table with her colleagues, decided to
interfere in this bizarre situation.

She walked up to me and spoke with a hint of strained casualness: "Why, thank you, Tariq. I'll take a kiwi."

She picked up the fruit with a playful smile on her face and held it up like a trophy for all to see: "First come, first served!" she said, addressing the whole room.

I don't know how keen she was on the fruit, but what I do know for sure is that she managed to defuse the tension that my surreal gesture had created—and she did it with such subtle tact and spontaneous gusto.

Eventually, we sat down, Sami and I, with our trays before us. It was a late lunch and we did not talk much, but we did take our time watching the others follow Cohen's lead, digging in one by one and helping themselves to those shiny heaped-up fruits: dates, pomegranates, figs, tangerines, grapes, mangoes, and berries—it was all there for the taking. Thanks to Cohen's opening gesture, no one felt the least bit awkward about taking their share.

———

Sami was decidedly not in the mood for a walk along the beach. He did not even conceal his aversion to the idea. ("On a day like this?" he said with an irritated wince, forgetting our e-mail exchange.)

He was aloof and curt outside the cafeteria. Mint tea was the only option, apparently. ("In a quiet place, a lounge maybe?" he suggested.)

There was an instant's hesitation as I debated with myself whether I should explain the particularities of my situation and my need for a daily walk—tell him that the walks were not an indulgence but a necessary compensation, my only antidote against the recurrent panic attacks.

I decided to let him have his way and together we headed for the hallway to pick up our umbrellas. We walked out of the building and toward the vegetable garden to gather a few sprigs of mint for tea.

At no point did it occur to me that he might have been deeply offended by my behavior in the cafeteria before lunch.

It was damp and dreary out and I knew I could never prevail on Sami to let me show him around the grounds. The fog was getting very murky and it felt unreal walking through our empty vegetable garden out back. There was a strange distortion of sound—our footfalls in the gravel paths amplified behind us like an echo.

I gathered some mint and we took the long way to the dormitory, walking under that mysterious Breton drizzle: as thin as spray, floating in the air with a bug-like erratic jitter, landing on our umbrellas with an infinitely faint clicking sound, like a swarm of tiny insects descending on us.

———

He sat at one end of the desk and I made the tea at the other.

I boiled the water in the electric kettle, put the candle stove and the pot on the desk, let the leaves steep for a few minutes.

Then I poured out the tea and invited him to sit in the bed-side armchair.

He thanked me and said that he was fine there. I reached across the desk and handed him his cup.

The semblance of daylight in the window behind him was so weak it seemed to flicker. It turned Sami's face into a vague shade of dun.

For the first time since his last visit at the Paris hospital, Sami wanted to speak to me about what he had only hinted at then: his investigations. He was gloomy and solemn, his voice unsteady. It was quite obvious that he had very important news to deliver.

I asked him if he felt ready to tell me, and he replied in the affirmative.

I remember putting my cup down on the floor, next to the armchair.

He began to speak: "What I'm going to tell you has not been officially confirmed by the police," he said, "and it will probably never be. This friend I told you about when you were in Paris: he's a criminology postdoctoral researcher. We did talk about—the tragedy. He's done an impressive amount of research on what happened, and he thinks he has formulated a hypothesis."

"A hypothesis?"

He took a folded sheet of paper out of his breast pocket, put it next to his untouched tea, and went on with his explanation as if he had not heard me: "Yes, he told me that he's narrowed down his research to a more specific assumption: there is an obscure, extremely powerful cult or group behind—what happened. That's his hypothesis."

"You mean a religious movement? Is that what it is?"

It was his turn to look bewildered—as if the insanity of the idea was just beginning to dawn on him now that someone else had presented it to him in words.

"Not quite," he said with a scowl, "and it's not—nothing has been verified yet. It's still a hypothesis. He needs to do some more research. He says it's very hard to eavesdrop on their Internet activity. They use Swiss proxy servers."

All at once, I grew panicky again. I wanted him to slow down and take the time to explain all this arcane information: "Can you start at the beginning and tell me what this is really all about? You're telling me this is about religious fanatics? I've never been involved in anything that remotely resembles that kind of craziness!"

I began to shiver, and my mind wandered off for a moment—I thought about the radiator in my room: did I forget to turn it on this morning?

(In fact, it was the anxiety tremors again—I had no way of controlling them. I believe that Sami was trying to be as clear and succinct as possible under the circumstances. And he was, of course.

The real problem was that his explanation was rendered foggy and confusing by my physical and mental reaction to the information. And it was not so much the information overload as the effect of the information—the emotional impact was simply unmanageable, with the negative feelings feeding into my cognitive confusion, which made it even more difficult for me to calm down and listen to him.)

Sami must have felt much at a loss about how to properly deal with my distress. He looked angry, but I think he was just afraid of breaking down.

He lowered his head for a few seconds, as if he was praying, then he looked back at me with his expression unchanged—that frown of strenuously contained sadness that could easily be mistaken for anger: "Are you all right?" he asked.

I stood up, took a blanket out of the closet, and wrapped it around my shoulders. Then I sat back down and told him that I was fine, asked him to go on.

"According to my friend, it's a crazy—it's a sort of fanatical *spiritual* cult or group, not a religious movement. They believe in human sacrifice—some sort of Tantric sacrifice. It's certainly not Satanism or Muti. His investigation is based on solid research and he has a very strong hypothesis. That's all he knows about them at this point, but he sympathizes a lot with your predicament and he has promised me—"

"You mean they believe in sacrificing..."

I could not finish my sentence. I was able to hear every single word resound between my chest and my throat with an unreal muffled echo (thump, thump, thump), like another man's words heard behind a wall.

He looked away from me again and just stared at the folded sheet of paper on the desk. There was not a single sign of hope in the face before me: it was grayish and indecipherable—like the quicksilver sky outside, the washed-out forms of the salt flats beyond the fence.

"The other details are in his notes here," he said, pointing at the folded sheet.

Then he looked into my eyes again, as if he had just remembered my last words: "They believe in human sacrifice, those monsters. They probably did it before. Then again, *that* assumption is not based on irrefutable facts. My friend told me—"

"They believe in Tantric sacrifice? Is that who they are? How does he know?"

"Network eavesdropping. My friend thinks that the cops have also been able to sniff them, very recently. They're extremely elusive and secretive. They don't even *use* Tantric symbols. They communicate with their own codes and symbols. Also, they make no direct mention of their horrible beliefs. They're all very rich, highly educated, and extremely well connected: the night of the crime, the executors gained access to the cellar area through tunnels. They were capable of doing that, those monsters. They used one of the cellars as a staging area. Nobody saw them get into the building. They used a sophisticated anesthetic gas to drug the babysitter. They were capable of disabling the electrical system in the staircase. My friend thinks the police still haven't developed a profile method—to understand their behavior. He thinks it's because their previous murders were too random and too far apart."

———

It was getting dark outside and he said he had to get going. He called a taxi.

When it was time for my friend to leave the dormitory, I could not help but step out and accompany him all the way to the seafront exit.

One of the security guards caught us up, though. He stopped me just outside the gate. I asked him if I could escort my friend to the taxi—I just wanted to see him off properly. He rejected my request emphatically, stepping between the two of us and stating that I "must remain inside the perimeter of the Community."

I promptly got back inside, with Sami and the guard at my heels. The taxi was idling by the side of the road. Night had now descended. The sea nowhere to be seen.

I shook hands with my friend and he told me that he would send me any new information by registered mail. Sami added that he would come and visit as often as his time permitted.

Then he turned around and walked away. The guard let him through the gate.

He walked up to the taxi, turned around, and flashed the victory sign. Then he disappeared inside the car, its taillights like red-hot stove burners in the fog.

On my way back to the dormitory, I remembered that I had to go to Rehabilitation to inquire about my next appointment with the speech therapist. (Among us residents it was universally referred to as the south building, a convenient way of avoiding the dreaded "R word," which we all associated with strain, struggle, and the specter of failure.)

———

It took a while for Sami's revelation to sink in, but when it did nothing was the same again—another step in the tower, another stop, another metamorphosis.

Thanks to my friend, I began to connect the dots between the planned escapade that started at the American Bar in the evening of August 29 and the tragic events that ensued. A new pattern of causality had emerged and I felt I had finally reached a point at which I was able to formulate an irrefutable hypothesis: at the center of my theory there were two seemingly unrelated individuals who had a significant connection to me right before the murders.

One individual who knew me and knew everything about me, including my late August visit to Paris and his daughter's vacation trip during that visit.

One individual who was forced into knowing me in order to draw my attention away from my sons and lure me into the trap.

Faisal Brahmi and Annaelle.

When my theory was fully articulated, I presented it to Dr. Cohen, but she refused to give her opinion: she told me that as a therapist her function was "to guide and not to evaluate or to judge."

As soon as I was able to establish connections between Zoé's father, Annaelle, and the timing of the murders, a meaningful pattern began to take shape in my mind; and with meaning came the sense of a predestined mission. Suddenly, every fragment of random pain began to take its rightful place in a design far bigger and far more significant than the fractioned spectral life that I was living here.

In beginning to assemble the seemingly haphazard narrative of our tragedy into a meaningful structured whole, I realized that I now had far greater control over my terrors: I began to gain a salutary sense of distance from my suffering and to contemplate the pieces of the puzzle that I was with a limited measure of equanimity, assembling them one by one into an emerging picture.

Thanks to Sami's visits and to my rather one-sided conversations with Dr. Cohen, I was also beginning to develop a certain sense of rage at myself: I was now capable of mustering enough energy and moral stamina to hate myself for being the cause of my sons' dark undoing.

With my emerging feelings of self-hate I almost simultaneously began to face the reality of self-pity, too; and so I often found myself wavering between two negative forces: disgust and anger at myself for being a criminally irresponsible father; followed by intense sorrow at the sheer bottomlessness of my misfortune.

Still, for all the ambivalence of my oscillating moods and Dr. Cohen's silent skepticism, I was convinced that I was about to turn the corner and finally descry a glimmer of hope in my tunnel of grief.

Riding that wave of nascent self-confidence, I realized there were significant moments of respite in my suffering during which I felt strong and purposeful enough—and determined to expose the murderers of my sons.

And so one day I decided that the time had come for me to confront Collin. Before I knew it, I was writing him an e-mail on my cell phone:

Dear Commissaire Collin,

It has recently come to my attention that police investigators as early as the fall of 2007 had access to information about a little-known cult or group that practices Tantric sacrifice. The authorities subsequently began to work from the assumption that they were potential suspects in the murder of my sons, Shams and Haroon Abbassi. If this is indeed the case, I must confess my utter astonishment at your failure to inform me of this "new" development in the case.

Sincerely,

Tariq Abbassi

His response was almost instantaneous:

Speaking in an artificially warm tone and using the passive voice, Collin informed me that the possibility of a conspiracy inspired by Tantrism was entertained from the outset of the investigation, even though the hypothesis was not fully verified.

The commissaire added that I should feel free to call the Commissariat and set up an appointment with him.

He hung up without saying good-bye.

———

My first coherent dream here:

The scene is Paris and the time is the fall.

I am walking with Zoé along the Seine, one of those low cobblestone embankments.

Khaleel is walking with us, too. He is silent.

The river is thick and reddish brown, like simmering hot chocolate.

I say to Zoé, "You see, the problem with my writing is that it causes such extreme reactions. People read the stuff and they think, "What the hell is this! Does writing have to be that extreme?" That's why I'm very skeptical about this new book I'm writing. I've already written a few chapters, you know, but I'm very, very skeptical."

No response from Zoé, whose expression I cannot even visualize.

All of a sudden we're walking underneath L'Arc de Triomphe, but its shape is altered and strange: it's much lower, thicker, totally unadorned, and reddish.

Then the square fades into another scene and I find myself standing on the very edge of the riverbank. The Seine is shallow here—more like a ford.

A bridge must have been washed away: there are huge clods of soil ripped out of the bank where I am standing and very large chunks of concrete sticking up out of the water.

Across the ford: slabs of concrete arranged like stepping-stones.

A few people, looking sad and scared, are using them to cross the river.

I stand here watching them, wondering how wise it is to embark on such a crossing.

Suddenly, I turn around and realize that I am not the only person standing on this riverbank: there are people waiting behind me, vaguely lined up, like a chorus line about to disband. Many of them have a dis-heartened look on their faces—a refugee look.

Off to the right, I spot mother. She has stepped out of the line and is trying to clamber down the riverbank.

Alarmed, I climb down there first and run to catch her before she slides down the slippery slope—my shoes are already ruined with mud and the water is lapping dangerously close behind me.

Without a single word exchanged between us, I stretch out both hands toward her as she comes sliding down.

Now I am carrying her on my back across the river, hopping along those wobbly stepping stones.

The scene shifts to an empty cafeteria with long tables and graying wooden benches.

Zoé and Khaleel are sitting at one of the tables, looking very amused and happy: mother and I are performing for them, dancing the Dabkeh together.

While we're doing this, I am throwing sporadic teasing glances in mother's direction, out of the corner of my eye: "You see," I say to her, "a mother and her son are allowed to dance together here!"

———

My first full conversation with Collin:

I saw him here in late spring.

He looked haggard, a bit disheveled, and grayer than when I had first met him.

It was impossible not to keep noticing (and feeling irked by) his eyelids: they were irritatingly red, as if they had been rubbed raw.

It was a beautiful windless day and we went out to sit on my beachside bench.

Although the tide was out, there were only a few clam diggers in the distance—scattered across the anthracite expanse of the sand-bars, like ragged monochrome forms in rubber boots, stooping in the tidal pools and in the long shadows of the furry rocks.

He was talkative from the start and still angry about the debacle at the Paris hospital.

"Why did they have to hurt *us*, of all people?" I asked him right away.

"So *you*'re the one asking the questions now. I'll let that pass because the investigation has been temporarily suspended. You've come a long way since your suicide attempt, which means you're going to be back under investigation—sooner than you think. About your e-mail inquiry, right now we don't want to jump to stupid conclusions and make complete fools of ourselves. Hence my silence about the voodoo nuts."

"Voodoo?"

"Voodoo, Tantrists, homicidal cult, theistic Satanists, hocus-pocus. Whatever. We call them that because we haven't been able to generate a criminal profile yet. Therefore, we don't have an official description for them. We didn't know who they were in the fall, by the way, contrary to what you wrote, and officially we still don't. So, why did they hurt *you*? Is that what you're asking me?"

"Yes."

"You tell *me*. After all, *you*'re the one in the know."

He fell silent but kept staring at me, as if he was expecting a response, but I think he was just trying to compose himself, to repress something within him that was threatening to break out into the open and run amok.

When he addressed me again, his tone was didactic—in a lamely casual manner, like someone doing a poor send-up of an educational show host: "That's the key question, don't you think? And the best way to deal with it is to say that they chose your children because you're familiar, that's why—but more on that later. We were—"

"But I have absolutely—"

"Shush! If you want *real* information, you need to remain calm and let me present it to you in its full complexity—just so you can get a sense of what we've been up against these past months. You have no idea—"

He looked away in anger, closed his eyes, clenched his jaw.

"Listen," he said, looking at me again, "we're working from the assumption that this whole business of the cult is a decoy meant to mislead us—subterfuge for the conspirators to hide behind. It's too excessive to be the work of an organized cult. You have a lot of enemies in Tunisia, Abbassi—powerful enough, vicious enough, and with influential connections in this country. I sent a note of enquiry to a confrere in Tunis. You're a left libertarian—some radical democracy fanatic. Apparently the activism of your younger years didn't sit well with a lot of prominent people down there."

Collin turned around for a second and pushed his cigarette into the sand.

"It's so obvious, why can't you see it? It all smacks of amateurish decoy tactics. Those crazy Tantrism shenanigans. They get that drug addict rigged out in some creepy New Age getup and make the murders look like a sacrifice—to some stupid god or other. Crazy nonsense. You have many powerful enemies in Tunisia, and those enemies have powerful connections here. That's who did it in my opinion."

"But how can they *do* a thing like that? I mean commit the act itself."

"You're an educated man, Abbassi. With power and money one can find a lot of people who *will* do a thing like that, as you put it. Have you ever heard of the Iowa ax murders?"

"No. What—"

"Google the Iowa ax murders—that's what. The city of Villisca, Iowa. Also, Google the legal concept of 'indirect perpetration.' Write down the information in your notebook—before you forget it. Now, let's be serious, shall we? Let's take a good hard look at this."

He broke off and leaned back a little, raised both of his feet, and dug the heels of his black Sebago loafers into the sand—maybe to give more power and emphatic finality to his statement.

Or maybe it was like this odd barrage of words thrown at me: a deliberately confusing flare of dramatic flamboyance to preempt my anger.

Whatever his intention, the effect was ultimately more ridiculous than intimidating—a sulky, stubborn teenager digging in his heels.

I jotted down his references then looked away for an instant—let my gaze and my mind drift off; a momentary evasion during which I found myself toying with the mental image of those city shoes: I imagined the sand slipping into them and Collin taking it with him into his chauffeured car, his Paris apartment.

Paris.

"Early on," he said, "we ruled out a direct link between you and the Tantrists. The babysitter was clean, and the anesthetic gas nearly killed *her*—not a likely scenario either. So that left us with the scenario of the two girls setting you up. But you refused to talk to Zoé, and your lover decided to have a nervous breakdown of her own. Not that we didn't try to go after her—Annaelle. But she had her fancy clinic, too: posttraumatic shock, acute depression, distortion. The works. The prosecutor threatened to throw the book at us if we didn't play by the rules. To this day she remains untouchable. But that won't keep us from digging into her past. And we won't stop digging until we find the link: from Annaelle to Zoé, then from Zoé to her father and from *him* to the Tantrists. You were set up by the two girls, Abbassi—I can smell it. We'll let them live their sophisticated high society lives and go on digging—invisibly. Total invisibility—that's the beauty of it."

"But Zoé *loves* my children. She would never—"

"What did I say from the start, Abbassi? Do you *remember* what I said? If you want real information, you need to listen first. Keep an open mind. Don't try to control the conversation with all these obsessive notions of yours. Theories you develop in a *room*, all by yourself. Zoé doesn't have to be *directly* involved in this—or even know any of the things that really matter. Think about it—indirect perpetration. I'm probably telling you more than you want to know here, but I want you to *think* about it, like an objective observer not an *adversary*: what did I say about her father *first?* Zoé's father saw you a couple of times during your visit. He lives in the same neighborhood. He knows everything about you. We grilled him several times and we went into his *house*. We gathered information on him: he is very sophisticated, he is very prosperous, he has powerful friends, *and* he is very suspicious. I'm not going to go into details, but he is suspicious. This is not a woman thing. The women are merely instruments in this sordid story. It's all about men, power-greedy men conspiring with angry and vengeful men. The two forces combined one night to wreck your life."

He stopped and began to stare straight into my eyes—with his red-rimmed sleep-deprived eyes—as if he had just noticed a crucial detail in them: "Other than the material in the diary and the photos," he said, "do you have any memories of being close to Mr. Brahmi? You know, male bonding between two fellow Tunisians—that kind of stuff."

"Mr. Brahmi?"

"Zoé's father!"

I was totally confused. I knew about the man who was Zoé's father from my diary, of course, but I was simply unable to connect any mental image of the man with the family name.

Collin was quite aware of my condition, but he kept *acting* impatient—put-on and performed impatience, the perfunctory impatience of someone who enjoyed feeling superior: "All right, all right, you don't have to answer me now; but since your writing skills are still very good, I want you to think about him and tell me in writing: did you used to go out together for a drink or to have a serious conversation? Things of that sort. You know, man stuff outside of your family get-togethers."

Then he started working on me—my guilt feelings, the bottomless chasm of isolation within me—the better to undermine any sense of attachment I might still have for Annaelle.

He shook his head with a mix of mock pity and genuine disgust—the angry metallic glint in his eyes piercing right through me: "Do you know," he said, "that Annaelle has consistently refused to see you? Do you know that?"

I could not trust myself to speak at first. I just shook my head. Then I added a few words: "I've never tried to find out," I said.

He looked away in exasperation for a few seconds—again, with a lot of theatrical flamboyance, but his anger was quite real: "Come on, Abbassi, you can do better than that—for your boys' sake. Now, regardless of what you can or cannot remember, I'd like you to take a hard look at the information and tell me this: why would an enamored woman commit such a reckless act of abandonment? The videos, the photos, the e-mails, the journal entries—I gave you back everything that is private. I even gave the doctors copies of your text messages that they passed on to you. You have full access to your past, Abbassi. I mean the new you—or whatever. And so with the benefit of hindsight, of whatever knowledge you have on last summer, I'd like you to tell me—tell me in a way that would be constructive for the investigation. Is this too much to ask?"

Suddenly, there was just too much information, too many words, too much emotional overload. And he knew it.

My eyes were beginning to glaze over from passivity and from the surreal performance of the man.

I began to wonder how long it would be before my anxiety tremors would start: "Tell you what?" I asked, and even as I spoke, I had no way of knowing if I was tossing the question back at him in defiance, in ignorance, or in sheer confusion.

Again, Collin marked a theatrical pause, followed by a gush of theatrical irritation: "Answer my question, that's what! Why would that junkie fall out of love as suddenly as she fell *in* love? So suddenly that she wouldn't even want to share her own *grief* with you? After all, love or no, there was that new common reality between the two of you, wasn't there?"

He paused again and as silence fell between us, it occurred to me that most of his anger was now focused on my inertia. I must have given him the impression that his words were bouncing off a wall of indifference, of deliberate apathy and unresponsiveness.

When he resumed his peculiar exposé, Collin was back in monologue mode—only now he sounded as if he was complaining to himself, maybe looking for sympathy within himself: "Our female colleagues spoke with her, they cajoled her, they pressed and pushed her. They damn near *massaged* the possibility into her head: would she be willing, at some unspecified point in the future, to get back in touch with you and start sorting out the outcome of what happened between the two of you? Closure and all that. All we got for an answer was no—with no elaboration. And whenever they pressed her for information on the why of the no, she would freak out. Then everybody would be on their back: the shrinks, the lawyer, the hierarchy. If you want closure for yourself and your family, you would do well to start cooperating with us. And so now that I trusted you and let you in on significant aspect of the investigation, allow me to ask you once again: why doesn't she want to meet with you?"

My reply was weak, shaky, like guess words in a sinister game: "She was never in love to begin with?"

He jotted down a few notes in a small dark-blue notebook, repeating my words as he wrote—haltingly, as if he was trying to memorize a quote: "She—was—never—in love—to begin with."

He looked up from his notebook with a bored flutter in his eyes: "Well, well," he said. "How sad. Assuming Annaelle never loved you in the first place, why would a beautiful younger high-society girl date an older man vacationing with two children? Based on what you have learned so far, can you recall noticing anything suspicious in her behavior? Anything that might be consistent with elaborate manipulation. A hidden agenda, you know."

Without waiting for an answer, he sighed and looked away again.

And now, after he had depleted my energies with the chaotic flow of information, Collin was ready to shift to something different from all the things he had said so far: "Mr. Abbassi, we've been doing some research about various religious and spiritual practices and we've found out something important about human sacrifice within the body of beliefs known as Tantra. I thought you might want to help us with the information."

I said, "So now it *is* about Tantrists? I thought it was the powerful Tunisians who murdered my sons."

"Listen, stop impeding me. Stop making snide, *ignorant* comments. Just cooperate, that's all I want you to do for me. This is a faltering investigation, and mainly because of you. We have nothing definitive yet. We're working with different hypotheses. So listen up and stop impeding me. What I'm about to say will probably shock and confuse you; that's why I need you to be composed and focused and provide me with any information you might remember from your files and things. Can you do that for me?"

"I'll try my best," I managed to say, and as politely as I could.

"Good. The people who—*chose* your children held a highly favorable opinion of your children—we know that for a fact at this point in the investigation."

"What?"

"Please just bear with me for a few minutes. I'm going to explain everything to you. As I said, I need you to stay focused and let me present the facts as they stand today. I'm sharing highly confidential information with you in the hope of bringing you on board—so that you can start cooperating with us instead of resisting us and withholding precious information from us. Your children were chosen because the cult members actually thought of them as privileged beings *worthy* of sacrifice—a source of divine energy that they needed to appropriate ritually in order to channel it into their world. From the point of view of the cult, the sacrifice in question has to do with a special kind of spiritual power—*occult* power, not worldly power. These people aren't after the power of men—they do have plenty of that already."

He took a deep breath and looked directly into my eyes before he resumed. Staring back at him in those few seconds, I could tell that besides his feelings of disgust toward my person, Collin had some doubts about my honesty.

"When we put ourselves in their minds," he said, "we must always remember to adhere to *their* own sense of right and wrong. To them, this is no double murder. In their crazed reasoning, the children they target for sacrifice are selected on the basis of certain criteria of excellence, if you will; and so sacrificing such highly worthy children is for them the best way to appropriate divine energy that they will channel into the world. When they conducted the sacrifice, the Tantrists firmly believed that the victims of their act were not victims, but elected individuals with a special destiny because of their distinguished status as objects of sacrifice."

His explanation was almost as formal as a lecture. This time there were no cheap antics in his didacticism: he was using his exposition as a defense mechanism, a way of putting as much distance as possible between his speaking voice and the sheer madness of the knowledge that he was imparting. If you wanted to communicate unspeakable horror, you had no choice but to rely on some kind of protective strategy. Collin's protection was to assume the role of a stiff and stuffy lecturer.

When he was done explaining, he stopped abruptly, staring into the shimmery stretch of mercurial slime beyond the shore—the waterless bottom of the sea looked stripped and sterile.

Then, after a long silence, he decided to speak again, his eyes still averted from me, his voice gruff and weary: "It's a Tantra-inspired sacrifice. Now you know. This is one facet of my hypothesis. The other facet is that your Tunisian enemies are involved in the planning and execution of the murders. Who are the people who set this up and how do they connect? We still don't know. And you know why? It's because *you* still don't know, apparently. Your shrink keeps telling us your memory is a total blank on what happened between you and that girl on the night of the murders. Ditto for the evening of August 29. You managed to wreck your memory minutes before your deposition at the Prefecture. We were still waiting for the doctor to come down and tell us if you were fit to be deposed. Next thing we knew, you were *definitely* not fit."

Collin was silent for a moment, looking off into the distance. When he spoke again, he was probably addressing me, but he sounded weary and lost in his thoughts: "There's nothing worse for us than a nut case like this. Those sick degenerates—they think of it as a sacred *offering!*"

I don't recall the expression on his face (I don't think I was actually looking at him when he spoke), but I do remember the crack of emotion in his voice as he uttered the last word. I will never know if it was weariness or pain that made his voice break.

And now he shifted gears, standing up brusquely and bearing down on me with the force of his rage, talking frantically again: "That's it, Abbassi, end of the lecture. I want you out of my sight, now. You know what you know, apparently, but my deputy will give you a list of keywords and references on Tantric sacrifice with a few instructions. When you've pulled yourself together tomorrow, I want you to sit down and think about the items in that list, about everything I told you—think hard and *write* down your thoughts: *anything* you can reconstruct in writing—from your files, the diary, or whatever memories you've been able to recall. Exotic jewelry, trinkets, figurines of gods or goddesses, books, certain words uttered, ideas half-spoken, gestures made. Anything that might help the investigation. Just make sure you put it down *on paper*—for your children's sake, your honor."

There was another long silence and he was still standing above me, but I did not know if he was looking at me. I was struggling so hard inside—it was all I could do not to curl up on that bench and close my eyes.

I kept looking away from him, tried to escape in my mind—gazing into the clusters of reeds by the path, imagining the silky platinum-blond gloss of their panicles; the shades of rust on the spiky tips of the sedge; the washed-out echoes of the clam diggers—remote and distorted, like television voices wafting out through an open window.

"My God, Abbassi, the kind of people you got yourself mixed up with—a solid citizen like you. What were you thinking? Were you even vaguely aware of what you were really doing? When you met that young girl? A midlife lucky break? A long overdue miracle? You didn't know that every miracle comes with a price tag, did you? When you met Annaelle? And the stunning thing is that you're still at it—this attitude of self-delusion. So far you have systematically refused to face up to reality and dig into your stunning array of documents—look back at your story with a critical mind. Be careful handling your material, though, because you are *not* rediscovering the two girls: you're quite literally getting to know them all over again. Take a healthy critical distance from them. Do not succumb to their destructive allure all over again; or try to *possess* them; or collect and *protect* them. That's vanity, Abbassi. Sad to say, it's your biggest weakness."

Another silence.

Eventually, I looked up and found him staring down at me. I started to stand up myself.

"Hold it!" he exclaimed, as he motioned me to remain seated. "We may be out here talking off the record, but you *are* being questioned, which means *I* get to tell you when to stand up. In your—*copious* documents, there isn't much about Mr. Brahmi that can help us solve the case. You can imagine how tough it is for my colleagues—having to dig into all that material and stay focused all the time. I even had them transcribe the messages you texted to Annaelle—you have copies of those, too. Poems. It's *your* turn to help us now. If you remember *anything* about him, be sure to let us know. My deputy will give you a couple of numbers later. Use them. Please. Every detail matters in this case."

He paused again, still staring at me with his red eyes.

"There's one more thing you need to know. You are, as of now, privy to highly classified material. So one last word of advice: mum's the word. Not your back-to-nature eco-shrink, not that freak show character you call your friend—the couscous chef. I'll hold you responsible for any leaks, understand? Let's go."

For a few seconds only, Collin walked two or three steps ahead of me—the first time he had his back turned to me.

The squat build and bow-legged soccer player's gait; the thick shoulder blades outlined behind his blue jacket; the decisive Martian swing of his powerful arms.

And just when he turned around (nervously, as if some innate part of him had already caught me in the act of observation), the thought occurred to me: this is a man who was perfectly capable of killing me with his bare hands, in a matter of seconds, and he probably never failed to remind himself of it every time he faced someone like me.

We walked back up the path and he said, "You're a piece of work, Abbassi, you know. They told me you helped in the kitchen today— cooked the tabbouleh. Pretty good stuff. If you can remember what goes into the pot, you'll remember the rest of your story, don't you think? Too many people counting on you *not* to, right? Jut like cooking."

———

"For your children's sake":

Collin's words kept echoing in my mind for many days after our conversation, as I wrote and thought about the things that were happening in and around me. Those same words loomed larger than anything on my mind then, smoldering in the depths of my soul, even during therapy.

It was the early summer of '08 and I was beginning to sense another shift in my condition: with the help of Dr. Cohen and her team, I gradually came to apprehend this capacity in me to reclaim my past with a genuine sense of identification, no longer as a mere aggregate of facts ordered in temporal succession (a set of remote dates and faces and places in another man's life).

My story was now evolving into an entity that I could grasp as something total in all its depth and humanity: what I began to discern in that summer about my life in Bordeaux and my character was at once troubling and fascinating in its ambiguity—this divided shadowy picture emerging, of a man endowed with an intensely rich inner life and yet almost entirely cut off from the world around him; devoid of any trust in the life stirring all around him, and the people inhabiting it.

Despite the shock of my confrontation with Collin and the ensuing suffering, it took me just a few days to muster enough strength and tell Dr. Cohen about the encounter, keeping the confidential information to myself.

I remember being agitated as I opened up, and when I was done telling her about Collin, she did not seem the least bit surprised that I had decided to bring *him* up after all. Instead, as if in deliberate digression, she observed that there had been considerable improvement in my speech lately, that I had "emotional vigor" in my tone of voice, too: "Your words have more clarity and punch in them," she observed, rather informally, asking me if I thought this was a "good sign."

A few days later, I agreed to give hypnotherapy a try—work with Dr. Cohen's colleagues at neuropsychiatry in combination with our usual psychotherapy sessions.

I felt that the timing was right for me and for the rest of my story: I was now able to delve into the content of my digital camera and begin confronting my past—that last night with Annaelle.

It was also around that time that I decided to definitively give up writing in Arabic and in French: in a twist of fate that I cannot even begin to comprehend, I suddenly found myself exiled in the English language, seeking refuge in the place of my exile with furious passion and despair, the way one seeks refuge in the most beautiful love affair—writing in English, thinking in English, translating my poetry into English, dreaming of English, and contemplating its endless shades of meaning and its immeasurable potentials for self-expression.

I still have not been able to remedy the turgidity and excessive formality of my prose, but I am working on it every day. I intend to seek the help of a renowned American speech therapist in Paris as soon as I leave the Community.

I think that my use of English as a medium of expression is at once a mark of the extremity of my trial and a harbinger of rebirth into a new world—something quite unprecedented within me, a fresh horizon of existence that I never even knew was there.

A new pact with life.

How she broke through to me:

The fact that I do not recollect how I got on to the subject of guilt and guilt feelings should be significant in itself; and so, in a way, it does seem to make sense that even now, several hours after the session, I still cannot remember how I entered into those shadowy regions—places in my life that I have been avoiding for months, hiding behind the pretense that I was piecing together a narrative about the life of a virtual stranger.

As for Dr. Cohen's role in what happened today and in the grief process in general, sometimes I feel so guilty about my terrible attitude of total closure toward her; and the infinite goodness and patience with which she responds to the closure and the distance. Along with having to work with the purely physical and cognitive challenges of my case, Dr. Cohen has to wage a subtle war against my extraordinary capacity for denial and repression—incredibly creative imaginary strategies and scenarios that I always manage to contrive in order to dodge the fact that the story of the death of my sons is my story. In her brilliantly unintrusive way, she always manages to put up a brave front of self-effacement, allowing all my strategies and subterfuges to play themselves out without passing any judgment or imposing any limitation.

The woman is tolerance and patience incarnate.

Also, beyond having to put up with my unavoidable self-protective tactics and smokescreens, there is the sheer confusion in my words and thoughts—sometimes even more difficult to contend with than the denial and the repression.

I don't recall the exact moment when I strayed from my notes, but at some point I started to talk about the spring and summer of 2007:

Tariq: "I think I'm beginning to grasp the meaning of that period. I must have felt it was a fresh start for me—and my children; before and after the encounter—with Annaelle. There was a great deal going on inside me. The diary takes on a very emotional tone in those months—urgent; sentimental, too."

Dr. Cohen nods and moves her face slightly forward, in that inscrutable way of hers—something possibly eager and expectant in the barely perceptible movement, or perhaps a signal that she is getting ready to close the session.

I remember having asked her from the start to open the window, on account of the unbearable heat. (My thoughts were intense and I did not want to break into a sweat.)

As for Dr. Cohen, she was jovial in the sleeveless lilac blouse, the flared knee-length skirt—her sensual arms so white.

There were scattered garden sounds and pleasant echoes wafting through the window—fitful guitar strumming on the green, a soft rustle of waves from the sea.

I think I'm beginning to see the full extent, the powerful meaning of this right now:

The sensation of genuine emotional attachment to my boys. Sitting before her, I told her that I was feeling it right now even as I spoke; that it was authentic and that I was beginning to sense it in a way that I had not felt since the injury.

I had been terrified of showing it for months—the attachment. This sense of a real connection arising within me—something totally independent from the writings and the photos and the videos.

T: "I suppose that in some way, during the last few months, I must have resented them very much—for having been there and dying so soon, just when we were really starting to relate (just when I was starting to relate to them and show them my feelings). Because of this secret feeling, I have come to hate myself even more. I just wish they hadn't been so desperately—alone, in that hell. So open like that—to anything and anyone. How can a man do an unspeakable thing like that? Do you know?"

Then she did it, the second our eyes meshed—the thing that shattered all the dams.

Cohen leaned forward with her hands on the edge of the desk, as if she was about to confide something so secret that it had to be whispered; and her face all of a sudden—a countenance so sad and yet utterly transfixed, like a mask of wax frozen in a statuary look of timeless sorrow: "It must have been dreadful," she murmured.

The thing I remember most of that moment and that expression is her face: lifted up on my welling tears, floating in broken bits on the surface of my eyes.

Then I was on my knees with my face pressed against the rug.

I don't know how long I remained kneeling on the floor, but it was long and loud and raw. I heard Dr. Cohen shut the window and later come around the desk to tell me that it was all so sad; that there were just no words for all the sadness; that sometimes it was so good to let the words go and lose oneself in the sadness.

At some point, I heard her speak again: she was saying that I was a man of great will and that I had all the necessary strength and willpower to see myself through this trial, to emerge from it stronger than ever before.

———

With the return of tears, my absence seizures grew less intense. Also, my ear ailments began to ease up considerably. It was an immense weight off my shoulders—the burden of all those pent-up tears.

———

On a blazing summer day, coming out of the water:

The gentle curves and shadowy hollows of the Breton country east of the gray-ribbon road—pulsating ever so quietly in the shimmer of the afternoon heat, sprawled like the soft forms of a sleeping woman;

the salt-and-fern fragrance of a land baked and burnished in all the hues of gold, copper and bronze;

and those wind-dwarfed, weather-braving lone pines—still now, in the scorched stillness.

And you are in the middle of it all, in and out—floating in the vacuum of this stretched-out instant (no sense of time or place or even country).

Only the remotest corner of your consciousness is vaguely aware that you have once again lost your bearings; that you have suddenly become oblivious to the material world and no longer know where you are.

But deep inside, you already know what you are about to tell yourself, once again, in the face of the blackout—this sudden distraction of the senses: does it really matter where and when you are?

As if, with the dazzling blue expanse stretching behind you and the vacant country spread out beyond the coastal road, the very idea of names and places, of countries and their mental moorings had vanished—fading all at once into the inner awareness that has taken over within the darkness of your mind, a second consciousness slowly unfolding inward like a receding wave.

Inner force of no name and no identity, moving like a tidal wave across the expanses of your soul, in a space where everything that is you has become voided by its power; and there is no longer you or anything you have known before: not the kindred scents of this blessed land; not the immensity of the ocean sky; not even the sensations of your feet in the shifting sand—the soft thrust and retreat of the water, the hushed downward rattle of the tiny shingles.

Suddenly, in the blank here and now of the moment, its utter nothing and no one, there is one distinct thing that happens to you—a visualized scene, to be precise; moving and yet inexplicably remote, as if some insubstantial part of you (infinitely finer, infinitely greater) were witnessing the successive fractions of this projected happening from an ungraspable eonian distance that has opened up within you.

Something in your expanding mind knows that the happening is real, a street scene, actually—not so much seen as visualized in your consciousness then projected outward through your mind's eye.

Or, if another word for this state were needed, perhaps you may simply want to say that you have come to grasp it—the scene; so surely that it feels like a living emanation from your mind:

A man and a woman walking together down a slanting alley, in an unknown city, in America—his arm around her shoulders in the autumn cold. Leaning into each other as they walked, legs striding in unison like a dance. Yet beautiful as they are (the spontaneous choreography of their merged bodies), there is something else about them that you find even more compelling— touching to the point of tears. An expression more than anything else—the one you see on the faces of children when you tuck them in their beds with a hug and a few tender words—home at last.

In the scintillating center of this marginal moment, this suspended splinter of time, you catch yourself wondering: the vision of this lover walking down the alley—this fraction from the other man's life—why do I keep dreaming of it?

(And even as you think of the vision from where you are now, sitting behind your desk, you realize that it did indeed emerge from the dark brooding margins of your mind, just like a dream—with no identifiable trace or mark from the pictures and the videos; not from the recorded voices either, crackling with unnatural distortion in the speakers of your machines; nor from the written words, dead and pressed between your pages like the fossilized tendrils of ancient plants.

The man's contented whisper and the woman's smile—dreamed and wordless and yet more real than any of the floundering efforts at reality-making that have engrossed you these past months—the ravishing slant of that stray wisp of dark hair, silhouetted against the woman's face like a thread of black smoke; her skin smell of honey gland and crushed carnation.

And the exquisite echo in your heart—a note plucked from the deepest, noblest chord within you; the tidal longing, quietly welling up—half-remembrance half-sense, like the phantom sensations rising into consciousness from the memory of a vanished member.)

Your body pauses and ponders, its material memory rising and falling like the drowsy sigh of the surf on this deserted beach. Then, acting on a cue as natural as the rhythm of your breath (with the wavelets still lapping at your feet, the sandy trickle trapped between your toes), it begins fading back into the confines of your conscious self—back to thoughts of your germinal self.

Your mind has retained an imprint of a hopeful knowledge that you will carry with you for days—the thought that you have come out of this vision (this "hallucination," as the boring minds call it) not only a stronger man, but an altered man also; invigorated with the sight of yourself as the other— the total stranger encountered in a nameless street that you do not even think of knowing or naming.

Finally, there comes the point of culmination—that one instant of total guilt-less bliss as you find your being suffused with the idea of how beautiful it was to have at last escaped (if only for a moment) the confines of yourself, to have stolen into the bliss of the other, to have wondered in silence: "Maybe there is a way for me too."

Maybe.

North '07

For many weeks after hypnotherapy, I remained cooped up in a vacuum of contemplation—thinking about the contents of my hypnotically induced recollections and the powerful new reality that they had introduced into my consciousness and my writing: how much of that reality was sheer self-suggestion, and how much was unadulterated memory surfacing amid the flotsam of trauma?

I pondered the question endlessly during the days that preceded these words; and however I looked at it, I always came to the same conclusion: the recollections and the words in which they are expressed may not be fully accurate, but I do find them to be as soundly grounded in reality as anything I have ever remembered and written, their truths self-validating and self-sufficient, like the certitude we derive from belief.

And there is Dr. Cohen also: although we have never discussed the subject of my hypnotherapy work with Dr. Masson and his team, I have a feeling that she is satisfied with the outcome of my treatment: the terms according to which I have gradually come to piece together the final chapter of my children's tragedy appear to be coherent enough to her and to the members of her team in the Psychiatry Division.

By the standards of their profession, I must be a good hypnosis subject, a very successful case.

And so as I write what I am writing at this point, I do it without the least doubt or trepidation: as I see it, the truthfulness of my words lies in the recollection, quite literally—the time and energy and dedication that it took me to pick up the pieces of my life where I had left them that night and make my sons' story whole again.

The doubt and the trepidation: with a measure of certainty, I can say that I have managed to outgrow them by now, having at last resolved to speak of the final day as I have come to grasp it through the work of hypnotically induced remembrance and whatever other information I was able to salvage from my instruments—the diary, the laptop, the external hard drive, the pocket camera.

———

It was yet another hot and steamy day, but the sky was clear, judging from the photos.

I spent the morning with my sons before I went out to meet Annaelle in the small churchyard where we had sat the other day after lunch.

(We had agreed to have lunch together then go to the art gallery by Parc Monceau: I had promised the gallerist to stop by and drop off some of my photos and video work.)

Seeing her there—facing away from the pale gate, tall and straight-backed in the bluish shades of the court—my initial reaction was puzzlement: Annaelle was dressed in the strangest outfit and, for all I knew, looked like an unmoving apparition in the dim labyrinth of some video game. Something in the way the colors of her outfit overlapped and juxtaposed against the alabaster sheen of her body made her forms appear flat and photo-like in the distance, with that same depthless quality one finds in an abstract Matisse.

Annaelle might have been heading for the beach: she had on the same leather sandals that revealed her feet's marmoreal translucence, was braless underneath the silk tank top, and her hair was arranged in an updo with an emerald-green Kente cloth.

But it was the silk wraparound skirt that I found at once fascinating and strange: it was split from the hips down by a fuzzy imaginary line where the colors in the front and those in the back faded into each other—murex-purple in the front with a tie-dye circular spot of gold just below the waist; shimmery silver-gray in the back with a crimson spot to match the one in the front.

I walked toward her, reaching for the camera in my pocket.

I took three shots.

The second and third were frontal and she appears to be cringing in them—an inward cringe.

Maybe she took the photos as a compliment, which they were, in a way.

———

(Here they are—stored in the piece of evidence that no one else possesses; the scandalous box of virtual memories where all the answers to Collin's questions are entombed—the remains of one fateful day deposited in the same electronic crypt: Annaelle in the churchyard, enveloped in Tantric color symbolism—from head to toe, quite literally; Annaelle and I leaning far back and laughing before the camera, like two crewmen hiking out on a yacht—with the petrified glass-eyed Jardin des Plantes leopard towering as close behind us as we could get him; the stealthy snapshots in Parc Monceau; the Billie Holiday sound-alike show at the American Bar; the moonstruck marble statue in Arènes de Lutèce—"that lady with the book," as she called her; and the maddening forms of Annaelle fixed forever in the ice-blue gaze of my camera—dancing in the pale night, her loosened hair a frozen crown of black seaweed, her naked body more glorious than anything ever set in metal or marble or words.)

———

(Lunch with her:

I was correct in my intuition about Le Verlaine.

When I called one of the numbers Collin had given me, his aide confirmed my initial assumption: a scanned copy of my debit-card record showed her that Annaelle and I did indeed have lunch at the restaurant on Rue Descartes (August 29, 2007).

At first, though, it was not clear whether I was going to get the information: the aide was curt and told me that she had to obtain authorization from her superior; but when she got back to me, she sounded nice and obliging, said she knew me.)

———

And even if you had to guess the place, even if you cannot recall the details of that last meal, you still feel proud and strong at the thought of the power you find in yourself to relive it again—not just as a pained observer, but also as someone who is beginning to outgrow his position as a compassionate outsider invested with the spotty memory of another person:

A man who can now identify with the deeply moving thought that she was a miraculous sight to meditate, the woman you now see in your unaided imagination, her body veiled behind a collage of strangely hued fabrics—those misty shades of the odd outfit she wore (as if her frame was not contained within ordinary clothes—only hastily covered in juxtaposed strips of cloth that looked like superficial strokes from an unusual palate).

Wondering: how much of that dizzy, joyful color display had infected you as you felt yourself open up to her, become one with the wonders that she had brought into your world.

To envision her presence then and there—the greatest gift of all (bequeathed to you freely and unconditionally by fate out of the nothingness of those sad meager months); the endless spectacle of her charms slowly unfolding before your eyes, manifesting like a living epiphany against the backdrop of urban indifference (the hectic shifting fresco of "real life" surrounding the two of you with its multicolored blur of feverish city crowds going about their chaotic business—the indistinct noise of the so-called "real world").

And so now you can, at long last, see: the totality of it, or if not the totality, then at least the parts that matter; and not with the obsessive eye of the painstaking archivist, but with a vision radically different from anything you have ever known—beyond the smothering certitudes of sense and sensation, trace and record, proof and point: Annaelle opening her eyes wide open—those strange and equivocal windows into her soul; Annaelle stretching her arms crosswise for emphasis; Annaelle shifting the angle of her eyebrows for appeal, or maybe to let you in on one of her deliciously incomprehensible witticisms.

And you think: how childishly lucky you must have felt on that day—touched by the hand of Providence; to be happy and alive under the sun, holding her hand as you stroll together down the crowd-choked sidewalks of Paris; taking the side streets with her and walking through that sloping alley with the mossy walls (a full backstreet decorated just for the two of you—with wolf lichen, dwarf ferns, and the tiny snow-specks of nameless flowers, a cavernous addition to the many small places of bliss that had suddenly sprung up in your life).

Then you both stop, as if on cue—to hear her say perhaps that this is where it was, the revelation in the storm, when she became sure how and where it would all end—her mad run under the rain, her meandering game of hints and guesses.

———

Another variation on the nightmare:

Standing in the landing with a big bundle in my arms—or maybe it is one of those string-tied butcher paper packages in which they wrap meat in the Tunisian countryside.

I feel cold and damp, even though I am dripping with sweat: "It's the walls," I say. "They're sweating with something evil."

The walls are indeed soaked with some nauseous brownish fluid trickling down in barely visible threads, dripping from the ceiling on the stair rail and into the stairwell—a steady ticking sound from a puddle at the bottom of the stairs, echoing in the death stillness of the twilight like a clock.

I look up, trying to find out where I am. That is when I recognize the somber depth of the form overhead: the barrel ceiling of Zoé's landing—its moldy patches and jaundiced walls, the russet marks of the trusses showing through the sodden mortar.

But the mold and the rust and the water spots are gone now: what I see are thick gobs of a maroon substance, like huge patches of soggy scab.

Then, inevitably, the magnified voice flares out from the bottom of the stairs, booming up the stairwell, bouncing off the walls:

"FREEZE! PUT DOWN THE BABY NOW! PUT YOUR HANDS UP ON THE WALL! DO IT NOW!"

I comply and put down the bundle, which, I now realize, is mushy inside, soaked through with something a shade paler than blood; only I cannot tell what it is, not in the dreadful grayish murk of this landing—thick with the sickly vapors, dim as a dirty aquarium.

I walk up to the wall and comply with the orders, but then the sensation hits me in the chest like a sledge hammer—the wet rusty reek in the walls, in the ceiling: "Blood—gouts of blood! The walls are dripping with it!"

Then I wake up with the smell still alive in my memory; the hard and horrid smell of congealed blood spill—a mix of wet rust and raw calf liver.

———

I remember taking a nap in Jardin des Plantes—curling on my side and going to sleep with my head in her lap (the soft sensation, before I drifted off to sleep, in the cheek that was facing down and the warmth in the nape of my neck; and Annaelle's words echoing in her belly, reverberating down to my muffled ear with a throb like womb pulsations—bass vibrations, the words coming out of her mouth transformed into soothing echoes of pure sound).

Strange how misleading the world of images can be: looking at her slim body in the videos and in the photos, one could easily assume that her lap was not a soft place to rest one's head.

But it was, and the memory that I have kept of it in my senses is that of a warm and welcoming concavity, like a firm but snug silk cushion.

I recall being very much at peace as I began to nod off—fitful throbs of Annaelle's womb sounds in one ear and in the other the wind rustling in the trees, the playground chatter of children (jingling in the dim distance beyond the cushioning presence of her body—formless and anonymous, yet sweetly familiar, like silverware clutter).

And when you woke up: did she notice (for the first time, perhaps) that same look Thouraya had reflected on so tenderly at poolside in Tunisia—those "unmistakable streaks of childlike sadness" in the depths of your face ("as if the whole world was nothing but a relentless letdown," she had said in your diary—a "rained-out picnic")?

You will never know. But you do remember lingering, with the back of your head cradled in the sweet warmth of her lap, those sad eyes gazing into the tree canopy, looking up incredulous and full of wonderment, your mind still a bit dazed and displaced from your nap; and Annaelle's face bending near to yours, with those hard-to-decipher eyes beaming, the tip of her finger trailing lazily around your lips, your eyebrows, the ridges and hollows of your face.

And would it be hard to guess what you were thinking in that blessed moment?

To linger in the lip of this instant and hold it still, still, like a wave frozen in its cresting, arrested above and beyond all aspects of time, wrested and redeemed from the cruel clangor of life beating in the restless arteries of the city—the hectic flux of the riverside traffic raging outside the garden.

Life in the quiet composure of the timeless moment: this sanctuary of *our* garden—the oneness of *Us* sheltered from the sad endless flow of the hours.

———

Then these thoughts were all gone.

And you treated yourselves to a dashing romp through the menagerie and the museum of natural history, with the shadows growing deeper and longer in the snapshots that you took; the petrified museum animals like stern long-faced parents, disapproving of your capering—stern and solemn in their eyes, as the two of you staged all sorts of crazy antics and wild poses before them.

In the middle of all the excitement: you knew that it would not be long before you had to run back to Zoé's, that you would never have the time to put on your evening clothes, that you would only be able to change your batteries and memory cards, pocket the American Bar voucher and dash into a taxi with her.

But none of that seemed to matter somehow, amid the charged libidinal heat and sweetness of it all—your silly, unseasonable bird dance in the garden.

———

It must have been a sort of senseless, one-sided hide-and-seek in pictures and words—a lone private game that probably began without deliberate design as I decided to steal in through the tiny rear gate by Musée Cernuschi, on the opposite side of the gate where I had left her on my way to the art gallery.

I remember that when I first spotted Annaelle she appeared to be strolling around aimlessly; and instead of calling my lover or heading her way, I started to play at being invisible, at stealing as many video and photo impressions of her as possible.

The distance between us, the shifting light conditions, and the inevitable unsteadiness in my hands were all factors that determined the unusual visual quality of those photographs: most of the Monceau pictures (with the exception of the last vignettes) look unstructured and expressionless—rambling and anonymous.

Also, in their deliberate toying with focus, framing, and exposure, those furtive photos seem to have been structured like stepping-stones toward the final close-ups at the footbridge; or maybe I imagined them as fleeting moods in which the impersonal imprints of her head and spear-like bodyline were always deliberately thrown off-center, very far left on the edge of the frame, appearing against the background as smudgy pictographic strokes and scatterings—sublimated into a strange and depersonalized presence in fuzzy color, a shifting attractor within the relative visibility of the world that she was just about to exit.

Regardless of what my intentions as a photographer were, I probably must have found it exciting to go beyond what felt like a threshold of danger—the mixed fear and thrill of exposure—using the trees, the bushes, and the monuments as screens between the two of us, hiding spots where I took my shots; pushing my luck just a little further with every shot, coming a little closer behind her with every snapshot that I took—for that long-sought instant of intimate knowing, perhaps, that scintillating second of utter clarity, when the nebulous scatterings of her fuzzy forms and colors would at last converge and crystallize in the center of my vision: the point where the lens, the screen, and my gaze would come together in one instant—the fickle place of convergence where the miracle of beautiful creation is born.

Then, quite unexpectedly, there came the vision that triggered the words I texted her: I was trying to take a profile snap of her walking across the sand, just as she was going around the corner of the monument opposite the pyramid. She had vanished behind the stone structure, and mysteriously (quite possibly through a process of subconscious association), I began to visualize her footprints as a trail of glowing holographic forms—pale traces shimmering like afterimages in the shadowy folds of the sand over which she had walked instants ago: I suppose one could say that they were like visual reflections of the images that had been tracked by my pupils through the membrane of the lens and the mirror of the screen; but in my recollection of that experience, I remember that those traces of her stood out as oblong roundish marks separate from my vision, radiating across the lawn with an irrepressible physical force all their own—a material presence larger than the imprints of real-life feet, like flagstones covered with some white glowing substance.

That was when the entire poem (after days of rambling fragments and notes in the diary) flashed across my mind's eye and emerged like a fully crystallized sand rose from the mental chaos in which it had been gestating.

I took my cell phone out of the knee pocket of my cargo pants. I wrote:

Snow Tracks

> *And just when you think the burning of her footsteps*
> *has ceased*
> *to glow—*
> *in the*
> *ice-frosted*
> *green*
> *of your*
> *garden,*
> *there you see them,*
> *through the wrinkled ice-sheet*
> *of your window:*
> *the scarlet embers*
> *of her spring kisses,*
> *burning in the holly—dropped from the tip of her lips,*
> *like carnival candy.*

I remember following her through the park and reading the poem at the same time—quite possibly several times, because it was not before she was halfway over the arch footbridge that I decided to send it.

I was standing very close by at that point, behind the low foliage of a tree and a bush between the brook and the bridge—looking up at her sideways through the leaves as she opened the purse for her phone.

Now, Annaelle was standing at the crest of the bridge with the phone in her hand, and it suddenly dawned on me that for all our sharing and conversations, the woman who stood before me was more mysterious than ever.

She had turned to face the stream to my left, her hips touching the stone balustrade, her jaw going slack as she began to read with an expression of utter void on her face. That was when I knelt down and took my first close-up picture of her through the drooping branches.

Then there was the second close-up: Annaelle resting her fore-arms sphinx-like on the balustrade, staring into the stream in what could easily be perceived as distress—a dark expression on her drained face, her stare hard as steel.

The blanched face, the clenched expression, the opaque mood: she stood there inscrutable and withdrawn, and I did not know why. She had read my poem only once.

(And yet hard stare or no, it is all so ineffably, so compellingly beautiful—the baffling complexity hidden within those shades of expression captured by your camera through the fuzzy phospho-rescence of the tree: the face seems somehow profoundly *haunted* with a nameless hermetic mix of mystery and revelation radiating from the sublime mask that was her face; the immense engrossing power of ambiguity so suddenly vested in this monumental face, this woman, who—there was no telling—was either about to swoon into the stream like a love-drunk opera heroine, or tear up the very stones on which she stood.)

———

I do not remember anything of what was said between the bridge and the colonnade by the pond, but I do know that it was rather tense for a moment when I joined her. (I can only assume that it had to do with her disquiet about any form of flirtation.)

Still, the mood was decidedly cheerful later at the pond, and just before we left the park at sundown, we decided to throw in a coin and make a wish.

(That closing picture in Parc Monceau:

The pond, shimmering with the last streaks of day, had your penny and your wish safely locked in it now; the crescent of columns hulking in silhouette above the water; a segment of low branch detached in the foreground to your left—shadows of ginkgo leaves like clusters of onyx coins in the afterglow.

That was your last established visual fragment in that park.

But what about the unrecorded words that you deposited in the bosom of the pond along with the coin? Your own private investment in heaven.

Were they words of giving? Were they words of taking?

Was there anything of the offering in your wish—for the sake of your children, for the sake of a world tattered by conflict, shorn of the blessings of true love?

Face it, just a few hours before the stroke of doom, you did not give a dam for your children or the world.

Your secret words by the pond: they were probably like the rest of the conceited thoughts and turgid reflections expressed in your diary during those last days of August—miserly cogitations of an infinitely selfish and self-centered man fooling himself with the false hopes of a new beginning.)

———

It was a night of mad self-indulgence—I know it from memory, from guesswork, and from agonizing self-scrutiny; and so there is really no need to go over all that again in writing—no need to blame anyone either, including myself. There will be none of that here.

Still, some things must be said, shameful as they are—like my allowing her to spike our champagne at the American Bar. (Was it just cocaine? I do not recall ever asking.)

That was perhaps the worst indulgence of all: the rush of alcohol mixed with unaccustomed drugs filled me with unaccustomed euphoria and daring—it made me foolishly oversexed and rash.

In short, for the remainder of my evening with her, I became the victim of my own impulsive reactivity—a man with no sense of consequences, like those "borderliners" one hears about in the news, people who find their foolish deeds suddenly converted into fodder for the media.

Despite the scrupulously reconstructed facts and flaws and fatal errors, however, those last hours of consciousness remain shrouded in a shifting fog of unreality—from the instant I stepped out of the taxi to the final crash; and I am not talking about fuzziness of fact only.

What I mean is the essential texture of the night itself: it was as if, imperceptibly, the thinnest veil of dark mist had descended upon Paris and slowed down the very unfolding of time, rendering every aspect of the city ineffably estranged—infinitesimally removed and distorted and opaque.

Vague nightlife scenes from a barely familiar theater—seen through the smudgy lens of a nervous camera, the cramped and twisted chambers of a drug-inflamed mind.

The first thing that I recall about getting back to the Mouffetard neighborhood is the silhouette of a lone saxophone player close by the bar—playing a tune I do not remember, a string of notes in shadowy pantomime (it was probably the same man I had seen with Zoé just a few days ago).

Then Annaelle and I going into the bar—the half-darkness of the main room and the subdued scintillations beyond, the soft lights of the space where the show was to take place.

———

The two of us must have cut an odd figure as we walked into the place—Annaelle in her strange outfit, and I with my informal clothes and my sun-drenched face, looking very much like the outdoorsman.

Despite its stellar reputation, though, the establishment was by no means conservative: I do not remember feeling unwanted or out of place as we made our way across the barroom and out to the back court, which was tastefully decorated to look like a courtyard bar with small candlelit round tables and nice flower and potted plant arrangements.

Management could not have chosen a better setup: with night falling fast, the day's heat wave had turned sticky and stifling, like a furry beast breathing down your neck—watching the singers perform inside would have been an impossible experience for all.

I know for certain that there was nobody around when we were seated, because that was when she spiked our bottle.

And so here we were—just the two of us at first, sitting in a corner table like a pair of shady companions, sipping drug-laced champagne by candlelight; and as for our anachronistic surroundings, they seemed sweetly chimerical with a queer after-hours feel about them: the bandstand before us—studded with equipment and instruments but empty; the thirties-style microphone—silent under the lightning-blue beam of the spotlight; and, shining behind and above it all like a dream apparition, an immense wall-size screen projection of the woman in whose honor the four-day international contest was organized: Billie Holiday—sad but deep and compelling in a strapless low-cut dress, a double-strand pearl choker, and a larger-than-life silk flower in her hair like a feather ornament.

———

By the time the first finalist stepped up to the microphone, most of the tables were taken; but it was not a full house.

Except for the one song that I filmed in full, the mosaic of low-resolution videos is technically imperfect and rather sketchy, but the clips are telling enough: the four finalists were all quite good, although judging by the full-song video I must have shown an immediate preference for the younger contestant, Sarah Bellamy—the one who eventually came out second. (There is no trace of the jury members in the photos and the videos—I suppose that they must have been on the conservative side and did not have a favorable opinion of Sarah's choice for her closing song. Maybe they thought it was arrogant and pretentious for a little-known singer to enter a song of her own composition—and introduce it in her own words, to boot, like a big star.)

At any rate, it must have been a tough call. The other singers were all very talented and offered an impressive range of Holiday classics—together, they covered a representative assortment of songs from Lady Day's repertoire.

Still, there was no denying that Sarah had left a compelling mark on the evening; and the young singer's power as a performer was not just in the deliciously pained crooning quality of her velvet voice, but also in the spiritual depth with which she borrowed the tunes and inhabited them.

I have no idea what became of Sarah or her song after the show, but what I do know with certainty now is that there is a particularly haunting sense of suffering and depth and darkness in her closing number: arresting qualities of soulfulness suffused with that felicitous combination of clumsy sentiment in the lyrics, the vaguely bluesy overtones of the music, the uncanny intensity of her own diminutive presence.

She stood there and sang in her island of light, driven by a power of eloquence well beyond her years, this young Frenchwoman who had come so close to incarnating the sound and mystique of the Lady herself—the angle and stiff swing of the right arm; the eyebrows rising and falling to mark shifts in mood and emotion; the head thrown back with abandon, eyes closed in ecstasy.

Sarah was probably in her mid-twenties, and the last piece with which she chose to conclude her performance must have smacked of hubris and self-promotion to the members of the jury—a choice that was probably detrimental to the young woman's score.

Sarah introduced that closing number herself, which none of the other contestants did: "For my last entry," she said, "I'd like to do something I wrote especially for this evening, in honor of the lady we're—remembering tonight. It's called 'Any More Heaven.' The lyrics are by Mike Strombel, who's with us in the house tonight."

And so the music began, and Sarah started to sway ever so gently, to the whine of the saxophone and the muted strains of the band.

Her short hair was dyed platinum blonde and done in a finger-wave style. The idea behind the hair color was probably to create a provocative contrast with Sarah's deep tan (enhanced by earth-toned makeup).

The rest of the lighting around her was dim and undefined, and it somehow lent a strange quality of chromatic distortion to the beam in which she stood. (Onscreen, the light appears like a diffuse layer of pale blue filtering her entire body.)

As she stood there in the low-cut satin dress, Sarah glistened with sweat, and the moisture made her body appear like glazed metal. (Captured in my video clip, paused and frozen on my screen, Sarah is this vestal figure of bronze—shining fitfully and imperfectly, but rare and beautiful beyond explanation; a haunting epiphany amid the vanished ghosts of that suffocating night.)

They say love smiles only
On the lucky and the strong.
I know I'm neither, honey,
Yet you stood by me so long.
You loved me soft, you loved me loud;
You loved me shy, you loved me proud—
More love than I ever dreamed,
More joy than I've ever seen.

And if it's anywhere given
To feel any more heaven,
Thanks, but no thanks—
I don't wanna find out:
The touch of your eyes
Is all I can imagine;

The gift of those skies
Is what my life's about.

For all the lyrics' gloss of potential hope, the rhythm and texture of
the song were a somber blue, the mood and expression very much
like Billie's later rendering of "I Don't Want to Cry Anymore" and
"Sophisticated Lady"—the frail but honest confessional tone of a
woman whose gaze was projected beyond the audience in this transformed court, lost in bittersweet contemplation of a vanished moment
of plenitude—the moment of authentic joy that outshines everything.

Stars? They shine and fade.
Lovers? The fast, the slow.
I sigh and watch the parade
Of wooers come and go.

The drop in Sarah's tone and expression after the starry-eyed illusion of the first two lines—to even deeper depths, with the velvet
voice at times muffling the words into articulate sighs and swoons
without the least break in pitch; the faint throaty cracks in her voice
emerging naturally and steadily within each phrase—a measure of
the timeless pain pouring out of her, the emotional scars of a voice
all too acquainted with the pits of hell after the heights of hope.

The mere thought of you outshines them all,
A sound from your lips—my only call.
More faith than I even dreamed,
More hope than I've ever seen.

Then back to the refrain: the world-weary voice spiraling down into
loneliness, determined to shun the very possibility of love.

And if it's anywhere given
To feel any more heaven,
Thanks, but no thanks—
I don't wanna find out:

> *The touch of your eyes*
> *Is all I can imagine;*
> *The gift of those skies*
> *Is what my life's about.*

———

The small tree-circled garden where we went after the show was at the far end of Arènes de Lutèce by Rue Monge—she called it the garden of "that lady with the book" (the marble statue of a studious woman with a book opened across her lap—a monument to Mortillet, symbol of the man's indefatigable dedication to the study of the past).

Our late-night caper there was Annaelle's idea, and as soon as we squeezed through the narrow gap between the trees and the fence on Rue des Arènes, we must have both agreed that if we stayed by the fence anybody passing by would overhear us.

That was how I ended up following her all the way down to the monument, the lowest and quietest spot in the Arènes—a slope that dipped gently into a low crescent-shaped lawn ringed by a semicircle of cypress trees with the marble statue at its center.

It was there that I spent my last moments with Annaelle—walking behind her under the full moon, trying to film her silhouette as she hurried along ahead of me (my only attempt to capture her on video that night).

(There are no visible traces or audible sounds of Annaelle in that downhill video fragment—nothing but indistinct buzz and gloomy scrambled grayness, a shaky stretch of opaque nothingness.

Then, all at once, there is my voice rising within this chaos of amorphous noise and murk—the only mark of meaning in the absurd quivering vacuousness of the screen: "Keep running, I don't care. I'm going to film the lady with the book."

Followed by more swishing noise and a few fragments of the monument—all very poor and spur-of-the-moment; far less coherent, visually, than the photos.)

Suddenly, Annaelle came out from behind the statue, and I immediately understood why she had decided to run ahead of me: she stepped out stark naked into the circle of grass with her hair down, the fleece beneath her navel black; and she commenced to dance—something vaguely oriental, something naïve and sweet and beautiful.

I kicked off my shoes and immediately felt the cool touch of the grass on my feet. I took a few pictures and put down the camera next to my shoes.

And then it seemed as if the drift of time had begun to decelerate—to freeze in slow motion like an ice circle in the stream—as I witnessed and absorbed and adored the fevered dance of her slender frame. There was something strangely solemn and formal about the poetry of that body in motion.

(Dancing in and out of the shadows, oblivious to your presence, with the moonlight casting a fitful bluish-gray glow on her skin, like the flicker of faraway lightning.

Mental images created in your consciousness thanks to the pictures captured on your screens: the flux of the seconds and the minutes and the hours frozen in the mosaic formations of the pixels. Moments lost to trauma but never quite forgotten—their pulse still beating somehow, still reverberating in the somber recesses of your sleepless unforgetting machines, the fertile folds of your shock-battered brain.

Ultimately, though, the same question arises—as it has, again and again, during these last few months of struggling recollection: do you have any of your own words for that fateful moment—any independent affective traces in your memory besides the ghostly dance of images from the screen?

Feelings, in short—things of the heart that you can claim as your own.

Home at last: is that what your naked self felt and said then and there—now that you think you know who you really were and what you really did in that moon-bathed garden in Paris?

A "sense of belonging," in sum. That was probably the live kernel of feeling that you found within you at the far end of the

Arènes, your final homing place after the unreal hubbub of a long and sultry day: the sudden dawning of a new kinship under the kind munificence of that full-moon sky. All at once, you must have felt accepted and admitted, freely and unconditionally, as you stood there and watched her deliver that dance for you—the ultimate token of intimacy, the sacred culmination of the gift that she was.

And the peculiar knowledge that came with the feeling: knowing with certainty that this gift was the most beautiful form of closeness that she could grant you; knowing also, in this frozen arrested moment of certainty and bounty and opening, that you were now willing to do anything for the woman—that there was something deeply, movingly redemptive about the knowledge itself and the absoluteness it had put in your heart.)

———

Inevitably, she ended up spreading her wraparound skirt on the lawn and we lay down together in yet another temporary bed, yet another borrowed place created by the two of us.

Only tonight it was different from when she had straddled me in the hotel room on that rainy day—the way she had seemed lost in her ardor then, as she rocked and raced after her pleasure, driven by a power at once awesome and touching in its honesty.

(That solitary hotel room—your first full act of love together:

You were so obsessed about keeping it all in your imagination and in your diary, hours after you had left the place: the delightful respite of that room magnified in fantasy and in writing, page after page; the dense shadows of that rented haven and the sweet ease with which she had turned it into yet another scene of her desire—the depth and despair with which she dug her fingernails into your shoulders, the way she hugged your belly so close and rocked herself and came with a strength you found almost eerie in its gushing anarchy, its untamed drive.

After which there came a moment when she became far less knowing in her movements, almost erratic; and she probably began to sense your confusion also, because when she lifted up her face from your shoulder, she looked at you with understanding in her eyes. And she put her hands in your hair, lowered her face toward yours and whispered the words you were to turn over with such sentimental fever in your diary, your side-notes, your hasty half-poems: "Don't worry, I *am* going to see you off—I just need to recover my wits.")

And now this most unlikely of rooms: the treetops for bed canopy, the scraps of moonlit sky flashing through the spongy somberness of the foliage. I was stretched out on yet another improvised bed—the vaguely Indian-looking skirt that I had found so unbecoming just a few hours ago, as I secretly tried to capture the meaning of her strange outfit while she stood alone and unsuspecting in the bluish shades of the churchyard.

Annaelle was deep and intent and intense as I lay on my back and let myself be taken, step by step, through all the gradations of bliss.

She knew me with such exquisite naturalness—measuring her time against my own hidden ebbs and flows, testing and teasing the fickle pulse of my pleasure; knowing when to hold tight and when to let go, always deferring the last rush—that most dreaded coming of the final flood.

Then there was a powerful change in the movement of her hand, and she began to squeeze me with gentle downward motions—taking her time all along, putting me every now and then in her mouth to keep me smooth and moist.

And that was how she made me get there as the sound of my voice resounded with strange unidentifiable echoes—the heat waves rising from my body, rushing outward with the last spasms.

My come gone to the last drop on her skirt. My seed scattered on the ground.

———

(After a while, she must have requested some time to herself for reflection, because I remember leaving her supine by the statue and walking back up alone toward the fence as the city slept.

I do not recall any conflict or tension in the last words exchanged between the two of us.)

When I found my way back to the street, the square on Rue Mouffetard was deserted, and another amazing illumination struck me with the same lightning swiftness as my vision in Parc Monceau.

Only now everything around me appeared to pulsate with new and unnamable shades of color and meaning—even the usual scraps of scattered paper litter seemed to sway in slow motion, like weightless fragments of gift wrap hovering in a vacuum field.

That was when I decided to sit down on the rim of the fountain, switch on my phone, and send her the second poem.

Moonset

You *are the sun, I know.*
But it is hard to confess:
That it is I who must wear your light,
to tunnel my way
into the maw of night.
Mistress of my dark climes.
Still, the moment of your going
never fails to come, always.
Though you do take the time
(before you begin to arise,
slowly, slowly, lifting)
to see me off and out—
feel me receding:

From bone-bright moonshine
to drum-skin translucence;
to the endless slow dissolving—
the final graying of the glow,
like a solitary speck of snow
melting into a sheet of water.

I entered Zoé's building and flipped on the light switch and nothing happened.

All the lights were out and I had to grope my way up the stairs in total darkness.

As I reached the third-floor landing, I saw a scattering of light fanning out from under Zoé's apartment door.

Everything else around me was pitch black—the building dead still in the dead of night, the twin dwarf trees by her door like a cloaked miniature figure in the middle of the planter.

When I opened the door, I saw Samia in the full glare of the ceiling lights—sprawled limply on the living room couch, her mouth agape and her face set in a frozen wince, a dried-up trickle of something thicker than saliva down the corner of her mouth. It was not sleep, I knew right away—and right away I knew something had gone dreadfully wrong with my children.

I left the apartment door wide open behind me and dashed down the corridor to their room:

Everything looked normal—their door still ajar, the way I always left it; but there was something horrifying about the altered air and my head was already full of its wet rusty reek in the half-dark, so different from the ether-and-overripe-apple smell of the living room— and everything in my body going down with horror, down into a place of frozen sleep and imploded nothingness. I was shutting down inside and I was knowing it as I shook and shrank before the door: it was too late, I knew it, and I had no struggling strength left in me already—nothing left to fight for my sons.

I pushed the door open and saw them—their bodies torn and twisted in the acrid twilight, mangled across the bed, the sheets so splattered with their flesh and blood that I could hardly make them out against the bedclothes.

And I did not even try to go any further—to see them at least and feel them and hold them and *be* with them, before they were taken away and ceased to be mine.

Instead, I ran out, choking on my own vomit, screaming through it; ran out and slammed the apartment door shut and put it all behind me; and I kept screaming—through the vomit, the foaming in my mouth, the primal pain.

I know there was not enough manhood left in me to keep the door open, because I remember being in complete darkness before I passed out atop that door-side planter: I fell face down on the plants and the world I thought I knew faded into a black nothingness.

———

The acute stress reaction must have resulted in a first-time seizure and the dissociative stupor that followed: I was unable to make appropriate responses to the nudges of the man who stood over me as I lay across the planter. (The police officer scrutinized me under the beam of a flashlight then he worked the key in the door and let himself in. A moment later, I heard his transceiver crackle inside.)

I think I tried to pull my legs into the planter at some point—or did I try to heave myself to my feet by holding on to the rim?

A long time had passed, it seemed, with the building still in silence and darkness—Zoé's door was closed again and I remember gripping the plants and groaning in the dark (I cannot say how long).

Then I heard deep guttural sounds in the stairwell—someone sitting on the stairs above (those were echoes of my own terrified fitful breathing, but I did not know that then).

I had no sense of inner space—the place inside me where my consciousness began.

Then, all of a sudden, the waves of hell commenced to crash into the building and once again, everything changed in a matter of seconds.

First, there was the shrill clang of the front door in the vestibule downstairs, the heart-rending clamor of the tactical unit in the stairs—their lights dancing in the staircase like silver shafts.

Those who had gotten in through the roof were already positioned on the flight of stairs just above Zoé's landing—pointing their weapons at me through the banister, shouting down incomprehensible warnings.

Two of them eventually made their way down to the landing and shouted more things at me in peremptory but less aggressive tones (as it turned out, there was a third man behind them holding up a round light on a staff).

When I did not respond, the two officers pulled me up from the planter and frisked me vigorously.

Their guns looked like absurd, unnecessarily complicated toys, their night-vision goggles crab-eyed on top of the robotic headgear, their Kevlared uniforms thick and bristly and prehistoric-looking, like the synthetic hides of amusement park dinosaurs.

Eventually, they let go of me, their voices distorted into a throaty gargling jumble as soon as they lowered their visors.

I gradually sank down and slumped against the wall between the plants and the stairs, where more black-uniformed figures were coming down.

Zoé's door was now wide open again and the landing and stairs teemed with them: RAID or GIPN men in tactical gear, called in by the attorney general to clear the building for the officers of the Brigade Criminelle. A few of them were talking into their mouthpieces—incomprehensible staccatos, SMR-distorted exchanges.

When their commander declared the building safe, they ordered the paramedics into the apartment to take Samia away.

Then it was the Brigade's turn.

———

I was still disoriented and had no sense of space or time when the two uniformed policemen helped me up from the spot where I had wedged myself by the stairs.

I still had no sense of the limits of my mind either. I was suffering from loss of vitality and my body felt hollow and weak, as if from electric shock.

I remember the moment when Collin stood before me in the semi-dark landing: he looked as if he was wearing two round pieces of mirror glass on his eyes—probably the reflections from somebody's flashlight on his oval rimless glasses.

He must have tried to address me in some way, but I was standing unsteadily between the two policemen and I did not say a word. He did not have time to wait for my words either—his men were already sealing the scene. (For some reason, with the light coming across the doorway now, I was beginning to see them all through a sort of reddish-black aura: they were all jarring and menacing and ominous-seeming, their sounds shrill and penetrating—these shadowy-red men caught in the insanity of their bustle like frenzied backstage actors.)

There was another man with Collin—possibly the police Prefect: the lead investigator, who was a commissaire de police, stepped aside and let him in first with a deferential gesture.

They were followed by Collin's aides then the experts of the Police Technique et Scientifique—somber men with sinister white gloves and stacks of brown bag envelopes; and their ponderous, incomprehensible equipment—it came in black cases of various sizes that made them look like musicians. There were two white-clad-and-gloved men each holding a stack of dull-white plastic receptacles with thick numbers stenciled in phosphorescent orange.

I stood there and looked on as the two policemen held me. (Was it a routine gesture or did they both decide that I might try to run away?)

And then, during those unreal minutes, something happened that I had always retained in my memory—in my dream-thoughts and in my waking thoughts, well before the work of recall under hypnosis—the only words from that evening that I remember hearing in full clarity: a man with a black-inscribed red armband was talking on a cellular phone—I recall the rectangle glowing a phosphorescent aqua blue in his hand as he tried to put all the din behind him, leaning far out over the rail of the banister, like a careless boy, his hand cupped over his ear.

Apparently, somebody somewhere in the outside world was worrying about the size of the building, and the red-sleeved man was working on allaying their concerns, even as he peered into the dark downward gape of the stairwell, as if he was testing how far out he could lean before he went over.

The officer was almost shouting into his cell phone, hopelessly trying to be authoritative and convincing in the middle of the madness: "We're working on the lights. The stairs are *very* roomy, believe me—it is an old building with a very wide roomy staircase. No, no. The landing—no. The landing is *huge*. We'll let you know when we're through."

He was so close that I could have reached out and touched him—this man whose inscrutable words are the only utterances I have kept safely locked in my memory all along.

All at once, I began to shake and whimper: "It's all gone," I remember saying.

The reaction of the two officers was to turn me around and help me sit down on the stairs.

One of them leaned over me and tried to tell me something, but all I could register were the distortions of his face through the translucent rim of the reddish-black aura—that face looked like an empty rubber mask wobbling without support.

His colleague was shouting something on his transceiver as the men of the Brigade ran in and out of the apartment.

As I sat on the stairs, I suddenly began to feel that I literally did not know where to turn, that I was literally about to lose my head: was the building going to be invaded by another onslaught of piercing cacophony? Or maybe it was just my head—my nerves imploding in the cavernous recesses of my mind.

I put my hands over my ears and sat with my face cradled between my knees.

Time kept pounding and grinding inside me—its horrid, inhuman relentlessness.

———

(And when they went to work inside, what were the exact words they uttered? The sounds they made? The acts they executed?

Even now you find it impossible to interrogate your memory for any details from the place of horror—the sightless scene that you have persistently refused to recall in spite of its obsessive recurrence in your dreams.

The relentless clicking echoes of the machines, the desperate-sounding voices of the men shouting out your children's names as if they were in pain or in horror. Dream fragments—your only substitute for reality.

The children. The children. Echoes of a moment you still do not dare revisit, or name, or define—nailed and hammered into your bones incessantly, through the primal language of dreams, wordlessly.

Or is it your present mind projecting, imagining—how it might have been, as you try to conjure up the remainder of your last day, relive it with less torment if you can—in some in-between world, a sphere of existence halfway between your nightmares and the labor of writing the night into a second life?

Is it the man putting evidence together in the here and now, or the guilty trauma patient? Or a form of impersonal memory floating back in flashes—some of them unnaturally sharp and intact, as if channeled through a miraculous rift in the cosmic weave of time? Uncanny flares of timeless recognition.

How easy and comforting it feels: to be able to imagine, within the span of one moment, that it was all nothing but one boundless nightmare stretching over several hours, with no sense or sound or substance; that it was never really your own life events unfolding—a mere play of shadows in a theater of borrowed dreams.)

I was drowning on the stairs: hugging my shins hard with my face pressed against my knees, I wound up instinctively trying to revert to the fetal position to keep myself from flying apart; but the pressure was choking the air from my lungs and creating further anguish.

Now the paramedic called in by the officer stood before us with an orange kit in one hand and a thermal blanket in the other.
She lay down the kit and put her hand on my arm.

One of the officers helped me to stand up. Then he walked down one flight with me, helped me sit down in the stairs, and stepped aside for the paramedic, who spread out the thermal blanket on the floor and had me lie down on my back.

I do not remember what she was telling me as I lay down in the dark, but I know that her words had to do with the pace of my breathing: she kept reminding me to breathe, to control my rhythm, to hold the air within my chest for a few seconds, to visualize my chest expanding with my breathing.

Many times she had to hold me down and keep me on my back when I grew agitated and wanted to go back to the fetal position.

She kept holding me and talking to me all the while.

That woman's presence was the only thing that kept me together during those dreadful moments following the seizure.

———

After a while (I don't know how long), I had to walk back up the stairs with the two policemen: it was time to face Collin.

I was quite probably still in a deep stupor, because I had no depth perception and no sense of time or place. The world around me was a shaky sequence of visual impressions blinking on and off like disconnected scraps from a film—sometimes shockingly sharp, sometimes fuzzy and depthless.

The lights were back on now, and my aura had turned even more somber. The men of the Police Technique et Scientifique were exiting one by one, looking grave and gloomy.

Collin wanted me to leave with him, right away. A policewoman standing by had a fresh shirt for me.

And now, under a light the color of rusty water, I found myself face to face with another form of silence—almost as dreadful as that of a while ago: the hush of shocked and shaken men filing out with the dark mark of unreality and disbelief etched into their leaden faces.

Collin was as livid-faced and harried as the others, and he appeared to be very much in a hurry.

Still, as he addressed me, he managed to come off as almost mild-mannered. And yet the firmness of his mind was starkly visible—in his body language, the relentless urgency of his gaze. He knew the hours ahead were going to be long and crucial.

When I could not begin to slip out of my shirt, he unbuttoned it for me and asked his assistant to help me with the fresh one. Even then I sensed an undercurrent of deep disdain in the intensity of his silence.

A significant part of the man was this ominous mass of inner out-rage that he was capable of using to get things done—a force tightly packed and walled inside him, like insulation material.

———

Among the memories I was able to retrieve after my injury, that first isolated minute outside the building looms like a freeze-frame on a screen; and yet even now, as I try to put the scene together, I can still feel in my body powerful residues of the living sensations:

I remember quite precisely how I felt out on the sidewalk—the shiver of loss and disorientation that ran through my frame; the stink of exhaust fumes from the idling vehicles on the square; Collin standing close behind the ambulance outside the door, instructing the two police officers to take me to his car—his face fiery in the red glow of the taillights.

The horrid reality of what had happened and what we were about to do must have dawned on me as I stood there: the realiza-tion caused my body to react with fright and I began to panic and wanted to turn back at the sight of all these vehicles, some of which were starting out ahead of us.

At any rate, I certainly resisted following the two men to Collin's car and stood on the doorstep, virtually within arm's reach of the ambulance. The two officers did not insist but they kept holding me, while the commissaire spoke with one of the paramedics through the passenger window.

Even so, Collin was intent on keeping me out of his way (I think he did not want me to see my sons brought out and taken away). He turned around and barked something at the men, and this time they did force me into his car.

And now I was sitting in the back of an idling police vehicle with a driver standing by and two officers keeping watch outside, and before long the man of power who controlled all these men of power got in with his assistant and we drove off into the early dawn—the last hour of quiet before the city began to stir.

———

The car was racing down the deserted street, yet I remember Rue Saint Hilaire with stunning intensity: the spikes bristling like spearheads on the fence of Jardin des Plantes; the rectangular stone frame of the diminutive corner gate mottled with moss and lichens; the somber mass of trees inside the garden—towering and brooding and forbidding in their height and their gloom, like mounds of charred rags and bones.

All of it sliding away behind us second by second as we sped down Rue Buffon toward Place Valhubert and across the Austerlitz Bridge, with the arched iron hulk of the trestle bridge looming farther downstream—the jagged skeleton of a prehistoric beast etched black against the blush-wine sky.

(There are many structures of familiar buildings that come back to me from the fleeting visual impressions of that crossing—buildings and monuments along the riverside that were silhouetted against the first streak of dawn: mental images that I was able to recall with increasing lucidity over time, well before I decided to use online satellite imagery to trace out the route we pursued.

Part of me must have known and retained where I was amid the chaos: we were driving over the same stretch of river that I had crossed with Annaelle on our first night out together.)

Our car glided down the ramp and we swerved left on the Pompidou Expressway, picking up speed again along the Seine—the early barges dark and bristly in the gray water.

Then we stop and I can see him—even now, as I try to write it all into sense; and I can feel the power and reach of my inner vision as it stretches further and further back—to encompass and magnify even the most marginal details; as if, by sheer mind power, I am able to conjure up every single step he took across the empty street and up toward the entrance of the Prefecture building where I was to be taken for questioning later—the officer waiting for him between the two square columns, standing unreal and incongruous by the closed door, with the colors on the becalmed flag above him coming to life and the limestone facade between ash-gray and pale red.

Collin spoke with the policeman briefly and made a lengthy call on his cell phone.

Then we had to leave.

———

We drove back along the river to the east end and the Institut Médico-Légal.

The driver parked right near the service entrance, and the four of us waited outside in the shadow of the dark brick structure, just a couple of steps from the door; and right here already, as the city braced itself for another day of suffocating heat, I came face to face with the same thing that had struck me cold in Zoé's corridor—I could smell it again, or perhaps not so much smell it as absorb its chilling power through some unconscious instrument of sense buried deep within me: the rank yet barely-within-grasp redolence of death—exuded through the walls and the windows in sly tentative emanations, like an acrid aftertaste.

Here was the place of all endings, then, and yet even as I stood among these gray-countenanced, blank-eyed men (their faces worn thin by the night of inhuman effort that I had inflicted upon them), something wayward and weak in me persisted in its refusal to acknowledge the one Truth that mattered: the stubborn fact that my sons were dead, that it was now my paternal duty to face them at last and see them through this terrible passage.

The back door opened and a woman appeared, her summer-brown face framed in straight blond hair that enclosed her features like a helmet of gold thread.

With her standing in the door now, some of the Truth started to sink in and my legs began to give out.

As my gaze met the woman's ice-blue eyes, I saw there was an expression of deep sadness in them—or perhaps it was commiseration. She was not dressed in her work clothes and yet it was obvious that she held a senior-level position at the institute. The woman greeted us from the doorstep and motioned me in, her face averted in what appeared to be embarrassment.

I took my first step forward, with the men crowding so close around me that I could feel their bodies press against mine.

There were many dim meandering corridors before we came to the room, which was, as far as I can recollect, vacant and shockingly white under the neon light. The woman was wearing her uniform now, and when she stepped up to the refrigerator after the few formulaic words that she had addressed to me, I failed to follow her and simply stood by the door. I began to shake.

The next thing I remember, my face was dripping with water and Collin's men had their arms hooked under my armpits, holding me up as their boss shouted at me.

In hindsight, I now realize that there was nothing at all in the commissaire's behavior that came even close to shouting. The truth is that the man was most likely trying to address me with a few words of encouragement—to bolster me up and jolt me into whatever physical alertness I could muster under the circumstances.

Still, I will never be able to dispel the distorted sensation that Collin's words and manner amounted to nothing less than a brutal injunction hurled at me with violence that spiraled downward into the depths of my soul, tore at the deepest roots of my being; and I will never forget the force of terror radiating from his face: that flare of anger in the arrowhead nose; that unexpected glower of aggressiveness in the flint eyes—raging emotion lighting up his face with a ruddy glow all at once, throwing him off balance and shifting his expression from the neutral objectivity of professional indifference to something far more personal, far more emotional.

And it was probably the unexpected emotionality of the shift, its unforeseen subjective coloring, that had now darkened his demeanor with a shadow of heartfelt rage—the very thing that he had worked so hard to contain all along.

I suppose some of that unspoken rage had quickly found a frail place within me and lodged itself in it: I must have passed out a second time right after Collin's words. At any rate, my last moments in the institute remain a blank in my mind to this day—a cognitive gap from which I have never been able to recover any memory.

But I do remember what happened just before I lost consciousness again: Collin's men dragging me toward the woman just as she rolled a stainless steel body carrier out of the roll-in refrigerator— the capsule-shaped white bag, the tray burning with white light.

Then the blackout: my mind still refusing to face up to reality— the consequences of my horrid act.

———

Between the morgue and Quai de Gesvres, there is an empty stretch of nothingness in my memory, followed by recollection (both intense and distorted) of an inner courtyard at the Prefecture.

I was walking between Collin and his aide, the two men flanking me relentlessly like two ghostly forms. Keeping pace with their stride proved to be almost unendurable: the pain and confusion of that unending uphill sensation, the ground shifting beneath my feet.

Inside the building there was a long succession of narrow corridors—dim and random and confusing; then a neon-flooded office where a third person (a uniformed police officer) commenced to attend to some paperwork behind a black desk.

They all seemed in a desperate rush.

And when the policeman was done, I had to go with the three of them—down a narrow flight of old stone stairs to a tiny low-ceilinged basement lit by a grimy bulb hanging from a cord, its light so dim and dusty it was no more than a feeble glow, like a lump of shiny wax dangling from a black string.

It all happened very fast and very mechanically from that point onward, as if the remainder of the procedure was the natural outcome of a long and careful rehearsal:

Collin and the other man keeping their distance, retreating far behind us already, their forms silhouetted against the wall by the stairs; the officer searching me before the holding cell; and then the final step: going beyond the pale line, I remember, that marked the threshold of the cell—the gravelly slide of the barred door, the deep iron clang as he locked me up.

It was scare tactics with a therapeutic twist, one might say.

By putting me behind bars, Collin was ostensibly adhering to the letter of the law, pure and simple: a suspect in my state had to be confined and examined by a doctor before any deposition could take place. Still, his choice of cell was highly unorthodox—and purely tactical in the end: a cheap ploy to shock me into the hard reality of his power, turn me into a constructively scared and cooperative subject.

My recollection of the physical features of that unnamable space is spotty and distorted, but I do remember that my reaction to it was instantaneous: I climbed onto a hard round-edged surface—some sort of concrete table by a bunk-like cement structure at the back of the cell.

Then I jumped off.

I recall the flash as I landed on my head, the darkness that followed for a short while before I began to hear the voices and look down at myself from the Other Side lying unconscious on the floor of that cell: contemplating the cold cement sensation of the bleak space behind the bars; the streamlined rounded aspect of the forms inside the cell; the three men's frantic bustle around my body.

Impressions defined and structured in accordance with their own logic, their own cognitive and geometric laws; otherworldly perceptive powers that beautifully defy scientific explanation.

And I have never tried to explain them, to this day. Instead, I keep on remembering and revisiting those empowering moments from the spirit world all the time.

———

Silence. After all the frenzied calls, the jangle of fretting voices bouncing off the walls.

Silence.

Followed by the paramedics—three of them, under the strange incandescence of that orphan light.

Their voices almost melodious, detached and distinct from the clicking and bleeping, the crisp rustle of the unnatural fabrics all about my body: humane sounds in the well—their human sounds—their plea to "stay with us" echoing like the grave reverberations of prayer, "remain with us, Mr. Abbassi."

"Are you still with us, Mr. Abbassi?"

None of it harsh or hurried at all, from where I was watching.

Even the dust-muted, grime-encrusted light bulb was beautifully metamorphosed—its glimmer a reticular radiation now—a floating orb of dull crystal lit softly from within, swaying in chiaroscuro amid the shifting shadows.

And the insubstantial iron bars—bending with such graceful ease, like seaweed in the depths.

———

They were good, they were brave; and when they got me into the Paris trauma center, I knew it was not over for me yet.

That first assistance intervention at the Prefecture was conducted with rigor and effectiveness—well within the "golden hour," as it is called in emergency medicine.

I will not even begin to describe what they did on the operating table—the mere memory of singed hair makes me sick to my stomach.

In fact, there is hardly any memory from that heartbreaking circle of sorrow that I would like to revisit—the marginal world of the OR.

As for what happened before and after surgery, what I can say at this point is that it was long, painful, and terrible—but never unendurable, in the way surgery was.

Still, there were three fortunate occurrences in the infernal chapter of my early hospitalization, and *they* are definitely worth remembering: my immediate recognition of Sami upon waking, his research into the events that took place in Zoé's apartment, and the brilliantly creative innovations undertaken by the neurorehabilitation psychologists shortly after I emerged from my coma.

Relatively soon after surgery, the doctors and the rehabilitation nurses discovered three highly promising cognitive characteristics of my posttraumatic state:

First, my working memory was not impaired; second, my writing, reading, and comprehension skills were miraculously still intact and fully functional—an easily explainable twist of fate according to the doctors, who seemed very good at explaining everything except my uncontrollable, unnerving shifts from French to a perfectly fluent but excessively formal and florid English; third, despite the amnesia, I was still capable of recalling certain events that occurred shortly before my self-inflicted injury.

Indeed, I still managed to retain distinct but disconnected memories from the evening of August 29 and the early hours of

August 30: segments from my evening with Annaelle (whom I was unable to identify by name or by description); significant episodic memories from the last excruciating moments in Zoé's apartment; the police intervention in the apartment and the procedures initiated by Commissaire Collin (after Sami, Collin was the second person I spoke with upon emerging from coma, and even though I found it strenuous to communicate with the man, I was able to recognize him immediately).

The hospital's neurorehabilitation staff had a brilliant strategy, and it ended up saving me from despair: one of the nurses installed a voice-to-text application on my laptop computer and had me equipped with a digital recorder. Because of what had happened to my body and my speech, writing to others and reading what they said became central to my daily existence—especially in the first phase of my contacts with Sami. That application on my laptop and the digital recorder became my main tools of complex communication with the outside world.

Eventually, they became great tools of empowerment and self-esteem, too—a source of hope amid the onslaught of shattering revelations, the unrelenting implosions of sense and logic that plagued my life in Paris and during the dreadful first months at Le Croisic trauma center—days when I felt I was witnessing my own erasure as a flesh-and-bone entity.

As the recorded events of the past unfolded on the page and onscreen, I found myself utterly mesmerized by the eerie narcissistic sentimentalism of the diary, the even eerier spaces of the photos and videos, with their spellbinding assemblage of sounds and images and words crying out for narrative structure and meaning and pattern: those astounding mosaics of digitized life that I now had to reconstruct piece by piece—incorporeal puzzle of the man that I used to be.

But before any reconstruction of my identity was even imaginable, there was that dreadful limbo of suspended existence between the intensive care unit and the neurosurgical ward—an experience that I struggled so hard to articulate into words:

As a man with traumatic brain injury, you turned into a virtual entity, wavering between worlds and modes of being (the physical and the mechanical), existing at the intersection point between your frail body processes and the cybernetic channels and chemical flows that were keeping them in a functional state.

And when you found yourself observing it all from the Other Side, a witness to your own precarious existence, contemplating your machine-dependent body in the ICU: the total vision of the machinic you and the web of artificial nerves connected to it (the new props of your life) was positively horrifying— the life that you had once arrogantly claimed as "yours"; the life that had once throbbed in your heart as you proudly walked the streets with the woman who was your new love, your guide into a new existence.

That life—how hard you fought against its waning, and how bitterly you mourned its withering away: you might have been silent, but the fury in your heart was like a raging volcano.

That life—how deeply and painfully you lived its encrypted metamorphosis into the cold winking digital codes of the machines, its forced denaturing as they prepared you for the OR.

The experience has left you scarred and humiliated in ways that you find so hard to name, much less comprehend and process: the insertion devices on your arms; the intubation of your throat and the catheter in the back of your head; the drop-by-drop flow of unnatural liquids that was now the life stream of your physical being—the sedative and the analgesic, the diuretic and the paralytic agent, the hypertonic saline and the anti-epileptic.

Something still active and rebellious in you (your Soul?) found all this so unnatural and constrictive, and it kept egging you from the start into screaming your rage and refusal to the doctors and the nurses, those insubstantial ICU shades bustling about you, working so hard to save your life: the needles swelling your veins as you tried (but failed) to shout your resistance; the claustrophobic panic invading every bit of your being even as you lay limp and helpless; the sad depressing sound of the mechanical ventilator hissing through you—the two-note monotony of its rise and fall a measure of this dwarfed new consciousness that you were now given, a nagging foreshadowing of the unreality to come.

The unquiet echoes of all the men and women swarming around you, speaking in urgent indecipherable tongues behind their masks, wrapped up in the dazzling green of their scrubs, like giant praying mantises, diligently going about the somber business of getting you ready to be saved.

The even more dazzling glare of that other green—the pale-mint wall of the cubicle curtain within which you were now confined: in the days that followed, you remember, every time the sedation started to wear off, you would wake up, every time, to feel its unbelievable power of restraint; this circle of pale cloth erected around your chemistry-and-machine sustained life (sinister theater of your semi-awake post-surgery terrors) was as powerful and repressive as a concrete wall—unsurpassable border between you and the world of flight and freedom that beckoned beyond the hospital.

Those terrors: waking up in the middle of the night to find yourself trapped in this enclosed space of machines and screens and connections and extensions; of floating lines and dots of red, green, and aqua blue winking in the darkness.

And the panic—primal, disconsolate, bottomless—the horror that comes from the insanely contradictory awareness that you are a non-body in a nowhere who is conscious of being non-body, of being nowhere. The raw primeval truth that you are not—even as you can locate yourself within the contours of some body, an entity in pained existence, somewhere.

The infinitely naked, infinitely frail infantile horror that arises with this unbearable contradiction: this utterly terrified consciousness (without thought) of being trapped in a space that you cannot size or fathom—only the colored crystals of the digits, the lines of your life circles and stipples and jagged lines, translated into the cold heartless language of the machines, the information flows whizzing in the wires.

And the dreadful pace of that respirator, like the muffled hiss of a frightened animal dying in its den.

And the fact of knowing and not knowing, just as you begin to awake—the impossibility of anticipating the fear that sends you howling in the middle of the night.

Then the echoes of alarm from the ICU hub: waves of panic from the personnel preceding them within the curtained well (or theater), and the widening tear of darkness in the curtain and the flood of light—the black mist of your chemical night eating away at everything that is.

———

Technology and my unflagging will to write everything into meaning were crucial in the days that followed surgery.

But my efforts would have been utterly vain if it hadn't been for Sami's presence—his active assistance, his encouragement and moral support.

Starting from our first conversations on my computer, his validation of my version of the truth and his briefing on what had happened to my sons was a source of great comfort and clarity when things became too painful and desperate, with the rehabilitation staff working relentlessly to reinvent reality and distort the truth of my narrative:

"Do not give up," Sami said during his last visit in Paris. "Do not let anyone twist and distort the truth. I believe every single word you say about the events of August 30—the dreadful passing of your boys. It was *not* an accident, but a most vicious, cowardly murder. I have it on good authority that the monstrous deed was plotted by a number of powerful and influential people. That's all I can say for now, because you need to get strong first before I can tell you what I know. Also, let's keep this strictly between us—we're dealing with extremely dangerous, extremely powerful people. They're already working on the staff in this hospital—threatening, bullying, manipulating, and distorting. A competent criminologist, a very close and trusted friend of mine, is working on elucidating the circumstances of these heinous crimes. Do *not* let them intimidate you into believing the easy version of history—the story that's going to make it easy for them to skirt the real crime simply because it's too big and too shameful. They're already developing all kinds of cunning pseudo-scientific strategies to brainwash you into accepting *their* story. Do not let their clinical posturing intimidate or mislead you. Refuse and resist, Tariq. Take heart from what I've told you. Together we'll find a way out of this terrible tribulation. Fear nothing."

I will never forget the painful effort that he had put into keeping everything under the seal of secrecy. All that terrible information locked inside his head: he knew he had to keep it to himself—for months if need be—until I got better and was strong enough to face the things that he knew.

I will never forget how brave and self-sacrificing he was in the months that followed Paris: being patient of our bizarre written communications, getting in touch with the postdoctoral student to confirm certain technical details, reexplaining some very painful aspects of the crime.

In the weeks that followed our first extensive conversation at the Community, I was able to use the precious information he had provided like material from a testimony, interrogating it for signs and clues, double-checking and parsing it with him whenever he came to visit me in Brittany.

During his third visit to the Community, I remember asking him the terrible question that I had contemplated for weeks:

We were sitting in my room and I asked him directly: "I have been thinking about our last conversation—things that you told me about Tantric sacrifice. You said something about 'invading their bodies,' and I never got around to asking you. What did you mean by that?"

He looked away in silence.

"Sami," I pressed him, "some of the events of that night are a total blank in my mind—a blank that's going to kill me. Is there anything else you're not telling me?"

He mumbled that "sometimes it's better to let things go." His face was twisted in pain.

"Please," I pleaded, "let's deal with it now—once and for all. I want to know, even if the information kills me. I just need to know."

Sami said, "They needed a lot of blood on that night—a symbol of energy. So they ripped their chests open. Then they took with them each boy's left hand—a sacrificial gift to some god. My friend had told me already. I just didn't have the heart to write it into the notes. I just couldn't find the words."

———

Some days I have such a strong sense of emotional closeness to them—my sons:

Contemplating the photos, the videos, the remote echoes of my own words and feelings coming to me from the other life; feeling so deeply and genuinely moved by those last days we spent together and by the heartrending pain and sheer sorrow of what became of us, what became of them. Our presence in each other's lives brutally terminated. The promise of a new beginning aborted for the three of us.

Still, all too often I find it impossible to reflect on what happened without thinking that the presence and the promise and the pain and the sorrow are simply too abstract to be true (the insubstantial product of words); that the hard reality of eternal immitigable apartness is the ultimate reality, somber proof that all the "feelings" that I am putting (struggling to put) into these words are nothing but awkward *attempts* at feeling—a maudlin, guilty pretense.

Those are the moments when I feel most unworthy of them, unworthy of life; when the entire world simply ceases to make sense and collapses into a heap of ruins; when my heart feels as frail and insignificant as a wad of crumpled cellophane, my mind addled and fallen and aimless.

What if it was all unreal? What if it still is?

But when hypnosis is working at its best, there are days when I can feel the channels of memory opening up, the flow of remembrance moving with ease; and I do not feel at all false or ashamed or unworthy when I write "I remember" or "I recall."

Those are the precious moments when I can feel that there is still hope for me:

Hope that maybe someday I will be able to teach myself how to really use these new words in my new life, this new enchanted tongue that was given me by Providence—use them without fear or impatience, without feeling cramped and clumsy and out of place; use them to metamorphose the story of my ghostly world of scattered ruins and remains, turn it into a hospitable narrative that is truly my own; use them to look back, quite simply, and smile at long last and see the life of the man who existed before me as the necessary antechamber to an altogether new enchanted space that I can inhabit by a pure act of magic, using those once terrible phrases like talismanic words of invocation, or maybe even empowerment: "I recall," "I remember," "I recollect."

As for Heend and your mother, now that they have turned twice dis-incarnate, as it were, in the course of your rewriting them—now that they too have become reconstructions, you can begin at last to see how unfair you were (and ultimately self-defeating) in not acknowl-edging the unconscious tangle of ambiguous emotions that had kept your mind so closely bound up with their lives—your unavowed but enduring kinship with their anger and humiliation.

Reading about them in the diary, contemplating their faces, and hearing their voices, you have come to realize how much your iden-tity was shaped by their mistrust of the world that was yours—a world created and ruled by an unbreakable horde of selfish fathers.

How lonely and cut off they must have felt during your years of cohabitation in Rades—and how paltry a share of that loneliness you took, when all is said and done.

Although this period of horror and confinement has taught you little besides the perennity of your guilt, it has at least served as irrefutable proof that the woman of ravishing beauty you call mother saw the fact of exile not as a dictate of fate but as an art of living: in her own confinement, she must have found something that far surpassed the anger and the humiliation—a country of her own making, a place of peace and unexpecting.

But there was nothing to be done about the hurt, and you both knew it. Now that you have come to see the past in a different light, you can at last admit the intolerable truth: that the secret throb of her voiceless pain was nothing less than the pulse of your existence; that the most meaningful moments of your life were ultimately those hours you spent listening to its infinitely subtle echoes—ghostly reverberations of the woman herself, unspoken replications of her injured soul rippling through your boyhood house.

How often you did this as a child, without admitting it to anyone, least of all yourself—practicing the craft of wordless listening, absorbing the unspoken words issuing from the heart of the woman with hurt in her eyes.

And now, years after you left the house and the woman, you find yourself listening to her thoughts again, guessing at her greatness and her sway; only you are openly expressing this to yourself now, in explicit words—confessing it, putting it in writing, without shame or pride. A simple statement on the way things were.

As for her letter, only the electronic version has made its way to you, but you find no difficulty in visualizing the original as if it were right here on your desk, imagining yourself holding it in your hands and reading it:

It is ponderous, its initial odor gone, yet you still remember the first time you opened the envelope: the smell of dry rose and jasmine petals wafting out of it in an ambiguous exhalation—both tart and sweet, a mix of stale snuff and rosewater.

Holding her words in your hand—the letter read and folded back so many times—you feel no shame and no guilt as you admit the long-repressed truth to yourself: your deep, fond kinship with these words.

In them (through them) you become conscious that you have come home in some way—to a place where you can finally assume some of the woman's burden, with no sense of shock or self-hate; a space where you can admit to yourself that through all those years you spent in Rades, the secret longings in her vast embattled heart were nothing less than a prefiguration of your most compelling feelings as a man: your darkest fears and your highest hopes.

And so as you remember her now, the woman you call mother, you cannot help but wonder: that inscrutable solitude of hers—hasn't it been your destiny, too? Something you have inherited, like a gift by will, from her diminished life as an outcast among her own people, a self-willed exile in her hometown; the woman who, in utter despair at the heartlessness of the one man she had trusted with the frailty of her love, decided one day to shut her heart and her door and embark on a long journey of impenetrable pride and silence—a self-willed prisoner in the lonely house by the sea.

Rades, February 12, 2008

NB *As a precautionary measure, I am e-mailing you a typed electronic version of this letter.*

Dearest,

I am writing again. I wish I could tell you that I am not doing it out of obligation, but I am. These words are addressed to you under extremely stringent circumstances—circumstances that I never anticipated, not in my worst nightmare. Indeed, besides having to deal with the grief raging inside me, I also find myself confronted with the painful task of reestablishing the truth in your tragedy; because ultimately, the truth must *be reestablished, however painful and contentious the effort.*

I hope you will forgive this abrupt opening and the apparent lack of feeling. Know that my mind is addled with excess *of feeling—for you, for our dear departed ones. But if I were to let my emotions be known at this point, they would surely end up flooding the entirety of my mind—and this letter would turn into an unending flow of senseless words. So hoping that you will be patient with me, I will limit myself to the facts for the time being.*

Allow me, then, to get to the heart of the matter: your boys (my beloved grandchildren) were not the victims of a barbaric sacrificial ritual conducted in Zoé's apartment. Shams and Haroon died in a car crash just outside the Paris beltway, shortly after midnight on August 30. You were driving them

back to Bordeaux in rainy weather, anxious to have them home and in bed—
Regina was to pick them up the same day.

But fate had other intentions. The car skidded off the highway and flipped
several times. You survived the accident, albeit with a major head injury, but
our two little angels did not make it. They died in their sleep.

There you have it. The reality of what happened finally set down on paper
by your loving mother, after many days of tears and excruciating hesitation.

Dearest, I don't want you to worry about my tears and my hesitation.
Even more importantly, I don't want your grief to be compounded by guilt.
Devastating as they are, the words that I have just written are meant to restore
the truth and make you whole again—whole by the truth and in the truth.
They are words grounded in objective facts, and facts are far more powerful
than our strongest defense mechanisms—even when those mechanisms are
validated by a devoted friend.

I do not want to dwell at length on Sami Mamlouk lest you think I am
biased and unfairly critical of your friend. My intention here is not to criticize
but to clarify some key information—present you with the facts as I have come
to learn them from Zoé and Mourad after they had spoken with everyone,
including Regina. I know and appreciate that he has been steadfastly support-
ive in these difficult times. He is loyal and selfless—I know that for a fact and
I respect it; but when loyalty turns into consistent denial of reality, the process
becomes a dangerous indulgence—one that you cannot afford at this point
in your life. Last summer, you spoke highly of his intellectual gifts. I don't
know why he keeps deluding both you and himself. Neither does Zoé, who has
known him nearly as long as you did and is baffled by his behavior. "He is
like a different man," she told me. Your brother Mourad, on the other hand, is
convinced he has solved the mystery of Sami's metamorphosis: he has developed
this sinister theory about power and professional ambition, but I disagree—I
think his assumption is blindly cynical, and I will not bother you with it.

Conspiracy speculation aside, I think it behooves us all to reflect on why
your friend seems to take everything you tell him at face value. Khaleel (your
sister Heend's husband) has his theory about that, which I will spare you, too,
since I personally find it too technical and obscure. Still, I believe some theory
should be put forth, for all our sakes. In my view, Sami's idea about allowing
yourself to "explore different imaginary scenarios" in order to resolve your crisis
is not only utterly unacceptable, it is deeply unhealthy. Those were the very words

he used when he finally accepted to speak with Zoé and Mourad: "imaginary scenarios." Having said that, I am sure that Sami's notion comes from a good place: he is full of good intentions and is not at all aware how irresponsible his idea is—how disruptive it can be for all, especially himself. Zoé told me that he is genuinely consumed with grief for you. But letting his grief interfere with your healing is extremely dangerous, and I think he himself is in urgent need of help.

In any case, regardless of how well-founded my assumptions are, I just want to be as clear as possible on Sami's role: while I am convinced that it is miraculous to have a person of his loyalty as a friend, I also think that the man has his limitations too—he is, after all, only human. When I spoke to him on the telephone, he was curt, and I am sure that the curtness was not a deliberate strategy—it was the outcome of mental confusion and sheer stress, if I may venture an opinion.

You're probably exclaiming, "Enough already!" But as I said earlier, my purpose here is not to criticize or pass judgment on your friend—I only want to clarify the facts and state where I stand with regard to them as candidly as is possible under the circumstances. Then I will proceed to the real purpose of my letter.

As far as the facts are concerned, not only does Zoé's relation of the events of that ill-starred night make sense, its healing quality for all of us is far more sound than any imaginary scenario. "Why more sound?" one may ask. Beyond matters of personal preference and subjective likes and dislikes, the answer hinges on one irrefutable fact: it was Zoé who accepted to sacrifice her peace of mind and put herself through the grueling work of actually researching the truth. Shortly before Mourad's visit to Paris and the fruitless trip to Le Croisic, your brother signed power of attorney over to her and she requested a formal fact-finding meeting with the investigator, Commissaire Collin, who had already seen you once in the hospital and had not been able to communicate with you properly.

With regard to Zoé's visit down here, I suppose by now you understand that in dwelling on her role in our life my purpose is not to add to your burden but to be fair and thankful in acknowledging your friend's immense efforts and the toll they took on her. The mere fact of thinking about what she had to go through makes me cry. As soon as she got here, she sat down with me and we went over all the details of what had happened that night; and even as she explained and clarified, she wept bitter tears. The woman is distraught: a friend (who is, in fact, very much of a big brother figure) has come to grief and *refuses to even see her; two children that she adores are dead—and one of them is her godson; her father (who probably saw himself as a father figure to you) finds himself dragged into a sordid plot with horrendous implications. The ramified emotional and mental "consequences" of this tragedy are extremely hard to endure, even for a woman of Zoé's stamina.*

Please allow me to say it again in order to clarify my position: the last thing I want to do at this point is make you feel weighed down by guilt. At the same time, however, I think it is both morally necessary and mentally salutary for us to come to grips with the pain and distress experienced by Zoé as she faced that commissaire. He told her unequivocally that he was investigating a case of negligent homicide. Collin said that he was unable to obtain any coherent information from you when he saw you in the Paris hospital. And after your transfer to Le Croisic, the references to a crime scene that you told him about in Paris evolved into a complex narrative about a sacrificial murder plot masterminded by Si Brahmi and his friends. (Could it be that you were working on a similarly themed story shortly before the accident took place?)

Anyway, Collin told Zoé that he knew what he was after. His investigation was focused on a highway tragedy with a view to substantiating only one hypothesis: negligent driving in the first degree. The theory of a murder plot hatched by a cult was very surprising to the commissaire, but even so, he told Zoé that after consulting with Dr. Cohen, he decided to help you obtain some information: he thought (and the psychiatrist agreed) that learning about the workings of real-life sacrificial murder might serve as a "reality-grounded corrective" and help you come to terms with your loss. Collin discussed the subject with you; he referred you to various online sources; and he even spoke with Si Brahmi. The information that he relayed to you about the latter was unequivocal: beyond a keen interest in esoteric movements and philosophies (an interest you both had in common), Zoé's father had no shady involvements with the occult—a man of irreproachable character who probably saw you as the son he never had.

Zoé told me that Collin was more than competent and thorough; he was also kind and humane—and the man seemed genuinely upset by the sad and unexpected turn your life had taken. He tried to reassure her that the murder plot hypothesis had no foundation in fact, but the damage was done: that dark dimension of her inquiry had left your friend shaken and distressed.

With all that said, let me make my position on "the consequences" as clear as possible: no matter how you regard your "share of responsibility" for what happened on that tragic night; no matter how much condemnation or hostility you receive from the people around you, I want you to try, as you read this letter, to set aside and rise above all considerations of culpability. And I want you to be assured of the one unchanging truth: my love for you. In the face of this nameless adversity, you must always remember it—my love for you, which is now stronger than ever before. And Zoé's love. And Heend and Thouraya and all your siblings, who now love you more than ever before. When this terrible trial is over, when you will have written your way out of amnesia and the distortions of "cognitive bias," you will learn and know how to find them again, how to cherish them again—more than ever before.

Meanwhile, there is your mother, who is struggling with the here and now, its ups and downs: using these words not to look back and judge and evaluate the happenings of one summer night; but to reach out and communicate with you honestly, even if it means having to go against the natural bent of time—writing in anticipation of your healing, trying to reach you despite many arguments to the contrary. Indeed, there are many knowledgeable people, here and elsewhere, who have tried to talk me out of this letter—with the same reasoning expressed in different euphemistic ways: the seemingly self-evident argument that it would be far wiser for me to wait before I tried to get through to you. So you see, I, too, have had my share of chaos and confusion during the last several months—struggling hard to carve out a path to clarity amid the thicket of conflicting opinions and advice. In spite of all the disarray, however, I have never lost sight of the possibility of an exchange of letters between the two of us: not only do I believe that I can get through to you; I am deeply convinced I can reach the very best in you. Throughout this strange period, I have remained steadfast in my belief that there is a great expanse of creation within you that is more open, more fertile, and more beautiful than ever before; that this expanse is an inexhaustible gift of love and understanding and compassion that you can still share with your mother, with your loved ones, and with the rest of the world.

Dearest, if there is any doubt in your mind about the power of my belief, know that it (the belief) is fueled by your own words—poetry written in the early days of your hospitalization in Brittany and which I am enclosing below as a token of my admiration:

Night Owl

Oh, you know: that hour.
The smeared rim of heaven
has turned to cold crystal;
it is the last champagne blush
in the opalescent sky:
The light-dregs of day
at the bottom of a lonely glass.

But the owl has descended,
preening on his perch;
a few last touches before the night hour—
his time of glory,
when all the rest of creation
will be floundering, floundering
in formless mud and murk.

Oh, you know, you know:
When his gaze begins to brim up
with a thousand sparks of amber,
crackling with the memory of a million noons—
the encapsulated sparkle of eons
at his command,
lighting up his voyage into the night.

Words always fail me at the sight of this poem: I literally cannot tell you how much hope your verse has filled me with—how much light and beauty it has brought into "the night" that has hemmed me in. And since words have failed, I will leave it at that, with the addition that it is your duty to remember the sincerity hidden behind the stammer in my pen, the quiver of my voice, the tears welling in my eyes—wordless testament to the power of your voice. Any man who is vast enough to contain and express these words is a man of great valor and worth, a great creator who is still willing to share the beauty inside him with his fellow humans.

Tariq, this poem is the only trace of the new you that I have: Zoé was allowed to have an electronic copy of it after she had begged Dr. Cohen to give her something of you (any token of possible hope) to bring back to me. So you see, this letter is also about me in many ways—a woman who, after many years of indifference toward the world, has come to openly acknowledge her feelings and commune with the best in her; a woman who would like to make you discover the changed mother that she has become—changed not just because of the tragedy that befell you on that dreadful summer night, but also because of what has been happening inside me, inside us all here in "time-forsaken Tunisia," as you used to call her in your angry student days.

But your anger was there well before university and the harsh hard days of political activism—and you had every right to be angry. And I must confess it to you now: you never said a word about it, but I know (I have known all along) that in your adolescence you spent many dark moments brooding about the environment in which you were born and raised—what it did to your mother and your sister; the unshakable power of its traditions; the rank seeds of resentment it planted within you. Those were days of deep rage that, in one way or another, you turned into self-imposed distance toward your mother—a desperate attempt to avoid thinking about the source of my pain and my humiliation.

But things will be different from now on. Now that you can begin with a blank page, as it were, and write your own life anew: there is tangible hope indeed that you might be able to put your old wounds to rest and start to live a life freed from the injuries that marred your beginnings here in Tunisia. Zoé had a long telephone conversation with your therapist, Dr. Cohen, who explained to your friend all the medical aspects of your case. Through Zoé's notes and Khaleel's explanations, I was able to learn a great deal about the hardships of your condition after the accident. But there is also a great lesson of hope that I learned from your injury: while the trauma can be confounding with its various losses (the amnesia, the cognitive disorientation, the personality change and crisis of identity), it is also a symbol of a new beginning—an opportunity for self-renewal and a unique occasion to see yourself and your past as you have never seen them before.

And so, at the risk of seeming insensitive, allow me to share these words of solace with you: if your tragedy has taught me anything, it is that a great loss, more often than we are willing to admit, bears within its darkest depths the greatest gift of all—the gift of self-surpassing; the capacity to rise above our sorrows and will ourselves into a state of being that transcends the prison-house of our somber circumstances: wisdom, insight, compassion, and the healing power of self-love are only a few of the attributes of that state of being. If you have any doubt about the validity of these words, just consider what has become of us after that August night: your mother is writing again, after the torpid silence of many long years—writing again, feeling again, my heart welling with the noblest sentiment; your brothers, overwhelmed with grief at your loss and your pain, came together right here under the mulberry tree and wept side by side (we have never seen anything like this, and I think it is for the best, considering how lofty they were during your visit last summer). While the sight of our men so aggrieved tore your sisters' hearts apart, it has also brought us closer together—a real family united in the tears and in the sadness, but also in something far nobler than the tears and the sadness. Indeed, from that moment onward, we began to drop our old masks and to show one another how vulnerable we were, how much in need of one another's healing touch. Unbearable as it is, your loss has allowed us to discover the gentler side of our nature—and it has brought Heend and the rest of us women closer to Zoé and Thouraya than we have ever been.

The two women stood firmly by your sister—not in spite of the complications of her grief (the details of which I will spare you here), but because of them. Heend kept telling them how she would never be able to get rid of the obsessive recurrence of one image: the painful impression that kept rising up in her mind's eye was the scene of your quick good-bye at the airport. I must confess that I never grasped the full complexity of her guilt until Thouraya and Zoé explained it to me—the extent of her remorse for having been so brief just before the three of you had departed. I believe that Heend is torn with guilt because she confuses her failure to be sisterly at the airport with her powerlessness to help you at present. We spoke recently and she told me that she had not done enough to "protect" you from your brothers last summer; that she knew and felt their deliberate distance toward you all along, their moral arrogance and callousness; that she stood by helpless and watched it all happen, as if she was "drugged." The ceaseless cycles of obsessive guilt: they can be terribly trying mentally, in their repetitiveness. I have done my best to console your sister—by saying that what she thinks of herself is utterly untrue and that you would never agree with it; by telling her that she is associating her helplessness in the present with far less dramatic situations from the past. But above all, the most important solace I try to share with her is what I have just told you about myself: it is never too late to begin again. It is never too late to be tender and "weak" again. It is never too late to feel again.

As for your brother Kareem, he came here to see me shortly after your accident and we sat down together in the garden, and we were both so silent that you could hear the sound of the sea like a field of ripe wheat whistling in the wind. And after I served him tea and waited again in the long silence, he put down his cup and looked deeply into my eyes. He told me that he had gone back to Korbous by himself for a few days—in order to forget. But all he did was remember: his walks in the cliffs down there kept reminding him of you—how much you had suffered during your student days, and how he had always tried to make you look on the bright side. Your brother had reflected on your summer visit: he knew that you needed someone you could relate to, but all he did was drop you off here without even a proper good-bye. He said that he would never forgive himself for having parted with you "on hostile terms." Those were your brother's exact words, and as he spoke them, I saw brotherly love in his eyes. This is what Kareem has become after the moral arrogance and the callousness of last summer. I did not want to add to his pain, but I could not let the moment slip by without making my point: I spoke to him about the sacred obligation of silat arrahim—the familial "bond of the womb" that connects siblings—and believe me, he knew exactly what I was referring to.

Last summer, you were in need of moral support—all the men knew it; and I don't want you to think that I did not see their failure to provide it: the cold arrogant aloofness of your brothers and Khayyam—their unwillingness to welcome you as their equal—was like a taste of ashes in my mouth. And yet I chose not to speak up—out of moral cowardice, I must confess.

The failures of our men and how to protect ourselves against them: the fundamental question at the heart of this letter. (As I mentioned earlier, I do not wish to dwell on the why of what happened to you and us in the early hours of August 30—this letter is not about the burdens of the past, it is about the possibilities of the future.)

And yet the future would be nothing but a nightmarish trap of recurrent flaws and failings without the benefit of a profound purging of the past. This is what I want to speak to you about now—the saving process of purgation, starting with something that is, unfortunately, very painful and contentious: the role that an older Tunisian man has come to play in your life—Si Brahmi. Before your accident, Zoé's father was only a minor character in the narrative of your life—a man you enjoyed meeting occasionally in order to share the pleasures of intellectual exchange. And now, with a suddenness and intensity that might seem inexplicable at first glance, the man has assumed a terrible position, becoming an ominous figure at the center of your tragedy. This crippling presence must fade out of your consciousness soon if you are to move ahead with the healing process. For the present Si Brahmi is nothing but a figure, precisely—a symbol of your many bruising, humiliating conflicts with your male elders when you were a student in Tunisia: people who ultimately sought to oppress you instead of admiring your youthful enthusiasm and the political acumen of your editorials and student speeches—members of the security services with their monstrous methods during your many detentions and interrogations; the reactionary faculty members in your university, including a powerful dean who seemed to enjoy making life impossible for you; the small-minded but highly vocal and influential members of your father's family, who disapproved of your struggle and could not keep their opinions to themselves. I said something earlier about the utter uselessness of dwelling on the pain of past wrongs that one is powerless to set aright. And yet, considering the present state of things, I also believe that in the long run you do need to delve deep within yourself and learn to rediscover some aspects of your relation to authority and its supreme incarnation in this country: malicious male figures that you were forced to contend with despite your deep aversion to confrontation. Unfortunately, those people were a significant factor in your youth—the sinister human forces that shaped your early experiences in Tunisia, determining your perception of power: many of them, sad to say, were conniving older males who permanently distorted your vision of the paternal image.

Your brothers and your brothers-in-law were aware of all this, of course— the long shadows of the past in which you stood; so thick and dark and daunting that you had consistently refused to discuss them with anyone, including Thouraya in the old days. When taking into account this traumatic

*background and your current life in a deeply alienating country, your broth-
ers' moral arrogance during your summer stay becomes all the more difficult
to comprehend, let alone justify. Your visit as a single father among us here
must have felt like a second exile. (Evidently, this feeling of alienness among
cold and cruel people is nothing new to you: after all, you are a man who has
admirably managed to maintain grace and a divine sensibility in the inhuman hell of European hate.) As for what happened here with your brothers, I
do not want you to think that I failed to grasp the reality of how isolated and
rejected you felt. I was a witness to your alienation among your own people,
and I was greatly pained by it; but I also failed to do anything about it and
will have to live with the consequences of my moral weakness.*

*But now, after everything that has happened, I know I cannot afford a
second act of moral cowardice: I must learn to confront reality and deal with
the fact that my beloved son is going through a terrible trial; that he has had
to confront situations over which he is incapable of exerting any control; that
in the name of psychotherapy he has been made to relive—over and over,
amid anguish and pain—a chain of events that have now become the sinister
tool of his confinement. Does the thought of so much misfortune pain me?
It certainly does, and the mere idea of your confinement brings back terrible
memories from your student days; and it makes me wake up in fright and sit
up drenched in sweat in the middle of the night; and it sends me roaming
around aimlessly amid the night shadows of my house, like a restless ghost.
Still, in spite of the torment, there is good reason to hope that someday this
will all be over; that your loss and your grief and your stranding in strange
places are the very condition of the deepening of your life experience, your evolution into a wiser more compassionate man. A year from now, when you will
have put all the suffering behind you, you will emerge from Le Croisic pained
and uncertain; but you will also come out with a greater understanding of
humanity than you ever thought possible.*

*In addition to that, there will be the reward of a clear perspective on
your past as a militant—the burden of rage and resentment imposed on you
by your elders. This is the only point on which I had to differ with Zoé when
we last discussed your version of events on the telephone: saying that your
"demonizing" of Si Brahmi is "unfathomable" misses the deeper significance
of your anger, for the complex expressions of your rage at him need to be
seen in a different, more symbolic light: they are the outcome of a buildup of*

unconscious anger against the authority figures you were confronted with in Tunisia. Remember, though, now that you have to revisit your life here with a renewed vision: it would be both unjust and self-destructive to polarize your own private history into two opposed energies: the repressive forces of an older generation and the promising energies of a younger one. Think of Si Brahmi, precisely. Zoé told me that you were always full of praise for his tolerant disposition toward your militant past. And remember all the militant professors who encouraged you and helped you exit the system here and seek refuge in France. Long ago, when you decided to leave this country, you chose (much to Thouraya and Heend's chagrin) to turn your back on those professors, staying in contact with Khaleel only—through your sister. Although I shared Heend and Thouraya's bewilderment at how radically you severed all ties with the "dissident scene" in Tunisia and in France, there is a dark side of me that sympathizes greatly with your self-banishment from the others—after all, that is precisely what I did long ago when I felt that everybody had betrayed my struggle to gain a legal and respectful divorce from your father (I raised a levee between me and the rest of the world, kept my door locked). But today that dark side is being radically reevaluated, as far as I am concerned. As for you, I am convinced that once you get out of this predicament, you will be able to revisit the hardships of your militant past, and see that there is truly no noble aspiration without hardship; and you will manage to set aside all denial and come to view your comrades in the struggle with pride—people and memories to "revisit" in the full sense of the term.

Without forgetting the hardship, then, I remain hopeful and strong in the face of all adversity; and if I am putting myself in this hopeful state of mind, it is not for you but because of you: through a magnificent poem written in great physical torment and mental anguish, you have taught me that it is quite possible for a man to carry the highest hopes within him even as he has to confront the deepest despair—a man who experienced hell before as a young student and who managed to write his way out of it, emerging rejuvenated in France. Now a second rejuvenation awaits you as you emerge reborn from the ashes of the old Tunisia you knew. I know this sounds sentimental, and I know that you probably find many of the ideas contained in this letter sentimental and very much at odds with the silent woman you knew. And yet, at the risk of sounding pedantic, my advice to you at this point in your life is precisely to be *sentimental! There is no better way to cleanse your soul of the impurities that have been deposited in it.*

And above all, remember: a great man will always know how to turn his worst moment into his finest. That is why I believe it would be unwise (and ultimately self-defeating) to see your present woes as a sort of accursed lot—something dark and evil thrown at you by the fickle hand of fate. Your sorrows, however crippling in their absurd indecipherability, are in the end a form of living proof—a ceaseless reminder (in the flesh, quite literally): to always rise to the battle of life and seek what is best in you through the battle—grace, acceptance, and belief in yourself. When you reach the end of this tumultuous experience in Le Croisic, I trust you will find the necessary equanimity to study the other life paths you might have taken well before the road to Brittany; and I have faith that in so doing, you will come to realize that an existence shorn of struggle is nothing but a barren field of banality and a dying without end.

Strive then to embrace your destiny as it is, my son, to endure and be graceful in your endurance. Ultimately, that is the only other road I can point to from where I stand, here on the shores of our beloved Tunisia: the path of self-trust as your unassailable refuge against the ravages of existence—this vast and contentious stage we call life, the ever-shifting scene of your triumph and your trial.

Acknowledgments

I would like to express my deepest gratitude to my friend Patrick Perez of the Nantes Police Department for his invaluable help with research on forensics and crime scene procedure. His patient explanations and clear illustrations helped enhance the vividness of the crime and investigation scenes depicted in this book. I am also grateful to Dr. Alexandre Vivier for his patient and expert advice on physical trauma and brain damage. His exhaustive reports were of inestimable value during the research phase. To those who were asked to read and comment on the typescript of my work—John Glendenning, Janine Ranger, Jean-Claude Ranger, and Mari Ruti—my continuing indebtedness.

Made in the USA
Charleston, SC
03 October 2015